THE ECLIPSE OF THE ZON – FIRST TREMORS

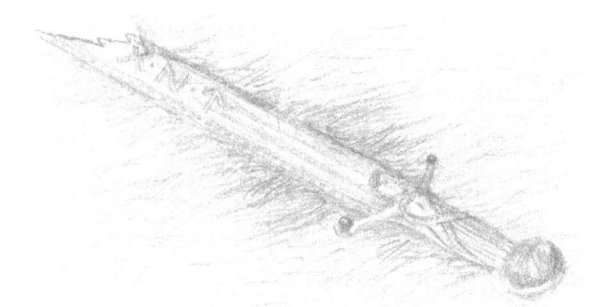

R M BURGESS

THE ZON website:

http://burgessrm.wix.com/empire-of-the-zon#!books/cnec#
empireofthezon

Follow
The Empire of the Zon on Facebook
and
ZonEmpire on Twitter.

Also by RM Burgess

The Empire of the Zon

Cover design and additional illustrations by Akhila Krishnan
© Akhila Krishnan and R. M. Burgess

Zon Huntress painting by Boris Vallejo

ISBN 10: 0997467304
ISBN 13: 9780997467307

a CHILD aLONe ...

ASGARA LOOKED INTO his dark brown eyes. He did not meet her steady gaze but blinked and looked away quickly. Her emotional acuity caused warning bells to go off in her head, but she was faint with hunger and ignored them. She took the apple and began to eat it hurriedly before he changed his mind. As she was eating, he sat down on the ground beside her. She felt him pet her hair and then her cheek as she ate the fruit.

"You are a beautiful child," he whispered. "Such pretty hair, such smooth skin."

Asgara kept eating as fast as she could. She was almost done with the apple when he put his hand under the blouse of her shift and began caressing her flat chest and stomach. She dropped the apple core and twisted away from him, saying, "I thank you for your kindness, sir, but I must return to my friends."

"Oh no," he said. "We have only just begun. One apple will not sate your appetite. I have something here for you to drink."

He produced a bottle of clear fluid and attempted to give it to her. When she did not take it, he held one of her thighs tightly and attempted to put it to her lips. As she struggled to free herself, his grip moved up her thigh.

"If you scream, the fruit vendor and his friends will come and beat you again," he whispered in her ear. "You had best come with me. We will make each other very, very happy."

"No!" she whispered desperately, as she continued to struggle. "Let me go! Please sir, I am good girl! I am sure that I cannot make you happy."

However, she did not scream, as she was afraid of attracting the vendors and being beaten again. Then she felt his fingers touch her underclothes.

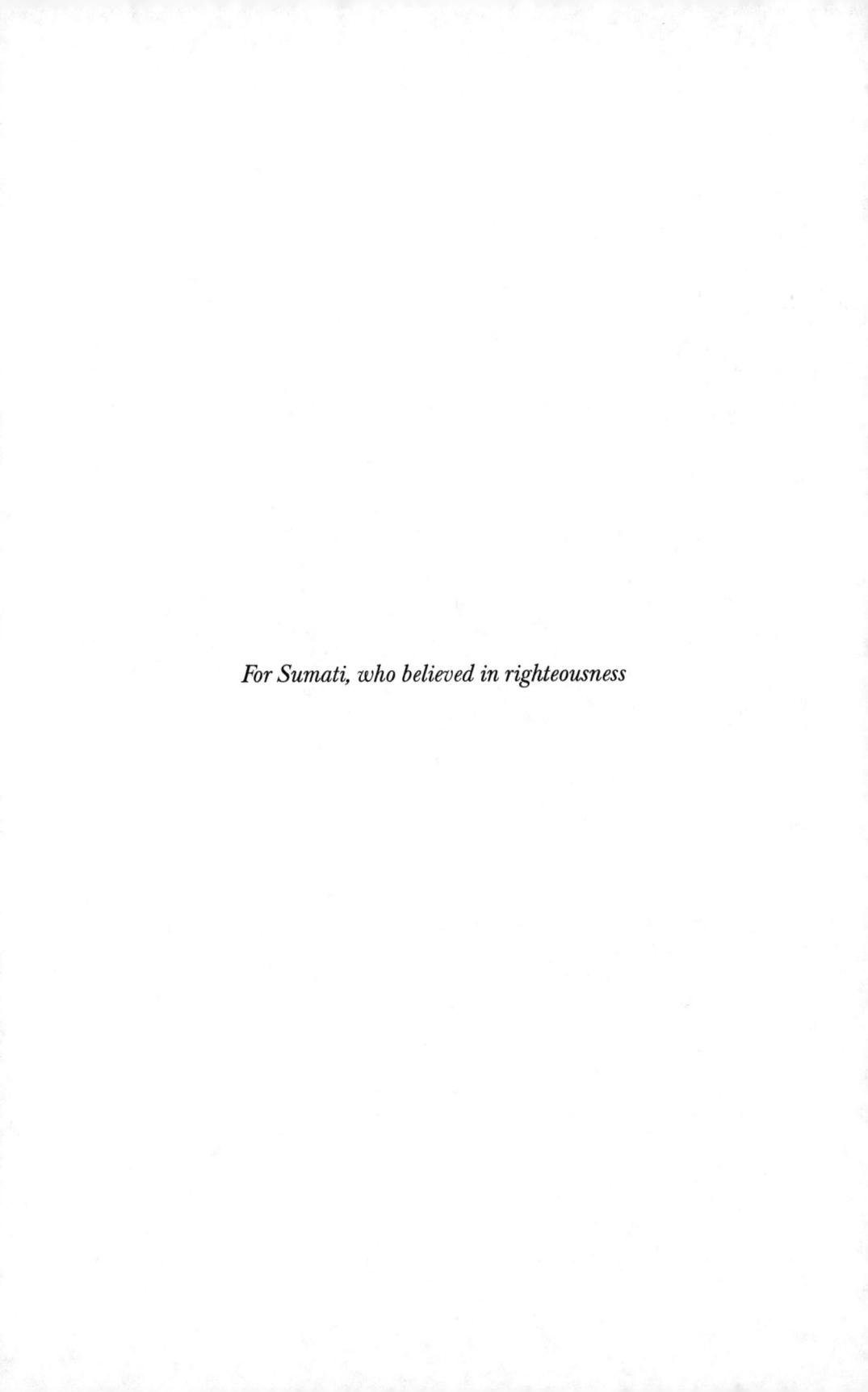

For Sumati, who believed in righteousness

ACKNOWLEDGMENTS

THIS BOOK HAS been a long journey with many fits, starts and wrong turnings. I began writing it in Philadelphia soon after completing *The Empire of the Zon*. Many of my readers helped me along the way with comments, suggestions, and support. But a few stand out for special mention—Snehal Awate, Marcelo Cano-Kollmann, Abhinav Chitturi, Ana Colovic, Rian Drogendijk, Ajai Gaur, TJ Hannigan, Eric Schoeniger, Haritha Saranga, Andreas Schotter, Steve Tallman, Helene Tenzer, Jenn Wood. All of you—named and unnamed—will see your comments live in this story.

The Eclipse of the Zon was originally written as one large book in two parts, roughly the same length as the *The Empire of the Zon*. But several readers suggested that this is too bulky and difficult to handle, especially in hard copy form. These comments prompted me to divide *The Eclipse of the Zon* and release it as two separate books: *First Tremors* and *Rising Dark*. I have tried hard to make each of these two parts into a standalone novel. However, reading the two constituent parts in sequence may be more enjoyable.

Once again, Akhila Krishnan produced the incredible art and the stunning layout that you see throughout the book. The final product is as much hers as mine. Leslie, my editor at Createspace, did a stellar job. She read every line and her incisive comments really improved the quality of the dialog and the cohesiveness of the plot.

I put the finishing touches to *The Eclipse of the Zon – First Tremors* in Luzern amid the snowy Swiss Alps. It was just such majestic scenery that inspired New Eartha. I welcome you to my world.

RM Burgess, Philadelphia

CONTENTS

THE EMPIRE OF THE ZON
SYNOPSIS

WHILE *THE ECLIPSE of the Zon* is a stand-alone novel, it continues the story begun in *The Empire of the Zon*. This synopsis provides a rough outline of the earlier storyline and may enhance the enjoyment of this book.

By the twenty-second century, women had become the dominant gender on Earth. Plagued with undereducated and recalcitrant males, the female leadership eventually concluded that men were net burden on society and unnecessary. This instigated them to build up a vast, genetically diverse semen repository and enact the Male Abortion Law, which required all male fetuses to be aborted. Over the course of a century, males died out, leading to the establishment of the Zon Sisterhood, a purely female society. The very name of the planet was changed to Eartha and the Zon calendar set the year zero at 1920, the year women got the right to vote. Hatred of the patriarchy and fear of its return was a founding cornerstone of the Zon psyche. Zon society gradually evolved into a culture that worshipped female excellence, especially physical beauty. Ultimately these characteristics were formalized, whereby passing demanding physical and mental tests became prerequisites for membership in the voting classes. Standards were set so high that only about 8 percent qualified to vote, roughly the same percentage as in the democratic city-states of ancient Greece.

However, the natural environment on Eartha had been ravaged during the countless millennia of the patriarchy. By the twenty-fifth century, it became clear that the damage was irreversible and that in spite of the best efforts of the Zon Sisterhood, Eartha would soon be unable to sustain human life. To preserve their civilization and way of life, the Zon selected their best and brightest to emigrate in search of other life-sustaining planets.

The Empire of the Zon follows one of these groups that arrived on a "Goldilocks" planet populated by technologically backward peoples that the Zon call "barbarians" or "savages." The Zon rename the planet New Eartha and proceed to conquer it using their superior technology, which the natives view as "sorcery." They rule with an iron fist, extracting heavy tributes from their barbarian vassals. And so their rule is bitterly resented, leading to periodic revolts that they crush brutally.

The Empire of the Zon opens about a thousand years after the arrival of the Zon on New Eartha. Nitya, a young barbarian girl, is accused of being a witch and sentenced to death in a native court. Lady Caitlin d'Orr, a Zon aristocrat and military officer, flouts official Zon policy by interfering in native justice and rescuing her. Escaping together and pursued by the barbarians as well as the Zon, Caitlin and Nitya are observed, tracked, and then befriended by Greghar, a mysterious man with secrets of his own. Greghar turns out to be the bastard son of the last true king of the barbarian realm of Utrea and is in hiding from Shobar, the usurper who currently sits on the throne. As Caitlin, Greghar, and Nitya travel and face challenges together, they grow close and begin to trust one another. Caitlin and Greghar are strongly attracted to each other, but both view the chasm between them as unbridgeable. In a moment of weakness, Caitlin offers herself to him, but clumsily characterizes him as her inferior. Greghar is stung into refusing her.

The period is one of strife and war. Caitlin's mother, Princess Deirdre d'Orr, leads the Zon military, along with her ruthless field commander, Diana Tragina, known to the barbarians as "Lady Death." Concurrently with Caitlin's escape, they face a major insurrection comprised of rebellions in two key barbarian kingdoms. In the northern kingdom of Utrea, the revolt is led by the usurper Shobar, and in the richest barbarian kingdom of Briga, Duke Artor Hilson calls for barbarians to unify under his leadership to throw off the Zon yoke.

Vivia Pragarina, High Mistress of the Zon Trading Guild, sells war matériel to Artor, while Shobar obtains advanced weapons from some disaffected Zon exiles. Both gain early and unprecedented victories. When Princess Deirdre discovers Vivia's treachery, the High Mistress arranges an ambush to have her killed. Artor overthrows King Harald of Briga, a key Zon ally, blinds him, and claims the Brigon throne. Barons flock to his banner. As the war rages on, the Zon desperately try to maintain their grip on their adopted planet and their way of life.

The fates of Caitlin, Greghar, and Nitya become increasingly intertwined with the titanic struggles raging around them. Caitlin falls into the hands of Nestar Crogus, the sadistic commander of Shobar's Skull Watch in Utrea, who tortures her and forces her to marry him. Greghar and Nitya, aided by a renegade group of Zon fanatics, manage to rescue her but find her near death. To save her life, they return with her to Zon forces.

Greghar joins the Zon war effort, helping to bring his uncle Lothar to their side. Lothar's sons, Pinnar and Bradar, support their father. Leveraging alliances in Utrea with Lothar and in Briga with Harald's wife, Queen Esme, the Zon turn the tide and the rebellious barbarians are defeated. Shobar takes refuge in caves in the Great Ice Range and Artor Hilson is forced to flee alone, disguised as a common soldier. The Zon restore Harald to the throne of Briga and place Lothar on the throne of Utrea. Lothar takes Greghar and Nitya under his protection.

With the peace, Caitlin returns to the Zon capital. However, in the eyes of the Zon public, it was her interference in barbarian justice that brought about the war and placed the Sisterhood in such grave danger. Under heavy public pressure, the military brings her to court martial, where she is found guilty and stripped of her rank and all her honors. Eventually she is sent to silencis, a rarely invoked Zon punishment of shunning whereby no one will acknowledge her presence. Sick at heart and consumed with grief over her mother's death, she decides that the one last service she can render the Sisterhood is to perpetuate the ancient House of d'Orr. Greghar's sperm has been extracted and stored in the Zon Repository. She uses it to become pregnant and deliver a daughter, Asgara. She places the d'Orr heiress in the Zon state nursery and leaves the Sisterhood for exile in barbarian lands.

ƆRαmαꞆIS PERSONae

Alphabetical, by country of residence

THE ZON

Centuria Lady ALEXANDRA **Sheel** – First Handmaiden to the Queen; an officer in the Cohort of Palace Guardians; scion of one of the Zon aristocratic houses

ALIUTA **Ednina** – a commoner; former nursery worker, retired to Ostracis

Princess ANDROMACHE **Saxe** – High Priestess of the Upper Temple "*Cognis*"; wearer of the Royal Tiara of Saxe

Centuria ANIKA **Rulina** – an officer in the Pentheselia Legion

LADY ASGARA **Paurina d'Orr** – daughter of CAITLIN **d'Orr** and **Greghar Asgar Nibellus**

Seignora BEDRIT **Svensina** – an officer in the Cohort of Palace Guardians; classmate of CAITLIN **d'Orr**

Centuria BLANCHIA **Rodina** – Executive Officer of the airship *Hydromeda*

BODIL **Axessina** – Zon Resident in Daksin

BRENDEL **Nevisina** –an airboat pilot; daughter of HEBE **Nevisina**

Princess CAITLIN **d'Orr** – scion of one of the Zon aristocratic houses; wearer of the Royal Tiara of d'Orr

DARBENI **Milsina Pragarina** – daughter of VIVIA **Pragarina**; Chief Executive of Pragarina Enterprises

Princess DEIRDRE **d'Orr** – late mother of CAITLIN **d'Orr**, known to the barbarians as "Princess Ice"

Cornelle DIANA **Tragina** – commander of the elite Cohort of Palace Guardians; known to the barbarians as "Lady Death"

Countess DOROTHEA **Sheel** – descendant of one of the Zon aristocratic houses; mother of ALEXANDRA **Sheel**

First Maiden DURGA **Bodina** – leader of the Engine Maidens

FELICIA **Andrina** – a huntress in the Cohort of Palace Guardians

Captain HEBE **Nevisina** – commander of the airship *Thetis*; mother of BRENDEL **Nevisina**

GISFIN **Ednina** – medica in the obstetrics department of the Zon Reproduction Institute; daughter of ALIUTA **Ednina**.

HELIODORA **Talerina** – High Priestess of the Middle Temple Magis

HILDEGARD – Queen of the Zon Sisterhood, Empress of New Eartha

IANTHA **Paurina** – daughter of MEGARA **Paurina**

JENA **Saracenina** – a huntress in the Cohort of Palace Guardians

JORDIS **Invarina** – Zon Under Resident in Daksin

First Principal MAYA **Kalina** – overall commander of the Zon military

Seignora MEGARA **Paurina** – an officer in the Cohort of Palace Guardians; best friend of CAITLIN **d'Orr**

Naorina **Wilkina** – personal maid to Lady **Vivia Pragarina**

Centuria Saskia **Warrina** – mechanica and Chief of Engineering on the airship *Hydromeda*

Lady Selene **Allerand** – Zon Resident in Briga; descendant of one of the Zon aristocratic houses

Lady Vivia **Pragarina** – High Mistress of the Zon Trading Guild

Yukia **Rabbina** – former hostess of *Lives of our Sisters*, a popular show on the Zon comm

BRIGA

Chevalina **Allura Wellithan va Alsor** – wife of **Trianus va Alsor** of Tirut

Alumus – Red Bishop and ecclesiastic leader of the Thermadan Mission, the largest of the barbarian religions on Tarsus (New Eartha)

Artor Hilson – hereditary Duke of the House of Hilson; masquerading as a common soldier using the name **Rator** after his defeat in the Great Insurrection

Axel – oldest son of **Harald V** and **Esme**, heir to the throne of Briga

Biarus – landlord of the Three Feathers Inn in Tirut

Binne Avedus, a rancher in Hareskot, Southern Marches; wife of **Seamus Avedus**

Cheval **Darthus va Haxos** – equerry to **Esme**; youngest son of **Ratto va Haxos**

Cheval **Cresus Hilson** – a great-nephew of **Artor Hilson**

Dhanraj – a Yengar youth from Hareskot, Southern Marches

Digaran – a deputy to Collector **Mantan Yandharan**

Dolomus – younger son of **Esme**, Queen of Briga

Esme – Queen of Briga; younger daughter of **Artor Hilson**

Sous Chevalina **Estia va Goset** – wife of **Hughen va Goset**

Gianina – a courtesan at the Blue Parrot in Dreslin Center; mistress of **Kierus Brontus**

Harald V – King of Briga and of the Royal House of Shelsor.

Baron **Horus Matalus** – Son and heir of **Marnus Matalus**

Sous Cheval **Hughen va Goset** – a Brigon nobleman; older brother of **Kitara va Alsor**

Cheval **Jagus va Alsor** – Younger son of **Nehemus va Alsor**, Baron of Tirut

Kelva – a madam in Dreslin Center

Cheval **Kierus Brontus** – Sword of Peace (commander) of the Red Sentinels of the Thermadan Mission

Kitara va Alsor – wife of **Jagus va Alsor** of Tirut; younger sister of **Hughen va Goset**

Lidill Ikren – a widow in Tirut; mistress of **Artor** when he is masquerading as **Rator**, a common soldier

Lupa – personal maid to **Esme**, Queen of Briga

Baron **Lutus Terendor** – Lord of East Brosia; commander of the Brigon Navy; cousin of **Artor Hilson**

Magnus Pontus – Royal Executioner of Briga

Collector **Mantan Yandharan** – a lawman in the service of **Nehemus va Alsor** of Tirut

Duke **Marnus Matalus** – a Brigon nobleman; installed as Duke of the Northern Marches by the Zon

Martius – master of the *Darling Thoma*, a Brigon merchant caravel

Myrne – wife of **Kierus Brontus**

Nambian – a deputy to **Mantan Yandharan**

Baron **Nehemus va Alsor** – Lord of Tirut and the Southern Marches

Nexius – first mate of the *Darling Thoma*, a Brigon merchant caravel

Noki – son of **Lidill Ikren** of Tirut

Cheval **O'fran Ulthro** – youngest son of **Olsean Ulthro** of Chenak

Baron **Olsean Ulthro** – Lord of Chenak; father of **O'fran Ulthro**

Pegrin – an Utrean courtesan in the Blue Parrot in Dreslin Center

Quirus va Alsor – commander of the Color Guard at Tirut Castle; nephew of **Nehemus va Alsor**

Baron **Ratto va Haxos** – First Minister to **Harald V** of Briga

Rubya – personal maid to **Kitara va Alsor**

Baroness **Talia** – Wife of **Horus Matalus**; older daughter of **Artor Hilson**

Seamus Avedus, a rancher in Hareskot, Southern Marches; husband of **Binne Avedus**

Tar – ship's cook on the *Darling Thoma*, a Brigon merchant caravel

Cheval **Trianus va Alsor** – Older son and heir of **Nehemus va Alsor** of Tirut

Cornel **Valder Mitrell** – commander of the King of Briga's Royal Black Regiment

Wytor – son of **Horus Matalus** and his wife, **Talia**

Zaibene – wife of Collector **Mantan Yandharan**

UTREA

Baron **Bradar Nibellus** – younger son of **Lothar Nibellus**

Baroness **Esgrin** – wife of **Bradar Nibellus**

Greghar Asgar Nibellus – son of **Jondolar the Just**, former King of Utrea and Queen Empress **Hildegard**

Guttanar of Estrans – a captain in the Skull Watch

Baroness **Guttrin** – wife of **Pinnar Nibellus**

Katog of Louth – First Minister to **Shobar Nibellus**

Jondolar the Just – late king of Utrea; father of **Greghar Asgar Nibellus**

Lothar Nibellus – King of Utrea; brother of **Jondolar the Just**; uncle of **Greghar Asgar Nibellus**

Lovelyn of Loftrans – wife of **Lothar Nibellus**; Queen of Utrea

Baron **Nestar Crogus** – commander of the Skull Watch

Nitya – a Yengar girl; ward of **Greghar Asgar Nibellus**

Baron **Pinnar Nibellus** – elder son and heir of **Lothar Nibellus**

Dagmar the Exquisite – the most famous courtesan in Nordberg

Shabor Nibellus – usurper of the throne of Utrea; ousted by **Lothar Nibellus**

Tadar Loksus – castellan of Nordberg Castle in the service of **Lothar Nibellus**

DAKSIN

Vokran II – King of Daksin and of the Royal House of Bhoj

Grand Sab **Ghaz Ib Makhtoom** – late father of **Kimr** and **Ghor Ib Makhtoom**

Sab **Ghor Ib Makhtoom** – a Chekaliga chieftain; younger brother of **Kimr Ib Makhtoom**

Jaan Bardhan – owner and master of the *Dream Weaver*, a Daksin merchant caravel

Sab **Kimr Ib Makhtoom** – Grand Sab of the Chekaliga alliance

Thamaran – an innkeeper at a trading post on the main Tirut–Siggar caravan route

Tah, Mujor and **Dai** – body-aides to **Ghor Ib Makhtoom**

THE ROYAL HOUSE OF BRIGA

Astor Dalton m Ariene

Marcus Matalus

Talia m Solarus Matalus ----- Ragnus Matalus **
                    brothers
            sister
    Gystor

Esme m Harald V Shelox

    Arel
    Dolumus *

* secretly fathered by Akunu, the Red Khalif

** killed by baillin d'or in "the empire of the Zon"

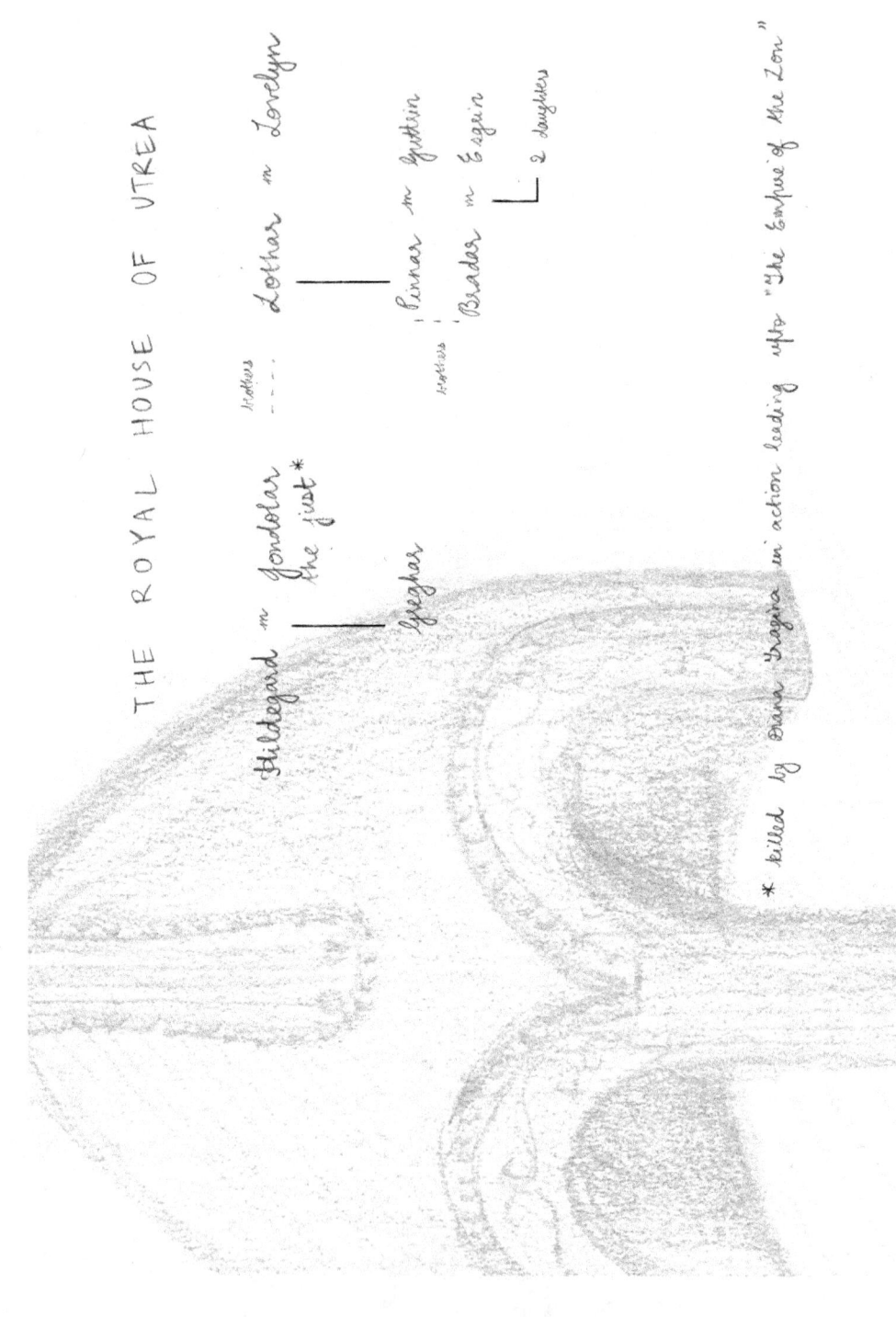

THE ROYAL HOUSE OF UTREA

Hildegard m Gondolar the first*

Gyeghar

Brothers

Lothar m Lorelyn

Brothers

Rinnar m Gyttin

Bradar m Espin

2 daughters

* killed by Diana Yragira in action leading up to "The Empire of the Lion"

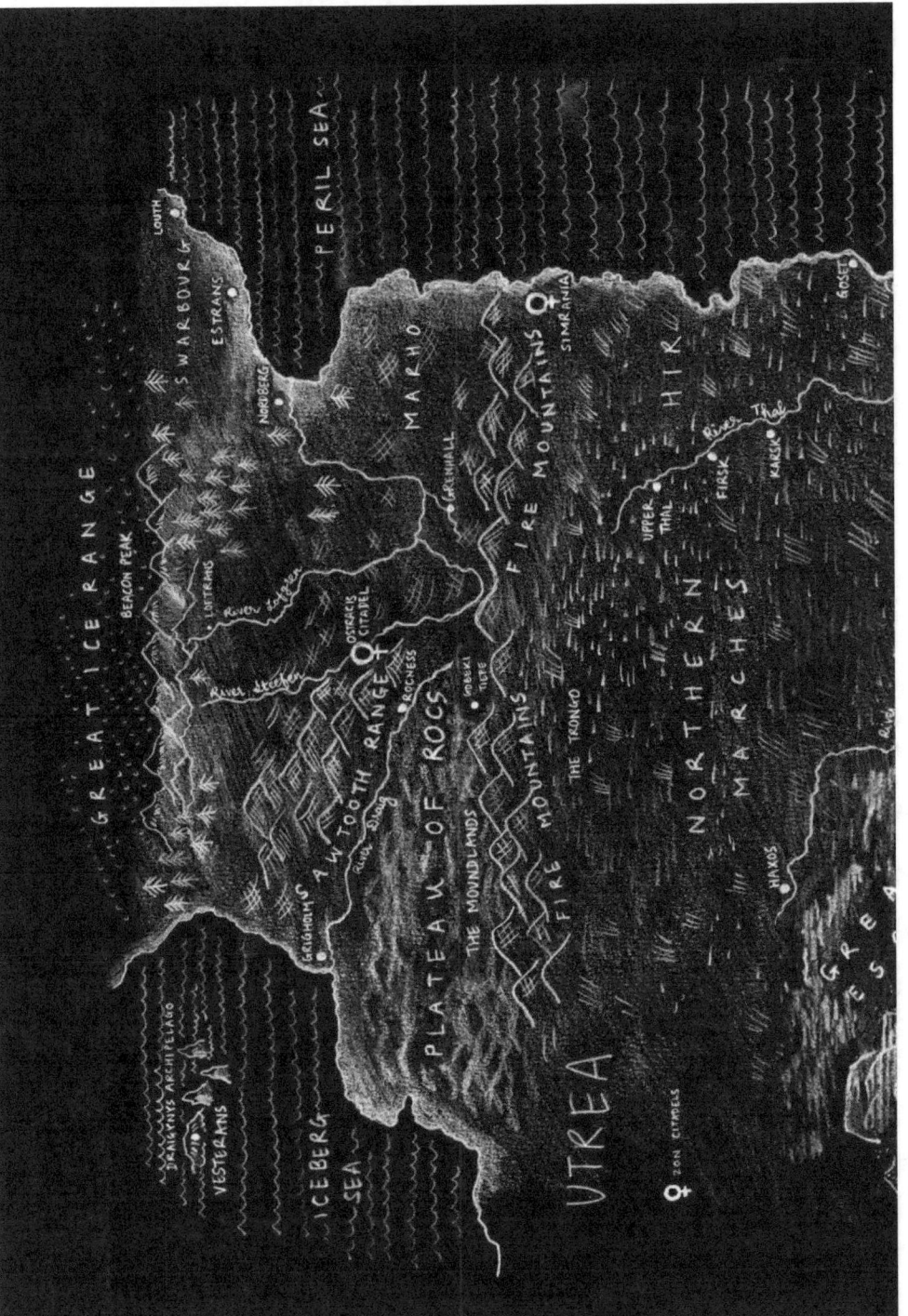

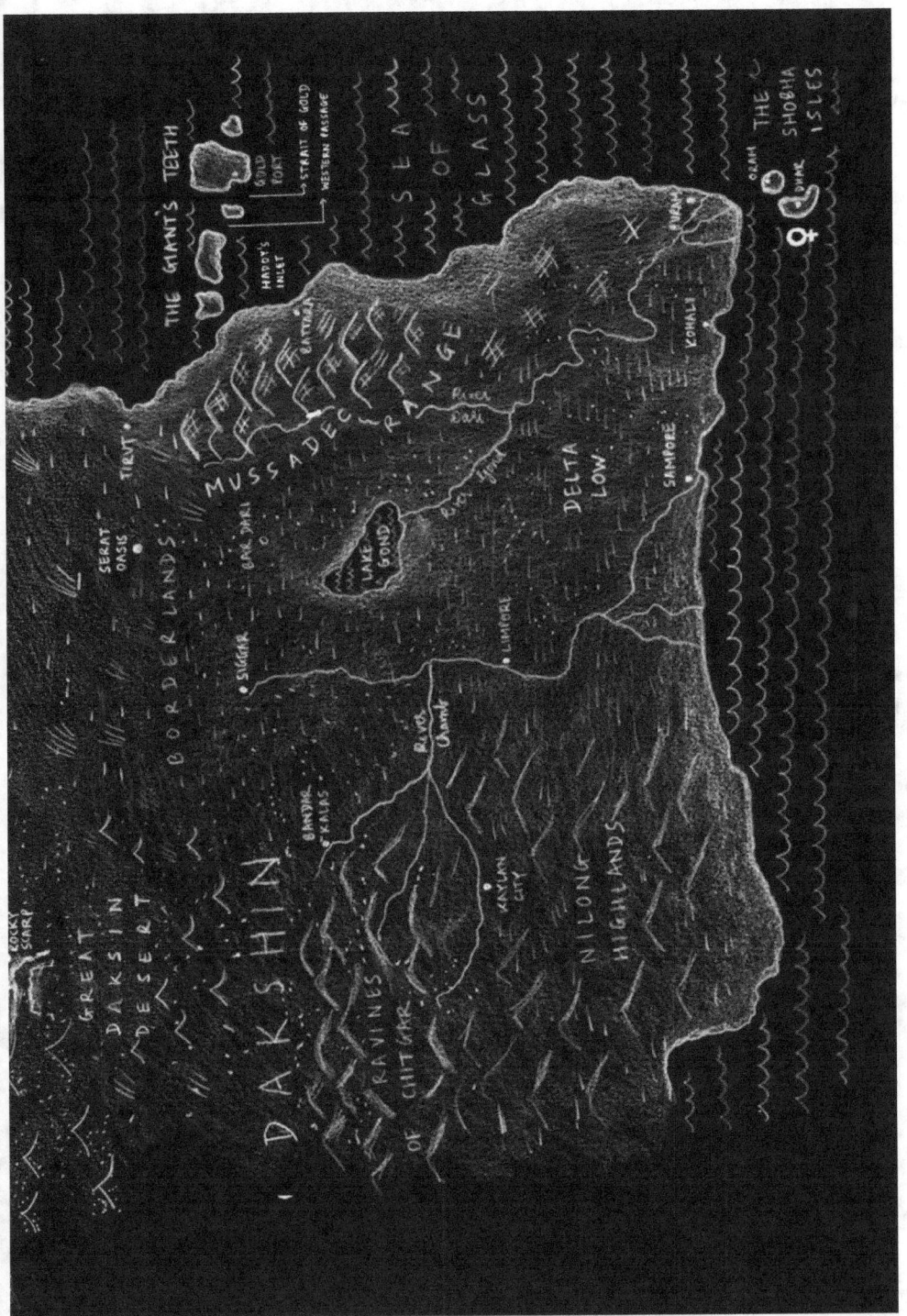

A UNION FORGED, AUTUMN, 1678 Z

LADY VIVIA PRAGARINA, High Mistress of the Zon Trading Guild, normally had a thousand matters in her head that made it difficult to fall asleep. But this night she fell into a deep slumber almost immediately. An hour passed and the bedchamber seemed to grow darker and there was a low hum. Without quite knowing why, Vivia snapped awake and sat up in her huge bed, the shoulder strap of her nightgown slipping down her arm.

There was a white-haired man in brown robes sitting erect on one of her comfortable bedside chairs. He wore a sword and held a stout staff. As she watched, his hand released the staff, but it remained standing. He gave off a faint blue aura. *I am dreaming*, she thought, trying to lie back down and turn her face away from the apparition. But she found that she could not move.

"Vivia Pragarina," he said, his voice gravelly and harsh. "You do not know me, but I know you well. Unknowingly you have thought of me often."

Vivia was not easily cowed. But the strange and unfamiliar nature of the situation had her on edge.

"Whoever or whatever you are," she responded with spirit, "I have never thought of you."

"Ah, but there you are mistaken. For your deepest, most fervent desires lead you to me. I am here because you have opened yourself to me. Indeed, you have been calling to me for years. It is just that you did not know it."

Vivia tried to move again and failed. She willed herself to be calm, thinking, *It is just a nightmare. It will pass, and when I will wake up I will laugh about it.*

"Your talents and capabilities are unmatched in the Sisterhood," he went on. "And yet you have been unjustly kept down. But I can help you get what you truly deserve. I can raise you to the heights you crave."

"If you know so much about me, then tell me—what do I crave? I have everything I ever wanted. I am rich, I have made myself and my daughters electrae, I have become an aristocrat, and my daughter Darbeni will inherit my title after I am gone."

"But it is not enough, is it? For if you were content, I would not have heard your call."

"I crave nothing," she said, her voice rising. "Nothing, I tell you!"

"Such vehemence! I thought you had higher aspirations, but obviously I was in error. Please forgive me."

She knew he was mocking her, but her ambition overcame her irritation.

"What you speak of is impossible."

"Why? You have immense popularity and the Queen Empress cannot rule forever."

"I am popular among the commoners. But they do not vote."

"Ah, but the voting electrae are just as easily swayed as the commoners. I can sway them for you."

Vivia was intrigued, but her hardheadedness did not desert her.

"Why would you do this? What do you have to gain?"

He remained silent for a while, contemplating her. She was in her prime, and her unblemished, unlined skin shone in the light of the yellow moon that spilled in through the viewport. Her gray-green eyes glittered.

"I have watched you, Vivia Pragarina, since you were born. You and I, we are of like mind, a match made for the ages. Worship me, be mine, and I will take corporeal form in your world. In time I will raise you up to immortality, eternal youth!"

"I am Zon. We do not worship men."

"I am not a man! I am one of the Chosen, an immortal."

"How many women have you despoiled in this manner?"

Her tone was unfriendly and insolent. However, it brought a smile to his face.

"It pleases me that I do not intimidate you. It is true, I have had sensual encounters with other women, but they were mere instruments. You are the only one who can complement me, the consort I have been seeking through the centuries."

She did not respond and they sat facing each other. Hours passed, but it no longer seemed to matter. The bedchamber remained in darkness, the only light stemming from his blue aura. Finally she spoke.

"Guide me."

Slowly, his visible image grew less distinct and his blue aura concentrated and grew brighter. Soon the human image disappeared altogether, replaced by a shining point of blue light. She closed her eyes, shutting out the view of her room, but the blue light remained, becoming even sharper.

"Come."

She heard the word clearly. She felt something tugging at her consciousness and fought a brief moment of panic. Then she allowed herself to be led and perceived a feeling of release. Now she was floating and saw her chamber from above. She saw her bed and the sheets in which she had just been sleeping.

She felt a lightness that she had never known before. The point of blue light moved toward the window and she found she could follow it. She drifted out of her palace, rising, rising, till she could look down and see the twinkling lights of Atlantic City from high above, as though she were in an airboat. Then the point of light moved away rapidly and she willed herself to follow it.

It was like nothing she had ever experienced before—all the mental stimulation of flight, without any physical sensation of movement. She could see the contours of the land below her, moving south over the green of the Great Amu-Shan plain, onward over the brown of the Great Daksin Desert and then over the rugged, broken terrain of the Borderlands. She knew where they were going, but she did not know how he had communicated with her. They arrived over an enormous city of imposing edifices, broad boulevards and gigantic plazas. But as they began to descend, it became clear that it was in ruins.

"Bar-Dari," said Vivia. "The ancient capital of the Dhalian Empire. I was brought here as a schoolgirl."

"Yes," he replied, his tone harsh. "A thousand years ago, your Queen Simran brought about the ruin of this great city."

They drifted lower and lower. Then there was a discontinuous jump and Vivia found herself floating in an enormous chamber, high above the floor. It was a house of worship, for there were the remains of dozens of lines of pews and an imposing central nave. But the high altar was in good condition, with hundreds of recent candles and masses of dried flowers.

"The Abaidan Mission House," he said. "The first great House of the One God."

"Your House," said Vivia.

"Indeed. Abaid was my mortal form. When the time came to relinquish it, I ascended to the highest peaks of the Great Ice Range. There amid the snows, I strove with every shred of my being to continue serving the One God. And I was Chosen. I became Malitha."

"You followed the Yengars, a people that Thermad hated. And you contravened his explicit teachings. For did he not say—*Immortality apart from the One God is impossible and such a quest is sinful.*"

"Thermad was naïve. The infidels have always offered blandishments to tempt the faithful, and draw the Mission away from the True Path. I saw that to continue the fight against the false gods and their servants, I had to adopt their methods. Without my centuries of guidance, the Mission would have been suborned by the unbelievers. It would have been overcome by the Yengars, the Gandharas, the Zon Sisterhood. Moksha and Ma would gradually have replaced the One God. By now, nothing would have been left."

"But you preserved the Thermadan Mission."

"Yes, I did. But our greatest test is before us. A new power has come forth into our world, born of d'Orr and Nibellus, Zon and One Lander. Allowed to grow to maturity, it will consume us. Join me in this battle, Vivia Pragarina. And rule with me."

"Your enemies are my enemies," said Vivia. "I will be united with you. Forever."

"Then lie on the altar."

She slowly floated down, till she sensed the candles and dried flowers about her. The altar was smooth, cold, and hard. She felt his caress, and it was lighter than any touch she had ever known. She lay back and luxuriated as he traced the lines of her body. Then he wove a cocoon of deeper darkness around the two of them and showed her how to worship him.

LATE AUTUMN, 1678 Z

The Zon Sisterhood and its institutions represent the pinnacle of human advancement. The preservation of Zon culture and values requires that the Sisterhood seal off its small population from the barbarian masses in impregnable citadels. It is our manifest destiny to eradicate the barbarian patriarchy and spread Zon civilization throughout New Eartha.

– From the Coronation Address of Simran the Merciless, 662 Z

HORESKOT IN THE SOUTHERN MARCHES

 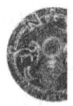

L OVE OF ANIMALS was a central feature of Zon culture, but horses occupied a special place in this pantheon. All Zon were brought up undertaking a range of equine activities, working in stables, grooming and caring for horses and of course, riding. Even the least athletic among them were good riders and Caitlin d'Orr was one of the best.

So when she saw a herd of horses in the distance, she touched Rufus's flanks with her heels, urging him on toward them. A few mares pricked up their ears, but most of the herd ignored their approach. They were obviously not wild horses, but nonetheless, they shied away as she came near, no doubt intimidated by Rufus's huge size. A few young males stood at a distance, eyeing her and Rufus defiantly. One bay in particular stood out. To anyone he was an attractive animal, but to Caitlin's Zon eyes, he was gorgeous. He had a white blaze and socks, and his mane was thick and dark. His coat was bright, and the morning light gave it a liquid shine.

"He's almost as handsome as you, Rufus," Caitlin whispered in her mount's ear. Rufus neighed as though he understood her. He sounded indignant to her indulgent ear, and she patted his neck.

As Caitlin watched, a slim boy rose from a rock outcropping behind the young horse. He was completely focused on his objective and had not seen Caitlin, screened as she was by the herd. He crept up on the young horse and Caitlin saw that he had a rope in his hand. He threw the loop around the horse's neck and managed to leap aboard. The horse snorted loudly and reared, but the boy hung on, one hand on the rope and the other around the horse's neck. The horse bucked wildly a few times, but when his unwelcome rider hung on, he took off across the dusty plain at a full gallop.

The boy hung on grimly—clearly he had ridden before. But Caitlin's experience told her that it was only a matter of time before he was thrown. She touched her heels to Rufus's flanks again, gave him just the hint of guidance with the reins and they were off in pursuit. Rufus was big, but he was also strong and very fast, a mature campaigner. The young horse began to tire and they began to overhaul the wild pair. The bay abruptly stopped, and as Caitlin expected, bucked again and again. The boy kept his seat for the first two leaps, but on the third he was thrown. He fell hard, fortunately missing a boulder, and lay groaning. The horse cantered back toward the herd, the rope still trailing from its neck.

Caitlin leaped off Rufus and knelt by the boy on the kneepads of her thigh boots. He had a light brown complexion and a shock of thick, dark hair. Up close, she saw that he was older than she had thought, for his slim build had made him appear younger.

"Lie still," she said to him in Brigish, for they were in the Southern Marches of the Kingdom of Briga. His eyes widened in surprise as she leaned over him, her red hair looking fiery with the sun behind it.

She gently rolled him onto his back and went through a basic field medical examination. There was nothing broken. The range of motion in his arms seemed to indicate minimal ligament damage. However, he had some significant contusions and an egg-shaped swelling was rapidly forming on his skull.

"It could have been a lot worse," she said to him.

"It is not my horse," he said, sounding dazed. The non sequitur indicated to her that he was confused and almost certainly concussed.

"What is your name?" she asked him.

"I'm Dhanraj," he said, faltering. As the shock wore off, the pain set in and he gritted his teeth.

"Where do you live?" she asked.

"Live?" he asked in response.

He was clearly not coherent enough to be any use, so she pulled out her communicator and tapped it to bring up a terrain map. The sensors indicated habitation a few kilometers to the east. He was not too heavy, so she was able to pick him up and put him on Rufus. She mounted behind him and they walked slowly eastward.

Caitlin's communicator had indicated a small collection of buildings and they soon appeared as small indentations on the horizon of the flat landscape. As they came closer it was apparent that there was a ranch with a small hamlet a kilometer further away. The location of the dwellings was made clear by a small spring that burbled out of the ground by the ranch and formed a stream that flowed down toward the hamlet.

Caitlin rode into the small yard between the ranch and its barn. There were some assorted chickens and ducks that scurried out of Rufus's way, clucking and quacking angrily. A square man with a craggy face emerged from the barn in response to the stir in the yard. He wore weathered clothing that had seen hard use and was patched and resewn in numerous places. His eyes were brown and kindly, and he surveyed Caitlin in silence, without hostility.

She swung down from the saddle and carefully lowered the boy on the ground. His concussion was worse than it seemed at first, and he swam in and out of semiconsciousness, sometimes babbling incoherently.

"I see you have Dhanraj, the Yengar boy," said the man. His voice was warm, but his tone betrayed some irritation. "I've told him a thousand times to stay away from the horses. Did one of them kick him?"

"He tried to ride the young bay," replied Caitlin in fluent Brigish. She tried to speak flat and slowly to disguise her singsong Zon accent. "He was thrown."

"The young fool!" the man expostulated. He wiped his hands on the seat of his pants. "I guess you had better bring him inside."

Caitlin picked up the boy and followed the man, carrying him inside the ranch. The living room was rough, but warm and welcoming, with comfortable furniture, a scoured wood floor, and stone walls. There was a very attractive fireplace, though there was no fire lit at the moment. Caitlin lay the boy down on the couch and straightened to see the man looking at her curiously.

"Who are you, stranger, and what brings you to Hareskot?" he asked.

"My name is Cat," she said, keeping her voice low. "My mother died, so I decided to travel."

"I am sorry to hear it," said the man, sounding surprisingly genuine. "I am Seamus. Do you know anything about healing, or should I go to the village and fetch the herbalist?"

"I think I know enough," said Caitlin. "I will need some ice if you have it, or some damp cloths."

"We have no ice," Seamus said. "But I will wet some cloths in the kitchen and bring them to you."

He returned a few minutes later to find Caitlin covering Dhanraj's legs with a blanket that had been draped over one of the chairs. She wordlessly took the damp cloths from Seamus and gently wiped the boy's forehead and before laying one on the contusion on his head. He breathed fitfully, but eventually fell into a restless sleep.

"Not much you can do with a concussion," said Caitlin. "Rest is what he needs. Hopefully he has sustained no internal injuries and will be over the worst of it by tomorrow. He is young; he should be fine in a day or two."

Seamus looked at Caitlin curiously, taking in her sword, dagger, thigh boots, and leathers.

"You are a woman, yet you are attired like a warrior," he said cautiously.

"The roads are dangerous," Caitlin replied. "A woman traveling alone must take precautions."

"Yes, in spite of the restoration of good King Harald," agreed Seamus. "The king's patrols have returned and they do good work, but they are few and stretched too thin. I carry a sword and a crossbow myself when I travel."

He paused.

"I was just going to have some lunch," he said, changing the subject. "You are welcome to join me. My wife is shopping in the village, she will not be back before tea."

"I will be glad to join you," said Caitlin, realizing that she was quite hungry. "Indeed, I will be happy to wait on you," she continued, recalling that barbarian women were expected to serve men.

"I wish you would teach my wife," he smiled. "Thirty years we have been married, but she still hasn't learned to wait on me."

He led the way to the kitchen and they sat at a solid stone topped table, and ate a simple, but hearty lunch of homemade bread and cheese, with some assorted vegetables.

"My wife, Binne, keeps me well fed," Seamus said, burping after he wolfed down a few hunks of bread with cheese. "Though I hope you will forgive our lack of meat—money has been tight for us this year."

Caitlin had eaten more delicately, and spoke only after she had cleaned her plate.

"This is better than I have eaten in many weeks," she said. "I thank you, sir—there was nothing lacking."

She stood up.

"If you will give me some oats, I will cook a gruel for the boy," she said. "He will be quite dizzy still and is unlikely to have much of an appetite. I will also need some fresh wet cloths."

Seamus showed Caitlin where the food and utensils were stored and gave her some more cloths. Then he left to return to the barn saying, "I must get back to mucking out the stalls."

Caitlin spent the afternoon in the living room with young Dhanraj, feeding him the gruel, changing the wet cloths and keeping him under observation. In the late afternoon she heard voices out in the yard and soon Seamus came in followed by a small, slender woman with curly white hair. She was smiling and her twinkling eyes looked like they were eager to be happy with whatever she came across. Caitlin took a liking to her at first sight.

"My, my, Seamus," she said, laughing. "I go away for half a day and return to find you in the company of a gorgeous belle. What would you do if I went away for a week?"

"Your husband has been very kind to me," said Caitlin, smiling. "He has also been very helpful in caring for this young boy who was thrown trying to ride one of your horses."

"Yes, yes," said Binne, clicking her tongue. "I met Dhanraj's parents in the village. One of the village boys saw you bringing him back here on your horse. They are very worried about him, but they are too old and frail to come here on their own. I assured them that Seamus would bring them tidings of their boy by tonight. We are happy to have him here till he is fit to be moved." She paused and gave Caitlin a very warmhearted look. "Of course, we would be delighted if you would stay and care for him till then. It is hard enough keeping this ranch going with the two of us—we are not as young as we once were."

Binne hung up her shawl as she spoke and went to work in the kitchen, while Seamus went back outside. A couple of hours later, delicious smells proceeded from the kitchen. Seamus returned, having made the trip to the village. He told Binne and Caitlin he had met with Dhanraj's parents and laid their fears to rest. Then he excused himself to go and wash up.

Dusk set in and Seamus was building a fire in the grate when Dhanraj finally came round. The boy was very confused and had no recollection of what had happened to him.

"Who are you?" he asked Caitlin, when he was able to sit up. "Why am I at Seamus and Binne's?"

"You are lucky I happened to come by," scolded Caitlin. "It was incredibly silly of you to try and ride that young bay. Even if you could ride him, it would be wrong to do so without asking Seamus for permission."

Dhanraj looked abashed.

"I love horses," he said, looking down at his feet. "But we are very poor. I could never afford to own one."

"You should have asked Seamus for work in his stables," said Caitlin severely. "Then he might have let you ride a horse."

"He cannot work out here," said Binne, bustling in. "His parents need him to care for them several times a day. I am sure they already miss him sorely."

Dhanraj looked guilty.

"I must return to them," he said, attempting to stand. He teetered and then sat back down.

"You will have to spend the night here," said Seamus firmly, standing up from the fire that was now blazing brightly. "I will take you to the village in the morning."

The four of them sat down to dinner in the kitchen. Binne had made a much more appetizing gruel for Dhanraj and there was a very hearty stew for the other three, washed down with a hoppy home-brewed ale. Afterward, Binne brought out a spice cake and an old bottle that contained *Kharvas*, an anise-flavored rye alcohol. It went down very well, but Caitlin had not drunk this much since her days carousing with her huntress girlfriends. Without realizing it, relapsed into her strong singsong Zon accent. Seamus exchanged a look with Binne, but they did not say anything.

Caitlin offered to bed down in the barn, but Seamus and Binne would not hear of it. Binne made a bed for Dhanraj on the couch in the living room and another one by the fire for Caitlin from a pile of blankets and pillows. Caitlin was far too sleepy to argue. She obediently took the nightdress Binne gave her and went into their bedroom to change. It was a floor-length shift, but she was so much taller than Binne that it barely covered her knees. Then she came out and burrowed into the bed Binne had made for her. After weeks of camping, the bed was incredibly comfortable and fire was warm. She fell into a dreamless slumber almost immediately.

CAITLIN WAS AWAKENED by sunlight streaming in through the window behind her head. She smelled aromas wafting out of the kitchen and arose, yawning and stretching. She went to the bath-house, performed her toilette, and dressed just as Binne called them all to eat. Dhanraj ate with good appetite and seemed quite recovered. So after they ate, Seamus hitched a pony to a small trap and set out with him for Hareskot village.

"So is it just the two of you on the ranch?" asked Caitlin, as they watched the trap rattle out of the yard.

"Yes, now it is just the two of us," said Binne, her normally cheerful face clouding over. She did not speak for a long while. Caitlin did not press her, but eventually Binne continued. "We were childless for many years, but we prayed hard to the One God and ultimately he heard us. In late middle age, when we had given up hope, he gave us a daughter that we named Marte. We were the luckiest parents in the world, for we could not have asked for a more loving and devoted child. She grew into a beautiful woman and many asked for her hand. But she would not consider anyone who would not live on the ranch with us." She sighed. "It is a hard life out here in the barren Southern Marches, and none were willing to accept those terms."

Binne stopped and clicked her tongue.

"But you don't want to hear the sad ramblings of an old woman," she said, trying to brighten up.

"No, no," insisted Caitlin. "I am very interested. Please go on."

"We should have forced her to marry someone from the towns, for many merchants' sons were taken with her," continued Binne hesitantly, not sure whether Caitlin was really interested or just being polite. "Then she would have been safe. For when the Chekaligas came earlier this year, they took our Marte." Tears started from Binne's eyes. "I wish that they had killed us both instead of merely beating us. It would have spared us the tortures imagining what they must have done to her and how she must have suffered. The men from Hareskot found her mutilated body a week later. At least we could give her a funeral and say good-bye, unlike some other parents whose daughters were never found." She paused. "I suppose that is a blessing from the One God."

"I thought that Briga and Daksin pay the Zon Sisterhood to keep tribes like the Chekaligas in the hills and ravines," said Caitlin slowly.

"I know nothing of politics and kingdoms," said Binne, wiping her eyes. "Perhaps the Zon Legions protect King Harald in Dreslin Center and King Vokran in Sampore. All I know is that here in the Southern Marches, the Chekaligas come when they want and take what they want."

"That is scandalous!" cried Caitlin. "You pay taxes—where are the king's troops when the Chekaligas come?"

"They come sometimes," said Binne, still teary-eyed. "But mostly they remain in their forts on the Daksin border."

They sat in silence for a while. Caitlin felt like putting a protective arm around Binne but did not want to presume on such intimacy. So she just sat there and shifted uncomfortably in her seat.

"I will go out on to the range and bring in that young bay," Caitlin said, breaking the silence that was threatening to become embarrassingly long. "He probably still has the rope that young Dhanraj threw around his neck."

IT DID NOT take Caitlin long to find the young bay. He was grazing a short distance from the bulk of the herd. He was feisty, but for a horsewoman of Caitlin's skill, he was not much of a challenge, and she soon had him under control. An hour later, she had him in a stall in the barn and after a few nervous shies, he allowed her to pet him.

She scoured the barn and assembled a grooming kit. After loosening the dirt in his coat with a curry comb, she used a hard-bristled brush in short strokes to remove it. The familiar action of rapid strokes in the direction of his coat growth was therapeutic. She lost herself in the rhythm and worked tirelessly till his coat was beautifully clean and soft. Finally, she used a grooming towel to work his coat into a high gloss.

Tired but content, she rested her back on one of the posts of the barn and surveyed her work.

"There," she said to him. "Look how attractive you are. Let us take you out to the corral and make Rufus jealous."

She led him out to the corral with her zircon lasso and shut the corral gate after him. Rufus intimidated the young bay. Although the huge red ignored him, he moved to far end of the corral. Caitlin leaned on the corral rails and called her horse. Rufus obediently trotted over, and she fed him the handful of oats she had in her hand. He nuzzled her, and she patted his neck, saying, "He's just a needy young lad. You're not jealous, are you?" Rufus was used to Caitlin talking to him, and he whickered.

Caitlin was brought out of her horse world by the sound of the trap. She walked back into the yard to meet Seamus and was surprised to see that he had brought Dhanraj back with him. Binne also came out of the ranch house. Both the women could see that something was terribly wrong. Seamus looked dazed, and while Dhanraj hung his head, they could see that his face was wet with tears.

As Seamus drew the reins to bring the trap to a stop in the yard, Binne spoke first.

"What happened? Why did you bring Dhanraj back?"

Seamus did not respond immediately. He climbed down from the trap and put his hand out to Dhanraj. The boy ignored his hand, leaped down from the trap, and ran into the ranch house. They heard him sobbing noisily through the open window.

"A pair of proselytizing Thermadan preachers came to Hareskot yesterday," said Seamus. "When they learned that there were Yengars in the village, they whipped the locals into a frenzy with their talk of heresy and servants of the Evil One. They goaded a mob of youths into attacking Dhanraj's parents. They beat them to death!"

"The poor old souls!" cried Binne. "They could barely walk! We know all the lads in the village. Surely they could not be so cruel."

"People will do all manner of cruelty if they think they are serving God," said Seamus tiredly. "I turned around and returned here as soon as I heard what had happened. I am afraid they will come here today, looking for Dhanraj. As you know, Cat was seen bringing him here yesterday."

"Did they see him with you?" asked Caitlin.

"No, I don't think so," said Seamus. "I had him hunker down in the trap. I did not wait around to answer questions."

"I am sure you are right; they will come here looking for Dhanraj," said Binne decisively. "If anyone comes, we must say that he died from his injuries. I will hide him in our secret cellar below the kitchen floor."

Caitlin said nothing, but helped Seamus take care of the trap and pony. They had barely completed this when they heard the clatter of hooves in the yard. They came out from the barn. Binne emerged from the ranch house, drawn by the same sounds.

It was a ragtag mounted group. At their head was a hard-faced horseman with a beaky nose, whose face was as leathery as his garb. His bearing radiated authority and he was clearly used to command.

His sword and the crossbow slung over his back looked well used. He wore a wide-brimmed hat, and there was a bronze badge pinned to his vest.

Beside him were a couple of black-robed, middle-aged Thermadan preachers astride donkeys. They had thinning hair and well-upholstered middles. Behind them were two more warriors, who wore red vests over their traveling armor and half a dozen youths on unkempt ponies, armed with staffs and axes.

"Collector Yandharan," said Seamus, addressing the leading man. "What brings you out here from the Serat Oasis?"

Instead of the leader, one of preachers responded, his tone arrogant.

"We met the Collector in Hareskot and he has accompanied us here. Along with our Red Sentinels, we are bringing the love of the One God, Lord Thermad, and the Thermadan Mission to the poor, rural folk of the Southern Marches. And to visit his fury on those who refuse to accept this love."

"I have gone to the House of the One God since I was a little girl," said Binne, speaking slowly but firmly. "I was taught that he stood for love, not rage or violence."

"You are unread and ignorant, old woman," said the other preacher, sneering. "You should read the Abaidan interpretation of Thermad. In Qura III, he tells us plainly, *'To the infidels, I offer a simple choice—acceptance of the One God or death.'* "

"We offered the love of the One God to the old Yengar couple in Hareskot," continued the first. "But the old man had the gall to tell us, 'I have worshipped Lord Moksha for over six decades, I see no advantage in giving him up now.'" He shuddered theatrically. "To hear the Evil One called upon so brazenly! It made my flesh crawl. Fortunately, the right-thinking youths of Hareskot put an end to their blasphemy."

Neither Seamus nor Binne responded to this speech. The second preacher laboriously dismounted from his donkey.

"The folk in Hareskot tell us that you have the Yengar couple's son here," he said, leaning on his staff mounted with the Thermadan triangle. "Give him up to us—for we must bring him the love of the One God."

"How do you propose to do that?" asked Caitlin, in a low voice. They had been eyeing her surreptitiously and now they all stared at her openly.

"Why, the devout will chastise him with rocks, sticks, and axes in the normal manner as they did his parents," responded the first preacher. "If he truly accepts the One God, nothing will harm him." He paused and eyed Caitlin suspiciously before turning to Seamus. "I smell sin here, rancher. Your women are bold and forward, with uncovered heads and faces. And this young one, dressed as a warrior—who is she?"

Seamus saw Caitlin's indignant expression and spoke quickly before she got them all into deeper trouble.

"She is our daughter and has just returned from travel." To prevent further discussion, he returned to their question about Dhanraj. "We did indeed have the young Yengar boy here. As you probably heard in the village, he was badly hurt trying to ride one of our horses. The One God has done your work for you, for he died of his injuries last night."

"Hand over his body," said the first preacher promptly. "It must be hung in the village square with his parents to show the good citizens the wages of serving the Evil One."

"We burned his body," said Binne hastily. "We hear that is what the Yengars do with their dead."

"So you performed the dark rites of the Yengars, did you?" asked the second preacher ominously. "I'm getting a very bad feeling about all of this. Collector Yandharan, you must search the premises. Our Red Sentinels will assist you."

"We are honest folk, we have nothing to hide," said Binne, trying to sound cheerful. "But you must allow me to provide you gentlemen with some refreshment before you begin your search. Seamus, pray seat them all on the porch, I will bring out some snacks and cold drinks."

The preachers looked at each other. It was hot, and they were not in the best of shape. The offer of cold drinks was attractive.

"All right," said the first preacher slowly. "I suppose there can be no harm in it. While we fault you for your uncovered head, your generosity to the servants of Thermad does you credit."

Binne disappeared into the kitchen, signaling Caitlin to follow her. The men began to dismount and make their way to the porch, while Seamus hurried to carry out more chairs from the living room, so that everyone could sit. Yandharan went into the living room with Seamus to help him.

"I thought your daughter was killed by the Chekaligas," he said to Seamus when they were out of earshot of the others.

"We thought she was," said Seamus nervously. "As you know, the Chekaligas are cruel, but unpredictable. They grew tired of her and released her. It is our great good fortune."

"I recall your daughter as being attractive," deadpanned Yandharan. "But she seems to have grown paler and much taller."

"Perhaps you are confusing her with someone else," said Seamus, licking his lips. "She has always been pale and tall—takes after Binne's mother's side of the family. They were Utrean."

"I see," said Yandharan. He pursed his lips and said no more.

While all the others seated themselves on chairs on the porch, Yandharan leaned on the porch railing. Binne and Caitlin came out with trays of cold drinks and small bowls of crunchy nuts. As the men ate and drank, the women remained standing and replenished their glasses and bowls. The preachers drank several glasses and crunched their way through several bowls of nuts.

Finally, one of them said, "Well, we must begin the search. Collector Yandharan, you are experienced in these matters—please guide our Red Sentinels and the devout youths who have followed us."

Yandharan slowly uncoiled himself from the porch railing. To Caitlin's experienced eye, he was the most formidable warrior present. She did not make eye contact with him but watched him out of the corner of her eye. Several times she caught him looking at her, but unlike the others, he did not ogle her. He seemed to be assessing her, carefully observing her weaponry and carriage.

Yandharan led the two Red Sentinels and the gaggle of youths into the yard. They began by searching the barn and other outbuildings and then came back to go through the ranch house. Throughout, Yandharan was deliberate and thorough. His face remained expressionless and he said little. The two preachers remained seated on the porch. They spoke to each other in loud voices and kept ordering Binne to bring them more refreshments.

It was over an hour later when Yandharan led the motley crew back to the porch.

"We have searched the premises thoroughly," he said indifferently. "There is no trace of the boy. We found a large pile of incinerated rubbish behind the barn—nothing out of the ordinary."

"Did you burn the boy's body on the rubbish heap?" asked one of the preachers of Seamus.

The rancher nodded without speaking.

"As the rancher says, the One God seems to have done our work for us," said Yandharan. "I assume you preachers will proceed on your tour toward the Serat Oasis and the local lads will return to Hareskot."

"What of you, Collector?" asked one of the preachers. "Will you not accompany us and do the work of the One God?"

"I am afraid my return will delayed by the more mundane work of the king," said Yandharan lightly, but unsmiling. "You have your Red Sentinels to protect you from the dangers of the road."

The preachers scowled. They gathered their robes about them, mounted their donkeys and departed without further word, followed by the Red Sentinels. The youths from Hareskot left in ones and twos shortly afterward, slinking away with downcast eyes. None of them made eye contact or spoke to Seamus or Binne. The Collector remained, leaning on the porch rail.

"Seamus Avedus, you have satisfied the servants of the One God," he said. "But that is not my province; I am here to serve the king. I find that you are on my list of tax delinquents."

Seamus smiled weakly.

"Collector Yandharan," he said, running his hands through his thinning hair. "We need some more time. It has been a difficult year for us. The Chekaligas came and took the most valuable part of our herd, so we had little for the auctions. But we will raise the money somehow and pay soon."

Yandharan shook his head.

"I understand your position, rancher," he said. Caitlin wondered how he could maintain such a level presence—there was no malevolence, but no empathy either. "But you must understand mine. The King's tax collectors come to Serat every year and when my cheval is in arrears, he must pay from his own coffers. When he has to do that, he becomes upset with Collectors like me and our heads do not rest easy on our shoulders."

Seamus looked wretched and had no reply.

"Collector Yandharan," said Binne, interceding. "We have interacted over the years—surely you must remember us? We have been diligent taxpayers, year in, year out. This is our first delinquency. We will pay, we only beg you for some more time."

Yandharan shook his head.

"I am sorry, madam," he said. "The numbers in my ledgers in Serat are cruel. If you do not have the gold, you must come with me to debtors' prison in Serat. Your ranch will be sold to raise the tax and then you will be released. If the proceeds of the sale exceed the tax you owe, you will receive the balance—you can depend on my honesty."

Binne looked crushed. Seamus put his arm around Binne's slim shoulders and held her.

"Come, my dear," he said to her, dropping the pretense that Caitlin was their daughter. "With our daughter gone, what have we to live for? What need have we for possessions? We may as well beg in the streets of Serat as work here."

Binne looked at Yandharan, who met her gaze steadily and without emotion.

"You are a good man, Collector Yandharan," she said. "You have always been fair to us. We know you are only doing your duty. Will you give us some time to pack? We promise not to take anything of value."

He nodded. Binne turned to Caitlin.

"Cat, I am sorry that we cannot offer you any further hospitality," she continued. "But I am sure Collector Yandharan will not mind if you stay here for a few weeks till the ranch is sold. It will give us comfort, knowing that it is being used by someone as good of heart as you."

"You may stay here," said Yandharan, addressing Caitlin. "But not under false pretenses. You are not their trueborn daughter—they have admitted as much. Who are you?"

Caitlin looked over at the old couple, who were now making their way slowly toward the ranch house. The impending loss of everything they knew weighed on them heavily and their shoulders sagged. They looked older, defeated. *They are good people*, she thought. *To be reduced to begging in Serat! They will not survive long in the streets, consumed with grief over their dead daughter.* She made up her mind.

"I am not related to them by blood," agreed Caitlin. "But I am Cat Avedus—their adopted daughter."

This stopped both Seamus and Binne in their tracks. They turned around and looked at her, surprised.

"And I will not stand idly by and allow you to take them to debtors' prison," she continued.

"How do you propose to stop me?" asked Yandharan. Caitlin expected to hear mockery or bravado in his tone, but there was none.

"With whatever works," she said determinedly.

"Don't push me, girl," said Yandharan, finally beginning to show some impatience. "If you foist a fight on me, you will rue it."

Caitlin had no intention of provoking a clash, but his calling her "girl" nettled her.

"You are very confident of your skills," she responded angrily, her hand on the hilt of the ancient d'Orr sword, Nasht. "Perhaps overconfident."

"I never fight unless I have to," he returned. "But if you force the issue, you will find me competent. So unless you can come up with the five gold talents of tax money, draw your sword or step aside."

Growing up rich and privileged, the sum seemed trivially small to Caitlin.

"Is that *all?*" she asked, stupefied. "You would drive two decent people to beggary for such a sum? *I* will pay the tax."

Caitlin turned on her heel and disappeared into the ranch house, passing Seamus and Binne on the way. Her saddlebags were by the head of her makeshift bed. She quickly drew out a leather sack, untied it, and counted out six gold talents. Retying the sack and secreting it in her saddlebag again, she reemerged into the yard.

Yandharan put out his left hand and Caitlin dropped the coins into it. He saw immediately that there were six coins. Before she could withdraw her hand, he caught her wrist saying, "Where did you get hold of such a large sum of money? And you think this bribe of a gold talent will keep me from asking inconvenient questions?"

Caitlin had not anticipated his action, but the assault on her person drew forth the conditioned response drummed into her by long training. She smoothly drew the long dagger from her left thigh boot, and Yandharan felt rather than saw its sharp tip at his solar plexus. To make her point, she pushed the tip of the dagger through his leather vest till it pricked his skin. He looked into her green eyes and saw something manic. *The bitch is crazy*, he thought.

"Release me," she hissed. "Or I will gut you. Take your money and leave."

He released her wrist and backed away slowly. But he looked unafraid and maddeningly calm. He casually unslung his crossbow, put in a bolt, and began to wind it. Caitlin drew Nasht, tensed, and prepared to rush him.

Seamus approached them quickly.

"Stop, stop!" he cried. "This is all a misunderstanding. Cat has just returned from selling stock at the Dreslin auction. The One God be praised, I had no idea she was able to get such a good price."

"Six gold talents?" asked Yandharan doubtfully.

"All of the stock that the Chekaligas left us," put in Binne, coming up to Seamus's side.

"I see," said Yandharan. He looked from one to the other. Grunting, he slowly began to unwind his crossbow. Caitlin waited till he had slung it over his back again before sheathing her sword and dagger.

Without warning, Yandharan flipped one of the heavy gold pieces away toward Caitlin's left. In spite of being completely unprepared, she instinctively extended her left hand and caught it easily.

"I will forget the attempted bribery," he said. "And I will forgive the delinquency. This time. Your taxes are paid." He turned and unhurriedly mounted his horse. Looking down from the saddle, he addressed Caitlin. "You are a remarkable warrior and athlete, Cat Avedus. If I were you, I would not flaunt those skills." He turned his horse's head and trotted out of the yard without a backward glance.

As Seamus watched Yandharan disappear down the road, Binne came up to Caitlin and looked up into her big green eyes. She was only chest high to her, so she had to reach up to put a hand on each of Caitlin's cheeks.

"You are an angel sent down by the One God," she said. "We will repay you. I don't know how, but we will."

Caitlin took both her hands in hers.

"You are good and kind people," she said. "I don't want money. I ask for something far more valuable in repayment."

"Ask and it is yours," said Binne. "If it be my very life."

Caitlin looked down at her kindly old face, such a contrast to the glamorous beauty of her dead mother. She was seized with a sudden urge to cry.

"I ask for a home," she said quietly.

Binne looked at her steadily and Caitlin thought at first that she had not understood her. Then to her horror, big tears appeared in her eyes and rolled down her cheeks. Binne did not bother to wipe them away but drew Caitlin into her arms and hugged her tightly, not letting her go.

"My dear, my dear," she sobbed. "The One God is too kind!" Still holding Caitlin, she looked up at her face. "Oh, you must forgive a silly old woman, for I cannot stop these tears of joy. From the first moment I laid eyes on you, I felt a special connection."

Caitlin looked over Binne's head at Seamus, who stood awkwardly, shifting his weight from one leg to the other. But the grin that split his face from ear to ear proclaimed his happiness.

AUTUMN 1685 Z TO SPRING 1686 Z

Intellectual as well as physical excellence being essential to the prosperity and security of the Sisterhood, suffrage is hereby limited to those who demonstrate superior capabilities in one or both of these realms. Intellectual brilliance will be recognized by admission to the *priestess temples*, and athletic virtuosity will be the basis of selection into the *huntress legions*.

– Proclamation of Thetis the Great, 456 Z

TWO

THE O'ORR HEIRESS

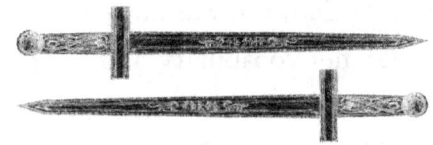

UPPER MOAT FALLS made a silver curtain in the growing light of an autumn sunrise. There was a nip in the morning air that caused Megara Paurina to raise her temperature shield and widen it to include the small raven-haired child asleep on a blanket beside her. She lay on the grass at the edge of the falls, watching the water cascade off the sheer cliff to form the Stevia River several hundred meters below. But out of the corner of her eye, she maintained a constant watch on another child gamboling a safe distance from the cliff edge. As she watched, the child climbed onto one of the low branches of a dwarf oak and walked out on it till it thinned so she could jump and cause it to sway under her weight. The rising sun caught in her mop of ash-blonde curls as they bounced prettily about her head. Now almost two meters above the ground, she did a few small hops and then a pirouette at the end of which she landed on one foot.

"Careful now, Asgara," said Megara, speaking as she would to a much older child. "There's no one to catch you if you fall, so don't get too adventurous."

"I'll be careful, Mother," the child replied, her childish pronunciation belying her articulation and composure.

Like all children in the Sisterhood, Asgara had been continually tested, assessed, and analyzed since conception. Even among the obsessively selective Zon, she was an outlier. Her analytic skills, her grasp of social cues, her vocabulary, and her physical capabilities and attributes were all virtually unmatched in the State nursery system, even among children older than her. But to Megara, her most endearing quality was her uncanny reproduction of Caitlin's presence. Every mannerism and characteristic—the way she tossed her head, the way she fluttered her hands, the way she walked, even the tone of her voice and the cadence of her speech—recalled her biological mother.

Watching her now, Megara thought of the day seven years earlier when she had become legal mother to Asgara, who was then less than a year old. She had taken a leave of absence and flown back to Atlantic City from her post at the Brigon Residency as soon as she heard of Caitlin's departure into exile. When she arrived at Temple Heights nursery and identified herself, they gave her the package Caitlin had left for her. In it were several presents and d'Orr mementos that Caitlin had left for her daughter and a checklist of when she was to have them. Also on the list was the code to access a legal document in her comm data vault that gave Megara title to all Caitlin's possessions in Atlantic City. And at the very bottom of the list, there was the code for a personal site on the comm.

Megara had sequestered herself in a small private arbor in the nursery grounds and tapped her wrist bracer to open the site. Caitlin's familiar persona appeared on the projected hologram, dressed in barbarian leathers.

"My dearest Megara," she said. "I have no doubt that you flew to Temple Heights Nursery as soon as you learned of my decision to go into exile. I knew I could depend on you, for in all of the Sisterhood, you are closest to my heart. It is on the strength of this intimacy that I remind you of your promise to take my place as my daughter's mother. I want the best for her and I fear my presence in the Sisterhood will drag her down, perhaps even into silencis. I could not bear to be the cause of her failing to achieve her enormous potential. Megara, you are brave, beautiful, intelligent, strong—you exemplify Zon ideals like my mother did. You can teach my Asgara to become a worthy heiress to the Royal Tiara of d'Orr. I hope that under your tutelage, she will grow up to be different from me, without my frailties and weaknesses.

"Let her call you 'Mother'. Keep my identity from her as long as you can. When you have a daughter of your own, let Asgara grow up as her womb sister. When they taunt her with my misdeeds, as they surely will, let her have you and yours to claim as her family so that she can repudiate me. Perhaps in time she will forget that she ever had another mother and escape the burden of my sins.

"Dearest Megara, we have shared much together. Now I share with you what is more precious to me than anything in the world. I am easy in my mind knowing that as long as you are living, our Mother Goddess Ma will smile on my daughter and she will lack for nothing."

Caitlin's voice sounded upbeat, but there was a tremor in it that suggested that tears were not far away. She had clearly been crying before she made the recording, for her big green eyes were red rimmed, and her lashes were still wet.

—

You are wrong, my beloved Caitlin, thought Megara now as the orb of the yellow sun began to rise slowly above the horizon. *You are Zon perfection, not me. A capricious Ma has cast you down, for reasons beyond my understanding. I could not make your daughter different from you if I tried— her blood is yours, and she brings you to mind with every little thing that she says or does.*

Her chronometer chimed, and she picked up the sleepy child by her side as she rose.

"Asgara, it is time to return to Temple Heights," Megara called. "You have a big day at the nursery today, remember?"

"Yes, Mother," said Asgara, jumping down from the dwarf oak and landing gracefully. "I am to present the bouquet to the queen and welcome her to Temple Heights Nursery."

"Before you do that, you must get cleansed, anointed, and changed. We must not be late."

Asgara ran over to the speeder, tapped the hatch, and waited till it hissed open. She jumped in and sat in her booster seat on the passenger side. She put her arms out as Megara came up, saying, "Give me Iantha. She is very tired from all the running we did, poor thing."

Megara marveled anew at how easily she gave her daughter to a child only a year older. Asgara had some difficulty, but with Megara's help she managed to get Iantha into her jump seat between the driver's and passenger seats. By the time Megara loaded the breakfast basket and slid into the driver's seat, Asgara had strapped in both Iantha and herself.

"Ready to go, Seignora Mother," she said, sounding so serious that Megara was taken in for a moment. Then she saw Asgara's impish look and burst out laughing. Asgara joined in, pleased at the success of her joke.

Megara reached over ran her fingers through the child's soft ringlets. As the speeder's engine purred to life, Asgara asked, "Can we fly
off the cliff, Mother?"

Speeders were designed to fly a few meters off the ground and did
not have the power of airboats. However, Caitlin's personal speeder
was an extremely expensive model. It had enough power to descend
from the cliff top safely, especially with a pilot of Megara's skill at the
wheel and the waters of the Stevia beneath them as a safety net. It
would still be a very rapid descent, a rush of excitement that Asgara
always asked for when they came up into the mountains.

"OK, here we go!" said Megara, opening the throttle. She drove
forward, directly for the cliff edge. As soon as they were over, the
speeder plummeted downward, her velocity rising rapidly. Asgara
screamed with excitement, and Iantha sleepily opened her eyes. It
was only a five second free fall before the ground detectors on the
speeder's keel made contact with the waters of the Stevia and the
engine roared to counteract the downward force of gravity. Megara
brought the speeder under control in a graceful arc, her engine roil-
ing the fast moving waters of the river. Then she drove fast for the
Vale Gate of Atlantic City. The sensors at the Gate identified the
speeder and Megara acknowledged a call from the huntresses on
duty.

Transitioning into Caitlin's life of luxury represented a big change
for Megara. Initially she had tried to resist, but she was only human
and found herself rapidly getting used to the enjoyment of great
wealth. She was never profligate and always made sure to put Asgara
before Iantha and herself. Abstaining from the material assets at her
disposal—Caitlin's magnificent suite in Palace d'Orr, her expensive
speeder, her lavish income—would have required a level of self-denial
verging on masochism. *It is only right*, she said to herself. *After all, if*

Caitlin did not want me to use her wealth, she would not have left it all to me. Anyway, it is temporary; it will be Asgara's when she turns eighteen.

She pulled up in the courtyard of the Temple Heights Nursery campus. The campus included the junior school that Asgara and Iantha attended. It was a hive of activity in preparation for the queen's visit. Several nursery caregivers were out on ladders, putting up bunting. Others were raising the Zon circle-cross banner and the queen's personal standard on the twin flagpoles.

Megara emerged from the speeder and waited as Asgara unstrapped Iantha and helped her out. Very patiently, the child led the littler one into the nursery foyer and approached the reception desk.

"My womb sister needs to be cleansed and changed," Asgara said to the caregiver on duty. "Then I must get ready, for I am to greet the queen."

Megara stood behind her, smiling at the caregiver who was used to Asgara's precocious ways. She came around and took Iantha's hand.

"Have the girls had breakfast?" she asked.

When Megara nodded, she said, "I will make sure Iantha is ready. Can you take care of Asgara? The queen's party will be here within the hour, and she must be ready well before then."

In the event, Megara had to do very little, since Asgara used the cleansing unit and was able to do almost all of the complex Zon toilette by herself. Megara helped her with some of the lotions and picked out a simple outfit of green silk that she had just bought for her.

Well before the queen was due, the entire population of the nursery campus, most mothers, as well as a large crowd of onlookers was assembled in the large courtyard or in overlooking balconies. While the campus was located in the aristocratic reserve of Temple Heights, it served many of the western districts of the city. It had over a thousand children during the day and over a hundred boarders. So the waiting crowd was large and enthusiastic.

At precisely the appointed time, the Imperial speeder pulled up, preceded and followed by speeders bearing the markings of the Cohort of Palace Guardians. Centuria Lady Alexandra Sheel, the tall, blonde First Handmaiden to the queen, stepped out of the lead speeder, followed by another two Palace Guardians. More Guardians emerged from the following speeder and formed a semi-circle around the Imperial speeder. Alex hit the hatch release and handed out Hildegard.

Turning to the assembly she announced, "Hildegard, Queen of the Zon Sisterhood, Empress of New Eartha!"

The entire assembly bowed as one. Someone from the crowd cried out, "Hail Queen Hildegard the Victorious!" The cry was taken up and soon hundreds were chanting it. *Will this be my epithet?* wondered Hildegard. She knew there was talk of writing the Hildegard saga, talk that had arisen without any prompting from her. But she had not discouraged it, either.

"The Imperial March" played on the speakers as the head caregiver stepped forward, holding Asgara's hand. They walked forward several paces together. Then the head caregiver stopped and Asgara continued forward alone, walking confidently up to Hildegard through the phalanx of tall Guardians. She was not awed by the stone-faced Guardians and smiled at Hildegard, eliciting a warm smile in return. As the final strains of the march died away, she reached up and held out a bouquet of wildflowers that she had picked by Upper Moat Falls. The caregivers had tied it prettily with multicolored ribbons. Hildegard reached down and took the proffered bouquet.

"Your Majesty, I am Lady Asgara Paurina d'Orr," said Asgara, speaking slowly and enunciating every word. "On behalf of all my mentors, teachers, and sisters, I welcome you to Temple Heights Nursery."

"Thank you, Lady Asgara," replied Hildegard gravely. "I am so happy to be with you and all your sisters."

Several in the audience were struck by the similarities between the child and the queen. *Look*, they said. *The child has the queen's hair and eyes! Such a good choice for a welcome maiden!* Hildegard herself could not fail to see them, but she checked herself thinking, *Don't be silly and read too much into a passing physical resemblance.* Nonetheless, she made a mental note to ask Repro for Asgara's genetic profile.

Asgara was supposed to retire at this point, but she lingered for a moment, rose onto her tiptoes to get closer to Hildegard, and said in a stage whisper, "My mother took my sister and me for a picnic breakfast to Upper Moat Falls. That is where I got your flowers."

"And who is your mother, child?" asked Hildegard. She knew that Asgara was the d'Orr heiress and that Caitlin had departed into exile.

"Seignora Megara Paurina of the Cohort of Palace Guardians," said Asgara proudly.

She turned and pointed to Megara who stood with the other mothers, tall in her ceremonial Palace Guardian uniform, her conspicuous raven hair bound into a bun, her plumed helmet under her arm. Megara shot a fond smile at Asgara but remained otherwise unmoving.

"I see," said Hildegard thoughtfully. "You are right to be proud of your mother—she is a fine example."

"She is the best mother in the world!" Asgara bubbled happily.

Then she backed away the prescribed three steps as she was taught, turned, and walked back to her place in the ranks.

The visit was a huge success. Hildegard's charisma was well known, and she made everyone she met feel special with her warmth and empathy. She was everyone's picture of the ideal Zon mother—she had just the right mixture of beauty and elegance, striking without being intimidating.

An hour later, a group of caregivers saw the royal party off and the speeders departed. Slowly the mothers began to leave and by mid-morning all was normal again at Temple Heights Nursery. Megara kissed both Asgara and Iantha and left to return to her post at military headquarters. She was walking toward her speeder when a commoner accosted her. She was wearing the black lipstick and eye shadow favored by the more hardline members of the Sisterhood.

"Seignora Megara Paurina?" she asked curtly.

"Yes," said Megara stiffly, looking down at the much shorter woman.

"I am Tyla Dorrina. I am a descendant of Princess Iren d'Orr and therefore related by blood to Lady Asgara d'Orr. I have filed a motion in City Court challenging your right to serve as Lady Asgara's legal mother and to control the wealth of the d'Orr estate. A hearing is scheduled for the fifth day of the cycle at ten o'clock in the morning. I am hereby giving you notice of an official comm channel that you will receive this afternoon. I will see you in court."

She turned and walked away rapidly before Megara could respond, leaving her staring at her back.

<hr />

"YOU WILL TAKE some *katsch*, I hope, Seignora Megara?" Countess Dorothea Sheel asked sweetly.

Megara nodded, shifting her position on the low-slung couch and adjusting her weapons belt to make herself more comfortable. Though she did not know why, she sensed she was sparring with the countess and felt at a disadvantage. While Megara was considerably taller, Dorothea sat on a high-backed chair so she could look down on her.

"Alex, please ask Mina to bring some *katsch*," said Dorothea to her older daughter, who sat on an identical high backed chair by her side. Alex was resplendent in her Palace Guardian uniform, the dagger insignia of her rank on her wrist bracers and metal choker. The emblems of her office of First Handmaiden to the queen were on her shoulders. Alex tapped her wrist bracer and within moments, Dorothea's personal maid Mina came in bearing a silver tray embossed with the Sheel coat of arms. She wore a uniform with a badge bearing the Sheel arms on her left breast.

Megara guessed that everything was being done to overawe her. She was thankful she had not bothered to change out of her own Palace Guardian uniform when she had received the impromptu invitation half an hour before. She glanced out through the french windows on to the terrace, where Asgara and Iantha were playing a boisterous game. Being older, Asgara had an insurmountable advantage, but Megara saw that she was quietly letting Iantha win every other time.

She took her *katsch* and blew on it. She wondered what lay behind this sudden, unexpected invitation. She had lived in Palace d'Orr for years, and while the Sheel mansion was only a short walk away, this was the first time she had been invited. The presence of Alex, her senior officer in the Cohort of Palace Guardians, made it even more awkward.

"Seignora Megara," said Dorothea, after taking the first sip of her *katsch*. "You are probably wondering why we have invited you here."

"Yes, ma'am," said Megara.

"We are a small, close-knit community here on Temple Heights. My daughters Centuria Lady Alexandra and Lady Tara grew up here as did I, and our ancestors before us. Our foremother, Cornelle Soefia Sheel, commanded the Cohort of Palace Guardians and sacked Dreslin Center during the Brigon Conquest six hundred years ago. For her service in the Conquest, Queen Caitlin the Unforgiving created Cornelle Soefia the First Countess Sheel and gave her this property, cheek-by-jowl with the grounds of Palace d'Orr and Palace Saxe. She built this mansion, and it has stood here ever since."

Megara looked at Dorothea, her powder-blue eyes puzzled, wondering where this was leading. She could think of nothing to say and glanced over at Alex who had the grace to look embarrassed at her mother's boastful recounting of their ancestry. Dorothea took another sip of her *katsch* and drew a breath before continuing.

"We aristocrats believe in duty and service to the Sisterhood. I wear the Order of Motherhood with a bar and Centuria Lady Alexandra wears the uniform of the Cohort of Palace Guardians. However, we also believe in the maintenance of social decorum."

Megara was pleased that she had worn her own Order of Motherhood and now touched the red ribbons trailing from it.

"I completely agree with you, Countess Dorothea," she smiled. "I am proud to wear both the uniform of the Palace Guardians and the Order of Motherhood."

To her surprise, Dorothea tapped the arm of her chair in irritation.

"I am afraid that I have been too subtle for you," she said sharply. "Let me speak plainly. Queen Simran the Merciless marked out this enclave on Temple Heights for the aristocracy over a thousand years ago, when she first drew up the plans for Atlantic City. Your taking up residence in Palace d'Orr is an abomination. We have just heard that it will be challenged in open court, making the whole Sisterhood aware of this disgraceful situation. You must leave and return to your barracks immediately."

Megara's eyes grew wide with shock, and for a moment she was tongue-tied with disbelief. Then she rallied.

"I reside at Palace d'Orr at the express wish of Princess Caitlin," she said stiffly. "She has given me full control of all her material possessions till her daughter's majority. That includes the private apartments at Palace d'Orr."

"You refuse to heed my friendly advice?" Dorothea asked nastily.

"I fail to see the friendliness," responded Megara, polite but firm.

Dorothea turned to her daughter and gestured her to speak.

Alex looked uncomfortable, but she did not disavow her mother.

"Seignora Megara, my mother may have pitched it a little strong, but there is truth in what she says. This part of Temple Heights has been the preserve of the aristocracy since the founding of Atlantic City. We must respect our traditions."

"I have spent countless days at Palace d'Orr since I was a little girl," returned Megara. "No one ever told me it was off-limits to commoners."

"Princess Deirdre was wrong to allow her daughter so much intimacy with a commoner," said Dorothea harshly. "She was a great heroine, but her social judgment was not the best. I begged her to separate Caitlin from you and to make her spend more time with my own younger daughter, Lady Tara. I knew that consorting with a commoner would lead to presumption of this sort."

Lady Tara, who failed to become an electra, thought Megara. *As you failed, Countess Dorothea.* But she was too polite to say it.

Dorothea went on.

"Just look at you!" she said. Her fingers ran over the Sheel tiara as she took very obvious note of Megara's lack of jewelry and the wildflowers in her hair. "Your very appearance conveys your lack of breeding."

"I am the legal mother of Lady Asgara, the d'Orr heiress," Megara retorted. "And I am an electra, no longer a commoner. I see no reason to move out of Palace d'Orr."

"You may be an electra," cried Dorothea. "But who was your mother? A common server in a café! Are the halls of Palace d'Orr to be debased with such low blood?"

"I am obviously not welcome here in the Sheel Mansion," said Megara, standing up. "I beg your leave to take the girls and depart. I thank you for the *katsch*."

"Alex!" said Dorothea, tensely. "Tell her!"

Alex's look of discomfort grew more acute.

"Seignora Megara, you know that your record is outstanding," she said, speaking slowly as though the words were being dragged out of her. "You will soon hear officially that you have been shortlisted for promotion to Centuria this year. You also know that as First Handmaiden to the queen, your file must pass through me."

Megara knew how difficult it was to be promoted in peacetime. Most seignoras spent their whole careers at that rank without promotion. A bad assessment by Alex would go into her permanent record and doom her chances of promotion forever.

"Would you declare me unfit, Centuria Lady Alexandra?" asked Megara formally.

"Seignora Megara, fitness for a senior rank requires a respect for hierarchy and a recognition of authority," said Alex pedantically. "You saw firsthand the disastrous consequences of Seignora Lady Caitlin's failure to follow orders."

Megara did not hesitate.

"I promised Caitlin I would be a mother to her daughter," she said resolutely. "If that means I am never promoted, that is a price I am willing to pay."

She went out on to the terrace, collected the girls, and left without another word.

⌘⌘⌘⌘⌘⌘⌘

MEGARA HAD WALKED over to the Sheel Mansion, so she now carried Iantha and held Asgara's hand as they retraced their steps toward Palace d'Orr. She was an incongruous figure, a tall military officer in uniform with her weapons, with the two small children. They had to pass Palace Saxe on the way. On an impulse, Megara opened a comm channel to Andromache and asked if she could come in. Andromache readily consented and the motors whirred to open the gates as Megara approached them.

Andromache's handmaiden stood inside the gates waiting for them. She led them into the palace and through several long corridors to a cozy study, with a vintage fireplace and old-fashioned over-stuffed chairs. As with most desirable chambers on Temple Heights, it had a viewport with a commanding view of the city. Megara entered the study behind the handmaiden and bowed formally to the High Priestess. Asgara followed her example and executed a very creditable bow. Iantha hid behind her mother, peering around her legs at Andromache apprehensively.

"Some *amphal* juice for the girls," Andromache said to her handmaiden in her cultured High Zon accent. "And Seignora Megara, will you take some *katsch*?"

"I have just had some, ma'am," said Megara. "I will only take a moment of your time. I need to get the girls home to dinner and to bed."

Andromache smiled.

"Why don't we ask my handmaiden to take them to the nursery with their juice?" she asked. "It hasn't been used since my daughter Althea was a girl, but I am sure there are things there to amuse children."

"Thank you, ma'am," said Asgara seriously. "That is very kind of you."

Andromache looked at her warmly.

"She is a very precocious young lady," said Megara, grinning. "It will not do to treat her like a baby."

"So I see," said Andromache. Asgara's mannerisms brought Caitlin to mind, though her confident demeanor was more reminiscent of her grandmother, Deirdre. A look of sadness crossed Andromache's face, for she missed both of them dreadfully.

Andromache's handmaiden returned bearing a tray with two glasses on it. On receiving Andromache's instructions, she led the two girls away to the nursery.

"Well, what can I do for you, Seignora Megara?"

Megara composed her thoughts before relating both Tyla Dorrina's challenge to her status as Asgara's legal mother and then the Sheels' demand that she vacate Palace d'Orr and return to the barracks.

"I am merely carrying out Caitlin's wishes," she finished. "She wanted me to bring up Asgara and to take her place in Palace d'Orr. She would not have transferred everything to me otherwise."

Andromache did not respond immediately.

"Caitlin often did not make the wisest choices," she said finally. "You know that yourself from personal experience. She is not worldly. Choosing you to be Asgara's legal mother is just another example of this."

47

"What do you mean, Princess Andromache?" asked Megara worriedly.

"My dear, you are a fine military officer. And I am sure you are a fine mother. As you know, I am a firm believer that birth is irrelevant in decisions about advancement. Why, I turned down my own mother's application to the Middle Temple Magis! And I campaigned vigorously for our Queen, who was born a commoner. But you are not a fit legal mother for the heiress to the Royal Tiara of d'Orr. And though I rarely see eye to eye with Dorothea, I agree with her that it is inappropriate for you to be in residence at Palace d'Orr. There are a few time-honored privileges of the aristocracy that I would like to see preserved."

Megara was completely blindsided by Andromache's response.

"What is your advice, ma'am?" she asked, dazed.

The ancient Saxe tiara on Andromache's brow emphasized her blue-blooded descent and for the moment, Megara was cowed. Andromache looked out of the viewport and drew a deep breath.

"You have fulfilled your promise to Caitlin. Asgara is walking, talking, a young lady, as you said yourself. Recuse yourself and name me as her legal mother. If Caitlin had acted sensibly, this is what she would have done in the first place. It takes an aristocrat to bring up an aristocrat."

Megara could not believe her ears. It was true that Andromache had never invited her to Palace Saxe, but she often came by Temple Heights Nursery to visit Asgara. She had always been friendly whenever they met and Megara had thought of her as an ally. *But all this time, she has thought me unfit to mother the d'Orr heiress,* she thought.

"I take it you will not support me in the lawsuit brought by Tyla Dorrina," Megara said dully.

"If you do as I say, the lawsuit will be thrown out," said Andromache, her tone kind. "I will pay you a good allowance. It will enable you to rent a flat in a nice area like Lumin Hills. I will give you one of my speeders to use. When the time comes, I will give you a tutor for Iantha to make sure she reaches her full potential and has the best chance of becoming an electra. You can retain the comforts you have grown used to. Just give up your claims on Caitlin's residence and fortune. And on her daughter."

By now Megara had gotten over her shock and recovered her poise. She looked at Andromache steadily, till the High Priestess grew self-conscious.

"Why are you doing this, ma'am?" she asked.

"I love Caitlin!" Andromache burst out. "I watched her grow up, she is my darling girl! I am heartsick at what has happened to her. I want the best for her daughter. I am a Royal Princess; I can teach Asgara to be one! How can you possibly do that?"

Megara took a deep breath before responding.

"There is more to being a Royal Princess than fine manners and a beautiful accent," she said quietly. "Caitlin may not be worldly, but she will always be a princess because of what she has in *here.*"

She pounded her chest as she spoke the last two words.

"I am not a highborn aristocrat," she continued. "And I do not know how to raise a child to negotiate the corridors of power. But I know I can teach her to follow her heart. That may not make her a queen, but it will make her righteous like her mother. In the end, isn't that the greater achievement?"

AS SHE WAS being tucked in for the night, Asgara looked straight into Megara's eyes in her direct way.

"You don't look happy, Mother," she said softly.

Megara put her hand on the child's cheek.

"Oh, I am fine, my sweets. Just lots of things to do at work, that's all. Nothing to worry you."

"But you were so happy when you picked us up from the nursery after work," Asgara persisted. "You took us for cream ice in the park and told us all those funny stories. We laughed and rolled in the grass, and I picked flowers for your lovely hair. Then we had to go to the house of those horrid ladies and you got sad."

"What house do you mean?"

"The house where Iantha and I played on the terrace. I watched you through the viewport. I could see that they were being nasty to you. I hate them!"

Megara leaned down and hugged Asgara.

"What a treasure you are," she said. "But you mustn't hate anyone. It only hurts you in the end."

Then she raised her head and, still hugging Asgara, asked her, "Do you like Princess Andromache?"

Asgara considered before replying.

"She's a nice lady," she said judiciously.

"Would you like to live with her?"

Asgara caught the serious undercurrent in Megara's tone and grew worried.

"Why would I do that?" She clung to Megara more tightly. "I don't want to live with anyone but you, Mother! You won't leave me, will you?"

Megara hugged her back.

"No, my sweets," she whispered. "As long as you want me, I don't want to be anywhere else."

THE MESSAGE FROM Cornelle Diana Tragina was so unexpected that Megara played it again to be sure. She was being invited to a personal one-on-one meeting with the commander of the Palace Guardians! Diana had never invited her to such a meeting before. So as she waited with Diana's handmaiden outside the cornelle's spacious corner office, she wondered if it could have anything to do with her recent conversations with the Sheels and Princess Andromache.

As the portal slid open, the handmaiden stood aside and indicated that she should enter. Megara entered and saluted stiffly, hand on heart. Diana returned her salute and waved her to a club chair by a viewport, rather than an upright chair in front of her desk.

"A tot of clove wine?" she asked. "The queen herself gave me this bottle at the last New Moons Rite at the Great Temple."

"Too tempting to resist, Cornelle," said Megara.

Diana brought over the two stems and sat down.

"You know that you have been short-listed for promotion, I take it," she said, tapping her wrist bracer and bringing up a document.

"Yes, Cornelle," said Megara, holding her breath.

"Do you know who else is on the short list?"

"My friend Jena Saracenina told me that she was on it," replied Megara cautiously.

"Yes, there are only the two of you." Diana paused and looked at Megara intently. "Your files have come up to me. From me they will go to the queen, but if the military has approved a promotion, her signature is usually just a formality."

Megara said nothing but took a sip of her wine and waited.

"Even among the Guardians, you are an exceptional warrior," said Diana, seeming to change the subject. "I have observed you in training exercises. You lead your squad very well, your officiae trust you. During the Great Insurrection, you led daring raids into Dreslin

Center. Into the bowels of the Great Stony Keep itself, extracting our ally King Harald from the notorious Dripping Dungeon. For all practical purposes, you commanded our forces in the Brigon Residency during the siege—Lady Selene mentions in her report that even the Centuria of the Residency huntresses deferred to you."

Diana paused, as though waiting for a response.

"I did my duty," said Megara uncertainly. She had never seen Diana bestowing such fulsome praise on anyone before.

"You wear the Order of Motherhood," said Diana, ignoring Megara's response. "And you have taken over legal motherhood for your disgraced friend, Princess Caitlin d'Orr."

She tapped her wrist bracer and pulled up another document.

"The reports from Temple Heights Nursery are flattering—your girls are among the best adjusted. It says here that they are in the foyer waiting to go home with you every day, and that you never let them down. You seem to spend every free moment with them. You even missed the Academy Graduation Ball last month, the biggest social event of the year for us huntresses, just to be with them—I checked with the nursery."

Megara was now completely at a loss and just stared at Diana wordlessly. Diana did not seem to want an answer.

"It is no secret, at least among the Guardians, that Jena is fond of drugs. It is also no secret that she has applied for motherhood twice and been turned down as unfit."

Megara sat straighter and took another sip of her wine. She felt she should defend her friend, so she said, "She has achieved the highest rating on barbarian weapons and served with distinction in the Great Insurrection."

"Under your command," said Diana, looking her straight in the eye.

Diana's pale colorless eyes were intimidating, but Megara did not look away.

"Yes, I rated her very highly," she said.

Diana let a pause grow into a silence.

"What has Centuria Lady Alexandra got against you?" she asked suddenly.

The question was so unexpected that Megara's mouth dropped open and she covered it with her hand.

"I...I ...I don't know," she stammered. "I served under her as an officia. We were both with you in the action at Upper Thal during the Great Insurrection. She is an excellent senior officer who provides a fine example for all her juniors to follow."

"I see," said Diana, thoughtfully. They sipped their wine and Diana changed the subject to Megara's girls, eliciting a much more voluble response. Soon after they finished their wine, she dismissed her.

The portal had barely hissed shut behind Megara when Diana opened a comm channel to Alex and summoned her. Diana's tone caused Alex to drop what she was doing and come immediately. She found Diana seated in the same club chair by the viewport. Her commander acknowledged her salute and motioned her to the chair vacated by Megara.

"I have the promotion short list here, Alex," she said without preamble. "How in Ma's name can you rate Jena Saracenina above Megara Paurina? Megara should have been promoted years ago and I am not even sure how Jena got to be a seignora."

Alex had been expecting this from Diana, so she was prepared.

"Seignora Megara's fitness for command is suspect, Cornelle," she said. "She aided and abetted Seignora Lady Caitlin in the actions that led to her disgrace. It is quite clear to me that she is not to be trusted. I am even concerned about allowing her to retain her rank of seignora."

"I see you have a strong opinion in this case, Centuria," said Diana dryly. "I wonder why you did not see fit to put these comments down in your assessment."

"I saw no reason to blacken her name further," said Alex rigidly.

"Yet you know that if the file goes up to the queen with your assessment, she will reject Seignora Megara, no matter what I write. And if that happens, it will go into her permanent record and she will never be promoted. She is a young officer, she could serve another hundred years with no hope of advancement."

Diana tapped her wrist bracer and closed all the documents.

"The queen trusts you, Alex," she said mildly. "That is a heavy responsibility. I never had reason to doubt your judgment in the past. But this case makes me wonder."

"I believe in my assessment," said Alex firmly.

"I see," said Diana. "Are you sure that this is not about Megara's taking up residence in Palace d'Orr? About her being Lady Asgara's legal mother and using Princess Caitlin's wealth?"

"I made my position clear, Cornelle," Alex said. But she did not meet Diana's pale gaze. "My assessment has nothing to do with Seignora Megara's actions over the last several years."

"But do you approve of her actions?"

"Seignora Megara is within the letter of the law in implementing Princess Caitlin's wishes," said Alex, still not looking directly at Diana. "Ill-conceived as they are."

"You aristocrats don't like her living on Temple Heights, do you?"

"Cornelle, I will not lie to you," said Alex with spirit. "You know as well as I that Queen Simran marked out Temple Heights for the aristocracy over a thousand years ago. This tradition is part of our heritage and harms no one. So no, it does not delight me to have Seignora Megara living in Palace d'Orr. But that has nothing to do with my assessment."

Diana leaned back in her club chair. Again she allowed a pause to extend into a silence. Even as the seconds ticked away, Alex would not look her in the eye.

"I'll tell you what I am going to do, Alex," she said finally. "I will not allow you to destroy Seignora Megara's career. I am going to take her off the short list with retrospective effect. That will erase your assessment, since she was never on the list for you to assess. She will remain a seignora for now, but in the future under a different First Handmaiden, she is certain to be promoted."

"As for Jena, I am going to assess her as unfit for command. It was a mistake to promote her to seignora, but at least we can avoid compounding that error."

"Cornelle, that is harsh and unfair," said Alex, a bit too quickly. "If you preserve Seignora Megara's option of a future promotion, surely you owe Seignora Jena that same consideration."

"My mind is made up, Alex," said Diana.

VIVIA PRAGARINA DELICATELY dabbed her lips with her linen napkin and looked fondly at Darbeni, her younger daughter and Chief Counsel. They were dining in Vivia's suite in the Pragarina Palace in the luxurious Lumin Hills district of Atlantic City.

"I just read your quarterly assessment my dear," she said. "Very precise and insightful, as usual. I am pleased to see that you have exceeded my expectations in the day-to-day operations of our enterprises. You are young, but—" here Vivia paused and put a hand on her daughter's wrist. "—I was just about your age when I bought my first Trading License and became a Guild Mistress. The other Guild Mistresses had no idea how deeply in debt I was, since I had borrowed a little from each of them. Then I took such risks! I traveled incessantly and traded with anyone that would talk to me. I *had* to in order to pay the Guild's usurious interest rates."

Vivia paused and smiled as she reminisced. "Why, I even went into the Chitgar Ravines to trade with the wild hill tribes—in the midst of their annual rampages! Alone in the tent of Grand Sab Ghaz Ib Makhtoom, the Chekaliga chieftain, I had nothing to protect me but the toss of my scarf. One misstep and he would have forced me into his dissolute harem."

"The shoe is on the other foot now," responded Darbeni. "Now we are the ones making the loans and charging the usurious rates. Even the government is in our debt."

"Well, it is not our fault that they insist on running deficits."

One of the kitchen maids appeared and rapidly cleared away their dinner dishes. Then Naorina Wilkina, Vivia's gorgeous personal maid, came in bearing two steaming cups of *katsch* on a silver tray.

"I have some bad news, I'm afraid," said Darbeni, sipping her hot drink. "Those wild Chekaligas are on the rampage again this year. They managed to break into one of our smaller Guild forts in the Daksin Borderlands. Unfortunately, we were unable to remove our property in time. Our losses amount to almost ten thousand gold talents."

Vivia's good mood evaporated in an instant, for there was little she liked less than to lose money.

"That will take a big bite out of last quarter's profits in our Daksin operations," she snapped. "Why were we not given advance warning? It is the Daksin Resident's job to know what is going on in her jurisdiction. This would never happen in Briga. Lady Selene is always on top of things."

She picked up her *katsch* and blew on it. "Bodil Axessina, our Resident in Daksin is just not up to the job. I noticed that she was slipping on my last trip to Sampore. We must get her replaced. Do you have anyone in mind?"

"The Under Resident, Jordis Invarina is excellent," replied Darbeni. "I know her well. She would make a great Resident."

"She is too young," sniffed Vivia. "The queen would never accept her. We must find someone who has more experience."

She drummed her fingers on the armrest of her chair for a while.

"Send freighter airboats down to the bigger Daksin Guild forts," continued Vivia, making up her mind. She counted locations off on her fingers. "Sampore, Limpore, Siggar. Let us ship our most valuable assets back to Atlantic City and reduce our exposure."

"I'll see to it," said Darbeni.

"And contact Lady Alexandra, the queen's First Handmaiden, and get me an appointment to see the queen. If the current deployments are insufficient to protect our operations, we must get the government to transfer some more military units down there."

"I'll contact her first thing in the morning."

Darbeni could see that the news had put Vivia in a bad mood and did not linger long after finishing her *katsch*.

THREE

ESTRANS CASTLE

ARON BRADAR NIBELLUS walked the sea-facing battlements of Estrans Castle with his cousin, Greghar. He proudly
pointed to the various improvements he had carried out and clearly
sought his cousin's approval. Greghar was glad to give it. He had
been overwhelmed by Bradar's hospitality, for he had been received
as royalty, with no hint of his base birth. There had been a flurry of
banquets with all the highborn members of Bradar's retinue and the
local Sward nobility. Even Bradar's coolly elegant wife Esgrin, had
been polite. Greghar had always been good with children and his
cousin's young daughters took to him immediately, clambering into
his lap and dragging him into their nursery to play.

Now Greghar stopped, leaned on a crenel, and looked out to sea.
The wind ruffled his ash-blond ringlets, and he ran his hand through
them. Bradar surveyed his cousin's profile admiringly.

59

"By the One God, Greghar," he said spontaneously. "You have the mien of a king! Both Pinnar and I agree—you have more ability and right than either one of us. You should be in Nordberg, not banished to the provincial barony of Rocness. A pox on the rules which prevent you from succeeding to the throne!"

"Whoa, hold your horses, cousin!" cried Greghar in surprise. "I am a loyal servant of your father, and I will carry out his wishes. Pinnar is his named heir—so when the time comes, I will be Pinnar's most loyal servant. I would not accept the crown if you offered it to me."

Bradar looked obstinate for a moment, but then he smiled as one with a pleasing secret.

"Well, hopefully such decisions are far in the future," he said, rubbing his hands. "For now, I suggest that we repair to the Sea Parlor for some afternoon refreshment. I have asked my chef to create a pastry fit for a king!"

"Lead the way, cousin," said Greghar, smiling.

They returned along the battlements, nodding at the salutes of the sentries as they passed. Bradar led the way to the Sea Parlor, a circular chamber toward the fore of the rocky promontory on which the castle was built. It had relatively large windows, no doubt because this aspect of the castle was considered impossible to attack. The castle walls here rose almost directly from a cliff edge that dropped a great way down to the sea. The cove at the foot of the cliff was itself protected by an impassable ring of rocks that made a seaward attack a virtual impossibility.

They entered the Sea Parlor to find Esgrin reclined in a regal, high-backed armchair, with her personal maid standing behind her. There was a striking young woman seated on chair beside her. She wore a crimson gown of fine musk-lace and her dark hair was piled on top of her head. Her gown went well with her skin that was the color of old ivory. Although she wore little jewelry, her green-hazel cat's eyes animated her face and sparkled brighter than any gems. She was sitting with her legs primly crossed and then stood with Esgrin as they entered, smiling at them.

From halfway across the parlor, Greghar bowed deeply to Esgrin and repeated this show of respect to the other lady. To his amazement, the lady burst out laughing and ran to him, holding the skirts of her gown in one hand. She threw herself into his arms, crying, "You didn't recognize me, did you? You have made me lose my bet with the lord Baron Bradar! I was so sure you would recognize me, whatever I wore."

"Nitya!" cried Greghar, picking her up and swinging her around. "You look so...so...grown up!"

He set her down and looked at her with undisguised pleasure. She put a hand on her hip, stuck her nose in the air, and struck an exaggeratedly sophisticated pose.

"I was rather hoping you would find me more than grown up," she said in the drawn-out Utrish of the court. "Do I not please your eye?"

"You are very...elegant," he managed to answer, not quite sure how to respond to this eye-catching woman. Her striking looks made him inexplicably uncomfortable. He caught himself wishing she would turn back into the little girl he had loved like a baby sister.

A disappointed look crossed Nitya's face, but she erased it in a moment and resumed a sunny demeanor.

"Oh, your aunt, Queen Lovelyn has trained me very well," she said brightly. "I know all the court protocol, better than you, I bet. And I have learnt all about walking, talking, dressing and dealing with brash young men."

"I am sure you are breaking many hearts in Nordberg," smiled Greghar. "I can see that my aunt has brought out the best in you—all the graces that I cannot understand, but only appreciate from afar."

His happiness showed so plainly on his face that she could not stay irritated with him. She poked his midsection hard enough to make him gasp.

"It's only me, silly," she said in her old familiar way. "You don't have to act all formal now."

Bradar came up, looking very pleased at their happy reunion.

"I know that my sister-in-law, Guttrin, and my own darling wife worry that people talk about your relationship," he said amiably. "But I say to hell with the gossips! We all know your behavior is above reproach. My dear mother has grown so attached to young Nitya—this was all her idea. She suggested that I invite you both here separately so you would not be seen together in the capital."

"Your lady mother is a queen in every sense of the word," said Nitya, looking at him gratefully. "I try and emulate her to the best of my abilities. She has been so much a mother to me that I am sure you are jealous!"

Bradar laughed good-naturedly.

"I can never hear too much praise for my mother," he said.

"Her good heart sometimes blinds her to viciousness of the world," said Esgrin, who had approached. She put an arm around Nitya's slim waist. "This young lady has grown into such an exotic creature, I can see why she has become the apple of your mother's eye. But her looks will only make the gossip more ferocious."

"I am sure her looks are the least of her assets in my aunt's eyes," said Greghar, displeased at Esgrin's words. "It is her loyalty, honesty and above all her virtue that commend her."

"Come, come," said Bradar, trying to lighten the conversation. "Let us sit. Tell your maid to ring the bell, my dear. I am sure the stewards are waiting to bring in the refreshment I specially ordered."

They all sat on the comfortable chairs. The bell was rung and a procession of stewards entered bearing large trays. They were set down and the covers were removed, revealing the pastry Bradar had promised and much more besides. Nitya rose as she had been trained and poured out the hot *shlaba,* a concoction of a northern yam and fermented mares' milk that all Utreans loved. She served the men and then Esgrin before pouring a small thimble cup for herself. It had a very strong taste that revolted Nitya's foreign palate. After a few polite sips, she rose again and helped Esgrin's maid slice and serve the fine pastry.

It was a noble creation, the crust so light that flakes rose into the air as they cut it. Again Nitya served Bradar and Greghar, before waiting on Esgrin. She served herself a tiny portion last of all. Greghar watched her strict adherence to protocol and her graceful movements with pride.

Bradar steered the talk toward the weather, a safe topic that they conversed on animatedly till the urn of *shlaba* was empty.

"Cousin, with your permission I would like to show Nitya the view from the top of Observation Tower," said Greghar as the stewards entered and began to clear away the dishes. "It will also give me a chance to show her the significant improvements you have made to the castle."

"Why, that is an excellent idea," said Bradar heartily, pleased with Greghar's mention of his work. "Estrans Castle has a most dramatic setting, and there is no better place to see it all than Observation Tower. Be careful on the spiral stair."

Nitya rose and carefully thanked and paid the full measure of respect to both Bradar and Esgrin. Then Greghar and Nitya left the

Sea Parlor, maintaining a decorous distance between them. However, as soon as they were out in the corridor, she clung to his powerful arm, nestled in his side, and whispered, "I am *so* happy to see you, Greghar! It has been so long! You cannot imagine how I have missed you." When he put an arm around her slim shoulders, she felt like the little girl he remembered, and he felt more at ease. Nitya sensed this, and they walked on to Observation Tower in blissful silence.

As Bradar had warned, the spiral stair had very high steps, and it was difficult for Nitya in her long gown. She lifted her skirts above her knees, but even so it was hard going in her high heels. About halfway up, her heel caught on an uneven step. She lost her balance and fell backward, but Greghar was right behind her and caught her. She put her arms around his neck and closed her eyes. For a brief moment she regressed to her childhood, when his powerful arms had been her sanctuary in a world that hated her. But for him, the close contact with her womanly body was discomfiting, and he quickly disengaged from her. He was relieved when they reached the top of the tower and emerged onto the viewing platform. There were two men-at-arms on watch, and they came to attention and saluted.

"You may take your ease for a short while," Greghar said. "We will keep your watch and call you when we are done." The men bowed and retired down the stairs.

Nitya sensed his discomfort and looked contrite.

"Have I said or done something to upset you, Greghar?" she asked diffidently.

"No, no," he remonstrated.

"But you don't seem at ease with me," she persisted.

"You are still the same determined little imp," he said. "It is just that you seem so different now. I could never have foreseen that the little girl I found dressed in rags in the Northern Marches would turn into such a fine lady."

"I am not yet twenty," she said mildly.

"Most women in Utrea are mothers at that age," he said.

"Can we not be as we were before?" she asked. "We were so close when we journeyed together! Princess Caitlin and you are the only ones in the world I can trust completely."

"Are they not kind to you in Nordberg?" asked Greghar, his face tightening. "Have you been ill-treated again?"

"No, no," said Nitya quickly. "I spoke truly when I said that your aunt, Queen Lovelyn, has been like a mother to me. So good and kind, fulfilling my every whim."

"I am sure you give her good cause to love you," said Greghar. "Loyalty such as yours is hard to find in the court."

"Yes, I try to serve her as best I can," agreed Nitya without false modesty. She paused and looked out to sea. The breeze pasted her gown to her body, emphasizing her womanly curves. Greghar felt a manly twinge and was inwardly embarrassed that Nitya could elicit such a feeling.

"But even with the queen's favor, I am foreigner at court with no family, connections, or money. Rumors of my being a witch continue to circulate. Your cousin's wife, Guttrin, misses no opportunity to poison your uncle the king against me. King Lothar tolerates my presence, but he does not love me. He makes it quite clear that he would be greatly relieved to be rid of me."

"My uncle may not be the warmest of men, but he is fair," said Greghar seriously. "He will not treat you unjustly."

"It is your aunt's love that I fear more than your uncle's coldness," said Nitya. "For the last year she has felt that I am now a lady complete, a fit wife for an aristocrat. She has encouraged several young noblemen, chevals, and even barons to court me."

"Is this so repugnant to you? You are not Zon."

"Becoming an Utrean noblewoman has its attractions," she replied. "But not in this way. The queen does not see it, for as Baroness Esgrin said, she sometimes does not realize how grasping people can be."

"Without fortune or family, a nobleman would only court you to gain the favor of the queen and perhaps the king," Greghar said, completing her line of reasoning.

"Exactly," said Nitya. "Some have been quite blunt. One powerful baron came with a proposal for me to become his son's *second* wife. But when we walked together, he said that in exchange for becoming a lady and having jewels and servants, he expected me to share his bed as well as his son's. And that no child of mine would ever inherit his ancient title."

"The villain!" exploded Greghar. "Who is this wretch?"

"Oh, I wouldn't tell you," said Nitya unaffectedly. "I wouldn't want you to do something foolish." She sighed. "I don't expect anything better from the courtiers, for I am quite aware that I am not a great lady. I am just a penniless orphan girl who has been pitied by a queen, and believe me, I *am* very grateful. But I would gladly return to the gutter and to the tortures I endured as a child, if I could give myself to someone who loves me."

Some Aeolian deity wished to underscore her words, for an errant gust of wind lifted the shoulder of her gown, revealing the vivid Thermadan triangle branded into her shoulder by one of her childhood torturers. Greghar saw it and fought the temptation to hold her. He unobtrusively moved a step away under the pretext of looking more closely at some lateen-rigged fishing vessels that were rounding the point of rocks out at sea. A hurt expression crossed her face, but again she erased it in a moment.

"Your aunt is infinitely patient, but I sense she would be very happy if I were to accept one of the proposals," said Nitya soberly. "I am often tempted to do so, just to please her."

Greghar continued to look out to sea, so she went on.

"Vasitha often appears to me in my dreams. He is the only reason I resist your aunt. He keeps urging me to be patient, telling me that my future does not lie in Utrea. Recently, he has grown more forceful, warning me that Malitha has recruited powerful allies and that a big storm is brewing."

Greghar turned and looked at her.

"Following his counsel has not led either one of us to happiness," he said grimly. "You would be best advised to marry one of noblemen my aunt recommends. Surely you can find one who appreciates you."

She felt tears sting her eyes at his words and his tone, but she held them back and smiled at him.

"Nothing is ever that simple," she said.

BACK IN THE Sea Parlor, Esgrin had rung for more *shlaba*. She and Bradar sipped it in silence for a while. Eventually, Esgrin put her cup down and dismissed her maid to give them privacy.

"It frightens me to have that unholy pair in the castle," she said flatly.

"Oh, come, you cannot be serious," Bradar expostulated. "I have known Greghar since boyhood—a lot longer than I have known you, my darling. And Nitya, she is such a guileless young thing! How can you not like her?"

"I hide my dislike because I fear her," said Esgrin. "And you should fear her too." She shivered. "Her skin is the color of old parchment, equally foreign to Utrea, Briga, *and* Daksin! She is a Yengar witch of the netherworld, not of our world. When you men gaze into those cat's eyes of hers, she bewitches you. She serves the Evil One, I am sure of it. Guttrin says that Animus the White Khalif has firm evidence of her guilt, and he cannot be wrong. And Greghar! Only a devil could have his looks."

"Greghar has always been a good-looking fellow," said Bradar, proud rather than jealous of his cousin. "Even when we were young boys, the girls always sought his hand at parties and dragged him behind the curtains for kisses."

"You men see nothing!" exclaimed Esgrin angrily. "Look at the unnatural glow on his skin. Look at his hair, so light-colored and such perfect ringlets. His facial features, finer and more delicate than any woman in Utrea. His blue eyes—only ice bears and Zon have eyes like that! Is it not obvious that the rumors must be true? That his mother was a sorceress who seduced your royal uncle and then disappeared? It is no wonder that the witch is happy to be his whore. What a nightmare to have them together under our roof! And you have let them wander off together, without a chaperone!"

A FLASH OF lightning split the sky, revealing the full extent of the stormy surface of the waves. The Peril Sea was always treacherous and the gale had come up suddenly, just after dusk. Shobar stamped about his quarterdeck, oblivious to the pouring rain. His lame First Minister, Katog, limped after him obediently, getting equally soaked without complaint. The crew was nervous, knowing that there were dangerous shoals in the area and that not all were charted. Every now and then they caught a glimpse of the towers of Estrans Castle, dominating a rocky promontory. The helmsman constantly stole glances at his chieftain, hoping to be asked to change course away from shore.

Shobar had a fixed expression on his face and there was a brightness in his eyes that showed a fixity of purpose that bordered on psychosis. Finally, he turned to his helmsman and the man almost started from his post in his eagerness to hear what he hoped was an order to turn back out to sea. He was disappointed for Shobar merely said, "Steer straight for the castle. There is a sheltered cove beneath its southern aspect."

The helmsman's fear of their predicament temporarily overcame his fear of his leader. He began to babble in disjointed phrases.

"Sire, the ring of rocks that protects the cove...the sheer cliffs from the beach to the castle walls...the sentries on the battlements ..."

Shobar ignored his words and spoke to Katog in a loud aside.

"How soon can you get a new helmsman? I may have to behead the current one."

The helmsman dared not let go of the wheel, but even so, he fell awkwardly to his knees.

"Sire, straight for the castle it is! I will carry out your orders to the letter! There is no need for another helmsman!"

Shabor ignored his pleas. After a few moments, the helmsman cautiously got to his feet and resumed his job, ostentatiously staring straight ahead. His fearful expectations were realized when the pounding surf on the ring of rocks protecting the sheltered cove came into sight. He gave himself up for lost, but recognizing that his chieftain's sword was closer than the rocks, he held true to his course.

More than a score of small coasters trailed behind them, each carrying about a hundred men. They followed the red lantern that was firmly secured at the top of their highest mast. Each captain had firm orders to follow the course of the vessels in front of him as closely as possible, with Shobar's craft leading the way. From time to time, Katog glanced back to make sure the fleet was close on their heels. *The captains must be as nervous as our helmsman,* he thought. *But no one can be as nervous as I am.*

The pounding surf on the hungry rocks was only a hundred meters away when suddenly a bright, glowing orb appeared just ahead of their bowsprit. Shobar seemed to be the only one not surprised.

"Follow that light," he snapped to his helmsman. "It will guide us into the cove."

The helmsman nodded and spun the wheel, changing course as the orb moved. His fear of shipwreck numbed his shock and he followed it without conscious thought. Before the unbelieving eyes of all on deck, the orb led them to a narrow gap in the rocks. It was barely wide enough for the coaster's beam and the helmsman jockeyed his wheel to point the nose of the bows directly at the shining orb. The coaster captain shouted a continuous series of orders at the men up in the rigging to make sure they sailed as though the orb was fixed on their bows.

The channel between the rocks was not straight and no human crew or helmsman could have guided a ship through it, except with extraordinary luck. However, the orb led the way flawlessly. It guided them so close to some rocks that they scraped their timbers, and away from tempting channels within which lurked submerged rocks that would have ripped out their keel. Shobar's captain, helmsman, and crew were selected for their skill, and they proved their worth. Concentrating mightily, they kept coaster's bows perfectly aligned with the orb. After more than half an hour of tense work, they made a final tack and sailed into the incongruously calm cove.

The anchors rattled down and now Shobar smiled. He clapped his captain and helmsman on the back saying, "You must trust your King, men."

They both fell to their knees.

"Your Majesty!" cried the helmsman. "Never again will I doubt your wisdom. You see so much farther and so much more than us simpletons!"

The crew worked efficiently and silently. They lowered boats with a minimum of noise and began ferrying the troops to the beach with muffled oars. In the meantime, other vessels of the flotilla began making their way into the cove, each guided by a similar bright orb. One of the vessels did not follow the orb closely enough and had her bottom ripped out by an underwater rock. She rapidly broke up in the rough surf. There was little chance for her crew and the troops she carried, thrown into the freezing maelstrom weighed down by clothing and armor.

"Fools!" was the only epitaph that Shobar gave them.

Even though the men worked as silently as possible and the gale was loud, Katog felt that it was impossible that the patrolling sentries on the battlements could have missed seeing them. There were now nearly two thousand men mustering on the narrow strand at the base of the cliff.

"Sire, should we get something from the ships to shield our heads?" Katog asked Shobar, respectfully. "It is very likely that the defenders will rain projectiles or boiling liquids on us."

"There is no one to hear us," said Shobar. "We will scale the cliff and attack a sleeping castle." He broke off as Nestar Crogus, the commander of his elite Skull Watch, approached and bowed low, allowing rain to run down his back.

"Sire, my men are ready to commence the ascent," he said. "One of my captains, Cheval Guttanar of Estrans will lead the point squad.

He grew up around here and climbed these cliffs as boy, hunting for kittiwake eggs."

"Good, good," said Shobar. "I want you to secure the battlements. Remember, once up there, kill all the sentries, but do so silently. They should give you no trouble, but the troops in the castle are another matter. At all costs don't rouse anyone inside till we are all up with you. Then the Skull Watch will lead us as we storm the castle and slaughter the garrison. I want the Yengar girl, Nitya, and Greghar taken alive and unhurt—I will handsomely reward whoever takes them. And the same goes for Bradar and his wife, Esgrin."

"It will be done, Sire," said Nestar, bowing again. He returned to his men.

"You stay behind me, Katog," said Shobar to his lame First Minister. "You and I will be the last ones up. Cheer up! Today is the first day of the campaign that will lead us to total victory!"

GREGHAR WAS IN deep slumber, but self-preservation had taught him to sleep with one ear open. So even the very light footsteps woke him, and he sat up. The sword Karya was in its scabbard hung on one of the head posts of his bed, and he drew it soundlessly. He recognized the slim, dark shadow and whispered, "Nitya? What are you doing up at this hour? Why are you here?"

She came closer. There was a flash of lightning, and for an instant he saw her as clear as day. She had the look he remembered from Beacon Peak—her eyes were bright and feral, and she radiated the faint bluish halo.

"He comes," she intoned in a voice that was subtly deeper. "We are not strong enough to fight him now, you and I. We must flee."

"There is no struggle, Nitya," said Greghar gruffly. "It is all in your dreams or hallucinations. The war is over. A good and just king is on the throne of Utrea, my father's legacy is safe. I have done my part in restoring him. I am King Lothar's servant and no one else's."

"He comes!" Nitya repeated insistently. "All in this castle will fall to him. We cannot stay!"

"This castle is impregnable," said Greghar. "If you want me to move, tell me what you think you know."

"He has been here," she said, and trembled. "I felt his presence. He has cleared the seaward side of the castle. There will be no resistance."

Her look and voice made the hairs stand up on the nape of his neck. He dressed rapidly and laced on his light armor. Within minutes, he was ready with his weapons and his pack on his back.

"Show me," he said.

"There is no time," she said, her voice rising. He looked into her eyes and was shocked by how wide her pupils had become, like a cat's at night.

"Show me, or I will sit right here," he said firmly.

She stamped her foot.

"All right! Follow me! You try my patience!"

She turned and led the way out of his chamber. She was dressed for the road in a traveling shift and walking shoes. She retied the sash of her shift as they walked down the corridor. The gale and accompanying thunder and lightning meant that they did not need to muffle their footfalls. She led the way unerringly up the stairs to the battlements. When they got to the top of the stairs, Greghar felt his skepticism begin to recede, for the heavy door was ajar. He drew Karya and said to her, "Stay behind me now."

Oblivious to the pouring rain, he padded out onto the battlements. He knew there was a complete watch detail on duty, and a sentry should have challenged him by now—but there was nothing but the moaning of the wind. Then in the next lightning flash, he saw a sentry. He stood with his back to them, facing out to sea. He did not turn as they approached him.

When they were a few yards away, Greghar called out to him in a low voice to avoid surprising him, but he did not respond. He glanced around at Nitya. She mouthed, "*I told you so!*" In the next lightning flash, Greghar looked down along the crenels and saw sentry after sentry, all facing the sea, standing as still as statues.

"Are they dead?" he whispered to Nitya.

"No, but they soon will be," she responded. Her bluish halo was brighter now. "Look there!"

She pointed down toward the tip of the promontory where a dark shape had materialized and slipped over the top of the ramparts. It was followed by many more. As they watched, more and more attackers materialized and quickly moved along the battlements, approaching the motionless sentries quietly. They stabbed them with daggers before toppling them over the walls to fall down the cliff into the rocks and sea below. Greghar recognized the distinctive helmets of the Skull Watch and clenched his fists.

He put his arm around Nitya's waist and pulled her into a narrow archer's gallery, so they were out of sight. They saw the attackers complete their grisly task, disposing of the entire watch. In the meantime, every passing minute saw dozens more men-at-arms swarming up over the walls.

"I must get back into the castle and alert Bradar," whispered Greghar.

"It is too late," she whispered back.

Sure enough, even as she spoke the Skull Watchmen began streaming into the castle, followed by Shobar's regular troops. All the gates and doors from the battlements into the interior were ajar. Then a particularly bright lightning flash lit the scene just as the last of the Skull Watchmen began entering the castle. Greghar saw Nestar directing troops to various entrances. Without thinking he unslung his crossbow, loaded a bolt and wound it, confident that the gale would cover any sound he made.

"Don't," said Nitya as he lined up his shot through one of the gallery arrow slits. "Now is not..."

Greghar ignored her and fired. With the wind and the darkness, it was a difficult shot. However, even though Greghar's aim was true, Nestar's luck held. Just as Greghar squeezed the trigger, the squad of Skull Watchmen he had left to attend Shobar appeared over the walls and raised their standard, a black flag with a white skull on it. Nestar immediately trotted off toward the tip of the promontory to receive his liege. The bolt passed behind him, missing by centimeters. Greghar swore under his breadth.

Now sounds of violence began rising from the keep and the other interior buildings of the castle. Screams and shouts rose in the night air, carrying up to the battlements over the storm. There was the odd clang of weaponry, but mostly it sounded like slaughter and rape. Cursed with an ear that had experienced many battles, Greghar could picture what was happening. They were crouched in the cramped gallery for almost an hour before they saw Shobar and Katog make their leisurely way into the keep.

Almost all of Shobar's men were now inside the castle. Confident that the rocks secured their rear, they had left just a small rearguard to watch the battlements. These men soon grew bored, however, and paced about the battlements, checking out the various corbels, machicolations, and galleries. Hunched against the rain, two troopers approached the gallery in which they were concealed. Greghar drew Karya and prepared himself. The troopers were a meter away from the entrance and clearly about to enter when Greghar stepped into the narrow archway and ran the leading one through.

Many things happened at once. As Greghar put his boot on the trooper's body to extricate Karya, the second trooper drew his sword. Seeing Greghar helpless before the sharp blade, Nitya put up her right hand and a surge of blue flame shot out, engulfing the second trooper from head to toe. At the same time, an enormous bolt of lightning struck the ramparts just behind them. It was so close that the ear-splitting thunderclap was almost simultaneous, completely drowning out the second trooper's thin dying wail.

All the remaining troopers on the battlements threw themselves to the ground in response to the lightning strike. Fearing a second strike, they were slow to rise. Nitya took Greghar's hand and hissed a single word, "Come!" She ran quickly and silently along the battlements to the tip of the promontory whence the attackers had come, Greghar close on her heels. As she expected, thick ropes were still attached to crenels.

Just as they reached the ropes, a second bolt of lightning struck the ramparts, its accompanying thunderclap deafeningly loud. Shobar's troopers stayed down, flat on their stomachs with their arms over their heads

"Let us go down to the cove below," she whispered urgently.

"What then?" asked Greghar.

"Trust me," she said, self-assuredly. "Can I ride on your back as you descend?"

"It depends on how much weight you have put on," he said, cracking a grim smile. Even as he spoke, he hoisted himself over the edge of the battlements and stood with his feet planted on the wall. The muscles in his powerful arms knotted as he gripped the rope to hold himself steady.

She clambered over the battlements and settled herself on his back, holding on to the straps of his pack. She recalled his fear of heights and whispered in his ear, "Don't worry, we will be fine."

"Slick rocks, freezing rain, a slippery rope: nothing to worry about!" said Greghar, using graveyard humor to conceal his anxiety.

He eased himself down, hand over hand. The closer he got to the beach, the less anxious he became. She held on, supremely confident of his strength. They reached the sands of the beach, and Nitya leaped off nimbly.

"There are boats pulled up on the beach," she whispered to him. "We must take one and get out to sea."

He looked at her doubtfully.

"In this gale?"

"You can sail, you said," she reminded him.

"In a ship with a crew," he responded in a low tone. "Not in a rowboat."

"There is a selection of boats here," she whispered adamantly. "Choose the best one."

Greghar knew he had little choice. He had no wish to climb back up to the castle.

"Follow me," he said resignedly.

He led the way, darting from boulder to boulder to avoid attracting the attention of the men-at-arms Shobar had left patrolling the strand. Nitya stayed close behind, following him like a shadow. Each time he took cover behind a boulder, he scanned the line of boats pulled up on the sand just out of the waves. There were several score boats drawn up, and he checked out each boat carefully.

Finally he saw a one that seemed to suit their needs. It was a cutter, and he saw a mast with furled sails strapped to the gunnels. It was small enough that he thought he could row it, yet large enough that it had some chance of survival in the mountainous seas out beyond the rocks. However, there was a trooper pacing back and forth, right by her prow, stamping his feet in an effort to stay warm.

"Walk behind me," Greghar whispered to Nitya, and emerged from behind the rock.

He walked up to the trooper with no attempt at subterfuge.

"Who goes there?" challenged the trooper.

"I am a servant of Lord Katog," said Greghar steadily, adopting the guttural Utrean dialect of the Swards. "He has asked me to place this captive wench in the holds of the king's ship."

"Where is this captive wench?" asked the trooper roughly. "I see no one..."

His words trailed off as Nitya appeared from behind Greghar's back. She had tied her wrists together with the sash from her shift. She looked bedraggled and miserable, her hair matted down in a sodden mass by the rain. The trooper approached them and looked at her appraisingly. He pushed some sodden locks out of her face and grunted.

"She's comely, I'll grant," he said, deliberating. "No doubt she will clean up to look quite the lady for my lord Katog."

"Don't just stand there, help me get the cutter in the water," said Greghar impatiently. "We don't want to stand around all night. My Lord Katog will be down shortly, and I have to get her into dry things, ready for him."

"All right, all right, keep your calm," said the trooper. He turned and helped Greghar push the cutter toward the water. Nitya leaped in and settled herself in the stern sheets. Once she was afloat, the two men climbed aboard and began to row. They pulled strongly, and the cutter moved smoothly over the relatively mild rollers in the cove. They soon came upon the mass of vessels at anchor.

Subtly, Greghar began pulling away from them and toward the rocks. It did not take long for the trooper to realize something was amiss.

"What are you doing?" he cried. "Do you want to kill us? It is death to go toward the rocks!"

Greghar did not listen but continued pulling strongly. He avoided the eyes of the trooper and kept his gaze fixed on Nitya. She was beginning to give off the bluish glow again, and the trooper's eyes widened.

"What sorcery is this?" he cried. He looked at Greghar in a panic. "Have you been bewitched? Speak, man!"

Greghar still did not speak but continued rowing strongly. The prow of the cutter was now turned completely away from the vessels at anchor and the trooper stood, crouched low to keep down his center of gravity, and moved toward Greghar, drawing a dagger from his belt. Greghar waited, hunched over his oarlock. Just as the trooper raised his arm to strike, Greghar swung his unshipped oar in a vicious arc. He struck the trooper's side with enough force to knock him off his feet. His dagger flew out of his hand and he flailed in the air as he fell over the gunnel into the sea. He sank under the surface with barely a splash, weighed down by his armor.

Greghar quickly shipped his oar again and took the other oar.

"I will row for the rocks, Nitya," he said loudly so she could hear him over the gale. "For that death is preferable to the one that awaits us if we return to the castle."

She did not respond as he set the oars and settled into rowing. The sound of the breakers on the rocks grew closer and closer. Greghar fell into a steady tempo, his ears telling him that the end could not be long in coming. Then all of a sudden, she spoke, her voice sharp and commanding.

"Stroke with your left oar, *now!*"

He could not believe his ears, but he obeyed her instantly. All of a sudden they were in a slightly smoother channel.

"Three strokes straight with both oars, now," she chanted.

Again he followed. She used the tiller with an expertise that surprised him and continued giving him directions. Sometimes she spoke so rapidly so he only had time for half a stroke, and sometimes she told him to take several long pulls. Greghar saw the rocks out of the corners of his eyes, and they were sometimes so near that he struck them with his oars. Once she had him use an oar to push off a rock and get them around a tight turn.

He worked tirelessly. He was now aware that failing to follow her instructions instantly and precisely would mean death for both of them. In spite of the cold, he could feel the sweat running down his face. The pouring rain and the spray off the pounding breakers actually felt good.

In his concentration, he had no idea where they were. So when they suddenly shot out into open water and into the trough of a large wave, he was taken by surprise. However, Nitya was not, and she rapped out her instructions sharply. Following them, he brought the prow around in time to breast the wave. Her bluish halo and bright, predatory eyes were disturbing, but oddly they gave him confidence in her instructions.

He rowed them a hundred meters past the treacherous rocks before setting to unlashing and stepping the mast. His veins were coursing with too much adrenalin to feel tired and he worked steadily till he had them under a scrap of storm sail. Only then did he make his way back to the stern sheets and take the tiller from her. She found a dry tarp in the locker beneath their bench and draped it around both of them. He glanced at her to see that her halo was rapidly fading and she held him close, the Nitya he knew once again.

"Where do you want me to take you, mistress?" asked Greghar, only half in jest.

She snuggled closer against the cold saying, "I've done my part, now it is up to you."

He smiled down at her, feeling their old bond rekindling. He was proud of how calm and unafraid she was as the cutter pitched wildly in the stormy sea.

"I dare not take this cockleshell much farther from shore. But I think she should make it to Estrans harbor—it is only a short sail south of the castle. We can try to buy horses there and ride for Nordberg."

"Your aunt, the queen, gave me quite a lot of money," she replied. "She did not want me to be dependent on Baroness Esgrin. Four talents, one gold and three silver."

"Between the two of us, we should have enough for the journey," he said. "I shall be much happier once we cross the border out of Swarborg."

INSIDE ESTRANS CASTLE, chaos still reigned. Shobar's men had met little resistance, but in the storm and the darkness, there was still mopping up to do. Many of Bradar's people were scurrying this way and that, trying to find ways out of the castle to escape the clutches of the victors. Native Swards were particularly afraid for they knew that their service to Bradar would earn them the greatest measure of Shobar's displeasure.

Shobar and Katog stood on an inner balcony, watching prisoners being herded into the main courtyard of the keep. Nestar came up to them and bowed low.

"Highness, the castle is yours," he said. His leathers and chain mail bore a few marks, but he appeared unhurt. "It will take several hours for us to search every nook and cranny, but that is a minor issue. This is your ancestral seat, we know this castle perfectly."

"That is well," said Shobar, masking his eagerness. "But where are the Yengar wench, Greghar, and my cousin, Bradar?"

Nestar looked worried and rubbed the back of his shaven head.

"Sire, we have Baron Bradar, Baroness Esgrin, and their daughters," he said, trying to sound confident. "The baron and his lady are in the Hall of Tiles. Your High Seat has been prepared with a masthead."

"Yes, yes," said Shobar irascibly. "But what of Greghar and the wench?"

"Sire, we are still searching for them," said Nestar, not meeting the gaze of his liege. "If they were in the castle, we will find them."

"Make sure that you do," said Shobar, clearly not happy. Jerking his thumb, he said, "Deal with those down there and take me to the Hall of Tiles."

"Take care of them!" Nestar called down to Guttanar, who was in charge of the men-at-arms in the main courtyard. He drew his finger across his throat. Then he bowed again to Shobar and said, "I will attend you to the Hall of Tiles, Sire."

They entered the Hall, its high walls covered with finely inlaid tiles. Shobar felt good to be back in the familiar environs of the castle in which he had grown up. Bradar and Esgrin had been allowed to change out of their nightclothes and were dressed formally. Bradar was unarmed, but not restrained. Several dozen Skull Watchmen surrounded them. They all bowed low as Shobar entered. He noted, however, that Bradar remained erect.

Shobar went straight up to Bradar, drew his sword, and without saying a word, struck him hard on the side of the head with the flat of his blade. Bradar staggered under the weight of the blow, lost his balance, and fell. Shobar followed him and kicked him several times as he lay on the floor. Then he sheathed the sword, turned on Esgrin, and backhanded her across the face, drawing a scream of pain.

"You will give me the respect I am due," he said, breathing heavily. "I am King of Utrea as well as Lord of the Northeast. You have dared to usurp my ancestral fief and sit in my High Seat! Well, now your family will begin to pay for its treasonous crimes. Today I have taken back Estrans Castle, the first step on my road of conquest."

Bradar slowly got up, but swayed on his feet. Esgrin remained on the floor, cowering.

"Put Bradar in manacles and leg-irons," Shobar told Nestar. "Then clear the Skull Watchmen out of the Hall."

A few minutes later, with only five of them in the Hall, Shobar stamped up to the High Chair. The men had lashed a crude masthead fashioned from a wooden pole to the back of the High Chair. He eased himself into its familiar seat, and Katog took up his station on the floor at his right hand. Nestar roughly pulled Esgrin to her feet and pushed the couple to the front of the High Chair.

"Where are Greghar and the Yengar wench, Nitya?" Shobar asked, looking down on them from the High Chair.

Bradar looked at him stupefied, too confused from the blow to his head to answer. Esgrin nursed the bruise that was beginning to form on the side of her face.

"My husband saw fit to have the witch in the Maiden's Suite," she spat out. "And the bastard in the Blue Room."

Shobar looked at Nestar questioningly.

"We have searched both those places, Sire," he said woodenly. "They are empty."

"Search them again, thoroughly this time. Look for signs of escape out the windows. Bring any effects you find."

Nestar bowed and departed. Bradar's dizziness got the better of him, and he made for a chair to sit down.

"If you get off your feet, I will take them off for you," threatened Shobar, rising and drawing his sword partway out of its scabbard.

Esgrin hurried over and took Bradar's arm, holding him up. He looked at her in confusion, and she patted his face.

"Sire," Esgrin said in a cloyingly sweet tone, "my husband and I have no designs on your fief. We came here on the express orders of my father-in-law. He is your enemy, not us. We are very happy to return to our estates in the Draigynys Islands and live there quietly, never troubling Your Majesty."

"I see," said Shobar, thoughtfully. "Well, we will see what my advisers tell me."

Katog almost spoke up, but Shobar did not look his way, and he kept his silence. It was a long silence, finally broken by Nestar's return with four Skull Watchmen. They carried a large trunk festooned with pink, girlish ribbons and a plain pair of leather saddlebags.

"Empty them out," commanded Shobar.

The Skull Watchmen first unbuckled the saddlebags and emptied them as commanded. They contained some of Greghar's clothing and a spare pair of ankle boots. Then they did the same for the larger trunk. Unlike Greghar's saddlebags, Nitya's trunk was neatly packed, so when it was upended, her things cascaded out in reverse order of the layers she had put them in. First came her makeup bag, then several fine gowns, and a few bags containing slippers and shoes. Finally, secreted at the bottom were sheer stockings and filmy lace and lamé lingerie, which now floated out and lay on top, glittering in the lamplight.

"You can see from her clothes that she is a temptress," said Esgrin sourly and hypocritically, being partial to naughty lingerie herself.

"No potions, no witches' paraphernalia," muttered Shobar, half to himself. "Yet I was assured…"

"Sire, there is no doubt that she is a witch," said Esgrin forcefully. "I have had it from Animus the White Khalif himself."

Nestar cleared his throat.

"We searched the chambers thoroughly, Sire," he said. "The windows are firmly latched. We opened them, and I sent men on to the ledges—there are no signs of exit or escape."

"There is only one way to find where they are," said Shobar. He addressed the four Skull Watchmen. "Put together a rough fire pit on the flagstones here. Get some wood and start up a small fire. Bring me some butter."

They leaped to do his bidding. In short order a small fire was kindled and Shobar dismissed the Skull Watchmen from the Hall. Then he took the pot of butter, went down on his knees, and fed the flames, muttering, *"Na-dwara, na-dwara, na-dwara…"* over and over again. Esgrin and Bradar, who was now coming around, looked on curiously, but both Nestar and Katog's expressions were apprehensive.

Suddenly, all the lamps and candles in the Hall of Tiles guttered and went out. Esgrin gasped and her hold on Bradar's hand tightened. Nestar's gripped the hilt of his sword and Katog's lips moved soundlessly. There was a hum, low at first and then again, louder. A thin trail of smoke arose from the small fire and gradually began to gain form and substance. But each time it seemed to coalesce, there was a crackling sound and it dispersed again. This happened several times until finally there were small blue sparks in the smoke. The sparks continued sizzling and hissing, even as the smoke settled into a shadowy trail that rose out of the popping flames. None of them dared speak.

Shobar's eyes were closed and he swayed from side to side in a trance. Then he began to nod and his expression showed fear.

"Lord Malitha! I beg your forgiveness! I had my men follow your instructions to the letter. The Yengar wench and Greghar were our first objects, just as you ordered. I know what the wench means for us. Every one of my men was looking for her."

There were a few loud pops, adding to the steady crackling.

"She must have sensed our presence," continued Shobar, his voice growing more plaintive. "She must have grown stronger and broken the bonds you placed on her. She communes with Vasitha to obstruct us. Now she has fled with the bastard Greghar to protect her. But tell us where to find them, Lord. We will do your bidding—we will place them at your feet. For your cause is our cause."

Again there was a series of pops from the smoke, like fire eating at wet wood. Shobar cringed and his head snapped sideways. Then he nodded again vigorously. There was a low hum and the flames in the rough fire pit died down. In just a few moments, the fire went out and the smoky outline faded away. Shobar's eyes slowly opened and he leaned forward to rest on his hands and knees. He shook his head to clear it and stood up shakily. Nestar came up to stand beside him, prepared to steady him if he stumbled or fell. Shobar looked around the room, regaining his surly expression.

"We will ransom Bradar and his daughters to his father in exchange for my old fief of Swarborg. But we will keep the Baroness Esgrin—I have plans for her." He paused. "Then we must be patient. Malitha will guide our swords to our next conquest. Remain faithful to me and you will all share in coming victories! On the battlefield and in the bedchamber."

FOUR

THE CRUELTY OF LOVE

CAITLIN HAD THOUGHT that her feeling of loss would diminish with time, but paradoxically it seemed to get worse. As the years passed, she missed her daughter more rather than less. She often dreamed of Asgara and sobbed in her sleep. Binne was a light sleeper and heard her. She tried to ignore it at first, but it happened so frequently that finally she woke Caitlin and demanded to know what was wrong. Caitlin was evasive, but Binne was insistent.

"You are now my adoptive daughter, it is only right that I share your sorrows," she said.

"It is not sorrow..." Caitlin began.

"You sob so deeply, night after night, as though your very heart is breaking!" exclaimed Binne. "This is not some passing nightmare."

Caitlin looked up at her with an expression that was so unhappy that Binne sat on her bed and put her arms around her. Caitlin slowly relaxed as Binne held her and stroked her hair.

"I have a daughter," she said. "I committed the mortal sin of lusting for a man. And I broke the laws of my people. Under this cloud, I had her anyway. That girl I brought into the world—she is the light of my life! But it became clear that she would inherit the burdens of my misdeeds, so I gave her up to another. Now she appears to me in my dreams, asking to be cuddled, begging for my love! I am a monster! A mother who abandoned her own daughter!"

"No, no," said Binne, holding her tighter. "You wanted the best for your daughter. A child born in sin often pays a heavy price, especially a girl. You have sacrificed your happiness for her future. You are not a monster. I said it when we first met and I will say it again—you are an angel."

Binne's words comforted her and she felt her tension slowly melting away.

YANDHARAN FOUND HIMSELF making more and more excuses for trips to the Hareskot area. It was a small village in an impoverished region of his jurisdiction and his wife Zaibene eventually began to question the need for so many trips. In response, he started lying about where he was going. Once in Hareskot, he inevitably paid a few "courtesy calls" on the Avedus ranch.

Binne and Seamus were initially suspicious and worried that he was still looking for Dhanraj. So they hid the boy when they saw him approach. But after the third or fourth visit they discerned what attracted him to their remote homestead. Their deductions were confirmed when he saw Dhanraj and made no comment.

So now when he drew up in their yard, Binne came out of the ranch house with a smile on her face.

"You look like you have had a hard ride, Collector Yandharan," she said. "Did you not stop to take refreshment in the village?"

"No," he replied, swinging down from the saddle and doffing his wide-brimmed leather hat to her. "It was getting late, I thought I better pay my calls before sundown."

It was still early in the afternoon and Binne smiled inwardly.

But she said, "Of course, of course, that makes good sense. Will you come in and take some tea?"

Tea was brought up from the Nilong Highlands in Daksin, toward the southern tip of the One Land. While it was a very popular beverage, it was difficult to procure outside of Daksin, and consequently very expensive. The Aveduses were not rich and drank a very weak brew, using only the tiniest of pinches in each cup.

"I will be delighted," he said, heartily. "And I will not tax your hospitality." He grinned at his joke. "I have brought you a bag of tea from Serat."

"Why, Collector Yandharan!" Binne said coquettishly. "I am a married woman. You should have brought me such presents forty years ago when I was a maiden entertaining suitors."

"Would that I could have done so," said Yandharan gallantly, with a slight bow. "I blame my parents, for I was not yet born."

"Such flimsy excuses!" cried Binne, leading the way into the kitchen.

Yandharan followed her, taking off his hat and hanging it on a peg. She put the kettle on, and he presented her with a sizeable gunnysack. The delightful aroma of the tea emanated from it.

"What a wonderful fragrance," she said sniffing it. "It smells like Kaylan tea."

"You have a good nose, ma'am," said Yandharan.

With her newly acquired riches, she made two fairly strong cups. Then she joined him at the kitchen table, wiping her hands on a dishcloth. She sipped the tea and sighed with pleasure.

"Such a fine leaf," she said appreciatively. "We are much in your debt."

"No, no, it is I who owe you thanks," he countered. "For your hospitality has made my many official trips to the area pleasant beyond measure."

Binne smiled and watched him sipping his tea.

"I take it Seamus and Dhanraj are on the range?" he said, after what he thought was a decent interval.

"Aye, and Cat is out there as well," said Binne playfully. She paused to observe him and was gratified to see the spark of interest that leaped into his eyes. "As a daughter and then as a wife, I have lived on ranches my whole life. But I swear to you that girl teaches me new things about horses every day."

"You are fortunate in your adoptive daughter," agreed Yandharan. He opened his mouth to continue, but then shut it and looked out the window. Binne did not help him fill the silence, but sipped her tea, waiting for him. Finally, he squared his shoulders and went on. "I am a man of means, Binne Avedus. I am not wellborn, but I have worked hard, and I have been frugal. I have properties and landed estates in Serat and in Tirut. I have a comfortable income quite aside from my tax commissions from the cheval."

Binne looked at him primly, over the rim of her cup. Her intuition told her where he was going, but she did not want to make it easy for him.

"I have known your daughter Cat for several years now. I have reason to believe that she does not despise me. So I now beg you for information. Does she speak of me? If so, does she express warmth?"

"She sometimes speaks of you," replied Binne guardedly. "She does not view you as an enemy."

Yandharan made a fist, but stopped himself from pounding the table. He took some time to calm his eagerness.

"I am not a rash or foolhardy man," he said. "I know that a mysterious woman like Cat, with no connections or family and an unstable disposition is a very risky proposition. But I cannot help myself."

"My dear Collector Yandharan!" exclaimed Binne. "I believe I see color attempting to show itself on your leathery face!"

Yandharan looked sheepish, but he plunged on.

"If I were to press my suit with Cat, would you and your husband smile on it?"

Now that she had got him to come out in the open, she sat back.

"It is our dearest wish to see Cat settled," she said. "But with the right man, a man who appreciates her and can make her happy." She paused and looked at him sternly before continuing. "She is one of a kind, our Cat. She is something of a dreamer, a bit naïve, intensely righteous and loyal to the point of self-sacrifice. She is smart as a whip, and more athletic than any boy. Her heart has already been broken once. We would not see her hurt again."

"Are you saying that I am not sincere?" asked Yandharan, in a carefully emotionless voice.

"No," replied Binne gently. "I am saying that you are married."

CAITLIN WAS LYING in the shallows where the stream took a sharp bend, forming a tranquil pool in the inner side of the elbow. Her head was on the grassy bank and her thick red mane cascaded loose on the grass. Her clothes were piled up on the bank behind her head and her eyes were closed.

She was not asleep, but thinking of Asgara. She was imagining what she must look like, and at what stage of development. *She must be a young girl now*, she thought. *Riding horses, taking ballet, and going to school. She must be a curious child, asking questions about everything. And Megara is incredibly patient; they must be so happy together.*

Her bittersweet thoughts were abruptly interrupted by a low hum that grew in volume. Her eyes snapped open and she looked around, but there was nothing to be seen and the sound ceased. She cautiously closed her eyes again and it came again. When it stopped, she saw a tall man with white hair and beard, dressed in brown robes. His dark brown eyes were so warm that they melted away her fears. Her eyes were tightly shut, but his form was clear and sharp and his expression was kindly.

"Princess Caitlin d'Orr," he said. "I am Vasitha, lover of your ancestor Simran d'Orr, the first Zon queen on New Eartha. In her time the battle lines were clearly drawn, but now there is evil everywhere in this world. The Dark rises and soon all the established powers in the One Land will be co-opted by it. You are one of the Companions, the last hope for the powers of Light."

She blinked several times to try and excise the vision, but each time she closed her eyes, he was there, waiting patiently with a kind expression.

Her lips did not move, but she heard her voice.

"I am a weak sinner, exiled by my people. I cannot be the one you seek."

"Caitlin, you are no more a sinner than your ancestor Simran. It is the Dark that has cast you down, for your righteousness is abhorrent to it."

"What must I do?"

"You must seek out the others. In Tirut."

"How...?"

But before she could finish her question, there was a crackle as his image became distorted. There was a low hum again and her mind's eye went blank. He was gone.

YANDHARAN MEANT TO ride back to Hareskot and settle himself in the inn. On a whim, he rode down to the stream that flowed toward the village instead of taking the high road. The stream was one of the few sources of moisture in the parched, semi-arid landscape and it was cooler under the shade of the string of juniper trees that grew along its banks.

He was about half way to Hareskot when he came upon the sharp bend in the stream. Some dense privet bushes screened him off from the pool itself, but what caused him to pull up sharply was the big red that was placidly munching grass by the bushes. He recognized Caitlin's horse, Rufus. He dismounted, hobbled his own horse, and walked around the bushes, not sneaking up, but not making a great deal of noise either.

Yandharan saw Caitlin and came to a dead stop. His eyes were drawn to the faded black marks on her thigh, rather than to the rest of her. On her pale skin the blemishes were still vivid. Lost in her own world, she whispered, "Tirut!" Yandharan had only been there a moment and was about to decorously turn and leave when she sensed his presence. Her eyes opened and rather than try to cover her nakedness with her arms, she reached behind her and drew her sword Nasht.

"I will wait for you behind the bushes," Yandharan said hastily, beating a quick retreat.

A few minutes later she came around the bushes, dressed and angry. The circumstances seemed to confirm the prejudices instilled by her Zon upbringing.

"Collector Yandharan," she said coldly. "I see that like all men, you view women as nothing more than objects of lust to be taken advantage of."

"I most sincerely beg your pardon," he replied contritely. "I had no idea I would find you thus. No sooner did I see your state than I turned and removed myself. My eyes saw nothing but the marks on your thigh. If I could, I would remove those from my memory as well."

She eyed him suspiciously.

"What brings you here, off the high road?"

"It is a cooler ride, and I am in no hurry," he said with alacrity. "Please forgive me, I cannot bear to have you think ill of me."

"Why should my regard be worth anything to you?" she asked indifferently.

"Please accept my deepest apologies," he repeated, looking deep into her eyes. "I beg that you will allow me to wait on you tomorrow evening after my duty calls."

"I will be in Hareskot tomorrow evening, picking up some things for Binne," she said, cool and aloof. "I will call on you at the inn, it will save you the ride out to the ranch."

ALONG WITH CAITLIN, Dhanraj had taken up residence in the Avedus household after his parents' death. Initially the Aveduses kept his presence a secret, but gradually the truth got out in Hareskot and the villagers eventually got used to it. He had not grown much taller, but he had put on a bit of muscle and was proud to walk around without a shirt when it was warm enough. With Seamus and Caitlin as teachers, he made rapid progress and soon became a full-fledged member of the team in the running of the ranch. Caitlin had helped him to break the young bay and to his delight, Seamus allowed him to ride the horse as his own.

The day after her encounter with Yandharan, Caitlin came into the kitchen of the ranch house after working hard all day out on the range.

"You have had a hard day, love," said Binne, when Caitlin asked her for the list of things she wanted from the general store in the village. "You may as well go in tomorrow morning, when you are rested and fresh. There is nothing on the list that is urgent."

Caitlin did not want to mention her meeting with Yandharan, so she merely said, "I will get it done today and laze around the house with you tomorrow. We will drink tea and chat all day."

She got the trap ready, and mounted the driver's box. It was a pleasant drive to Hareskot, where she drew up in front of the general store. She bought everything on Binne's list and added some more small luxuries that she paid for with her own money. Caitlin noticed some young ranch hands lounging about the square. Anxious to get on to the inn and away from the stares of the lads, she made up larger loads to minimize the number of trips to the trap.

The ranch hands had been drinking and they now approached Caitlin as she emerged from the store with her last load. While most of them stood back in the street, two made as if to enter the store.

They passed Caitlin a little too close, brushing her side. Then they lurched into her, almost causing her to drop her bags and fall.

"Watch where you are going, you stupid woman!" one of them shouted. Then he turned to his friends back in the street. "Look at how she's dressed, boys. No Thermadan modesty! She's lusting for it! These infidel women are loose, and the One God smiles on the faithful who violate them."

Caitlin did not want to provoke an incident that could lead to an investigation, so she took a temperate approach.

"I mean you no harm," she said mildly. "I will leave peaceably."

The House of the One God was across the square. The deacon, a short, wiry man with iron gray hair, came hurrying over.

"Boys, boys," he cried. "Pray do not use violence in the name of our faith. Lord Thermad and the One God stand for love and acceptance. Allow this woman to go her way in peace."

"You were rebuked by the traveling preachers, Deacon," replied one of ranch hands. "Acceptance of the One God and his Prophet Thermad or death—that is the Abaidan teaching!"

The deacon looked at the tough, muscular group with trepidation.

"You have been misled, lads—" he began.

"Return to the House of the One God and prepare for your Feast Sermon," said one of the hands forcefully. "Or you may find that your deacon's robes don't protect you as well as you might think."

The deacon lingered for a moment, but when one of the ranch hands took a step toward him, he turned tail and hurried back to the House of the One God as fast as he had come.

The ranch hand by Caitlin reached forward to cup one of her breasts.

"Keep your hands to yourself," Caitlin said, knocking his probing hand aside.

"Ah, a frisky one," he said thickly. He winked at his friends. "The ones that fight are always the hottest."

They were interrupted by the sound of a horse's hooves. They all looked up to see Yandharan sitting tall in the saddle, looking down on the scene expressionlessly.

The ranch hands were frozen into place by the appearance of the Collector, who looked intimidating in black leather, the bronze badge of his office reflecting the evening sun.

"Perhaps you will tell me what is going on here, Cat," he said, his tone unflappable.

"I am buying some provisions," she said, her face wooden. "I was just making pleasant conversation with these gentlemen here."

"I see," said Yandharan. "Well, I am pleased that there is no need for the law to become involved."

As Yandharan swung down from the saddle, the ranch hands turned away and retreated toward the livery stable to retrieve their horses.

"Why don't we go to the inn?" said Yandharan. "We can relax in the bar parlor, and the innkeeper can serve us some of his fine ale."

Half an hour later they were seated by a window in the bar parlor of the inn. The trap was temporarily in the innkeeper's barn with Yandharan's horse. Caitlin now sat facing Yandharan, sipping the ale he had ordered. She had never been in the inn, since she rarely came to village and then only to buy things. It was still early in the evening, so there were only a dozen or so men in the parlor, mostly hands from the surrounding ranches. If what Binne had told her was right, it would get crowded later after the evening service at the House of the One God.

In spite of the sawdust floor, the sour smell of fermentation hung in the air and Caitlin had to curb her urge to wrinkle her nose. It was difficult to relax, as she was conscious of the men in the bar stealing furtive looks at her. The ale was quite a nice local brew, and she tried to focus on it.

"I am pleased that your run in with the ranch hands did not turn violent," said the Collector gravely. "Otherwise you may have had to draw your sword. And a sword once drawn usually tastes blood and that leads to the courts."

"Those boys—" began Caitlin.

"They are grown men, not boys," cut in Yandharan. "They pester women incessantly and get away with a great deal of mischief under the excuse of 'youthful exuberance.' It does not help that some of the local girls and even some of the younger married women encourage them. Or that 'bad boy' behavior sometimes gets them what they want."

Caitlin did not respond. She wanted nothing further to do with the local lads. She stared at her ale and tried to blank out the new patrons entering the inn every few minutes, all of who stared at her before proceeding to the bar. Yandharan finally noticed her discomfort, drained his ale and stood up.

"Let us go outside," he said gruffly. "The yellow sun will soon be setting. I never tire of watching it turn into an orange ball at dusk as it sinks below the horizon."

Caitlin left her half full glass of ale on the table and walked out of the bar parlor with him. She heaved a sigh of relief when she got outside, away from the covert stares in the inn. They walked down the short main street to the ford over the small stream that marked the boundary of the village. Beyond it, the dry, treeless landscape extended to the horizon, intermittently punctuated by large barrel cacti, some as high as twenty meters. They stood side by side and watched the sun go down. Caitlin was lost in the memories of golden sunsets she had watched as a girl from the terraces of Palace d'Orr, often with her mother and Megara. *What wouldn't I give to go back to those simpler times*, she thought.

Yandharan cleared his throat, pulling her back into the present. She turned to him and was confused by his look. Then he shocked her by taking her right hand and holding it firmly in both of his. She drew her dagger with her left hand, but he did not flinch. He went down on one knee and gazed up at her with that look.

"Cat Avedus," he said in an ardent tone that she had never heard him use before. "Your beauty is obvious to all that look upon you. But in the years that I have known you, I have come to recognize things of much greater value—your goodness of heart and purity of spirit. To know you is to love you. I am a man of good character. I have saved and invested wisely; people might even call me rich. I offer myself and everything that is mine to you."

She looked at him, but her mind was far away. *Greghar looked at me like that*, she thought. *He never spoke, but that was the look in his eyes!* Greghar's face appeared in place of Yandharan's and she felt an ache deep within.

While she did not respond, Yandharan took heart from her sad smile and the fact that she did not jerk her hand away from him.

"I do not ask for an immediate answer," he said, still holding her hand and still on his knee.

She slowly came back the present again, looked at him, and the smile faded from her face. She realized that he expected her to say something. But what should she say? Her instinctive response was to refuse him, but how? Would he be insulted? Would he turn violent? She still had her long dagger in her left hand, and as a precaution she did not sheath it. But she did not attempt to free her right hand either.

"Collector Yandharan—" she began.

"Please call me Mantan," he said. "It is my given name."

"Mantan," she began again. "I know you saw me unclothed yesterday, but I had no wish or plan—"

"No, no," he interrupted her quickly. "That event is expunged from my memory. I wish to dress you in the finest silks, to adorn you with jewels, to take you from your hardscrabble surroundings and give you the life of luxury that you deserve."

Now her face grew hard.

"The last time a man spoke to me like that, he tortured me when I refused him. You saw the ugly marks of his violence on my thigh. I'll wager *that* is not expunged from your memory."

Now she did jerk her hand free and back away from him. She tightened her grip on her dagger and her right hand was now on her sword hilt. He remained on his knee and continued to look into her eyes without anger.

"I will never touch you again without your consent," he said quietly. He got to his feet. "Who are you, Cat Avedus? I am not a member of the high nobility or the Merchants' Guild, so to me the Zon are near-mythical creatures. Even as an officer of the law, I have seen Zon in the flesh only a couple of times in my life. I have never heard of one living among us."

Caitlin said nothing but stared away, not meeting his eyes.

"Yet you are the image of the Zon huntresses of the folktales—tall, beautiful, more of a warrior and an athlete than most men. Your accent when you first came to Hareskot was suspiciously like the clichéd Zon singsong of satire."

"What do you want from me?" she asked. "I cannot marry you."

"Is it because you are Zon?"

"No," she said. She said nothing further for such a long while that he began to think she would not continue.

"It is not because of what I am," she said finally. "It is because of what I feel. I love another. I am the mother of his child."

"I will pretend I did not hear that," he said doggedly. "Please do not give me an answer now. Take your time, a day, a week, a month, a year. I will wait for you." He paused and waited till she met his eyes. "And please remember, if you ever need help—my sword and my wealth are yours."

CAITLIN TRIED TO sit still as Binne brushed her long, red hair, bringing out its lustrous shine and highlighting the blonde streaks. Two cups of tea sat on the side table beside them. Seamus had gone out on the range, but Binne had reminded Caitlin of her promise to spend the day with her in the ranch house.

"There!" said Binne giving Caitlin's mane a final, spirited stroke. "Turn around and let me see you."

Caitlin stood up and turned around. She tossed her head to make her fiery locks bounce about her head. Binne reached up, saying, "You are so beautiful that I must crack my knuckles on your temples to ward off bad luck!"

When they sat down together on the couch and picked up their cups, Binne grew more serious.

"Collector Yandharan was here the day before yesterday," she said, careful to keep her tone neutral. "He wished to speak with you. Did you see him in the village yesterday?"

Caitlin did not know how to start.

"He seems to like me," she said warily. "I don't know why. I have never given him encouragement."

"He asked me whether Seamus and I would approve of his proposing marriage to you," said Binne, watching Caitlin carefully as she spoke.

Caitlin looked at Binne's kindly face and knew that she could trust her.

"Binne, I was brought up to believe that relationships between the sexes invariably involve the violent subjugation of the woman. And I have experienced this firsthand—my body was broken by a man. Yet I see the relationship you have with Seamus, and it is full of love, partnership, and sharing."

Binne's eyes grew wide as she heard Caitlin speak of her torture.

"I am afraid there is a lot of luck involved, Cat," she said, gaining control of herself. "I did not have much of a dowry settled on me, so the only man who formally proposed to my father was a merchant fifteen years my senior who already had two wives. It was my great good fortune that I met Seamus at a horse auction and we fell in love. His parents were alive then and opposed the match, but he was stubborn—he insisted on marrying me. He is a good man, and we have had a long and happy marriage. The One God has blessed me."

"I have heard that barbar—I mean, men often take more than one wife," said Caitlin.

"Yes, it is common enough. Soon after we were married, we had a string of good years. Seamus was seen as a man of means, but I was not getting pregnant. Several local girls were proposed to him as second wives, some with handsome dowries. I told him that he was free to take another wife, but he would not hear of it. All these years, he has been faithful to me, but he is a rare man. Unfortunately, many men are as you describe. They drink, take as many wives as they can, beat them, and spend all their money in bars and brothels. That was my sister's lot, poor thing."

Caitlin nodded her head in agreement.

"I think Collector Yandharan was asking me to become his wife," said Caitlin. "I didn't know how to react."

"Have you had no pleasant experiences with men?" asked Binne. She took Caitlin's hands in hers. "You have a daughter. She must have a father."

A spasm of pain crossed Caitlin's face as she thought of Greghar. He was never far from her thoughts. She missed everything about him—his steady presence, his smile, his humor, the sound of his voice. He was so sharply etched in her memory that she could effortlessly bring him before her mind's eye.

"I love him," she said. "But he would not have me."

"The fool!" exclaimed Binne, putting her arms around Caitlin. She held her and they sat in silence for a while. *My Cat is a consort for a king,* she thought. *What coldhearted fiend would take such advantage of her generous nature? To lie with her, leave her with child and then desert her!*

"Collector Yandharan is a good man, my dear," Binne said at length. "To the best of my knowledge, he is honorable, honest, and ethical. He has a reputation as a man of moderate habits and upstanding morality. He has never been known to consort with women of easy virtue. And bear in mind, my dear, that in his position he has countless temptations thrown his way."

Binne paused to sip her tea.

"Are you recommending him, then?"

"I will be honest with you, dearest Cat," Binne said, looking troubled. "Collector Yandharan has a wife and children. When I questioned him, he maintained that he would never forsake them, that he is proposing that you join his family as his second wife."

She paused, searching for strength. She knew that what she was about to say would recall her grief, so she steeled herself.

"If my own daughter Marte were still alive and received this proposal, I would have welcomed it. I would have counseled her to accept him, for men such as Collector Yandharan are rare. I cannot imagine that he would discriminate between his wives or consequent progeny. Even his junior wife would enjoy a privileged, indeed an exalted position in Serat society and throughout the Southern Marches."

"I see," said Caitlin. "I realize now that I should be flattered to receive the attentions of such a man."

She took a sip of her tea and smiled. But Binne was not done.

"The One God knows that I loved Marte more than life itself. Not a day passes when I do not wish that the Chekaligas had taken me and spared her. But I love you too, my sweet Cat. No two loves are the same, so I do not compare."

Impulsively, Caitlin hugged Binne, reminded again of how thin and spare she was.

"I was a stray creature, and you welcomed me into your home and hearts," she said. "I will never forget that."

Binne smiled with genuine pleasure.

"There is a certain something about you, Cat. You wear no crown, but you have what I can only describe as a regal air. I have never seen a queen, but if I ever did, I would expect her to carry herself as you do."

Caitlin laughed, but not wholeheartedly.

"Your love for me makes you see me as more than I am," she said.

"No, no," insisted Binne. "When I was a little girl, the Baroness of Tirut visited Hareskot. It was the biggest day of my childhood, for there was such a huge fair in the village to mark her visit! My father brought us all in to see her. She was dressed in the loveliest gown of Tirutan cami-silk and wore a coronet of gold. She had an air about her, but she was nothing in comparison to you! Hers came from hauteur and pride, whereas you treat everyone as an equal, and it is just *there*."

Binne petted Caitlin's shiny hair.

"The first time I laid eyes on you, I felt you were a princess incognito, to the palace born. Yet you live on our remote ranch and work hard all day for a share of our simple fare with never a single complaint. I hope I live to see you restored to your rightful station in life. You were meant to be more than a Collector's junior wife."

"You come up with the craziest ideas, Binne," said Caitlin uncomfortably.

MEGARA WAS GOING over fitness reports in her office when she heard the ping of an incoming comm. channel. She opened it and saw it was from Centuria Blanchia Rodina, so she said, "I am at your service, Centuria."

"Seignora Megara, you have been ordered to take command of a detachment of three Guardian squads assigned to the *Hydromeda*," she said. "There is an airboat waiting for you outside. Please collect your personal effects and be aboard the airship in half an hour. We weigh within the hour."

"What is the emergency, Centuria?" asked Megara in surprise. "Has war broken out?"

"You will be briefed on board. This is a secret mission. Do not contact anyone. See me as soon as you board."

"But I need to contact my girls—" began Megara.

"Do not contact the nursery!" snapped Blanchia. "That place is a fount of gossip. Children spread rumors like wildfire, and we will have every mother in Atlantic City spreading crazy stories within an hour of our sailing."

"I will only tell my older daughter, she is very discreet—"

"Seignora Megara, I am beginning to have serious doubts about your judgment," said Blanchia icily.

"I hear and obey, Centuria," said Megara unhappily.

One of the *Hydromeda*'s airboats was indeed waiting outside and Megara was flown to Palace d'Orr. She was used to deployments and packed the few personal effects she needed in minutes and was on board the airship in less than thirty minutes. Blanchia was waiting for her on the egress deck and led her quickly to a conference room before she could ask any questions. There were three Guardian squads already mustered there, with two other seignoras. One of the seignoras was Jena. She waved to her as Blanchia clapped her hands for silence.

"Please be seated," she said. The thirty-six Guardians sat down with a scraping of chairs, and she continued. "We weigh in twenty minutes. We are bound for Daksin. King Vokran has invoked the Treaty of Wolf's Head and asks that we deal with some wild tribesmen who have been harrying his subjects in the border areas abutting the Southern Marches. We are under strict comm silence, so no personal communications are allowed until further notice. Any questions?"

"How long will we be away, Centuria?" asked Megara.

"Seignora Megara, you will be informed in due course. At the moment, I can only say that the mission is of an indefinite duration."

ASGARA SAT IN the foyer of Temple Heights Nursery with Iantha. They had dressed, packed their toys, and were ready to go home. They eagerly watched the portal each time someone came in, expecting Megara any minute. She was never late, and when the large chronometer showed ten past the hour, Asgara got up, took Iantha's hand, and approached the reception desk.

"My mother is never late," she said. "Something must have happened to her. Can you open a comm channel to her?"

The caregiver on duty knew Megara's habits. So she smiled at Asgara and said, "Of course, dear. Let me try."

The comm channel pinged and pinged, but there was no response. Finally, the caregiver closed it and looked down at the disappointed girls.

"I am sorry, but she is not answering. I have left her a message. Why don't you both return to the play area, and I will come and get you if she comes."

"No, she can't be long," said Asgara determinedly. "We will wait here."

Just then the outer portal hissed open and Andromache entered, followed by her handmaiden. She swooped down on Asgara, picked her up, and kissed her, saying, "How is my darling girl?"

Asgara wiggled free of Andromache's embrace and smoothed her dress when she was on the ground again. She bowed formally as she had with Megara at Palace Saxe.

"Good evening, Princess Andromache," she said very properly. "My sister and I hope you are well."

Andromache laughed happily saying, "You are such a precious thing! I know we will have a wonderful time together. Come, my handmaiden will take all your things to my speeder."

Asgara stood her ground and did not move.

"I am sorry, Princess Andromache," she said. "We are waiting for our mother. You will have to ask her about inviting us out."

"My dear girl!" exclaimed Andromache. "Have they not told you? Seignora Megara has been transferred to the Daksin Residency. She will be gone for years! I cannot have you living in the nursery all that time. You are to live with me in Palace Saxe."

Asgara's eyes grew wide with horror.

"That is impossible! She would never leave without telling us!" she cried.

Andromache squatted down in front of her and took her face in her hands.

"You must not blame her, Asgara. I am sure she had many things on her mind. Military officers have very stressful lives. They must focus on the task at hand."

"I don't believe you," said Asgara adamantly.

"Let us try and open a comm channel to her," said Andromache in a conciliatory tone.

"We already tried that," said Asgara dully.

"See? I told you that she has other things on her mind. Don't worry. We will have lots of fun together, you and I."

Andromache's handmaiden gently took Asgara's day bag and toy bag from her arms and tried to steer her toward the portal. But Asgara stood firm. She pushed the handmaiden's arms away and ran to Iantha, who had grown worried and started to cry.

"Where's Mommy?" she wailed. "I want Mommy!"

Asgara hugged her, whispering, "Don't worry, sweet pea, everything will be fine." She looked up at Andromache. "We will come with you and wait for our mother to call us at your house. She *will* call."

Andromache gave her a sympathetic smile.

"You are such a loyal girl! It is wonderful to see how well you take care of little Iantha Paurina. But I am afraid that she will have to stay here in the nursery. I cannot care for you both."

"I will not leave without her," Asgara said, her expression becoming fixed.

In her mind's eye, Andromache saw Caitlin as a child, taking a stand on something she considered righteous. Asgara's expression and manner were so like her mother's that Andromache felt her eyes misting. *It will be such a comfort to have her growing up at Palace Saxe,* she thought.

Andromache's handmaiden now returned with a few more caregivers. They gently but very firmly separated the two girls and carried Asgara away toward the portal and Iantha back into the nursery. Iantha began to scream, "Asgara! I want Asgara!"

Asgara sobbed inconsolably.

IT WAS THREE days before the comm silence on the *Hydromeda* was lifted, and Megara immediately opened a comm channel to the nursery. She was quickly put through to the playroom that Iantha shared with fifteen other girls. The caregiver took Iantha to a booth so she could have private time with her mother.

"Where are you, Mommy?" Iantha asked. "We waited and waited for you and you never came."

"I am sorry, baby," said Megara, trying to sound cheerful. "I had to go away on important work. You know Mommy works for the military. Sometimes we have to work far away."

"When will you come back?"

"I don't know, sweetheart. But I will talk to you as long as I can, as often as I can. I miss you too." She blew her daughter a kiss.

"They took Asgara away," said Iantha, tears welling up in her eyes. "I keep asking for her, but they say she can't come. Why, Mommy? Did I do something wrong?"

"You did nothing wrong!" said Megara, trying to keep the worry out of her voice and face. "I'll find out what happened, my sweets. Let Mommy talk to the caregiver now."

The caregiver took Iantha back to the playroom and then returned. She told Megara that Asgara was living at Palace Saxe. When she was dropped off at the nursery, Princess Andromache had left strict instructions for her to be kept away from Iantha to help her "adjust to her new life."

Megara thanked the caregiver and closed the channel. She tried to open a comm channel to Andromache. It pinged and pinged and then bounced over to her handmaiden, who said that the High Priestess was too busy to take comm channels.

Growing desperate, Megara opened a comm channel to the Temple Heights Nursery's head caregiver and asked to speak to Asgara. When she identified herself, she was told that Princess Andromache had left instructions that all outside communications for Lady Asgara be routed through the High Priestess's staff.

"I am Lady Asgara's legal mother," said Megara, finally growing angry. "If you will not allow me to speak with my daughter, I will get a court order to force you to do so. And I will contact the Live Sites. I am sure they would love to interview you about how you are keeping a military officer on active duty from communicating with her daughter."

The head caregiver decided she did not want to become involved in this tug-of-war. She patched through the channel to Asgara's playroom and a few minutes later, Megara had her hologram in front of her.

Asgara was so delighted to see her that happiness simply radiated from her.

"I knew you would call," she said joyfully. "I knew you would not forget us."

Megara knew she had to prepare Asgara for the worst and that meant telling her the truth.

"Asgara, I am away on duty. I don't know how long I will be away. But I want you to know that I love you and Iantha more than anything in the world. Nothing will stop me returning to you. *Nothing!*"

"I know that, Mother," said Asgara.

"And now I must tell you the truth, my sweets. I know they will tell you, so I want to tell you first. I am your legal mother, but I am not your real mother. Your real mother is Princess Caitlin d'Orr. She is my best friend; she lives in my heart, and we grew up like womb sisters. I promised her I would be your mother, and I have tried my best. I love you as much as my own daughter, Iantha. You are both equally dear to me. Your mother told me to keep her identity from you till you were older. But now it cannot wait. I am sorry I lied to you."

"I know that," said Asgara, sticking her chin out determinedly. "But I don't care. I have no mother but you. I am a Paurina, not a d'Orr."

"What do you mean?" asked Megara in surprise. "Who told you?"

"The older girls tease me about her," said Asgara, a line of anger showing on her forehead. "They say she sinned, that she was punished, and that she is a wicked woman. I told them that I don't care how evil she is, because she abandoned me, so she is not my mother. I hate her! *You* are my mother, not her! And you are fine example—the queen said so!"

"Your mother is not a sinner, my child," said Megara, growing tearful in spite of her resolution to be cheerful. "She has suffered a terrible injustice. She is a heroine, the best of the Sisterhood. You must not hate her, for she loves you more than anything in the world."

"Then why did she abandon me?"

Megara racked her brains for a way to put it that would make sense to Asgara. But she could not think of anything.

"Don't blame your mother, my darling," she said finally. "One day you will understand."

❦

IT WAS A gray and blustery day in Firsk with a steady drizzle and even a trace of sleet. By mid-morning the winds were up to gale force. Horus Matalus had spent several mind numbing hours deep in the vaults beneath the Gray Fort with his Treasurer, going over the fiefdom's accounts. He ascended the steps and emerged to ground level and was immediately approached by his head steward, who bowed before addressing him.

"My lord cheval," he said with a note of urgency. "The Zon have arrived for the tribute. They are in the audience chamber."

"Already! They are not due till next week!"

"Indeed, my lord. But I dared not question them." He dropped his voice to a whisper. "They are led by Lady Death."

He was bewildered by his master's reaction, for Horus smiled with genuine pleasure. He hitched up his sword belt and hastened to a long mirror in an adjoining anteroom. He ran his fingers through his hair and posed sideways, drawing his stomach in.

"Lead me to the audience chamber," he said. "Announce me with due ceremony."

"Shall I summon a troop of the Blues and Spades Regiment, my lord? Lady Death is escorted by a squad of her huntresses."

"No, no. Announce me and then have luncheon laid out in the Morning Room. I shall meet with them alone."

"Very well, my lord," said his head steward, poker-faced.

Horus allowed his head steward to precede him through the private entrance into the large audience chamber of the Gray Fort and waited in the vestibule.

"His Lordship, Master of the Barony of Firsk, Defender of the Northern Frontier, Cheval Horus Matalus!" he heard his head steward announce in ringing tones.

Horus entered with a measured step and ascended the dais to the receiving chair. He took his seat before raising his eyes to his visitors. Diana and a squad of Guardians were seated on the benches in the audience chamber. They wore combat uniforms and carried their full complement of weapons. Diana stood up and for the first time in their long association, gave him the formal Zon half-bow. Horus's mouth dropped open with surprise, for this salutation was traditionally reserved for native royalty and far above his station. Her Guardians followed their commander without hesitation, but one or two of them looked as astonished as Horus. Unsure of how to respond, he stood up and bowed deeply. He straightened to see Diana looking at him with amusement.

"Lady Death, I did not think that our trifling tribute was worth the time of a senior officer like you."

"All tributes are valuable," she replied.

"I have just assembled the tribute payment in the Treasury," said Horus after a brief pause. "We have not had a great year, but we will meet our obligations to the Sisterhood. I am delaying payment to my troops and postponing some repairs to the fort in order to do so."

"I am sorry to hear that, Horus." Diana hooked her thumbs in her weapons belt in her characteristic manner. "It will not serve our interests to have an ally weakened, especially one that holds a strategic position like you." She paused and glanced at her squad seignora, Bedrit Svensina before going on. "How much do you need to pay your men and make your repairs?"

"About half the tribute payment, Lady Death."

"Then pay us half today. You can pay the remainder in small installments over the year."

"I am deeply grateful, Lady Death," said Horus, bowing again.

Horus's head steward re-entered and cleared his throat.

"Luncheon is served, my lord."

Horus looked at Diana for a moment before responding.

"Lady Death, I beg of you to accompany me. There are some matters I would like to discuss with you."

"Very well," said Diana. She turned to her squad seignora. "Seignora Bedrit, please return to the 'boat. The squad and you can lunch on board while you await my return."

The squad stood and saluted, hands on hearts. But Bedrit stood her ground.

"Cornelle Diana, it is most irregular for us to leave you alone in a barbarian establishment."

"I appreciate your concern, Seignora Bedrit. However, in my assessment the risk is very low."

Bedrit saw the determined look on Diana's face, and said no more. She saluted and led her squad out of the audience chamber.

"Allow me to lead you," said Horus. "I do not believe you have seen the Morning Room on your previous visits to the Gray Fort. It has a pretty view."

Diana nodded and followed him. The Morning Room was on the highest level of the fort, well above the surrounding walls and battlements. It had an eastern aspect and its wide windows commanded a glorious view of the River Thal that snaked around the fort, serving as its moat on three sides. The front ranges of the Fire Mountains rose steeply on the far side of the river with fir-covered slopes and snow-capped peaks.

"You did not exaggerate, Horus. This is indeed a gorgeous view, even on a miserable, gray day like this. I can only imagine how beautiful it must be on a sunny summer day."

"I played in this room as a boy. I have known it all my life, and I still find it spectacular."

He advanced on the sizable sideboard, where a sumptuous lunch was laid out. His head steward stood with two servers, anxiously awaiting him. Horus pointed to particular local delicacies and the servers made up a plate for Diana. The head steward poured out two crystal flutes of crabapple wine, a well-known Firsk specialty. Horus oversaw his staff as they handed the plate and flute to Diana before dismissing them with a curt wave.

Once they were alone, he raised his flute to her.

"Lady Death, I welcome you most warmly to my home. You do me great honor. And I thank you again for your kindness with regard to the tribute payment. You cannot imagine how much it will help me."

"Think nothing of it, Horus," she said. "Besides, it will give me an excuse to come back to the Gray Fort to enjoy this view on a sunny day."

A smile lit up her face as she spoke. Her behavior toward him was markedly different than in the past, friendly rather than enigmatic.

He stared at her transfixed, thinking, *She is the most beautiful woman who has ever lived.*

She raised her flute.

"To the Defender of the Northern Frontier," she said.

Horus searched her face for mockery but found none, so he raised his own and responded, "To the Shieldmaiden of the Sisterhood."

They clinked and the crystal gave off a musical ring. The wine was the very best vintage and Diana swirled it her mouth appreciatively. They sat together at a long table with a view of the river and the snowy mountains and enjoyed the repast. As was her wont, Diana ate sparingly and delicately. Horus began as usual by piling his plate, took a few large forkfuls of food, and swallowed with minimal chewing. He burped and looked up with embarrassment, but the look on her face was kind.

"I am pleased that you are now the Master of Firsk, Horus," she said.

"All this is the outcome of the peace accords that ended the Great Insurrection. I fondly recall all the time we spent together during those negotiations, Lady Death."

"Yes, those were good times." She smiled. When she continued, her voice took on a husky note. "You can always make me laugh, Horus." *Our times together were happier than I knew at the time,* she thought. *I have missed teasing him.*

He pushed his plate away leaving the rest of his food uneaten. He was nonplussed by her warmth and racked his brains for something she would find interesting or witty. But nothing occurred to him and he cracked his knuckles to fill the silence.

"Lady Death," he said, finally. "I know that you must despise me, for you have witnessed many of my displays of cowardice. But I have asked you here to tell you that I have been inspired by your example;

by your calmness and bravery in battle. I have tried to better myself by emulating you."

He paused again but her expression remained kind, so he was emboldened to go on.

"Over the last few years, I have led our Blues and Spades on several expeditions into The Trongo to root out the outlaws that prey on our law-abiding people—and cut deeply into our tax revenues. I think I carried myself with honor, leading from the front. I do not want to boast, but the men now compete to serve in my personal guard. In the old days they had to be forced to do so." He pulled up one of his sleeves, revealing a long scar. "I killed the villain who gave me this. He was a huge brute. I wish you could have seen me."

"So do I," said Diana. She sipped her wine and looked out at the driving sleet. "I am sure your wife and son are proud of your accomplishments. I trust they are in good health?"

Horus tossed back the rest of his wine and refilled his flute.

"Talia spends most of her time in Karsk. She claims she is tending to her sick mother. She keeps our son, Wytor, with her."

"You must miss them."

"Lady Death, I do miss my son. But I can bear my wife's absence very well, for my marriage is not a happy one."

"I am sorry to hear that, Horus. Your marriage contract was an alliance of your house with the House of Hilson. It is a shame that the two of you have not developed a working relationship."

"Talia is forever prating about the superiority of the Hilsons and the greatness of her father. She poisons our son against me. When she is here, she misses no opportunity to belittle me in front of our guests, and even my own staff. To tell you the truth I am well pleased that she stays in Karsk, surrounded by her Hilson relatives."

"There *are* a lot of them," said Diana, laughing. "Even more than your wenches."

Horus joined in her laughter, but he soon grew serious again.

"Lady Death, it is true that I have enjoyed the favors of a few women—"

"From what I have heard, there were more than a few," said Diana, interrupting.

"I will not defend myself on that score. But since the time we spent together as platonic friends, I have become a new man. I have been celibate since the end of the Great Insurrection."

"Come now, Horus, it has been years since then! Even if you have stopped sleeping with serving wenches, your wife is an attractive woman. Is she unwilling to do her conjugal duty?"

"Talia does not refuse me outright, but she shrinks from my touch. I don't want to simply rut with a woman who makes it clear that she finds me repugnant."

They sat in silence for a moment. Then Diana changed the subject and pressed him for details about his battles with the outlaws in The Trongo. It was a subject that he was happy to discuss and he was soon explaining the dispositions and tactics of the various engagements, using spoons, forks, saltshakers, and pepper mills. She listened with great interest, asking occasional questions, and teasing him when he grew boastful. He relished her attention, and she found herself laughing with him rather than at him.

An hour passed before Diana leaned forward and brushed the top of his hand with her fingers.

"I enjoy spending time with you, Horus," she said.

"Lady Death, please consider—"

"But I must go now."

She rose and left him without a backward glance.

FIVE

BETRAYALS, IMAGINED AND REAL

BRADAR LED A very dispirited party across the viaduct and over the drawbridge into Nordberg Castle. His older daughter, a girl of eight, rode beside him as they entered the castle, while the younger one rode in a wagon behind them. He had been allowed a very small troop of outriders. Even this small number was depleted by the scouts he had sent ahead to warn his father.

Baron Tadar Loksus, Lothar's castellan, was waiting for them in the bailey, and he bowed low as Bradar and his older daughter dismounted. Bradar was gratified to see that his warning had been taken seriously, so the castle was on a war footing. Even as he dismounted, wagons loaded with grain continued to rumble in, stocking the castle for a long siege.

"You father and your bother await you in the Throne Room, my lord Bradar," said Baron Loksus. "I will escort you there. The queen has asked that your daughters be sent to her suite—one of her ladies awaits your pleasure."

"Yes, yes, please have my girls taken to see my mother," said Bradar with a distracted air. "And lead me to my father. I must see him without delay."

Lothar sat on the Masthead Throne and Pinnar stood at his right hand. Both of them looked relieved to see Bradar. Pinnar advanced on him, hugged him and conducted him to their father. Both sons kneeled.

"Rise, my sons," said Lothar. His tone was gruff, but he was gratified by their formal show of respect and it showed on his face.

They rose, found seats, and looked up at him, perched above them on the throne.

"I was more than happy to yield the frozen wastes of Swarborg to get you and your daughters back," said Lothar. "I am pleased to see you alive and unhurt. I trust you can say the same of your children?"

"Yes, Father," said Bradar. "But I wish you would have bargained harder to get Esgrin back as well! I would give anything to have her by my side. And the children are disconsolate without their mother."

"We tried negotiating for her, son," said Lothar heavily. "I offered gold and even some strategic islands in the Peril Sea. But his negotiators were very clear. 'Our King has taken Baroness Esgrin off the bargaining table,' they said. 'We can accept no offer for her freedom.' The One God knows what he wants with her."

A fearful look appeared and grew in Bradar's eyes. Both Lothar and Pinnar saw it, and became uneasy for they knew Bradar was not one to be easily frightened.

"Shobar is being guided by a specter," Bradar said. "The specter gave him the keys to Estrans Castle. And it was the specter that wants Esgrin. Only the One God knows its evil intentions! You must give me an army to march on Swarborg! I must rescue my poor wife from the clutches of this evil being."

"A specter!" said Lothar. He thumped the arm of the throne impatiently. "Tell me—were you in your senses when you saw it?"

Bradar licked his lips nervously.

"Shobar struck me on the head with the flat of his sword," he said. "But I had recovered my wits. I am sure I saw it rising out of a fire."

Lothar shook his head and Pinnar followed suit.

"A blow to the head will do strange things to a man's perceptions," he said. "Your scouts have already told us that Greghar and the Yengar girl Nitya disappeared shortly before the attack. It is far more likely that Greghar has turned traitor. Bribed by Shobar or bewitched by the Yengar girl, it does not matter."

"Are Greghar and Nitya in Nordberg Castle?" asked Bradar, incredulous. "Why are they not here? Surely they can help us with our plans to retake Estrans."

Pinnar put his arm around his brother's shoulders.

"Our father thinks it very strange that they were the only two to escape the battle," he said. "My wife Guttrin has reinforced his doubts. Both Greghar and the Yengar girl have been imprisoned in the Overhang Galleries."

Lothar stood up and stepped down from the throne.

"The time has come to give Greghar and the Yengar girl some stronger incentives to talk. I do not relish torture, but I have quite lost my patience with them."

"Father!" cried Bradar. "Surely you cannot be serious! Shobar slaughtered Greghar's half brothers and sisters. He has no cause to love him. He put his life on the line as your champion during the Great Insurrection. And if he's a traitor, why would he come back to Nordberg Castle?"

"Estrans Castle is impregnable from the seaward side," said Lothar grimly. "Only treachery could have allowed Shobar to take it. Greghar's disappearance with the Yengar girl just before the attack confirms his guilt. As for allying himself with Shobar—why, every man has his price."

"Father, think of all the time we spent with Greghar growing up," said Bradar in despair. "You taught him to sail, you were his first sword master—you were his idol. In Estrans he looked me in the eye, man to man and there was no deceit in his look. I cannot believe he has turned traitor."

"It is no use, brother," said Pinnar, putting his hand on Brader's arm. "Our father's mind is made up. We must accept his judgment, for he is our king as well as our father."

Lothar led the way as they mounted the steps on to higher and higher levels of Nordberg Castle. Finally they reached the iron doors leading to the Overhang Galleries. Over a dozen men-at-arms stood guard outside the doors. They pounded their pikes on the floor as the king entered with his sons. Their captain bowed deeply saying, "Command us, Sire."

"Rise, rise," said Lothar irritably. "Lead us to the prisoners."

The captain rose, and signaled his men. Two of them unbolted the iron doors and the captain led the way with his men, entering the Galleries ahead of their eminent visitors. Greghar was at the far wall, his arms chained above his head. He looked up as they approached.

"I am glad to see you safe, Bradar," he said, relief obvious in his voice. "I am sorry there was no time to warn you. I give you my word that I had no inkling of the danger till it was too late."

"Yet there was time for you to make a very convenient escape," said Lothar.

"Sire, I know you do not trust the word of a baseborn one such as me," said Greghar. "But I nonetheless renew my pledge of fealty to you. My life and sword are yours to do with as you please."

"Father—" began Bradar.

Lothar silenced his younger son with a gesture.

"Your birth has nothing to do with my mistrust," he said. "Your actions speak louder than any words."

He crooked his finger and the captain rapidly approached.

"Where is the Yengar maiden?" he asked.

"Sire, the queen came and took her from here," said the captain nervously. "I tried to reason with her, to tell her that the maiden was here by your order, but she commanded me to release the girl to her custody."

"You were right to obey," said Lothar, exasperated. "I am not so unfair as to place you between king and queen. But send a man-at-arms to bring her back here. He is to tell Her Majesty that it is my express command."

"Yes, Sire," said the captain, gesturing to one of his men, who turned and left at the double.

They did not have long to wait for the man-at-arms to return. Lovelyn of Loftrans, Queen of Utrea, swept in behind him. Nitya was beside her, dressed in a long fashionable gown, her hair piled on her head in a fine coiffure adorned with diamond studs. She wore teardrop diamond earrings and a gold necklace that had the Royal Nibellus coat of arms worked into its centerpiece. Two ladies-in-waiting attended them.

"Sire, we have come at your command," Lovelyn said with a flourishing bow. Nitya and the queen's ladies emulated their mistress, the entire movement executed with fine choreography.

"Madam, I am surprised to see your jewelry on this menial servant, this...this...beggar," said Lothar, controlling his rage with an effort. "And I am displeased to see her changed into this finery, out of the modest attire in which she arrived. Her treachery has cost the lives of hundreds of our loyal liegemen and soldiers."

Nitya made to speak, but Lovelyn put her hand on her shoulder, and she closed her mouth.

"Sire, I have nurtured this girl and brought her into womanhood. She is as much my daughter as Pinnar and Bradar are my sons. I know her, and I will stake my own life on her loyalty to us. And Greghar!" She went up to the far wall and put her hand on the side of his head, her fingers in his ash-blond ringlets. "How can you doubt him, Sire? Do you not recall your own hand in bringing him up?"

"Madam," said Lothar, still trying very hard to keep his tone civil. "I love you deeply and respect your opinions. However, I remind you that your judgment in these matters has sometimes left something to be desired. Your good heart is one of your most adorable characteristics—but it sometimes misleads you. You have taken this orphan Yengar girl to your bosom, but I am afraid that she has turned out to be a grasping snake and has bitten you. She takes whatever she can from you, but hates your very existence."

Nitya threw herself on her knees, unmindful of her fine gown.

"Sire!" she cried. "Please do not speak so! I have no use for these material things!" She crawled forward on her hands and knees. She took off the necklace and the earrings and then the diamond studs from her hair, one by one. She laid all the jewelry at his feet. Freed from the studs, her elaborate coiffure unraveled and her shiny hair cascaded down around her shoulders. She looked up at him and saw his set and unconvinced look.

"I could not love the queen more if she were my own mother," Nitya went on, her voice breaking. "I cannot bear you to say these things." She sat back on her heels and tore the gown down from her shoulders. She knew this would only stoke Lothar's anger, but she was too distressed to care. The dark scar of the Thermadan triangle branded into her shoulder stood out in sharp relief. "I have one unmarked shoulder, Sire. It is yours to torment. I can bear hot iron, but not the lacerations of your words."

The veins stood out in Lothar's neck, and his face went red. He ignored her and beckoned one of his wife's ladies.

"Gather the jewelry," he said briefly. As she hurried forward, he addressed his wife. "Madam, one of my men-at-arms will escort you and your ladies back to your apartments. I will take your wishes into account as I make my decisions. I know that you have my well-being and the welfare of the kingdom at heart—and for that, I thank you."

Lovelyn looked down at Nitya, anguish in her eyes.

"Ma'am, my own mother could not have done more for me," said Nitya quietly. "You must obey the king now."

Lovelyn left slowly and reluctantly, looking over her shoulder at the door. When she was gone, Lothar turned to Greghar again.

"Well, nephew, I ask you again. I want to hear every detail of how Shobar managed what no human could do. For I am certain he will soon turn his attention to Nordberg."

"Sire, I have told you everything I know and I will tell you again. Nitya grew disquieted and led me to the battlements just as Shobar's Skull Watchmen came over the walls. The sentries were in some sort of trance and could not raise the alarm. We concealed ourselves and made our escape, for it was too late to rouse the castle."

"Entrancements, specters, twaddle!" exploded Lothar. "Can no one give me a straight answer? I have asked you kindly and you have refused to answer me. The time for kindness is gone. Captain! Suspend him."

The captain now came forward with several of his men-at-arms. They unlocked Greghar's chains from the wall and led him to stand on one of the trapdoors. They reattached his manacles to a chain that was linked to a hinged ring set in the ceiling. Bradar and Pinnar both looked as though they wanted to speak, but were hushed by their father's evident rage. Greghar looked impassive, resigned to his fate.

The men-at-arms waited for their captain's command and when he made an unlocking motion with his hands, they drew back the trapdoor bolts. The trapdoor fell open and Greghar dropped a meter before the chain jerked taut. He hung there with the cold waters of the Lofgren far below him. Gusts of wind came in through the open trapdoor. Lothar raised his voice to be heard.

"Tell me how Shobar was able to take Estrans Castle!"

Suspended at this great height, Greghar's eyes bugged out of his head with fear. His whole body was rigid with panic.

"I...I...I..." he tried to speak, but his terror made his tongue heavy.

"I am waiting," said Lothar harshly.

"I...don't...know," Greghar managed to bring out.

Lothar looked at his captain dourly and nodded. The captain in turn jerked his thumb at his men-at-arms. Two of them put a pike in one of the links of the chain and moved it back and forth. Greghar began to swing from side to side in ever growing arcs. His rigid control gave way, and he began to throw up, spewing into the air and all over himself. Lothar let his men-at-arms swing him and watched him retch for a considerable time before snapping his fingers. They used their pikes to steady Greghar so that he was suspended immobile again.

"Please kill me, Sire!" cried Greghar. His face was streaked with traces of his retching. "My life is yours to take. But do not torture me thus!"

"Tell me what I want to know," said Lothar relentlessly.

"I have told you all I know," said Greghar wildly. "Now I only pray for death."

Lothar waited a long moment. Greghar expected no mercy and looked at Pinnar and Bradar, sending them a silent look of farewell. Finally he looked to bid goodbye to Nitya. She was staring at him, but her look was not sorrowful or frightened. She had her feral look again, her cat's eyes glowing brightly. She had a very faint bluish halo, but everyone's eyes were on Greghar, so no one else noticed her.

"Drop him," said Lothar through his teeth.

"Don't!" screamed Greghar. It seemed like he was begging for mercy, but Nitya knew he was screaming at her to spare his uncle.

The men-at-arms reached up with their pikes and undid the hinge on the ring set in the ceiling. Freed from its anchor, the chain rattled out and Greghar began to fall. After the terror of the suspension and swinging, it was almost a relief to know that death was coming and he relaxed. Unseen by anyone, Nitya made a small movement with her right hand. The falling chain whipped back and miraculously, one of its links caught on the bolt knob of the open trapdoor. Greghar found himself jerked to a stop and suspended again, but much less securely. He hung there, swaying gently in the breeze. He heard Nitya's calming voice in his head and with her words, his terror drained out of him.

"Climb up the chain," her voice said. "Breathe deeply. Don't worry. I won't let you fall."

He obeyed. Once calm, his great strength made the climb a fairly easy one. He reached the trapdoor and then used its reinforcing slats to climb up to the edge of the chasm in the floor. He pulled himself up and lay on the floor of the Overhang Galleries, panting. He did not look up, for he expected them to stab him with their pikes and drive him over the edge again.

His uncle's voice seemed to come from far away.

"Return them to the state in which they arrived," he said mechanically. Now Greghar looked up in surprise. Lothar had a strange look in his eyes, as though he was in a daze.

"Take the Yengar wench with you and leave Utrea," he said, mechanically.

⊰⊱

GREGHAR STOOD BY the fore starboard rail of the caravel *Darling Thoma*, secure on his sea legs. Nitya stood beside him, her hair streaming behind her in the fresh breeze. She held on the rail with both hands, looking down at the foaming bow wave, a look of happiness on her face. Every now and then a droplet of spray struck her face and her smile stretched wider.

"I can see why you love the sea, Greghar," she said. "I could sail like this forever."

They had bought a passage on a merchantman bound for Tirut and were now a couple of weeks out of Nordberg. The captain, a taciturn Brigon called Martius, had not been keen on taking passengers. But when Greghar offered him a gold talent in advance, with another promised on their safe arrival, he grew much more accommodating. They were now ensconced in Martius's own cabin at the stern. The cook was a one-eyed, ebony-skinned giant of a man that everyone called Tar, and Nitya charmed him into letting her help him. By the second day, she was effectively the cook, with him working as her assistant. The dramatic improvements in their meals so cheered the crew that she soon had them all literally eating out of her hand.

They took her everywhere in the ship, showing off their knowledge to her. Much to Greghar's chagrin, they even took her high up into the rigging and had her perched precariously in the crosstrees, taking delight in her expressions of wonderment. While she was as agile as a monkey, the men were quite careful with her. There were always two or three on hand to steady her in case she slipped or fell.

They began by calling her "my lady", but she checked them saying, "I am no great lady, I am just a simple girl like your daughters or sisters. Please call me Nitya."

However, this they would not do. They compromised by calling her "Miss Nitya," often winking broadly at one another behind her back as they did so.

So now Greghar smiled at her professed love of sailing.

"I have heard the hands talking," he said to her. "They think you are a baroness or at least a chevalina. 'Of course, she is a noblewoman traveling thus to avoid pirates,' they say. 'Her manners and accent are unmistakable.'"

Nitya looked at him sadly.

"Perhaps I can unlearn all that your aunt taught me," she said. "And my father before her. Then I would fit in with people of my class."

Greghar watched a gull dive and snatch a fish from just below the surface before responding.

"And what class is that?" he asked.

"Why, I am a servant, a beggar," she said. "Your uncle said so himself."

"He was angry at the time, I am sure he did not mean it."

"And what of you, Greghar? What do you think?"

Greghar did not speak for a time but concentrated on the jib tell-tales that streamed true.

"You know what I think," he said. He changed the subject. "Martius is a fine seaman. He is squeezing every last bit of speed out of this wind."

Martius was also a cautious seaman. He steered by the coast, rarely venturing out of sight of land. The Fire Mountains were on their starboard bow and Greghar looked at the snow-capped peaks, recognizing the profile of the land.

"Simrania is just behind that peak right there," he said, pointing.

Nitya followed the line of his finger.

"There seem to be thick clouds over them," she said.

"It is not cloud," said Greghar. "It is ash spewing out of the volcanoes."

"Yes!" said Nitya. "I remember Mount Brimstone was constantly discharging smoke and ash."

"There are some here, closer to the sea, that make Mount Brimstone tiny by comparison. This high mountain that you see on the shoreline has been known to erupt and send torrents of lava and ash into the water, causing the sea to boil."

Nitya shivered deliciously.

"What a sight it must be! Have you ever seen it?"

"No," said Greghar. "One of my father's old sea captains grew up around here and told me about it."

AS THEY SAILED steadily south, it became a bit warmer and the seabirds grew more plentiful. However, the winds grew less favorable and they advanced more slowly, tack by tack. Then the weather began to deteriorate: heavy swells gave way to foaming whitecaps.

"Things are going to get worse," said Greghar to Martius.

"Yes, it is going to be bad," said Martius, nodding. "It looks like there is a severe gale brewing."

He summoned his first mate, Nexius.

"Get the topmen up there," he said. "Reef down to bare poles. Break out the storm jib."

"Aye, sir," said Nexius. "I'll see to it immediately."

The winds continued to rise by the hour and the wave troughs grew deeper. Even with the tiny spread of storm sail she now carried, the *Darling Thoma* was driven into the rising seas. They lost their view of land and all they could see around them were the immense waves with their foaming heads. All hands worked hard to secure the ship: battening down the hatches, checking the sheets and strapping down moveable items, especially the heavier ones. The howling winds made verbal commands virtually impossible, so every man was guided by crude hand signals, the observations of the seas and the actions of his mates.

Nitya insisted on staying on deck as well, getting soaked to the skin. Greghar tried to get her to go below, but she demurred, saying, "If we sink, I would rather know firsthand." He relented but insisted on lashing her to a stanchion by the mainmast to keep her from being washed overboard. As they plowed through the moving mountains of water, colossal waves often broke over their bow and the deck disappeared beneath the frothy water before it drained out of the scuppers as they rose on the next swell. Nitya was sometimes waist-deep in swirling eddies of green seawater. She committed everything in the wild scene to memory.

Then there was a sudden bolt of lightning and an almost instantaneous burst of thunder. Sheets of icy rain followed, accompanied by powerful wind gusts that seemed to change direction from moment to moment.

"It is a squall!" Greghar shouted to Martius. "We must take in the storm jib! It will catch the gusts and drag our bows away from the oncoming seas."

"Can you do it?"

"Yes, but I will need some men to give me a hand."

"Go now! I will send men to join you in the bows."

Greghar made his way forward from the quarterdeck, passing the stanchion where Nitya was lashed on the way. Tar stood by her, working with the deck crew, and put his knuckle to his forehead in salute as Greghar passed. No sooner did Greghar reach the bows than Nexius appeared with a seaman by his side.

"I will need your help on the jib sheet," said Greghar without waiting for Nexius to speak. "Once we release it, it will take all our strength to fight the wind gusts and bring the storm sail back on to deck."

Nexius and the seaman nodded. Greghar released the anchoring knot, but the storm sail stayed stubbornly taut.

"The sheet is tangled in a jib boom pulley!" Nexius cried, pointing.

Before Greghar could respond, Nexius leaped on to the bowsprit and made his way out on to the jib boom to free the sheet. As he did so, the bows began to rise on an upswell. As the bows continued to climb, everyone on the *Darling Thoma* looked forward and realized that the wave before them was a monster, rising so high that it seemed to blot out the sky. Greghar and the seaman grabbed the rails to avoid sliding down the deck. Nexius threw himself down and wrapped his arms around the pole of the jib boom.

After what seemed an age, the ship crested the foam-streaked wall of water and teetered atop it for a moment before beginning her plunge into the incredibly deep trough. The wind carried away the voices of all those who screamed. The *Darling Thoma* hit the bottom of the trough with an immense groaning of tortured timber and then buried her bowsprit in the shoulder of the following wave. There was a cracking sound that was loud enough to be heard above the din of the storm and when they rose again, it became clear that the jib boom had broken. It canted down at a crazy angle, dragging the storm jib into the water.

Every seaman aboard knew that the sagging sail in the water would soon lay the *Darling Thoma* on her beam-ends, making it impossible for her to survive in these seas. Martius came to the bows with a hand axe and raised it above the bowsprit, his intent clear.

"Wait!" said Greghar. "I think I see Nexius. He is still on the jib boom. We cannot cut him loose."

"There is no choice," said Martius. "It is him or the ship."

"Give me a chance to get Nexius and cut the jib boom loose. Get me two bowlines."

Martius passed the word and in less than a minute another seaman appeared with two long bowlines, each a lifeline with an adjustable loop at the end. Greghar fastened one around his chest.

Martius cupped his hands over his mouth to be heard over the storm.

"Nexius's life is in your hands, Greghar," he said.

"And my life is in yours," replied Greghar, handing him the ends of the two bowlines. "Pull Nexius back aboard as soon as I get the loop around him. I'll raise my arm to give you the signal."

"When do you want us to pull you back?"

"Not till I finish chopping off the jib boom."

"It may drag you under."

"Perhaps," said Greghar. "Then you must hack off the whole bow-sprit and send me to my maker."

He turned and dived into the churning maelstrom. Greghar was a powerful swimmer, but it still took everything he had to make the twenty meters to where the splintered jib boom trawled in the waves. He grabbed a trailing jib stay and rapidly pulled himself to where Nexius hung on at the very tip. The first mate was half drowned and frozen. Ironically, the cold stiffened his grip on the jib boom and kept him from being washed away.

Greghar fastened the loop around his torso, pried his fingers loose from the wood and raised his arm, giving the seamen on the bows the signal. They rapidly pulled Nexius back toward the ship and hauled him aboard, barely conscious, but alive.

Greghar did not wait to see the result of his action. He drew Martius's hand axe from his belt and chopped off the restraining stays before beginning to hack on the splintered wood. It was slow going, for he could only get in two or three strokes before being submerged in each trough. The crew watched from the listing deck, each one praying for him to succeed.

With a final heavy stroke, the end of the jib boom suddenly parted and Greghar fell with it into the churning sea. As he disappeared from view, the seamen in the bows immediately began hauling on the bowline he had lashed around his chest. They pulled mightily, but they could not bring it in. Greghar felt himself being borne away with the broken end of the jib boom and realized that he had become enmeshed in one of the trailing stays. Consigning the hand axe to the deep, he frantically ran his hands over his body, searching for what restrained him.

Nitya screamed as Greghar disappeared below the surface and clutched at Tar's powerful arm saying, "Save him, Tar, don't let him die!"

The black giant needed no urging. He quickly joined the seamen by the bow rail and added his enormous strength to the tugging team. Submerged in the green water, Greghar felt the cord squeezing him as they pulled. As the blackness closed in, he finally located a stay hooked around his ankle. He desperately drew his dagger and managed to get the sharp blade on it. He felt the steel bite as he lost consciousness.

His last, despairing effort parted the stay. As Greghar floated free, the crew hauling the line got traction. Within minutes, they had him back by the ship's side and Tar hauled him aboard. The cook got on his knees and put his mouth to Greghar's mouth. He alternated blowing hard with pumping Greghar's chest. Finally Greghar coughed and retched, bringing up water. Martius and the hands in the bows heaved a sigh of relief.

"Get back to work," Martius barked at Tar and the hands. "The ship will not sail itself."

The squall passed, but the storm lasted all day and most of the night. By the time it blew itself out and they sailed into a wan sunrise, the crew were exhausted. Except for a brief respite after his effort, Greghar had been up with Martius the whole time and could barely stand. Nitya had taken a short nap as the storm began to abate and now helped Tar light the galley fires. As they worked, she thanked Tar for saving Greghar.

"I did nothing, Miss Nitya," he replied. "Greghar is the brother of Varu, Lord Moksha's incarnation at sea. The waters cannot kill him."

She looked at him sharply and he smiled.

"We Yengars must watch out for one another," he whispered, winking his one good eye.

The hot breakfast that Nitya put together had the crew queuing up for seconds and thirds. As she served them, she praised them warmly for their efforts in the storm and they basked in her smiles.

Greghar waited for Nitya to finish serving the crew and the officers so he could take his breakfast with her in the stern cabin. He ate as ravenously as the hands and did not speak till he had cleared a heaping plate.

"This is a very good," he said, wiping his lips with a serviette. "The hands were raving about it, and they were right."

"They are happy with the food," she agreed. "But they are moved by how you risked your life to save Nexius."

Just as they finished their breakfast, Martius knocked and entered.

"We will be putting into Goset," he said. "We've got a jury-rigged bowsprit in place, but I'd like to get permanent repairs done in case we run into more foul weather."

"I thought as much," said Greghar, nodding. "How long will we be in port?"

"Hard to say," said Martius, scratching his beard. "It could take a few days, it could take a fortnight. It depends on the repair facilities they have there and how willing the shipwrights are."

GOSET WAS A small fishing harbor with only a couple of wharves. It took Martius some talking to get a berth in order to bring shipwrights on board and begin repairs. The harbor was sheltered from the open sea by a spit of land that rose to a substantial height. Goset Castle stood on its tip, with sheer cliff faces on three sides and land that dropped away steeply in front of its only major gate.

The *Darling Thoma* had scarcely been in port for a day, when a quartet of men appeared at the gangplank asking for the ship's passengers. Greghar came on deck and leaned over the rail. He recognized the livery they wore as that of the local lord. The leader of the group stepped forward and said, "I am Head Steward to Sous Cheval Hughen va Goset. I wish to speak with the passengers on this vessel, an Utrean lord and lady."

"My ward and I are passengers on this vessel," said Greghar cautiously. "And we are Utrean."

Nitya appeared at Greghar's elbow and added, "We serve King Lothar of Utrea."

The Head Steward looked relieved.

"My master requests the pleasure of your company at a small reception. Would it be convenient for you to be ready by six this evening?"

"We should be delighted to wait on the sous cheval," she said before Greghar could respond. "It is almost three hours till six—that will be ample time for us to get ready."

"A carriage will call for you," said the Head Steward, bowing.

Greghar said nothing, but Nitya got the feeling that he was not best pleased. Nonetheless, he got ready, laced on his light armor since he had no formal wear and belted on Karya. The beauty of the ancient sword immediately set him apart from the common run of warriors. Sailors were great hands with needle and thread, and they had worked their magic on Nitya's attire. Soliciting donations from the entire crew, they had collected scraps of fine linens and even some silk. In the short span of time at their disposal, Nitya's traveling shift was lengthened and beautified into a presentable gown.

She could not get anything other than monosyllabic responses from him all the way from the dock to the small castle. The carriage jerked to a halt in the courtyard and the footmen opened the carriage door. As the lady, Nitya emerged first.

Sous Cheval Hughen va Goset stood in the courtyard to receive them with two ladies by his side. His son, his daughter-in-law, and his two young daughters stood a rank behind them. A small crowd of relatives stood behind them in the third rank. Several liveried servants were on hand. Greghar led the way to the receiving party with Nitya on his arm. She was acutely aware of the ladies' condescending looks at her makeshift gown, but she held her head up high.

"I am Greghar Asgar of Utrea," he said, carefully not taking the Nibellus name. He indicated Nitya. "And this is—"

"Your lady, I take it," said va Goset heartily.

"No, no," remonstrated Greghar. "She is my ward."

"We heard from your crew that you are Utrean nobility," said va Goset. "What are your connections? Perhaps we have heard of them."

Nitya now spoke up, her upper-class Brigish accent a contrast to Greghar's Utrish pronunciation.

"We both serve in the court of King Lothar of Utrea. Greghar is nephew to the king."

Va Goset's face broke into a wide smile.

"Nephew to the king! I don't know your Utrean traditions, but in Briga that would make you an archbaron at least!"

"Our traditions in Utrea are different," said Greghar ambiguously.

"I bid you both a most warm welcome," said va Goset. "Now, allow me to introduce my gracious wife, Sous Chevalina Estia."

Sous Chevalina Estia was short and thin, with a pinched face. She nodded to Greghar and Nitya, not nearly as happy to see them as her husband.

"And this is my sister, Chevalina Kitara va Alsor of Tirut," he said, taking the arm of the other lady who had been with him to receive them. Kitara was significantly younger than her brother and sister-in-law and was by far the prettiest of the women assembled there. She had mischievous brown eyes, a pert figure, and pouting lips that were painted bright crimson. Her gown hugged her curves and was cut to display her cleavage, even though she affected Thermadan modesty by wearing a scarf loosely over her dark hair. She gave Greghar and Nitya a quick bob of a curtsey but managed to make it look slightly mocking rather than respectful.

Va Goset now proceeded to introduce his son, daughters, and daughter-in-law, and then his kinsmen. Greghar and Nitya murmured the appropriate phrases to afford each one the recognition they were due.

"Now that we all know one another, let us proceed to our Reception Hall," he concluded. "We have some of our local delicacies laid out. Come, do follow me."

It was the Head Steward who actually led the way into the Reception Hall. The chamber was modest in size and appointments compared to the apartments in Nordberg Castle. However, both Greghar and Nitya made sure to look around with admiration and make several complimentary remarks.

There was a small orchestra seated in a corner and they began to play a gentle melody as the party walked in. The Head Steward supervised a motley staff of assorted maids and other downstairs help that had been pressed into service to attend them. They circulated with trays of the local *Gosetter* wine and small canapés.

"This wine is from our own vineyards," said va Goset, raising a glass. "I toast you both and drink your health."

"We thank you for your most gracious welcome," said Greghar, returning the toast. "And wish you and yours long life and happiness."

As soon as the return toast was drunk, Kitara stepped forward from va Goset's side.

"So, my lord Greghar, we have established that you are Utrean royalty, the nephew of King Lothar," she said playfully. "And you certainly look the part! But what of your 'ward'? Will you not name her for us?"

"She is Nitya, lady-in-waiting to Her Highness, Queen Lovelyn of Utrea," he said, maintaining a decorous tone.

"Oh my, we are greatly honored to welcome such distinguished guests to our little castle," Kitara said, again sounding slightly ironic. "I must steal you away to listen to your tales of the Utrean court."

Both Greghar and Nitya laughed politely. Led by va Goset, they circulated and made small talk with those he presented, mainly his kinsmen and favored local gentry. As the evening wore on, Kitara was as good as her word. She joined the group around them and with consummate skill, eventually managed to get them to herself in a corner, partially screened from the center of the Reception Hall by a pillar and a tall potted plant.

"My dear Lady Nitya," she said after some routine pleasantries. "You must tell me all of your protector's secrets. For he is so handsome that he has quite stolen my heart away."

Kitara now put her hand possessively on Greghar's forearm, a move that Nitya found incredibly forward as well as intensely irritating.

"He is quite serious," she sniffed. "He has no time for frivolous women."

"Oh, Greghar, surely that is not true!" exclaimed Kitara in mock horror. "For I am quite frivolous and if you have no time for me, it will break my heart."

Nitya expected Greghar to frown and brush Kitara off. But to her surprise he smiled warmly.

"I am quite forgiving of frivolity," he said. "Especially in a pretty girl."

"I am not a little girl," said Kitara, laughing coquettishly, with a glance at Nitya. "I am an experienced, married, and well-connected woman. My husband is the younger son of the Baron of Tirut."

"I wonder that we have not met him," said Nitya, hoping to embarrass her.

"Oh, he is far away in Tirut, so I am quite free to pursue my fantasies. In any event, he is not nearly the warrior Greghar is."

Her fingers traced some of the scars on Greghar's arm. In response, he took Kitara's other hand in his and squeezed it. Color rose to Nitya's face, for she had never seen this side of Greghar.

She had seen enough flirting in the Utrean court both as an object and as an observer. So she knew how it could range from exquisitely subtle to utterly crass. Even so, she had never seen a wellborn woman throw herself at a man like this. *Surely Greghar can see that Kitara is behaving like a strumpet,* she thought. *Why is he making such a fool of himself?*

Kitara and Greghar continued to make lighthearted conversation that progressively became laden with suggestion and innuendo. Nitya took no part in the conversation and stood with a set expression, her arms folded over her breast. Finally, when Kitara leaned seductively toward Greghar, causing his arm to brush her bosom, Nitya had had enough. She turned on her heel and was on the point of leaving them, when they were joined by va Goset. Kitara immediately addressed him effusively.

"Brother, you cannot allow our august guests to spend their time in Goset on their uncomfortable ship. You must invite them to stay with us at the castle."

"Of course, my dear sister," said va Goset immediately. "It will be our honor and pleasure."

"We thank you most sincerely," said Nitya, in her most polished Brigish. "But our crew will not hear of it. They are like our family, and we must stay with them."

"Oh, Greghar, will you leave us bereft?" asked Kitara theatrically.

Looking over at Nitya and seeing her thunderous expression, Greghar said quickly, "Of course our crew are dear to us, but we will doubtless spend more time with them when we return to sea." Turning to Kitara, his tone changed to one of overdone gallantry. "So if you will add your invitation to your brother's, we will have no choice but to accept."

"I invite you to stay with us," she said in a breathy tone. "With all my heart."

Greghar turned to va Goset.

"Sir, we are pleased to accept your kind invitation." He gave him a small bow. "I would be grateful if you could send one of your stewards to our ship to fetch our things."

"But—" began Nitya.

"My dear, it is for the best," said Greghar easily. "Think how nice it will be for you to have a firm bed after all those weeks in a hammock."

"I quite liked my hammock," muttered Nitya to herself as va Goset expressed his happiness at their acceptance. As soon as va Goset turned away, Greghar put his hand on the small of Kitara's back, and she gave him an amorous look. Nitya saw their intimate exchange with a stifling mixture of helplessness and fury.

GOSET CASTLE HAD no grand guest apartments, so va Goset had to make some whispered arrangements with his Head Steward during the dinner regarding improvised lodgings. As a result of these, the castellan was moved to share accommodations with the captain of the men-at-arms and his tower apartment was given over to Greghar. Va Goset's older daughter, a demure teenager, was moved in with her sister, and her chamber was given to Nitya.

The dinner was a painful affair for Nitya. Kitara contrived to get herself seated by Greghar, while Nitya was seated with va Goset's daughters near the foot of the table. Greghar and Kitara carried on an animated conversation with each other, being careful to include va Goset and his wife. Nitya could not hear their words, and so she imagined the worst. *What does he see in her?* she thought despairingly. *She is pretty enough and her figure is riper than mine, but she is nothing compared to Princess Caitlin.* She tried to concentrate on making conversation with the girls by her side, but they were too overawed to do much more than nod and smile.

She did not get the chance to talk to Greghar after dinner for the men retired for brandy and she was left with the ladies. She did not encourage Kitara's attempts to start a conversation with her, and after a short interval she was led to the room she was to occupy. On the way, she questioned the maid who accompanied her. To her chagrin, she discovered that Greghar's designated apartment was on the other side of the castle from the room she occupied. Nitya made her point it out to her from the gallery outside her chamber.

Her few possessions had been brought up from the ship and were already in the room, ready for her. She changed into her nightclothes and lay on the bed. She had grown used to the movement of the ship and the stillness of the bed made her dizzy. She meditated on the chant of power, grew steady and soon lost track of time. It seemed like she had barely shut her eyes when she was awake again. She rose and made her way to the window. She was on the landward side of the castle that faced full west, but even here she could see the lightening of predawn.

She did her morning ablutions and dressed. She found a hairbrush on the vanity and spent a good ten minutes working her hair into a high gloss. *The queen always said I have beautiful hair and eyes*, she thought, missing Lovelyn and feeling a sharp pang. She wished she could go to her for comfort and advice.

She had grown used to rising early with Greghar in their cramped cabin on the *Darling Thoma* and then serving him breakfast after he got ready. So as dawn broke, she made her way across the courtyard to see him in the tower apartment on the seaward side of the castle. She heard activity in the kitchen, and there were a few sentries on the battlements, but otherwise the castle was still asleep. She climbed the steep stairs that led up the rectangular tower, glancing out the arrow slit windows at the gray sea. From some angles, Goset harbor was visible and she could see the *Darling Thoma* in the distance, still moored at a wharf.

It was a long climb to the tower apartment, and she paused to catch her breath on the landing at the top. The door was heavy and banded with iron. She pushed it and found it locked. She knocked softly, for she knew Greghar was an extremely light sleeper. There was no response, so she knocked again, and this time she allowed a full minute to pass. When there was still no response, she grew concerned. *Have they done something to him?* she thought worriedly.

She closed her eyes and visualized the bolt on the inner side of the door. She concentrated hard and with her eyes still closed, saw it slowly sliding back. She pushed the door again and now it swung open silently on well-oiled hinges. With only a few very narrow arrow slit windows, the apartment was still in semidarkness in the breaking dawn. As she entered, she was aware of a sense of foreboding. A veil of darkness seemed to seep out of the windows at her approach. But it happened so quickly that she ascribed it to the rising sun, scolding herself for being oversensitive.

Greghar was instantly aware of the opening door and he sat up in bed as Nitya entered. He put a finger to his lips and whispered, "How did you get in here? Go back to your room, I will see you at breakfast."

"Why are you whispering?" she asked in a low tone. She came forward toward him, noting his discomfort and confused by it. "Why did you not open the door when I knocked? And why do you not have your nightshirt on? It was a chill night."

"I think I drank a bit too much last night," he hissed. "I need to rest a bit longer, so please leave me."

She now noticed a large shape under the covers by him. As she stared, it moved, and a dark-haired head emerged, yawning.

"What is the matter, Greghar?" asked Kitara sleepily.

"Nothing," he said hastily. "Go back to sleep. I thought I heard something, but I was mistaken."

He made a quick movement with his hand, making it absolutely clear to Nitya that he wanted her gone. It was quite unnecessary, for her face had fallen, and she was on the point of rushing out of the room of her own accord. But Kitara was awake now and saw her. She sat up, drawing the sheets to cover herself.

"Why, it is little Nitya," she said lazily. "Why do you look so shocked? Surely you have had your share of passionate adventures in the Utrean court?"

"I am pleased to say that I have had no such adventures," said Nitya, as stiff as Kitara was relaxed. She was furious, and it showed plainly on her face.

"My, my, what a jealous hussy you are," said Kitara, her tone light and teasing. "You have had Greghar in your bed, but he is too much of a man for just one woman, surely you see that. You must learn to share him."

"Don't you dare speak to me like that, you...you...you whore!" spat Nitya. "You would not understand the relationship I have with Greghar. Women like you think everything between a man and a woman is sexual."

"And isn't it?" asked Kitara knowingly. "Come now, you ladies-in-waiting are the worst hypocrites. I bet that all the Utrean queen's equerries have enjoyed your favors. That's the way it was when I was at the court of Briga. Why should things be different in Utrea?"

"I think that is quite enough," broke in Greghar. "Nitya, you had best go now. I will see you at breakfast. I can explain everything."

"How could you, Greghar?" Nitya cried, bursting into tears. She turned and rushed from the room, followed by Kitara's gay laughter.

NITYA WANTED TO leave immediately and return to the *Darling Thoma*, but the castle was still secured for the night. So she returned to her room and stewed till she thought the hour civilized enough to take her leave. She went down to the parlor and found va Goset and Estia at breakfast.

"Good morning, sir. Good morning, my lady," she said, addressing them formally. "I thank you for your hospitality. However, I must take your leave and return to my vessel, for I miss my shipmates dearly."

"You cannot leave us!" exclaimed va Goset, his tone cheery. "Has anything not been to your satisfaction? Tell me what's amiss and I will do my best to make you feel at home. Come, take some breakfast with us, and we will discuss the matter."

"I am not hungry, sir—" began Nitya.

"Nonsense," said Estia, in a surprisingly civil voice. "Young girls are always hungry. Sit with me and allow me to serve you some of our honeyed porridge. Everything will seem brighter once you have eaten."

Nitya looked at her in astonishment, for she had not been particularly welcoming the previous day. However, now she looked on Nitya kindly as she sat by her and served her solicitously.

"I saw how Kitara was trying to put you down at the reception last night," she said in a tone low enough that her husband did not hear. "But you must not let her upset you. She is ever so vain. She is used to being the belle of the castle whenever she visits. No doubt she sees an attractive young girl like you as competition."

Nitya looked at Estia gratefully. She did not know how to respond, so she just smiled. Estia patted her hand.

A few moments later, Greghar entered. Va Goset stood to welcome him and brought him to the table. He called on his Head Steward to bring out fresh rolls and hoped that Greghar had rested comfortably. Nitya refused to meet his eye. She ate her porridge as quickly as possible and took her leave with as much politeness as she could muster.

She ascended to the battlements and walked along the crenels, looking out at the seascape. Nitya contemplated the *Darling Thoma* down in Goset harbor and closed her eyes, imagining the morning scene aboard. When she opened them, Greghar was at her elbow, standing silently with an abashed air. Her own expression grew set, and she deliberately looked away to sea, trying to ignore him.

"I am not good with words," he said. "But you must allow me to speak to you."

"What is there to say?" she asked bitterly. "You are a free man and may act as you please. Obviously, you are more comfortable with women of your own class. Your uncle spoke for you when he called me menial and a beggar."

"Nitya, don't speak to me of class," he said, sounding remorseful. "I am a bastard. I have no pedigree. I am in no position to look down on anyone."

"But here you are a royal!" she snapped. "The nephew of King Lothar!"

"You styled me thus," he protested. "I would never have claimed that connection." He tried to put his hand on her arm, but she drew away. "I had no wish to hurt you. Quite the reverse."

"Well, if this is what you can do without trying, then I pray to never face your malice," she retorted. She crossed her arms over her breast and hugged herself tightly. She continued in a low tone, almost muttering to herself, "Anyway, the fault was mine, not yours. It was wrong of me to presume to be your sister. I am a Yengar, the butt of everyone's hatred. I have no right to expect kindness from you."

"You are being unfair, Nitya," he remonstrated. "At least listen to my side."

She leaned back on a crenel and waited for him to speak. The breeze played with her hair and gave it a wind-blown look. The loose "gown" that the hands had created for her could not completely conceal her curves, and her green-hazel eyes were half-closed, emphasizing her striking looks. Everything had become so complicated; how could he explain himself?

"Nitya, you are more than attractive," he began. "To my eye, you are a woman of rare beauty. But—"

"You must do better than that, Greghar," she cut in indifferently. "You forget that I have been flirted with and flattered by many Utrean noblemen. '*You gorgeous thing, come to my bed, be my mistress, and I will cover you with jewels.*' I have heard these words many times before. The more I refused them, the harder they tried. I knew they cared nothing for me—it was just a contest, for the first one to bed me would win such acclaim for his manhood! But in spite of what Kitara said, my virtue is intact. I do not ask you to believe me, for there are many in Nordberg who boast of taking my virginity."

He clenched in fists in frustration.

"Oh, hang what Kitara said!" he exclaimed. "I do not doubt your virtue for an instant." He paused to marshal his thoughts and started again. "When I saw you in the Sea Parlor of Estrans Castle, I could not believe how much you had changed. I treasured my memories of you as a child, someone that I tickled and laughed with and loved as a baby sister. I had a hard time adjusting to your striking new avatar, as I wished for the girl I had cuddled in my cloak in the cave on the Sawtooth Range."

"I tried to be that girl, Greghar," said Nitya. "And to respect what I thought was your love for Princess Caitlin. I was ashamed of my feelings for you because I thought I was betraying her. But I see now that I need not have worried."

"I have told you before, and I will tell you again," he said doggedly. "I do not ask to be placed on a pedestal, for I am no saint. I have had my fair share of women, and I make no apologies. As for Princess Caitlin, to her I am just a low barbarian, far beneath her—she told me so herself. If ever there was warmth between us, it has long cooled. We are nothing to each other now."

They stood together for a while in uncomfortable silence.

"Try to see it from my perspective, Nitya," said Greghar finally. "The girl I knew was a powerless waif who needed my protection. When you first used your power at the Ice Bridge, it nearly killed you. Now you burn men alive without a second thought and effortlessly use telekinesis. You fluently project yourself into others' minds, bending them to your will. You say you are not a witch, but I am damned if I can see the difference."

He paused for breath before continuing.

"Of course I wish to return to the closeness we shared, Nitya. But I am also afraid of the woman you have become. You are so powerful now that I am just a tool in your hands."

Nitya looked at him steadily without speaking. He felt the hairs on the nape of his neck rise. When she spoke, her voice was flat.

"Whereas Kitara makes you feel strong and manly, doesn't she? Will she give up her husband's wealth and title to share your exile?"

"I do not ask that of her," said Greghar. "But she has offered to take us to Tirut in her carrack if we will wait another week. That is when she returns to her husband."

"You may stay and enjoy the favors of your paramour," said Nitya angrily. "I will leave in the *Darling Thoma* as soon as she is ready to sail."

"Her carrack is much bigger and faster than the *Darling Thoma*," said Greghar, coaxing. "We will get to Tirut sooner if we go with her, even though we leave later."

"I will not sail in a ship with her!" Nitya's tone was resentful.

"Nitya, be reasonable," said Greghar. "You don't need me anymore. Why do you begrudge me a little fling?"

Her head snapped back as though he had struck her. Her shoulders slumped and all the fight went out of her.

"You don't see, do you?" she whispered. "Vasitha has warned me again and again—it is a sin to use power for worldly ends. I have blackened my soul. I have distanced myself from the grace of Lord Moksha. But every time I used my power, it was for you." She did not sob, but large tears formed in her eyes and slowly coursed down her cheeks.

He took a step toward her to comfort her, but she put up her hand. He stopped short with a look of dread, as though he expected her to burn him. *He really fears me,* she thought miserably. *Have I really changed so much?*

"Go!" she said. "Go to her. I cannot give you what she can."

GREGHAR STOOD ON the same spot on the battlements two days later, looking down on the harbor. The *Darling Thoma* was slowly making her way toward the open sea. He squinted, trying to focus on the tiny, antlike figures on the deck. It was no use—they were too far away for him to recognize anyone. Feeling slightly foolish, he raised his right hand and waved, hoping that one of the tiny figures was Nitya and that she would wave back. But he could discern no response.

He had felt extremely low since his conversation with Nitya. She had taken great pains to avoid being alone with him again and left to return to the ship that same afternoon. *Emotional, melodramatic woman!* he thought. *I never promised to be a celibate. I have acted no differently than any red-blooded soldier of fortune. Yet she acts as though I have betrayed Princess Caitlin, a woman who has probably long forgotten that I exist.* But no matter how many times he ran this through his mind, he could not assuage his feelings of guilt.

"Why so thoughtful, love?" Kitara's voice intruded on his thoughts. He was jerked out of his reverie and saw her leaning on the same crenel that Nitya had leaned on, looking at him languorously. She put out her arms. "Come hold me, the breeze is a bit chilly, and my gown is thin."

He obeyed and held her. The feeling of her body was enjoyable, but his pleasure was soured by the view of the *Darling Thoma* over her shoulder. She sensed his uneasiness and guessed its source.

"Don't worry about her, love," Kitara said, snuggling up against him. "She is just a teasing hypocrite who wants to keep you dancing to her tune. If you ignore her, she will come running back to your bed."

SIX

FIRST STRIKES

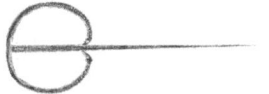

ASGARA WAS UNFAILINGLY polite but cool in her dealings with Andromache. The High Priestess showered her with affection and presents, but her busy schedule meant that she could not give her much time. Asgara was usually picked up from Temple Heights Nursery by Andromache's handmaiden and spent many evenings at Palace Saxe tended by the staff. She had been used to telling Megara every detail of her day, and having her hang on every word. Now she was almost always asleep by the time Andromache came home. From being the center of Megara's world, she found herself a minor satellite of Andromache's constellation.

However, this was a weekend, and Andromache had personally gone to spend time with Asgara in the Palace Saxe nursery. She had brought her own *katsch* and a glass of warm milk for Asgara, who sat drinking it in silence.

"Isn't it a beautiful day?" asked Andromache. "My mother and I would often sit together in this very nursery when I was a little girl."

"On nice days, my mother would take my sister and me into the mountains for picnics," replied Asgara. "I always made her dive off cliffs in the speeder. It was so much fun!"

"Typical dangerous huntress exploits," said Andromache with a sniff. "And most inappropriate for young girls."

"My mother would never endanger us," responded Asgara with spirit.

"Well, my dear," said Andromache, changing the subject. "You and I are doing something very exciting this evening. We have been invited to dine with the queen!"

"She said that my mother is a fine example," said Asgara. "I pointed her out when the queen came to Temple Heights Nursery."

The constant references to Megara as her mother grated on Andromache's nerves. She had to remind herself that the little girl was not trying to bait her.

"I work closely with the queen," said Andromache. "I am her foremost adviser. Seignora Megara is just a—"

She stopped, sheepishly realizing that she was trying to impress Asgara, competing with Megara for her affection. She drained her *katsch* and stood up.

"I have a surprise for you," she said. "I have bought you a beautiful new outfit for our visit to the queen. You will look so pretty in it!"

She tapped her wrist bracer, and a few moments later her handmaiden entered, bearing the new outfit. It was a child's size version of a formal adult gown, beautifully cut and finished. It was far prettier than the simple clothing that Megara used to dress her in.

She looked at the gown suspiciously.

"That is not mine," she said.

"I had it made for you. They used one of your dresses as a pattern for size." She ran her fingers over the soft fabric. "It is musk-lace. It will caress your skin. Try it on."

"I did not wear special clothes when I met the queen before. My mother said that those who are impressed by fine clothes are not worth impressing."

Andromache was tempted to say something cutting about Megara, but she held her tongue.

"We show our respect for the queen by arriving in her presence suitably dressed. Not every little girl is invited to dine at Chateau Regina. You are very lucky to have this opportunity."

Asgara finally consented to Andromache's handmaiden dressing her in the new gown. She stood before the three-dimensional mirror and scowled.

"I look silly," she said.

"Oh nonsense, dear," said Andromache. "You look fabulous, a very proper heiress to the d'Orr tiara."

Asgara's scowl deepened.

"I am a Paurina, not a d'Orr," she said.

Andromache wisely did not respond but let her handmaiden finish dressing Asgara and lead her to the speeder. They were driven to Chateau Regina in silence.

ALEX LED THEM into a reception room of the residential north wing of Chateau Regina. Hildegard received them there herself, dressed semiformally, as though she had just returned from work. However, the atmosphere was very relaxed. She greeted Andromache as an equal. When she addressed Asgara, she did not stoop or pick her up but spoke to her as she would to an adult.

"Lady Asgara, I am so happy you are able to accept my invitation," she said. "I trust you are well?"

Asgara curtsied as she had been taught at Temple Heights Nursery.

"I am well, Your Majesty," she said. She looked into Hildegard's gray-blue eyes and seemed to struggle with herself before blurting out, "But I miss my mother, Seignora Megara, and my sister, Iantha."

Hildegard put her hand on Asgara's shoulder and squeezed it. They seemed instantly at ease with each other.

"Come, supper is laid out on the balcony," said Hildegard. "Our chef will be expecting us to be there by now." She leaned to speak to Asgara in a mock whisper. "I dance to everyone's tune here, Asgara. I am not my own mistress." She straightened. "Isn't that true, Alex?"

"It is always a pleasure to serve you, ma'am," said Alex. Her words were formal, but her tone was warm. "You are very easy on us."

They followed Alex out on to Hildegard's large private balcony. Alex pulled a chair out for the queen and indicated chairs for Andromache and Asgara. The chair for Asgara was prepared with a booster on it.

"Thank you, Alex," said Hildegard, and her First Handmaiden withdrew.

The supper laid out was sumptuous but prepared specially with a child in mind. However, Asgara waited till the queen asked her to help herself and then served herself a decorously small portion of each item. She waited till the queen and Andromache served themselves. Only when the queen urged her to eat did she take the first bite.

"Asgara is very excited to meet you again, ma'am," said Andromache, feeling left out of the wordless intimacy between Hildegard and Asgara. "She was telling me about how she met you when you visited Temple Heights Nursery."

"Yes," said Hildegard. "She pointed out her mother to me. Seignora Megara is such fine officer, is she not? An impressive military record and such striking good looks as well!"

"Iantha and I have the best mother," said Asgara, nodding. "She was always the first to arrive for pick-up at Temple Heights Nursery. All the other girls used to envy us."

"I make sure my handmaiden is there every day precisely on time for pick-up," said Andromache, sensing an unspoken rebuke.

They finished eating, and Hildegard suggested that they move to a comfortable arbor at the edge of the balcony, overlooking the city. The queen seated herself and looked up at Asgara.

"Will you sit by me, Lady Asgara?" she asked.

Asgara did not answer but smiled and plopped down beside Hildegard. The queen looked down on her fondly. Andromache sat facing them, not quite sure what to make of their spontaneous closeness. Hildegard had never been particularly close to Caitlin.

"Well, my dear, I have a surprise for you," said Hildegard. "Your mother is in Atlantic City. I have invited her here to see you."

Asgara's eyes went wide. She looked from Hildegard to Andromache and back again, suspecting a joke or a trick. Hildegard stroked Asgara's ash-blonde curls, thinking, *Who could ever have predicted that Deirdre and I would share a granddaughter!* She tapped her wrist bracer, opening a comm channel to Alex.

"Alex, I take it she has arrived?" she asked. "Please bring her out to see us."

Asgara waited with bated breath. The portal hissed open and Alex entered.

"Seignora Megara Paurina of the Cohort of Palace Guardians," she announced, and withdrew as soon as Megara entered.

Asgara squealed, leaped to her feet, and raced forward. She threw herself into Megara's waiting arms. Her legal mother picked her up and hugged her tight. Neither spoke, but their joy was plain to see. Hildegard looked on benignly.

After a few moments, Megara put Asgara down and saluted Hildegard, hand on heart. Then she bowed formally to Andromache.

"I apologize for my lack of self control, Your Highness, High Priestess," said Megara. "I meant no disrespect."

"What kind of a society would we be if we decried a mother's love for her daughter?" asked Hildegard, smiling.

Asgara held Megara's arm tightly and beamed at Hildegard. Then she looked up and immediately saw through Megara's attempt to conceal her look of worry.

"What is the matter, Mother?" she asked.

"Nothing, my love," said Megara.

"Come, come," said Hildegard. "Please sit with us. Will you take some supper, Seignora?"

"I had a bite on my way over," lied Megara, seeing that they had already eaten. She sat down, and Asgara immediately climbed into her lap and put her arms possessively around her waist.

"How did the trial go, Seignora Megara?" asked Andromache.

Megara ran her fingers through her thick hair distractedly.

"It could have been better," she replied.

"What trial?" asked Asgara.

"It is nothing, my darling—" began Megara.

"You are a very bright and perceptive girl, dearest Asgara," cut in Andromache. "Seignora Megara has persisted in keeping the truth from you. But I really think it is best for you to know that facts."

"I have not..." Megara's retort trailed off, and she sat back, weary and resigned.

"Tyla Dorrina, one of your d'Orr relatives, is challenging Seignora Megara's status as your legal mother," said Andromache. "The wealth and comforts of your life in Palace d'Orr are yours to inherit from your real mother, Princess Caitlin. Tyla's relationship to you is quite distant— she is descended from a younger daughter of your ancestor Princess Iren, making her your fourth cousin. But she believes her blood gives her a stronger claim to care for you and use the d'Orr fortune."

"I am not a d'Orr," said Asgara, her voice growing shrill. "I am a Paurina and Seignora Megara is my mother. Let them take Palace d'Orr and everything in it! I will live with my mother, if we have to camp in the wilderness."

"Asgara, Asgara, you are being silly," said Andromache gently. She turned to Megara. "Tell us about the trial. Was judgment rendered today?'

"Yes, ma'am," said Megara. She kissed the top of Asgara's head. "The judge ruled that the tradition laid down by Queen Simran with regard to Temple Heights supersedes the title Princess Caitlin has given me to her assets. Since I am not an aristocrat, I can no longer reside in Palace d'Orr."

"Is that all?"

"No, ma'am," said Megara. "She ruled that the d'Orr estate is indivisible, so she also struck down Caitlin's transfer of her assets to me. But Tyla Dorrina is a commoner—she is not even an electra—so the judge awarded her nothing but an official note of commendation for bringing the matter to the attention of the court. All d'Orr assets are frozen and all incomes will accumulate untouched until either Princess Caitlin returns or Lady Asgara comes of age."

Hildegard cast a glance at Andromache so fleeting that no one noticed it. The High Priestess sat primly with her legs crossed, hands on her knee, one on top of the other. She had a cool smile on her face and looked the very picture of aristocratic elegance. *I know that look,* thought Hildegard.

"Was Tyla Dorrina alone in her suit?" asked Hildegard.

"No, ma'am," said Megara. "Countess Dorothea appeared and filed a supporting brief."

"I see," said Hildegard. She paused and now cast an obvious glance at Andromache. "Surely you must continue to serve as Lady Asgara's legal mother. Princess Caitlin's rights as a Zon mother are unalienable under the law and she has chosen you for that responsibility."

Megara and Asgara hugged each other tighter. Megara smiled tiredly. It had been a hard few days for her, struggling to understand the arcane minutiae and proceedings of Zon law. She had been out of her element, facing lawyers and the judge, all quoting and interpreting the complex legal doctrines that had developed over more than a thousand years.

"Yes, ma'am. She has accepted that I am Lady Asgara's legal mother. But she has also taken into account that my posting to Daksin is of unspecified duration. Apparently, in such cases, a legal mother's status may be transferred to another party, if a suitably meritorious candidate can be found."

They sat in silence for a few moments, looking down on the twinkling lights of the city.

"The foremothers who framed our laws were wise," Hildegard said at length. "There is no more meritorious candidate in the Sisterhood than Princess Andromache. Lady Asgara is fortunate indeed."

Asgara had buried her face in Megara's side to conceal her angry tears. Her words were muffled, but quite clear.

"You cannot separate me from my mother!"

BRADAR WEPT FREELY as he hugged Esgrin tight. She did not return his embrace, but she did endure his display of affection with good grace. Lothar, Lovelyn, Pinnar and Guttrin were also in the chamber. His parents and brother looked on indulgently, while Guttrin could not conceal her impatience.

"I cannot believe my good fortune," exclaimed Bradar. "I am so happy to have you back, my heart is about to burst with joy!"

She smiled but did not respond.

"They released you and sent you here with an escort," said Lovelyn. "You are sure there was no talk of ransom?"

"Indeed, ma'am, that is what I expected," replied Esgrin. "So I kept my ears open throughout, trying to fathom their motives."

"And?" asked Lothar, prodding her for details.

Esgrin turned to him.

"I am afraid I have little information, Sire," she said. "They did not speak of money, only of their interest in fulfilling their destinies. Perhaps Shobar had second thoughts, recalling that he is related to you by blood."

She smiled, thinking of her nights with Shobar, so different from the routine of her marriage bed. But it was not Shobar's rough love-making that filled her thoughts. His selfish rutting was only the prelude to the intense carnal pleasures she shared in her dreamscape with her incubus. Enveloping her in a cocoon of darkness, he thrilled every one of her senses. And the way Shobar looked at her each morning told her that he knew. Even now she shivered as the memories of that illicit lust made her knees weak.

She turned her attention back to Bradar. He still held her as though he was afraid that she would disappear if he released her. He kissed her, and she kissed him back dutifully. Finally, she managed to partially disengage herself so only his arm was around her waist.

"My dear," she said to him. "Recall the blissful times we spent together in Estrans Castle before Shobar's attack. I hope that those are the only memories that I retain of our stay in Swarborg."

Bradar, Lovelyn, and Pinnar continued to be unstinting in their exclamations of delight at Esgrin's return, and even Lothar allowed himself a rare grin. Guttrin was more restrained, not happy to find herself under Esgrin's shadow again.

That night Bradar was as gentle as ever, and Esgrin feigned great pleasure. He was duly gratified, delighted in his wife and in his marriage. Then he fell into a deep sleep and would not rouse even when she shook him. Satisfied, she lay back, closed her eyes and eagerly awaited her unnatural tryst. Shortly after she drifted into slumber, her incubus came and he did not disappoint her.

Bradar awoke in the morning to find Esgrin yawning and stretching like a cat, her demeanor marked by a languorous fulfillment. It unsettled him and made him jealous, but he could not understand why.

THE SUN HAD set, but it was still a gray twilight. As Queen Esme of Briga walked down the cold corridors of the Great Stony Keep, she looked out through the narrow arrow slit windows on to the twisting streets of Dreslin Center and beyond to Outer Dreslin outside the walls of the capital. She stopped for a moment and watched a lamplighter going about his business, lighting each street lamp quickly and efficiently before moving on to the next.

As per her normal practice, Esme entered the nursery, where two nursemaids and one of her ladies-in-wating were with the royal children. Crown Prince Axel had just finished his post supper homework and his young brother Dolomus sat by him. The princes worked every day with a young tutor who had just graduated from the Thermadan religious school in the capital. Harald had insisted on having all candidates interviewed by Lady Selene Allerand, the Zon Resident, and this tutor was her selection. He was very earnest and Esme could find no fault with his wide-ranging lessons on reading, writing, arithmetic, history, and geography.

The women jumped up on the queen's entry. Axel and Dolomus rose and bowed formally to their mother.

"We were just going to change their young highnesses for bed," said the more senior of the nursemaids, bobbing a curtsey.

"Carry on," said Esme. "Don't mind me. I will just sit here."

She seated herself on a window seat and watched as the nursemaids changed the boys. As she did every day, she observed the boys with a loving mother's eye. Young Axel was almost as tall as her now. He had Esme's vivacious personality and dancing eyes and was developing the classic Shelsor nose inherited from his father. Dolomus had a round face and small eyes and was already showing signs of pudginess. He had a mean streak that was particularly apparent to the servants who were subject to his whims. The court was rife with rumors that he was Alumus's son, and Esme was sure that they originated with Alumus.

"So how was your day, boys?" she asked.

"Wonderful, Mother," said Axel. "Tutor Granus taught us the history of Willum I, our ancestor who established the House of Shelsor."

"And what did he tell you?"

"We are an old house," said Axel proudly. "It was over six hundred years ago that Willum rose up against the old despot, King Ullavus. He defeated the tyrant's army in the Battle of Motsk. Then he marched in triumph up the Amu-Shan and the capital opened its gates to him."

Ullavus had raped and killed a huntress serving the Zon Ambassadress to Briga. When the Zon Queen Caitlin sent an airship, demanding ten thousand gold talents in damages for his act, he paid it and boasted afterward that it was a small price to pay for the pleasure of violating a huntress. The queen accepted the payment, but she never forgave him. She bided her time, fomenting unrest among the barons in the Northern Marches. Eventually they rose in revolt, led by Willum Shelsor then a minor but charismatic chieftain. When Ullavus sent the mass of his forces against them, the queen sent airboats to support the rebels. It was the microwave disintegrators of the Zon airboats that destroyed Ullavus's vast army at the Battle of Motsk, but Queen Caitlin declared Willum Shelsor the victor on the field. After the battle, she flew to Dreslin Center and took the lightly defended capital. She personally led the Guardian squad that captured Ullavus and had him roasted alive in Castle Square, earning the epithet "the Unforgiving." Then she ordered her Guardian commander Soefia Sheel to sack the city. Centuries later, Queen Caitlin's descendant Princess Deirdre would sack Dreslin Center once again at the end of the War of Brigon Succession.

Willum Shelsor arrived to find a cowed city, much of it in ruins. The queen was waiting for him with a new, gold-winged Eagle crown crafted in Atlantic City. She placed it on his head, proclaiming him Willum I in the Royal Audience Hall before a hastily assembled and sullen gathering of Brigon nobility and gentry. On the same day he swore an oath of fealty, accepting her as his mistress. This completed the Zon conquest of Briga, reducing it to a vassal state of the Sisterhood. The Zon ambassadress was elevated to the position of Resident. Within a year, construct-bots completed the Zon Residency and it had been the real seat of power in Briga ever since.

Growing up in the House of Hilson, Esme had been brought up to scorn the Shelsors. She now recognized that the truth lay somewhere between the polemics she had been taught, and the version written by the Shelsor scribes. But she thought it best for Axel to believe the official Shelsor version for now.

"Yes, he was an ancestor to be proud of," she said to Axel.

Both boys came to her for hugs before being taken to bed by the nursemaids. They were interrupted by the raised voice of Esme's lady-in-waiting, who had moved to station herself in the nursery's anteroom. She now retreated into the nursery saying, "No, no, Your Virtue, this is most improper..."

Alumus paid no attention to her and came in with a smirk on his face. He had grown plumper over the last few years and lost some more hair. He was just as arrogant and had grown more presumptuous with the king's blindness. But this intrusion was beyond anything he had attempted thus far.

"My dear," he said, addressing Esme familiarly. "I am here to see the princes. I believe it is my right, at least for one of them!"

"Red Khalif, even the king begs my leave before he enters the nursery," said Esme stiffly. "Your presence here at this hour is most unseemly. I must entreat you to leave us immediately."

"Come, come, my dear," he remonstrated, striding up to her.

As she shrank from his touch, she saw a faint blue aura around his form. She blinked, thinking it was something in her eyes, but it was still there. He put an arm around each of the boys and the aura seemed to pulse. Her maternal instincts aroused, she regained her courage and stepped back up, attempting to take his hands off them. Alumus released Dolomus, but his grip around Axel's shoulders tightened. Too angry to think of calling for help, she struggled to remove his arm from Axel's shoulders. Alumus took advantage of her focus on Axel to put his free arm around her waist and press her body against his.

She was now forced to physically wrestle with him. She managed to extricate Axel and put him behind her. Then Alumus put both his arms around her waist and drew her into his arms. Wild with anger at his unwelcome attentions, she drew the thin dagger from her bodice and stabbed him in the bicep. He screamed in terror and backpedalled away from her, clutching his wounded arm. His blue aura was gone.

"Oh! Oh!" he cried, panicked by sight of his blood leaking through his fingers. "You have killed me, you have murdered me!"

"Stop sniveling, you worthless piece of dung," she snapped. "It is a scratch. You will be fine tomorrow. Now get out of here before I call the Life Guards."

Alumus continued to wail, but he left the nursery at a half run.

Esme looked around at the boys, the nursemaids, and her lady-in-waiting. They all looked at her wide-eyed and open-mouthed. She wiped the bloody blade of her dagger on her skirts and returned it to its sheath.

"His Virtue appears to have suffered a minor mental breakdown," she said. "We must keep this episode secret. It would do great harm to the Thermadan Mission if it were to become public knowledge. I am sure that none of us wishes to harm the Mission and all its good works."

The nursemaids nodded dumbly and led the boys away to their bedchamber. However, her lady-in-waiting stammered, "But Your Highness, he treated you as though...as though..."

"He was not in command of himself," said Esme firmly. "You will not repeat this to anyone. Do I have your word?"

"Yes, ma'am," she said without raising her eyes.

Esme was shaken by the encounter with Alumus, for it represented a new and disturbing escalation in his behavior. If he treated her in such a manner in front of her personal staff, she worried about what he might do in public. She desperately wished she had someone to talk this over with. She had over a dozen ladies-in-waiting, but there was no one she could trust. And in spite of their intimacy, this was one secret she could not confide in Harald.

THE SMALL AUDIENCE chamber of the Great Stony Keep was warm and well lit. There was a cheerful fire in the grate and hundreds of candles brightened the room. The King's Head Steward had been in the chamber for over an hour. He went around, fussing over every place setting, making sure the wines and other beverages were presented in the most showy manner and even checking on the brass and silver on the King's Life Guards' uniforms. The conference table was set for five.

Alumus, the Red Khalif was the first to arrive. The Life Guards at the door announced him in stentorian tones, "His Virtue, the Red Khalif!"

The Head Steward hurried forward, bowing deeply.

"Your Virtue, please follow me," he said.

Alumus was led to his seat and took it with assurance. As he sat down, he gingerly felt his left bicep and winced. His bad mood was firmly writ on his face.

Baron Ratto va Haxos, the king's First Minister arrived very shortly thereafter. He was announced by the Life Guards and led to his seat at the king's left. He nodded curtly to Alumus and received a cold stare in response. There was no love lost between them.

They sat in uncomfortable silence for several minutes before the Life Guards at the door pounded their halberds into the floor and announced King Harald V and Queen Esme. Harald wore eyeball-shaped infrared sensors that the Zon had implanted in place of his burned-out eyes. Esme held his hand tenderly as she led him to the aerie-shaped chair at the head of the conference table. She took the long way around the table to avoid passing by Alumus, fearing the familiarity he might attempt to presume. Never one to conceal his feelings, he glared at her as she progressed around the room and helped Harald to his place. Then she took her own seat at his right hand and looked around the table.

"Well!" she said brightly. "We are all here and it is still a few minutes before Lady Selene is due."

The words had barely left her mouth when the Life Guards at the door pounded their halberds again and announced the Zon Resident in Briga. Lady Selene was her usual tall, commanding self. Her two trailing huntresses wore ceremonial Palace Guardian uniforms, but their long-barreled laser pistols and well-used longswords were all business. She did not appear to notice anyone other than the king and queen. As required by protocol, she gave the royal couple the half bow they were due and remained standing while everyone at the conference table remained seated. Even from her position of apparent subordination, her demeanor conveyed the unmistakable message that she was in charge.

Harald's infrared sensors conveyed her tall and svelte outline to his brain. His vivid memories of her did the rest.

"Lady Selene," he said. "How wonderful to see you again."

"The king and I welcome you," said Esme with a smile. "We thank you for accepting our last-minute invitation and apologize for the lateness of the hour. Please be seated and join us."

One of the huntresses drew back the chair at the foot of the table. She pushed it back with well-rehearsed skill so that it was in perfect position as Lady Selene sat down on it.

"I am ever at Your Majesties' service," said Lady Selene. The Head Steward bustled up with a silver tray laden with a range of drinks. She selected a stem of Brigon apple wine and smiled. "As usual, your hospitality is flawless."

"It is our Brigon show of good manners," said Alumus, his bad mood making his nasty tone even sharper. "We are hospitable even to those we revile."

Baron va Haxos cleared his throat, as he always did prior to speaking in company. But Alumus went on before he could speak.

"You can have no doubt as to why you have been summoned." With his animal cunning, he knew that emphasizing her formally inferior status would nettle her. But her long experience stood her in good stead, and she concealed her irritation. In turn she knew that he could not bear to be belittled. So she completely ignored him and turned to Baron va Haxos, smiling sweetly.

"My lord baron, I am very keen to hear why you have called this meeting."

Alumus turned as red as his robes. However, Lady Selene was used to outmaneuvering him and took little pleasure in it. She gave all her attention to va Haxos, who smiled with bluff good humor as she gave him the floor.

"Resident Lady Selene, we wish to discuss the security situation in the Southern Marches," he said. "A detachment of our Desert

Patrol has just returned to Dreslin Center. They brought the bodies of two itinerant preachers of the Abaidan branch of the Mission and some Red Sentinels. They were horribly tortured, and their bodies are badly mutilated. The Patrolmen say that large bands of Chekaliga tribesmen are now ranging freely over the Daksin Desert and the western drylands of the Southern Marches."

Esme raised her stem of apple wine and sipped while va Haxos spoke. She was inordinately pleased at Alumus's discomfiture but strove to keep a neutral expression on her face. As soon as va Haxos paused for breath, she spoke.

"Lady Selene, the king and I are very concerned," she said. "We hope that you will be able to reassure us that you will soon have the situation under control."

Lady Selene did not respond immediately. In her habitual deliberate manner, she sipped her wine and kept her face expressionless.

"We are monitoring the situation," she said, setting her stem down. "We stand prepared to support any action you choose to take."

They waited for her to continue, but she said no more and allowed the silence to grow pregnant. Finally, Harald spoke.

"Lady Selene, what do you advise?"

"I recommend that you proceed with the Royal Black Regiment to Tirut. Ask Baron Nehemus va Alsor of Tirut to muster some of his regiments. Turn these combined forces on the Chekaligas."

"All this for some looting scum from the ravines?" asked va Haxos.

"Our reconnaissance indicates that the tribes have united for the first time since the days of Good Queen Sonia. There are tens of thousands of them and they are acting like they are implementing a unified military strategy in Briga and Daksin. You will need a powerful military force under strong leadership to defeat them."

"In years past you have chased them back to their lairs using your airboats," persisted va Haxos. "This is your responsibility and is stipulated in our treaty."

"We have had some technical difficulties," said Lady Selene, uncharacteristically vague. "The weather has affected our flight operations. We are working to get things under control. But in the meantime, it would be wise to take no chances. Marching to Tirut with the Royal Blacks will also remind Baron Nehemus of the power of his liege lord."

"Indeed," said Harald. "The Tirut barons' taxes are the biggest source of crown revenue."

And their tribute payments to the Sisterhood are not to be scoffed at either, thought Lady Selene.

Harald looked at Esme, her form outlined to his limited vision. He put his hand on hers and squeezed it affectionately. Their partnership and mutual understanding had deepened over the years, and she immediately knew what he wanted.

"The king and I value your counsel, Lady Selene," said Esme. "We will do as you suggest. We will march with the Royal Blacks to Tirut, expecting that you will support us with your airboats as soon as the weather permits. And Baron, we assume you have no objection to mustering one of your regiments in Haxos and bringing it to Dreslin? I am second to none in my appreciation of the Life Guards and the Moles, but they are too few to secure Dreslin. We leave you in command of the capital and I am sure you will rest easier with a loyal garrison."

Va Haxos bowed his head to the royal couple.

"It will be my pleasure," he said. "I will send a rider to Haxos today."

LATER THAT NIGHT, just as Esme's personal maid Lupa finished preparing her for bed, there was a knock on the outer door of her chambers. Lupa went out into the anteroom and returned in a hurry, saying, "Your Highness, it is his Majesty! He begs leave to enter."

Esme rushed out into the anteroom to receive him. Since his blindness, Harald rarely came to her chambers, preferring to request her presence in his chambers as often as he could.

Esme stood by the door and curtsied deeply as Harald entered, led by his valet and holding the arm of one of his Life Guards. Lupa followed her mistress's show of respect.

"Your Highness," Esme said formally, cognizant of the presence of their servitors. "You should have sent for me. I am yours to command, and I would have flown to you."

"Yes, my dear," said Harald. "You are my most constant support, my lodestar. I fear I take you for granted. It is only right that I wait on you from time to time."

Esme came forward to take his arm and with an eloquent signal with her eyes, dismissed the Life Guard. Leading him into her bedchamber, she kissed him warmly on the lips. They were easy in each other's company as their body servants helped them change into their sleepwear. Lupa and the king's valet laid out trays of water and hot milk with luscious herbs on the side tables before withdrawing and leaving them alone.

Esme led Harald to her bed, and they made love unhurriedly, tenderly. Afterward he relaxed in her arms and petted her curls as she helped him sip some warm herbed milk.

"My darling, I thank the One God every day for his kindness in allowing me the joy of your company," he said. "I don't know what I have done to deserve the happiness that you give me."

She smiled in the darkness and held him tighter, knowing that no other response was necessary. They slept.

Esme did not know what awakened her, but she sat up in bed with a nameless dread. The night seemed so dark that she could not even see her hands. She looked at her nightstand and thought her eyes were playing tricks on her, for there seemed to be a strange blue aura around the unlit lamp. Then all of a sudden, Harald coughed. A pall of darkness seemed to rush out of her window and when she looked at her nightstand again, the lamp was black, sooty, and normal. Harald coughed again, long and hacking.

She looked down at Harald. The night was cold, and the fire had died down in her grate, but his face was covered with sweat. She felt his forehead and found it to be ragingly hot. Worried now, she rang her bedside bell for Lupa and swung her legs out of bed, putting her feet into her fleece-lined slippers. Lupa came in silently, bearing a lamp. She quickly lit a few lamps in the bedchamber before putting a warm robe on Esme. As she did this, Harald began coughing again, and this time it continued for several minutes.

"Get the healer," said Esme to Lupa. "And ask the duty Life Guard officer to come here. Hurry!"

Lupa left and Esme went back to the bed with some dry towels. She gently dried Harald's face and said, "Rest my love, the herbalist is on his way."

"No use," gasped Harald, his eyelids still shut tightly over his sightless eyes. "I have seen the Evil One, he has marked me for death. Hold me my darling, your touch is the only thing that can comfort me."

"It was just a bad dream," she said. "Don't dwell on it. You are strong; you are in good health. We will soon have you well again."

"My dearest," Harald said, his voice reduced to a whisper. "It was not a nightmare, for I was not sleeping. He woke me before speaking to me. And he told me his name—Malitha."

Esme held his head to her breast and prayed to the One God as hard as she could. A short while later Lupa led in a huge Life Guard captain followed by the healer with his bag of potions and implements. Esme reluctantly relinquished her place by Harald's head to healer, torn by his plaintive cry asking her not to leave him.

"He is very ill, Your Highness," said the healer to Esme after a quick examination. "We must bleed him to drain the ill humors, there is no other option."

Esme nodded her head and he began assembling his instruments. As he was doing so, she turned to the Life Guard officer.

"Take a troop of Life Guards to the Residency," she said. "Hail the Seignora of the Watch and ask to speak with Lady Selene. Tell her that His Highness is deathly ill. Convey my request that they send one of their Zon healers."

The officer bowed and left. Time passed in a blur for Esme. It seemed far too soon when Lady Selene strode into her bedchamber, her thin gown flowing around her graceful figure. The Residency's senior Medica followed her. The healer was still bleeding Harald, and there were several brass bowls with his blood. He was deathly white and still sweating heavily.

"Get out!" snapped Lady Selene at the healer. "Leave immediately. You are killing him, you fool."

The healer looked to Esme for support but found none there. He gathered his implements and potions sulkily. He bowed to Esme, pointedly ignored the Zon, and left with bad grace.

The medica set to work immediately and within minutes had placed a range of sensors on Harald's body, all cued into a data pack.

Esme, Lupa, and the Life Guard officer looked on in fascination as the data pack flickered to life. It projected a wide range of holograms, numbers, and colorful images that changed constantly as they monitored Harald's biological systems. The medica worked the data pack, generating a range of different configurations. The data pack was synced into her wrist bracer and patched through to the main processors at Repro in Atlantic City. All the data from Harald's body was analyzed and cross-tabulated against the billions of records in the Zon medical data store.

The medica read the results of the analysis and shook her head.

"Well?" asked Lady Selene.

"I have never seen a case like this, Your Ladyship. I have all his vitals, and I know exactly what is wrong with him. He has a high fever, his heart rate is elevated, his blood pressure is far too high, and the inner lining of his throat is inflamed. I detect a swelling of his brain tissue. But I can find no cause, no pathogen. He should not be ill at all, but yet he is."

"Can it be some unknown allergy to something he ingested?"

"The sensors have analyzed every cell and every system in his body. Every single cell is healthy, with no defects other than routine wear and tear, and his bodily systems are dealing with this as normal. His digestive system is processing everything he ingested, and there is nothing out of the ordinary. There is no evidence of an adverse reaction to anything he consumed. I am sorry, ma'am, but my analysis says that he should not be ill."

Lady Selene tapped the toe of her chic slipper. Worry clouded her attractive features.

"Is there anyone you could discuss the case with in Atlantic City? I can open a comm channel to anyone you name, even the queen's personal medica."

"I would be happy to discuss the case with the chief of pathogenic diseases in Repro, ma'am," said the medica. "I know her, we studied together."

"Do so," said Lady Selene briefly.

As the medica began talking in a low voice, Lady Selene went up and sat at the head of Harald's bed on the left, across from Esme who sat on the right. She laid a hand on his forehead, her cool, long fingers tracing the pattern of his eyebrows. His eyes opened, and he turned his head to look at her, his infrared sensors recognizing her shape. He raised a hand and put it on hers.

"Lady Selene," he said, his voice hoarse. "I...I..."

"Shhh," said Lady Selene in a soft tone that Esme had never heard her use before. "I have come. I am with you. Rest easy."

He relaxed and smiled. For a moment, she could have sworn his fever seemed to abate. But then his brow grew hot again, and his jaw clenched as the throbbing pain in his head returned.

"I love my Esme, Lady Selene," he said. "She is dearer to me than anything in the world. But long before I met her, you were my ideal woman, perfection, unattainable. If you had feelings for me, why, I would..."

Lady Selene glanced over at the medica, a mute question in her look. The medica stopped speaking into the comm channel and shook her head slowly. The Resident looked down at Harald and passed her free hand over his cheek before putting a finger on his lips.

"You are everything a woman could desire," she said in the same soft tone. "You are gentle, kind, and generous. You have worked tirelessly for the good of your people. If I were free to love, my heart would lead me to you."

Harald lay back, his eyes closed, and his features relaxed again.

"I am the luckiest man in the world," he said in a rasping whisper.

He coughed again, and this time he brought up dark blood. Esme immediately reached for him and buried his face in her bosom. After his fit of coughing finally subsided, his fever seemed to suddenly abate. As he grew cooler, he went limp, and Esme held him tighter, as though her grip could keep the life in him. Then a red light flashed on the data pack and it emitted a low whine. Esme did not need the equipment to tell her that he was gone.

The medica smoothly disengaged Esme from Harald's unmoving form. Lady Selene took her in her arms. Held by the tall Resident, Esme's shoulders began to shake, and her harsh, wracking sobs filled the chamber.

It was still dark outside, but the early morning routine of the castle had begun. One of the princes' nursemaids entered the bedchamber hesitantly. She was obviously frightened by Esme's noisy grief and the presence of the intimidating Zon. She stood in silence for a while and then finally got the courage to touch Lupa's sleeve.

"What is it?" whispered Lupa, clearly irritated.

"It is His Highness, Prince Axel," the nursemaid said, her voice low but quivering. "I went to wake him just now. But he just lies there in his bed with his mouth and eyes open, staring at the ceiling. I think he is dead."

IT WAS MANY hours later that Lady Selene, the senior medica, and a couple of escorting huntresses stood on a terrace of the Great Stony Keep to take their leave. The gray morning was made even more cheerless by the driving snow flurries. Esme had insisted on coming to see them off, and she held herself rigidly, dressed in a formal gown and bedecked with furs. Lupa had dressed her lovingly and worked hard on her makeup, but nothing could cover the grief writ so plainly on her face. Her formal demeanor was fragile, and Lady Selene knew that it would take very little to bring her anguish pouring out again.

"Thank you for coming so quickly and trying to help," said Esme, her voice tight as she tried to hold herself together. "I will call a meeting of the Privy Council as soon as possible. You will receive an invitation."

"Thank you, Your Highness," said Lady Selene, giving Esme slightly more than the half bow she was due. As she began to walk up the ramp into the airboat, Esme went on.

"Did you mean it when you said that you loved him?"

Lady Selene stopped, turned her head, and inspected Esme's face carefully as though she was striving to read her thoughts. Her look was neutral, but sympathetic.

"He was dying. It was the least I could do."

Esme said nothing further. But her normally expressive eyes were dead as she watched the Zon board the airboat and take off. On the flight back to the Residency, Lady Selene stared ahead in silence, and her expression discouraged all conversation. The pilots went over the flight details in hushed voices. As soon as they landed in the Residency, Lady Selene went straight to her chambers and dismissed her handmaiden with a curt, "I am not to be disturbed."

Still fully dressed, she lay down on her wide bed and ran her fingers through her hair, caressing the vivid white streak. Then she hugged her bosom and allowed the deep well of feeling to course its way to the surface.

"Oh, Harald," she whispered. For the first time since she was a little girl, she burst into tears.

SEVEN

DARK CLOUDS

CAITLIN SAT IN the kitchen with Binne and Dhanraj, drinking a cup of the Kaylan tea that Yandharan had gifted them. She looked outside, her brow knitted with worry. Twilight was fading and the pale light was diminishing rapidly. Binne had already lit the lamps in the kitchen. Caitlin stood up with her cup and walked outside, listening hopefully for the sound of hoofbeats. A few moments later, Binne and Dhanraj came out to join her.

"It is not usual for Seamus to stay out past dark," said Caitlin. "Did he say where he would be working today?"

"Down by the southern drylands," said Binne. "I am sure there is nothing to worry about."

Caitlin did not reply, but her fears were not assuaged. It was true that Seamus sometimes did stay out late, working on the range. But for some reason she could not explain, she felt worried. The feeling would not go away, no matter how much she reasoned with herself.

"Come, eat some supper," said Binne. "You have had a long day yourself. You must be hungry."

"You go ahead and eat with Dhanraj," responded Caitlin with a smile. "I will wait for Seamus; that way no one will eat alone."

Binne patted Caitlin's shoulder affectionately and returned to the kitchen with Dhanraj. Caitlin went around the ranch house through Binne's lovingly tended little kitchen garden. She walked a few hundred meters southward and scanned the outlook. The landscape of dry scrub was mostly flat, and she could see all the way to the horizon, turning purple now in the gathering gloom. Then she thought she saw a movement. Her eyesight was very keen, but it was so far away that she wished she had her long vision with her. She peered intensely, squinting with the effort and became certain that there was something moving. But it seemed more like the aimless movement of an animal than the purposeful movement of a person.

She made up her mind and went back into the barn. She led Rufus out of his stall and saddled him quickly. She drew her laser pistol from one of the saddlebags and stuck it in her belt. Then she mounted and headed southward out of the yard at a fast trot. As she closed the distance, it became clear that what she had seen was a horse and that it carried a rider. But the rider was slumped forward on the horse's neck, and it plodded on with little zest, pausing every now and then to munch on some scrub.

Caitlin touched her heels to Rufus's flanks and they flew over the terrain to their goal. As she approached, her heart grew cold, for she recognized Seamus's vest and his horse, Tagan. She leaped off Rufus and took Tagan's bridle to steady him. The slack reins slipped out of Seamus's hand. With an effort, he raised his head and looked at her.

His vision seemed to be impaired, but he did know her, for he said in a harsh whisper, "My dearest Caitlin; the One God is kind, he has allowed me to see you before I go."

There were two shafts projecting from his back, with the distinctive black-and-white wild-coot feathers favored by the Chekaligas. Caitlin gently lowered him from Tagan's back and laid him on his side. She drew her dagger from her thigh boot and cut away his vest and then his shirt to examine his wounds.

"Leave me," he rasped, the effort of speaking clearly taxing him. "Go immediately. Take Binne and Dhanraj, leave everything, and ride for Serat. All the Chekaliga tribes are massed together. I have never seen the like. Hareskot will be overwhelmed. You must warn Collector Yandharan. He can protect you."

"Hush," she said, examining his wounds and probing gently with her fingers. She had a sinking feeling as her examination revealed the full extent of his injuries. She doubted whether even Zon medicine could save him, for the arrows had penetrated vital organs. It was a miracle he was still alive. But she could not leave him.

"Go, daughter," he insisted. He savored the word, but his voice grew fainter. "Live for me."

She sat down on the hard ground and cradled his head in her lap. She leaned over him and kissed his grizzled cheek. He felt her lips, her warm hands, and her silken locks, for he smiled.

"You are so dear to me...so beautiful..." he said.

He shuddered and was still. She saw his eyes turn sightless and knew he was gone. She closed his eyes but held him, still rocking him gently.

She fell into a grief-stricken trance and lost track of the passage of time. When she looked down at his face again, his lips had turned purple. She put her hand on his forehead and found it was cold.

———

The darkness of night had descended and when she looked up, she saw the sky brightened by countless twinkling stars. She rose and took a trenching tool from her saddle. She rapidly dug a shallow grave and laid him to rest. She fashioned a rough triangle from the Chekaliga arrows she drew from his body and stuck the crude marker on his grave.

"May your One God take you to his bosom," she murmured after she covered him with earth. The simple words seemed inadequate, so she recited the Goddess Psalm in a low tone.

She mounted Rufus again, took Tagan's reins, and set off for the ranch house at a fast canter. She slowed as she approached, for even though the ranch house screened the yard from her, she could see the brightness cast up by burning torches. Now she drew her long vision from one of her saddlebags and looked carefully. She saw a number of the fleet, small horses favored by the Chekaligas. She hobbled Rufus and Tagan and approached the ranch house cautiously on foot. She got to one of the rear windows of the living room and peered inside. The drapes were drawn, but she could not make out any shadows. She used her dagger to jimmy the latch and open the window. She pulled herself inside.

The living room was dark, no lamps were lit, and the grate was cold. But faint torchlight filtered from the yard. Caitlin crept up to the front curtains that faced the yard. She carefully peeked through— and saw six heavily armed Chekaliga scouts. Their faces painted were painted with dried blood indicating that they were on the warpath. Caitlin had heard that they used the blood of their slain enemies. Binne and Dhanraj lay on the ground while one of the scouts poked them with the blunt end of his spear.

The leader of the small group of Chekaligas motioned for his man to stop chastising Binne and Dhanraj.

"The couple at the neighboring ranch told us you have a beauteous daughter," he said. "Where is she? Give her to us, and we will let both of you live."

"Your tribesmen already took our only daughter," said Binne, raising herself on one elbow. "We have no other young woman on this ranch."

"Why would these folk lie to us?" asked the leading Chekaliga.

"We had only one daughter," said Binne again. "She was indeed beautiful. Inside and out."

The Chekaliga leader spoke to Binne again, but now he sounded less certain.

"Old woman, we will waste no more time on you," he said. He turned to his men. "Kill them and set fire to the house and barn. We already have their herd of horses."

A couple of his men drew their curved scimitars and approached Binne and Dhanraj. Binne looked tired, but calm. She faced her tormentors without fear. Dhanraj looked frightened, but he was controlling himself with an effort and attempting to not tremble.

The men raised their swords when all of a sudden there were two hissing laser blasts, so close together that they sounded like one. Both men's heads were vaporized and Binne and Dhanraj were sprinkled with small spatters of blood. As the bodies toppled to the ground there were more laser blasts, and two more of the Chekaligas were killed. They now realized that the blasts were coming from the ranch house. The one remaining scout turned to run for his horse, but he did not duck or weave, and Caitlin shot him in the back.

Alone now, the Chekaliga leader stood his ground and drew his curved sword.

"Come out and face me!" he cried. "I spit on cowardly scum who kill brave warriors from the safety of an ambush."

He spat in the dirt to emphasize his point. Caitlin now stepped out of the ranch house. Her long laser pistol barrel was black with repeated firing, but the shots had been short range, so she had used little power. The power meter was still comfortably in the green.

"You speak of cowardice," she said. "You who prey on the defenseless."

"Draw your sword," he challenged. "If you have even a spark of courage."

"You are nothing but a locust, a scourge. You deserve to be destroyed like the insect that you are."

She shot him and he fell, his dying expression a twisted look of hatred.

Binne and Dhanraj slowly stood and dusted themselves off. Binne turned to Caitlin. Her look was sad rather than hopeful.

"You have returned alone," was all she said.

Caitlin met her eyes and did not reply. She did not need to, for her silence was eloquent.

"Did he suffer?" Binne asked.

"Not long," lied Caitlin.

"The One God has always been merciful to us."

"He urged us to go to Serat, to warn Collector Yandharan and seek his protection. He said that all the Chekaliga tribes have risen and that he feared Hareskot would be overwhelmed."

"I will put things together for the road," said Binne, striving to bury her grief under a burst of activity. "I will ride Tagan. Dhanraj, saddle your bay. Let us be mounted and on our way as soon as possible."

IT WAS THE first snowfall of the winter in the Great Vale. The surrounding mountainsides had been white for weeks, but now it came to Atlantic City itself. It began in the night, and with gentle persistence, it accumulated almost a meter by daybreak. The Zon meteorological systems had forecast the snow for several days, and the public works crews were ready. All the thoroughfares and even the byways in the city were plowed and dry. However, the high banks of snow by the roads and sidewalks as well as the icicles everywhere brought the reality of winter home to every city resident.

Hildegard stood patiently as her Second Handmaiden adjusted her crown so that it sat just so on her coiffure. When she was satisfied, she stepped back. Alex looked on approvingly.

"Your Highness, you look marvelous," she said. "Your escort is formed up outside. We are a few minutes early."

"Let us go then," said Hildegard. "There are bound to be a big crowds, and we will have to drive slow."

They escorted her to the Imperial speeder and at Alex's signal on the comm, the procession of vehicles moved off. They slowly drove out of Chateau Regina, descended down the broad avenues and on through the Lower Wards. There they turned right on to Sanctuary Drive that rose steeply to the ridge of Temple Heights.

The Princess Deirdre Memorial had just been completed. It was by the Great Temple of Ma on the perimeter of the aristocrats' reserve, a stone's throw from Palace d'Orr. Hildegard was there to preside over the dedication ceremony. All the Rapids to Temple Heights were full and thousands more were walking up Sanctuary Drive. As the imperial vehicles approached the top of the drive, the crowds began to grow thick. Alex put down the top of her speeder and stood up. She hit the klaxons a few times to clear the way. Hildegard's immense personal popularity ensured that the crowds made way for her column with good humor. They waved to her and blew her kisses, gestures of affection that she returned with grace and sincerity.

The administration had only put up a small outlay to build the memorial. However urged by Vivia, the Trading Guild had added on a substantial sum. Then the Guild Mistresses used their control of the media to call on the public to add in their voluntary subscriptions. The response from the public had been overwhelming. The final amount raised was so large that the planned memorial took on a gargantuan scale. Even with the deployment of an army of construct-bots, it had taken years to complete it.

The completed memorial was built of pink and white stone to match the Great Temple, a structure that it rivaled in size and grandeur. After the Long Trek Memorial, it was the largest monument in Atlantic City. Hildegard walked up the wide steps to the strains of the "Imperial March", surrounded by her flawlessly attired Guardians. At the top of the steps she turned to face her people. With the soaring pillars of the entranceway as her backdrop, she raised her hands palms outward in the traditional manner. This caused the cheers of the mammoth crowd to swell to such a volume that they were heard throughout the city and even spilled over its walls.

Andromache came from within the Memorial to receive the Imperial party, handmaidens and Temple priestesses trailing behind her. She bowed her head and Hildegard took her by the hand and led her to the top step. She raised Andromache's hand, fingers intertwined with her own. The crowd loved it, and they roared their approval of the royal pair.

Hildegard touched her wrist bracer, syncing to the public address system and signaled Alex who stepped forward and spoke.

"My sisters, our beloved Queen Empress Hildegard will address us now," she said.

Hildegard smiled and looked around into the crowd in her inimitable manner.

"My sisters," she began. It was the clichéd opening phrase, but when Hildegard said it, each member of the multitude got the impression that she was being addressed personally. "We meet today under bittersweet circumstances. We are here to mourn. We are here to remember. But we are also here to celebrate. To celebrate a life that was so big that it could not fit into one person. Princess Deirdre d'Orr lived many parallel lives and represented all that is best in us. Tens of thousands of you have posted your most intimate feelings about her on the comm, and they form a tapestry of incredible complexity, a testament to superhuman abilities, sisterly compassion, and motherly love. Deirdre was a huntress, the greatest of her generation, perhaps of all generations. She was a priestess, with intellectual powers so great that she did in her spare time what many of us struggled to achieve all our lives. Her love for her sisters was boundless and in the end, she unhesitatingly sacrificed her life for it."

"So today, we remember her. Rather than mourn her loss, I ask you to rejoice in the fact that we had her at all, even for a short while. While I am proud to say that Deirdre d'Orr was my dearest friend, I do not claim her. She belongs to all of us."

When Hildegard stopped speaking, there a moment of pin-drop silence, as though the throng expected Deirdre herself to come walking out of the Memorial. Then like a tidal wave approaching land, there was an upsurge of full-throated cheers hailing Deirdre that carried on and on. Gradually, the cheers coalesced into a staccato two-word refrain, "Deirdre...saga, Deirdre...saga, Deirdre...saga..."

Andromache leaned over and spoke into Hildegard's ear.

"Ma'am, they will not be satisfied until you commission a saga for her."

Hildegard nodded and raised her hands again, palms outward. Gradually, the cheering subsided.

"My sisters! I am your queen, but I am also your servant. You elected me, and I am ever responsive to your wishes. I hereby commission a saga for Deirdre and will appoint a panel of scribes to make it a reality. She was the descendant of Thetis the Great, Simran the Merciless, and Caitlin the Unforgiving. Let us hail Deirdre the Magnificent!"

The crowd took up the cry, "Deirdre the Magnificent! Hail Deirdre the Magnificent!"

Hildegard stepped back to take her seat on the throne that had been placed there for the occasion and a chorus of white-robed priestesses filed in to take their places at the top of the grand steps. Following the singers, synthesizers were quickly set up, and two priestesses seated themselves at the instruments. They struck up the opening notes of the Goddess psalm and the chorus took it up, singing the ancient Artha-Pranto words beautifully.

They sang several more hymns and finished with a new ode composed in Deirdre's honor. At the insistence of the crowd, they sang it once again before retiring. Finally, Alex rose and approached the top step again.

"My sisters!" she announced, her voice cold and official. "Lady Vivia Pragarina will address you now on behalf of the Trading Guild."

Vivia came up confidently and tapped her wrist bracer to sync it with the public address system.

"My sisters!" she said. She tried to emulate Hildegard's warm empathetic tone. "When the government came to the Trading Guild with a request for funds, I made it my personal business to canvass each and every Guild Mistress. It was the least I could do for Princess Deirdre d'Orr who was a lifelong supporter of the important work of the Guild. Like all electrae, she dedicated her life to serving the commoners. I am pleased to say that I was able to convince the Trading Guild to put up the sum of five million gold talents toward to the construction of this magnificent memorial and the incomparable display that you will shortly see before you." She stopped and looked over her shoulder to make sure that everything was ready before proceeding.

"I hereby declare the Princess Deirdre Memorial open. High Priestess Princess Andromache has consecrated it to our mother, Ma. It is now yours."

As Vivia pronounced these words, jets of water rose from both sides of the mighty pillars of the memorial. They grew in volume and rose higher and higher till they seemed to touch the sky. When the massively powerful fountains reached their full height, subtle lighting came on, creating prismatic rainbows in the cascading water. There were thousands of "oohs" and "ahs." The crowd was clearly pleased with the grandeur of the memorial and this accompanying display. Standing behind the speaker's position, Alex was puzzled by the faint blue aura that Vivia seemed to give off. *It must be light reflected from the laser display*, she thought.

The chorus now took up the recessional and the Imperial party began its dignified progress back to their speeders. Andromache now accompanied Hildegard, while Alex supervised the formation of the Imperial column. They moved off at a stately pace. The crowds again parted good naturedly to let them through.

"Both you and Vivia sounded so sincere when you spoke of Deirdre, ma'am," said Andromache, settling into the cushions. "You almost had me convinced."

"Andromache, I know that in the end Deirdre despised me for what I have done. But her love for the Sisterhood was indisputable.

In that we were united. I hope that unlike Vivia, my feelings are genuine."

SEVERAL DAYS AFTER the departure of the *Darling Thoma*, Greghar and Kitara sailed out of Goset in her carrack, the *Southern Belle*. She was one of finest ships in the Baron of Tirut's fleet, big and fast with a handpicked crew. The baron's daughter-in-law was worth a lot to pirates, so she was well protected.

They were now well on their way to Tirut. Greghar always rose early and had come up on deck from his officer's cabin just before dawn. But Kitara was a late riser and was still abed in the master cabin. Greghar missed Nitya's cheery company, for they both loved to watch the sunrise from the deck.

"Sail ahoy!" sang out the crow's nest.

"Where away?" called up the officer of the watch.

"Bearing due southwest," came the answer. The officer of the watch quickly went up the ratlines to take a look for himself.

Greghar knew it would be quite a while before the sail would be visible from the deck, but he preferred not to go aloft. He noted that while the weather ahead of them southward was quite clear, there was a thick fogbank developing on their port quarter to the east.

"What do you make of her?" he asked the officer after he had returned to the deck from the masthead.

"Difficult to say," was the reply. "She is hull down. But I would bet a day's wage that she is the *Darling Thoma*."

Greghar felt his heart beat faster. He had been expecting them to overhaul the smaller, slower vessel any day now. He had rehearsed a dozen different lines he would use to address Nitya when he saw her again, each time discarding it for something new. He still continued to rack his brains for something that would make things the way they were before.

An hour passed slowly. A seaman brought Greghar a hot breakfast, and he ate mechanically. Eventually Kitara came up on deck, dressed brightly and unsuitably in a billowing gown, but with a warm shawl against the wind. She had draped the shawl loosely over her hair in her habitual affectation of modesty. The crew was made up of her father-in-law's men, so she stood beside him demurely, as she would beside any wellborn guest. However, when no one was looking, she flashed him a look at her cleavage—she was an old hand at stoking a man's desires to keep him on a string.

It was now clear beyond doubt to all the seamen that the ship they were overhauling was the *Darling Thoma*. The captain had come on deck soon after the sail was sighted and he looked keenly at the caravel, now less than a nautical mile ahead.

"These merchantmen are such poor sailors," the captain said to Greghar. "Look at how she lies athwart the wind! Her sails are flapping disgracefully. I would have my sailing master flogged if we looked like that."

"Martius is a right seaman," said Greghar slowly. "This is not like him at all. She is being sailed as though she is seriously short handed."

The captain shrugged his shoulders.

"Whatever the reason, it is no concern of ours."

Greghar went over the port rail and peered into the thickening fogbank. He returned and took the captain aside, out of earshot of the others on the quarterdeck.

"I suspect the *Darling Thoma* has been taken," he said in a low voice. "And she is being used as bait to lure us into a trap. The ship that took her must be hidden in the fogbank to port."

"Then we must steer clear of her!" said the captain.

"Keep your voice down," hissed Greghar. "We do so at our peril. If we steer to starboard, we will have little searoom to maneuver and the coastline is dotted with shoals. If we steer to port, we head toward the fogbank where our enemies are doubtless waiting. We will be caught between two hostile ships."

"What are you saying?"

"Our best chance is to pretend to take the bait," said Greghar. "Let us sail up and hail the *Darling Thoma*. But first call the ship to arms. Get a boarding party ready below and crossbowmen in the tops. Do so in stealth, so that the prize crew on the *Darling Thoma* suspects nothing. We must attack first, board, and retake her before the ship lurking in the fogbank can come up and spring the trap."

"Who are these enemies that you speak of?"

"Pirates more than likely," said Greghar, though his own suspicions lay elsewhere.

The captain nodded.

"Yes, half the fishermen of East Brosia moonlight as pirates." He beckoned a seaman and sent him to request his officers to gather in his cabin below. "We will do as you suggest. I'd rather be armed and ready than surprised and taken."

The captain and crew of the *Southern Belle* were veterans of many sea actions. The ship was readied for battle, but nothing was apparent to watchers on the *Darling Thoma*. They reduced sail as they closed, and slowed till their bow wave was no more than a ripple. Greghar peered intently as they approached, looking in vain for anyone he recognized. There were several men clustered around the helmsman and he recognized several items of clothing, but not the wearers.

"Ask for Captain Martius," whispered Greghar to the captain of the *Southern Belle*, who nodded and turned the suggestion into an order.

The *Southern Belle*'s officer of the watch used a voice trumpet when they were within hailing distance.

"Ahoy, the *Darling Thoma*!" he cried. "Our master wishes to speak with Captain Martius."

"He is not with us on this voyage," came the response.

This lie was enough for the captain and he committed the *Southern Belle* to battle.

"Hard a-port!" he roared. "Fire away from the tops! Boarding party to the rails!"

The prize crew on the *Darling Thoma* attempted to steer away, but the *Southern Belle* had a full crew and moved much more adroitly through the water. Crossbow bolts flew through the air from the tops, claiming victims on the *Darling Thoma*. Then the men of the *Southern Belle* saw a black-hulled carrack emerge from the fogbank, a death's head flag breaking out from her masthead. The sight of the enemy ship spurred them on and even before the hulls ground against each other, the *Southern Belle*'s boarding party vaulted over the rails of the *Darling Thoma*.

Greghar was over first with Karya in his hand. As their adversaries met them, he noted the death's head of the Skull Watch on their collars. He fought with speed and ferocity, hacking his way through the ranks that met them. The outnumbered prize crew was quickly overwhelmed, but several darted down below.

"Take charge of the *Darling Thoma*," Greghar shouted to the officer of the watch who had led the boarding party. "Set the sails and gather way. Put that black ship between the *Southern Belle* and us. We'll see how *they* like being caught between a hammer and an anvil."

With that he threw himself down the companionway into the bowels of the ship. His intimate knowledge of the *Darling Thoma* served him well. He rapidly overhauled two Skull Watchmen who were blundering through the dim and unfamiliar interior below decks. Without a word, he ran one through the back. As the one fell, the other turned and drew a wicked-looking greatsword from a back scabbard. Even in the dark, Greghar recognized Guttanar.

"I know you," rasped the Skull Watch captain. "You are the filthy mercenary we saw in Grenhall. I should have killed you then. But no matter—I will kill you now."

Guttanar was a good swordsman, but he was no match for Greghar. And Karya was much better suited to the confined space below deck than Guttanar's ponderous greatsword. Greghar quickly outmaneuvered him, forced him back against a bulkhead and disarmed him. He put Karya's tip to Guttanar's throat.

"Turn around," he said. Guttanar reluctantly complied and Greghar bound his wrists. "Lead me to the *Darling Thoma*'s crew."

Guttanar did not respond.

Greghar pushed Karya's tip through Guttanar's leather vest till he pricked his skin.

"I can cut off choice pieces of you, Guttanar," he said in a low tone.

Guttanar shrugged, but led the way to for'ard lockers. The hatches were secured with heavy ropes. Greghar sliced them with Karya's blade and swung them open. The survivors of the *Darling Thoma* poured out.

"Collect arms and go above," Greghar shouted to them. "We have retaken the ship, the men on deck are our allies! Our enemies wear the death's head on their collars."

The crew streamed up the companionways, but they seemed strangely subdued in their freedom. Martius came out last, carrying

Nitya. Her face was covered with dried blood, and her blouse was stained dark red.

"Is she—" Greghar's voice was strained.

"She is alive," said Martius. 'But no thanks to these brutes." He indicated Guttanar with an angry movement of his head. "They beat her mercilessly. And if you had not come when you did, this monster planned to torture her."

"I must see to the battle and make sure we are safe—" began Greghar.

"I will care of her ladyship in the captain's cabin," said Tar. The big, black form of the cook materialized at Greghar's elbow. "You do what needs to be done to see off these vermin."

BY THE TIME Greghar came on deck, the black Skull Watch carrack was beating a hasty retreat back into the fogbank. *Black Sprite* was spelled out on her stern in big brass letters. The *Southern Belle* stayed on her course parallel to the *Darling Thoma* till the Utrean ship disappeared from sight. Then she hove to and Martius brought the caravel to within a cable length of her before doing the same. Greghar had conferred with Martius and now took up a voice trumpet.

"We have freed the *Darling Thoma*'s crew," he called. "They have lost some men, but there are more than enough to sail her. We will retain your boarding party in case the pirates return, and return them to you in Tirut."

There was no immediate response from the *Southern Belle*. They could see Kitara speaking to her captain, resplendent in her bright gown and shawl. At length, they saw the captain conclude his conversation with Kitara and pick up a voice trumpet.

"Chevalina Kitara requests Lord Greghar to return to the *Southern Belle*," he called.

"My best compliments to Chevalina Kitara," called back Greghar. "But my ward, Miss Nitya, has been grievously injured. I must see to her. I will wait on the chevalina on our arrival in Tirut."

They saw Kitara and the captain confer again. Eventually, the captain threw them a salute, Kitara waved one of the ends of her bright shawl, and the two ships made sail. The larger and faster *Southern Belle* quickly forged ahead and soon left them far astern. The *Darling Thoma*'s crew had other concerns than hastening to Tirut. All of the seamen that were not directly needed topside were clustered outside the captain's cabin, talking in low voices. Tar opened the cabin door just as Greghar came down the companionway. They parted to allow him through and he caught snatches of their conversations. "*The bravest lady I've ever seen...unarmed, she faced down the brutes...couldn't squeeze the information they wanted out of her...kept getting up each time they knocked her down...when he cut her with the dagger, I swore by the One God...she's the pride of the* Darling Thoma, *our Lady Nitya...*"

"How is she?" Greghar asked.

"She is awake and asks for you, my lord," replied Tar.

This brought sighs of relief from the worried crewmen as Greghar went into the cabin. Nitya was in a hammock. Tar had lovingly propped her up on pillows and dressed her wounds. He had cleaned up her nosebleed and dressed the cuts on her neck and the bruises on her temples with *mustar* oil. She looked pale and tired, but calm.

"I am pleased to see you have come through the battle well and unhurt," she said before he could speak.

"Nitya, I...I am so very sorry," he said, all his prepared speeches forgotten. His obvious distress rekindled her love for him. She took his hand and his look of gratitude extinguished the last of her anger.

"We are together again," she said, smiling. "You saved my virtue and probably my life."

"You have saved me time and again," he said. "Why did you not incinerate the swine?"

"I have sinned enough," she said, gentling her tone to take out the sting. "I did as you once advised me and thought of my father."

"What did they want?"

"What do you think? They are Shobar's men. They wanted me to bring Vasitha to them."

"What can they do to him? He is immortal."

"Immortality is not just a negation of mortality," she said vaguely.

She was tiring, so Greghar did not press the point. He leaned over her and kissed her forehead.

"Rest," he said, rising. "The fates have put that vicious thug Guttanar in my hands."

GUTTANAR AND THREE other surviving Skull Watchmen from the prize crew were on the waist of the *Darling Thoma*, arms trussed behind their backs. They were hemmed in by every off duty seaman, all muttering dangerously. Two officers held them in check or else they would have torn the Skull Watchmen limb from limb.

As Martius and Greghar came up and they parted to let them through. The captain raised his hand and the crew subsided into silence.

"You have attacked and taken my ship," he said. "And we are not at war. That makes you pirates. By the laws of the sea, it is my right to string you all up from the yardarm. And normally I would have done just that."

He paused and the hands began remonstrating.

"That's too good for them, sir!"

"Give them to us, we'll know what to do!"

"We'll give them what they gave Lady Nitya!"

The captain let them go on for a while, relishing the fear in the eyes of the Skull Watchmen. Only Guttanar stood with his chin jutting out, as if daring them to do their worst.

"You see how lucky you are that I do not give you to my men," said Martius at length. "By I agree with them, hanging is too good for you. So I'm going to keelhaul you first. Once you are well pickled in brine, I'll hang you."

"You may do what you like with three of these men," said Greghar as soon as Martius finished. "But I have a score to settle with that one." He pointed to Guttanar.

"It is your victory," said Martius, with a slight bow. "He is yours."

Greghar came forward till he was just a pace from Guttanar. The Skull Watch captain was broader, but Greghar stood a good half a head taller.

"You like beating women don't you, Guttanar? In Grenhall, you needed to bind your victim before you beat her. Now you have savaged and cut young Nitya, a mere slip of a girl. Such courage!" He paused and looked around at the seamen who were muttering angrily again.

"Well, I don't need you bound. I will give you the opportunity to defend yourself." He drew Karya, and with two perfect cuts, sliced Guttanar's bonds. The Skull Watch captain swung his arms to get the circulation going again.

"Bare hands against your sword," he said. "I will fight you even so."

Greghar sheathed his sword, unbuckled his sword belt, and threw it to Martius. He closed on Guttanar without another word. The hands rapidly formed a tight circle around them.

"No on touches him but me," Greghar called out.

Guttanar looked arrogant as he put up his hands and took his guard.

"Your men will doubtless kill me in the end, but it will be a pleasure to thrash you," said Guttanar.

He had barely gotten the words out of his mouth when Greghar's foot lashed out. The steel toe of his boot struck Guttanar in the crotch. As he doubled over, Greghar hit the back of his head with double-handed hammer blow. Guttanar fell to the deck. Greghar picked him up by the collar of his leather vest and hit him as hard as he could in the face. Fierce satisfaction flowed through him as he felt bones in Guttanar's face break under his fist. He released him and Guttanar collapsed again on the deck. Greghar now straddled his chest and began to pound his head and face, urged on by the seamen, who loudly began counting his blows.

"Stop! Stop immediately!" The commands were so sharp that Greghar instinctively ceased and looked around. Nitya leaned on Tar, and she was livid.

"Are you as much a brute as him?" she demanded. "I thought that we were civilized folk, that we were better than them. But it seems that there is nothing to choose between us—that the only difference is who is stronger on the day."

She scanned the seamen.

"And look at all of you, urging him on," she cried. "You are like brothers, like fathers to me. But now you make me ashamed."

The men shrank back before her rage and formed a wide semicircle. They hung their heads and would not meet her eyes. At length, Martius came up to her.

"What would you have us do, Miss Nitya?" he asked.

"Surely you can spare an open boat," she said. "I will buy you a replacement in Tirut. Let us give them some provisions and oars and set them adrift."

Guttanar was unconscious, but the other three Skull Watchmen looked at Nitya eagerly, their eyes lighting up with hope.

"I don't know, Miss Nitya," said Martius, scratching his beard. "By the laws of the sea they have committed piracy and should be hung."

"You are captain," replied Nitya. "The law on the *Darling Thoma* is your word. Remember, most of those that boarded us are dead already."

"What say you, Greghar?" asked Martius.

Greghar got to his feet, leaving the motionless Guttanar lying on the deck.

"If Nitya wishes them freed," he said. "I have no objection."

Nitya insisted on remaining on deck till the four Skull Watchmen were lowered to sea in an open boat. Guttanar had still not regained consciousness and was lowered into the boat in a harness. Only then did she consent to Tar helping her down to the captain's cabin again. Greghar followed them down. When Tar withdrew, Nitya finally sank back into the pillows and showed her fatigue.

"You push yourself too hard," said Greghar. "I don't know how you can endure so much physical abuse."

"I am a Yengar. I've had a lot of practice."

She took his hands in hers. They were raw and his knuckles were split from beating Guttanar. He looked at her bruises and cuts and sighed.

"You should have let me beat Guttanar to death," he said. "I swore to myself that I would get him for what he did to Princess Caitlin. And now to you."

"Hatred and anger are corrosive," she said, beginning to feel light-headed. "They damage you, not their object. My father always said that the most powerful are those who can master their emotions, not those who are slaves to them."

"So you let Guttanar and his thugs beat you. And now they are laughing at us."

"I knew you would rescue me," she said, yawning. "And I don't think they will be laughing for long. The Chekaligas are on the war-path and they control this coast."

She fell asleep before he could respond.

EIGHT

THE ROAD TO TIRUT

MEGARA TRIED INCESSANTLY to open comm channels to Asgara but found herself mysteriously sidetracked much of the time. She suspected that Andromache was putting obstacles in her way, but she had no proof. Eventually, she grew frustrated enough to apply for a permit for Asgara and Iantha to visit her on holiday. When Megara managed to reach Asgara and convey this information, it sent her into a fever of happiness and anticipation. She knew these things took time, but she still could not control her impatience. She secretly hoped to be on her way to see Megara within a day or two.

A week passed without any change. She tried to get one of the caregivers to open a comm channel to Megara for her, but they always seemed to find excuses not to do so. She wondered why Megara did not open a channel to her and began to worry that something had happened to her. *Maybe she is sick or injured,* she thought. She scolded herself for thinking such things, superstitiously uneasy that her thoughts might bring them to pass.

When ten days had gone by, she could not bear to wait any longer. She waited up till Andromache came home and tiptoed to her great study. It was late and past her bedtime, so Andromache looked surprised when she saw her. However, she smiled a welcome.

"I'm so happy to see you, my dear," she said, tapping closed the hologram she was working on. She stood up. "What is keeping you up? Did you have a bad dream? Come, I'll tuck you in. Perhaps we can cuddle together for a while."

"I am worried about my mother," said Asgara as Andromache took her hand and began walking back to the nursery of Palace Saxe. "She said she would apply for a holiday permit for Iantha and me to visit her. That was over a week ago, and I have heard nothing since then."

"Oh that," she said, stroking Asgara's curls. "Yes, she applied. It was turned down, and her appeal was turned down as well. The huntresses don't appreciate how important it is to keep our children away from danger."

They reached the nursery. Andromache tucked her in and lay down on the bed beside her.

"What danger is there?" asked Asgara. "We were taught that Daksin has been peaceful for over a century. What harm could come of our visiting our mother for a couple of weeks?"

"Things have changed, darling," said Andromache. "There is unrest down there now. That is why several of our best military personnel—officers like Seignora Megara—are down there. But Seignora Megara is young and impulsive. Blinded by her own desires, she would expose you to risk. I am pleased that it has all turned out for the best and you will be remain safe and sound in Atlantic City."

"How do you know all about my mother's application?"

"I am your local guardian, sweetheart."

"I see," said Asgara. She smiled at Andromache and closed her eyes. Andromache lay with her for a few more minutes, until she thought she had fallen asleep. Then she got up and went back to work in her study.

Asgara cracked her eyelids open just a fraction to watch her leave. She waited patiently for over half an hour. Then she silently rose from the bed, dressed herself and packed methodically. She cinched the shoulder straps to make sure her pack was comfortably on her back. She opened her viewport and climbed out. The nursery was on the ground floor, so she was able to drop into the garden without difficulty. She walked around the palace, keeping in the shadows. She knew where the security cams were, so she was able to avoid them.

Asgara made her way to the front portico of the palace. She knew that Andromache's handmaiden would be going home about now. She was pleased to see that the speeder the handmaiden used to ferry her to and from Temple Heights Nursery was parked in the portico. She planned out a path that would take her to the speeder without exposing her to the security cams. Then she cautiously crept forward and perched herself on speeder's far side running board.

A few minutes later, Andromache's handmaiden came out of the front portal of the palace. Asgara heard her call "Good-night," to someone and get into the driver's seat. Asgara tightened her hold on the door handles as the speeder moved off. It stopped to allow the outer gates of the palace grounds to open and then moved off again. As soon as it emerged outside the gates, Asgara jumped off into the grass, careful to avoid the outer security cams.

She waited for the taillights of the speeder to fade away in the distance. Then she began to walk purposefully for Atlantic City airfield.

She had gathered a great deal of information from the caregivers about its location and protocols. She was sure she could get to the airfield before first light.

It was still dark when she got to the airfield. It was in peacetime mode, but the perimeter fence was four meters high, topped with coils of electrified razor wire, and there were still huntresses on duty at the open gates. Asgara crawled up the dry drainage ditch by the approach road and waited very close to the gates.

It had been a very long walk for her young legs, and she was exhausted. Lying in the soft grass, she fought to keep her heavy lids open. Finally, just as the eastern sky began to show signs of light, she heard a speeder approach from inside the airfield. It drove up to the gates and stopped. From the information she had gathered, Asgara knew this was the changing of the guard detail. She peeked over top of the ditch and saw that the speeder was only a few meters away from her. The two guard details were chatting on the far side of the speeder from her. She crept up and got on the running board of the speeder as she had done before.

At length the speeder began to move. It made a U-turn and headed back into the airfield. Asgara saw they were passing the airfield hangars, heading for the duty barracks. Afraid that she would be carried all the way there and be seen, she tensed herself and let go, curling into a ball as she did so. She fell on the smooth grass, but the speeder was moving very fast, so she still severely scraped her elbows and knees before she came to a stop. The pain was very sharp. Safely out of earshot of the rapidly disappearing speeder, she allowed herself to lie in the grass and cry.

Finally, wiping her eyes, she picked herself up and hurried toward the hangars, staying low. The cavernous chambers were open, but their interiors were dark and forbidding. The dozens of airboats parked in serried rows looked like dormant monsters. She found a large, open trash bin full of metal scrap and climbed into it. It was hard and uncomfortable, but she was so tired that she fell asleep almost instantly.

When she awoke, she was confused for a moment before she remembered where she was. The scrapes on her knees and elbows were covered with dried and caked blood. The pain was dull and throbbing, and tears ran down her cheeks as she gritted her teeth to keep silent.

Outside it was bright daylight, but she had no idea what time it was. The hangar was full of noise, with the clanging of machinery and the sound of loud voices. She peered cautiously over the rim of the bin. No one was looking her way. There was a meter or so of clearance between the bin and the hangar wall. She quickly climbed out and secreted herself in this space.

She wiped the tears off her cheeks as she waited, not realizing that she was streaking dirt and oil from the metal scrap all over her face. Time seemed to pass very slowly and she was beginning to get hungry. She was on the verge of giving up hope of finding transport to the Daksin Residency. Then two mechanicae stopped on the far side of the trash bin. She pricked up her ears.

"Just finished work on the K-1784," said one. "She's all set."

"About time," said the other. "Cornelle Diana is coming by this afternoon to pick her up. She had better be battle ready."

"Where is she headed?"

"She's filed a flight plan for the Tirut Guild fort and then on to the Daksin Residency—"

They strolled off. Asgara waited till their voices died away before stealing a look around the trash bin. The airboat parked twenty meters away had "K-1784" painted on her hull in big black letters.

The rear hatch yawned open. Asgara did not hesitate. Standing very erect to appear taller, she sauntered over and clambered into the airboat. Inside, the metal deck was set with seating and the cargo hatch leading down into the hold was open. She climbed down the ladder into the hold and settled herself against the hard steel bulkhead, concealed behind some crates. Eventually, her tiredness overcame her discomfort, and she fell asleep again.

SERAT OASIS WAS built in a slight depression and had very poor defensive features. The reason for its location was the large spring-fed oasis from which it took its name, the only significant source of water for hundreds of kilometers. Caitlin, Binne, and Dhanraj rode through the gates along with many others: riders, cart traffic, and travelers afoot. Once through the gate, they dismounted and led their horses. Binne touched the arm of one of the guards at the gate and asked for directions to Collector Yandharan's house. The guard looked them up and down and found them acceptable before replying.

"The gates of his residence will be closed," he said. "They will not admit you unless you know the password."

Nothing in Caitlin's experience had prepared her for Serat, a town of over a hundred thousand residents. This immense population was crowded into a space only slightly larger than the Atlantic City neighborhood of Temple Heights, whose residents numbered a few hundred. Inside the walls there were no avenues or boulevards and no open space of any kind, just dark, winding streets and narrow alleys. Mud-brick hovels, many with two stories, were crowded together, their upper levels leaning forward precariously, blocking out almost all light. The drains were open and filthy and everywhere there were large piles of festering refuse. Mangy curs sat in piles of trash, growling and snapping at ragged children who searched for scraps. The stench was incredibly strong—Caitlin had to fight hard to keep from retching, and even Binne and Dhanraj were repulsed.

"Every time I come to Serat, I bless our life in the country," said Binne.

They proceeded down the broadest of streets, just wide enough for them to walk their horses. Beggars were everywhere, many horribly disfigured or mutilated. Ragged urchins followed them, pleading for alms. The few women they saw were heavily veiled. In deference to Thermadan norms, Binne had donned a long cloak with a scarf over her head and had gotten Caitlin to do the same. Even so, Caitlin knew she was the focus of hundreds of staring eyes. She wished she had a squad of huntresses at her back. Men sidled up as they passed and reached into her cloak, attempting to touch her intimately. No sooner had she brushed off one attempt than there was another one, each bolder than the last. Finally, she drew her long dagger and pricked a prying hand, drawing blood, a cry of pain, and a curse. After that, they kept their distance. Even the urchins hung back and ceased their entreaties. Stopping twice more to ask for directions, they reached the gates of Yandharan's house without further incident.

This was a slightly better area of the town and while there were just as many piles of rubbish scattered about in the street, the houses were of better quality. Yandharan's residence stood out from its neighbors in that it was built of dark granite rather than mud-brick. It stood tall and straight, the ten-meter high façade supported by impressive columns. There were two five-meter-high doors of dark wood set in the stone, and one of them bore an immense brass knocker. It was difficult to get a full measure of the residence in the narrow alley, hemmed in on all sides by other structures. But it was clearly more of a palace than a house.

Binne stood on tiptoe, raised the knocker, and struck it several times. There was a pause before a voice called out from within, "Password?"

"I don't know the password, but we must see Collector Yandharan," said Binne.

"Go away, woman," came the voice from within. "Unless you know the password, you must go to the Collectorate and seek an appointment there."

"But—" began Binne. Caitlin put a hand on her shoulder and spoke in her stead.

"Tell Collector Yandharan that Cat Avedus is here to see him. If you don't, you will pay dearly, I promise you."

"Wait," came the voice from within, clearly irritated.

They did not have to wait long. Barely a few minutes later one of the massive doors swung open. Yandharan stood there in his collector's uniform, flanked by two armed men who also wore bronze badges on their leather vests. A couple of liveried servants stood behind them. He came forward, sweeping off his broad-brimmed hat, causing his deputies to follow his example.

"Welcome, welcome," he said, his voice betraying his enthusiasm. "I am pleased to see you. Come in, come in, you look like you have had a long, hard ride. You must be very tired. My servants will take your horses. Would you like to clean up before I offer you some refreshment?"

"Before we do anything else, we must give you warning," said Binne. "The Chekaligas are on the warpath again. They have killed my husband, Seamus." She paused and caught her breath as a sob forced its way up. "He told us as he lay dying that there are more of them than ever before, all their tribes massed together. It is war this time, not just raiding. You must prepare yourselves and rouse the king's soldiers from their border forts."

"I am sorry to hear about your husband," Yandharan said. "He was a good man, tough and dependable. A true son of the Southern Marches."

He sighed and Binne sniffed. Caitlin felt a pain in her gut as the words conjured up the vision of Seamus dying in her arms, saying *Go daughter, live for me.*

"Every year we beat them back," Yandharan continued. "And they always return the following year. They have never attacked a town the size of Serat, but there is no point in taking chances." He beckoned to one of his deputies. "Nambian, alert all the town gates and double the watches on each one of them. Make sure they are prepared to close them and secure the town as soon as they see any suspicious movements."

Nambian saluted and left.

"Now follow me," said Yandharan. "Let me offer you the hospitality of my house."

He turned and led them in, still beaming. The scene inside was in stark contrast to the filth and poverty outside. The doors opened into a spacious inner courtyard with a bubbling fountain and some date palms. There was an inner verandah that ran around the courtyard on all sides, and stately stone columns supported a second story. Yandharan led them across the courtyard and through a long corridor with flagstone floors. Eventually they emerged into an interior, smaller courtyard, and he led the way into a suite of spotlessly clean rooms with dark, heavy furniture.

"You may use this suite for as long as you like," he said. "There is water in the bathroom. Please let me know what else I can do to make you comfortable."

"We are quite overwhelmed, Collector Yandharan," said Binne.

"I will return in a little while," he replied, smiling. "As soon as you have cleaned up, we will sit down to a meal."

They looked at each other for a few moments after he left.

"We owe this warm welcome to you, Cat," said Binne, putting her arm around her waist. "Whether you like it or not."

They washed off the grime of the road and stretched themselves out on the comfortable beds. They were all tired and an hour passed very quickly. They were on the point of nodding off when Yandharan returned.

"Will you take some refreshment now?" he asked solicitously.

The mention of food made them aware that they were quite hungry. In their hasty departure from the ranch, Binne had packed as much food as she could. But it was a long ride to Serat and they had eaten sparingly to make their supplies last. Yandharan led them along another corridor, and they found themselves in a high, vaulted dining room with grander furniture and fittings. It was well lit with a large window looking out onto yet another interior courtyard. The long dining table was laid for five with silver and crystal settings.

An attractive woman stood by the table, dressed in a flowing, high-necked gown. Her hair was completely covered in a beautiful mihr-silk scarf. She was small, no taller than Binne, with large, liquid brown eyes, but at the moment there was no warmth in them. She looked at them from under lowered lashes. Two small children, a boy and a girl, peered at them from behind her skirts.

"May I present my wife, Mistress Zaibene," he said formally. "And my children." Zaibene nodded curtly, but the children remained hiding behind their mother.

Binne curtsied and Dhanraj bowed deeply, but Caitlin was nonplussed as to how to respond. Her instinct was to give Zaibene the incline of the head that Zon officials accorded barbarian gentry. However, she was in exile from the Sisterhood and had no official status, so this did not seem appropriate. In the end, she returned Zaibene's nod with one of her own. Zaibene's eyes grew hot with anger at this presumption.

Yandharan observed all this and spoke quickly in an attempt to smooth things over.

"Mistress Zaibene is a va Alsor of Tirut," he said. "Her great-grandfather was Baron of Tirut and her grandfather was a Cheval. She did me great honor by accepting my suit." He went to her side and put an arm around her shoulders. "We are both pleased to offer you the hospitality of our abode."

"My dear," he continued, smiling down at his wife. "I have spoken to you of these folk. This is Binne Avedus of Hareskot, her adopted daughter, Cat, and Dhanraj, her ward."

"Collector Yandharan has told me of you," said Zaibene, addressing Caitlin and ignoring the other two. "I understand that you have no property, family, or connections, but that you have a way with horses. And with men."

Yandharan looked embarrassed at his wife's show of bad manners.

"Let us sit down to eat," he said quickly, to head off what he feared would be a sharp retort from Caitlin. "My dear, let us seat ourselves, so the others may know where to sit."

Zaibene looked toward a doorway and an unseen nurse hurried out to take the children. Yandharan seated himself at the head of the table and Zaibene sat at his right, looking none too pleased. He motioned to Caitlin to sit at his left, with Dhanraj beside her. Binne seated herself by Zaibene, looking at her nervously. Zaibene rang a silver bell, summoning the steward. He oversaw a crew of servants bearing heaping platters of food as well as wine in ice-filled buckets and numerous carafes of other drinks. They went around the table serving each of those seated and then placing everything on a massive sideboard. The steward remained by the sideboard, ready to replenish anything.

Both Binne and Dhanraj were ill at ease, never having been served before, but Caitlin was very relaxed. She made eye contact with the staff and murmured thanks in a manner that gave them consequence. Zaibene only acknowledged their presence to snap at them if they did not meet her expectations. They approached her with obvious trepidation and flinched when they felt the lash of her sharp tongue.

Conversation during the meal was stilted. Caitlin responded to Yandharan's polite questions about the ride from Hareskot as briefly as possible. Binne spoke of the weather, and Dhanraj ate the sumptuous repast with single-minded determination. The meal culminated in a rich dessert made from dates served with a sweet Mussadec wine from the mountain range of that name, which abutted Tirut. The dessert was much too sweet for Caitlin's taste, and the wine was too cloying, but Binne and Dhanraj were warm in their appreciation.

No sooner had Binne put down her dessert spoon than Zaibene stood up, prompting the others to follow suit.

"Let us adjourn to the audience chamber to discuss what has really brought you here," she said.

Yandharan rose after her and took her arm to lead the way down another corridor. The audience chamber had a high-backed chair, flanked by a normal chair, facing numerous chairs set at a lower level.

Binne and Dhanraj looked around with awe. Yandharan seated himself in the high-backed chair, looking self-conscious. Zaibene took the chair by his side and waved them to the lower chairs. As soon as they were all seated, Zaibene addressed Caitlin.

"Collector Yandharan has told me of his offer to you. As you know, among the nobility—and even among many propertied commoners—it is customary for the first wife to decide on the suitability of any subsequent wives." She paused. "I see you have brought your foster mother here to formalize the engagement."

Caitlin opened her mouth, but before she could respond, Zaibene turned to Binne and continued.

"I will not mince words. Your adopted daughter has used her wiles to bewitch Collector Yandharan." She waved Binne to silence and went on. "She is a trollop trying to gain wealth and consequence by connecting herself to my husband and through him to my noble family. Doubtless, you are encouraging her. Well, I am mistress of this house, and I will never allow this to happen!"

Binne grew angrier and angrier as Zaibene spoke. She flushed and lost all her diffidence. Caitlin saw her look and put a restraining hand on her arm. Secure in her sense of Zon superiority, she had to struggle to keep from laughing. She did not entirely succeed and a faint smile played on her face.

"Collector Yandharan," she said. "Your wife and I are of like mind, it seems. My company does not please her, and I am sure that I could not be happy in hers."

Yandharan looked at Zaibene reproachfully.

"My dear, you promised you would approach this audience with an open mind."

"I have!" she snapped. She made a motion indicating Caitlin from head to toe. "Just look at her! Dressed in tight leathers, displaying her body to entice and ensnare. Take your pleasure of her in a bawdy house, sir, but do not ask to bring her into this respectable house."

Binne stood up and addressed Yandharan.

"We came here to bring you warning of the Chekaliga rampage, not to be insulted. We have no wish to discuss your proposal to Cat."

Zaibene raised her eyebrows, but it was Yandharan who responded, his expression awkward, but kindly.

"I am sorry if we have misconstrued your intentions. Please forgive me; obviously my hopes overcame my judgment. However, you are always welcome in our house—my wife takes all my friends to her bosom, as I take hers."

Zaibene forced a smile and did not contradict him. Binne's expression did not soften.

Even as Yandharan spoke, there was a thunder of boots and his two deputies rushed into the dining room.

"A thousand pardons, Collector," said his deputy Nambian. "But you must come immediately. We are under heavy attack by Chekaliga tribesmen. We have never seen anything like it—there are thousands of them! They sent in scouts mingled with the refugees and killed the guards at the Desert Gate. They are streaming in through the open gate and will soon be running wild in the west end of town."

"Why wasn't the Desert Gate on alert?"

"It was, sir," said Nambian. "But the watch was looking outward. They did not expect to be assaulted from within the town."

Yandharan did not waste time with further unnecessary talk.

"Digaran," he said to his other deputy. "Form an escort from my personal guards and get my wife and children out of town by the Tirut Gate." He turned to Zaibene. "My dear, you must leave this instant. Choose some of our staff to wait on you on the road. Take men, for most of them can wield a sword in a pinch. Go to Tirut;

you can take refuge in our house there. Tell the baron that Serat is under heavy attack and may fall. Perhaps this will rouse him to send us some troops—after all, Serat is his son's fief."

Zaibene turned and left the room without a word followed by Digaran.

No hug or kiss, not even a wish of good luck, thought Binne. *Does she care so little for him?* However, Yandharan did not seem to notice. He turned to Caitlin, Binne and Dhanraj.

"I am grateful for your attempt to warn us of the danger. I regret that I am unable to show you the full measure of my regard. I can offer you passage to Tirut in my wife's caravan. I recommend that you leave Serat with her. It is not safe here."

"What will you do?" asked Binne.

"Serat is the fief of Cheval Jagus va Alsor, the baron's younger son. I serve Cheval Jagus, but he is rarely here, so I am responsible for the people of Serat. I must stay and fight."

"The Chekaligas have taken my trueborn daughter and my husband from me," said Binne. "I would rather stay and exact some measure of redress, however slight."

"I urge you to accept my offer, madam," said Yandharan to Binne, attempting to control his impatience. "I cannot spare men to watch over you."

She opened her mouth to respond but then closed it. She came over to Caitlin and gave her a quick kiss.

"Will you come with me, my dear?" she asked. When Caitlin shook her head, she did not argue, but looked over at Dhanraj enquiringly.

"If Cat remains here, I will stay and fight," said Dhanraj.

Binne took her cloak and scarf and left by the door through which Zaibene had departed.

"It seems we are destined to be together for now," said Caitlin to Yandharan. "In battle, if nowhere else."

Yandharan turned to Nambian.

"Nambian, send out heralds to call all able-bodied men to the Collectorate to get weapons. Take this Hareskot lad with you—he will help you distribute the arms. Form as many armed units as you can. Put one of our men-at-arms in charge of each one. Send these units to stem the Chekaliga advance." He paused. "And ask the heralds to call on women, children, and the infirm to escape by the Tirut Gate."

He turned to Caitlin.

"Come with me, since you have chosen to stay," he said, clearly impatient to take charge of the battle. Caitlin patted Dhanraj on the back and followed Yandharan out of the dining room.

THERE WAS A troop of men-at-arms waiting for Yandharan in the outer courtyard of his residence. They formed a cordon around him and Caitlin as they emerged into the street and began making their way to the west of town. There was screaming everywhere and people rushed about wildly, many carrying their prized possessions. Caitlin recognized a beggar that she had seen on crutches on the way in, now miraculously running at full speed. They passed several fires, and more fire arrows arced over their heads. Yandharan's men-at-arms cleared the way through the alleys, and they made their way rapidly into the area of town where the confused battle raged.

They came across several bodies, some with arrows sticking out of them, but most bearing the marks of swords or daggers. They all drew their weapons. The distinctive war cries of the Chekaligas grew louder. One by one, the men-at-arms slowed and allowed Yandharan to pass them until he had taken the lead. Caitlin held her position on Yandharan's right shoulder. Their tension mounted with every step.

They turned a corner and blundered straight into a troop of Chekaligas. The alley was so narrow that two could not walk abreast. The lead warrior slashed at Yandharan, but the Collector parried and lunged, his blade easily penetrating his opponent's leather and thin chainmail. As Yandharan was extricating his sword, the second warrior stepped around his comrade, hacking down with his scimitar. A mere centimeter from Yandharan's neck, the Chekaliga's blade clanged on Zon steel. Yandharan felt Caitlin's shoulder pad against his own as she stepped up, deflected the Chekaliga's sword, and ran him through.

Even as she freed Nasht's blade from the dying Chekaliga warrior, Yandharan dragged her down with him to the muddy ground of the alley. His men-at-arms had lined up their loaded crossbows and fired as soon as they had clear shots. Yandharan and Caitlin felt rather than saw the bolts whistle over their heads, and the remaining Chekaligas went down.

Yandharan helped Caitlin regain her feet, giving her forearm a squeeze of appreciation as he did so. He continued forward, stepping over the Chekaligas' bodies. They did not seek further fighting but ducked into houses every time they heard Chekaliga shouts or war cries. The third time they did so, Yandharan led the way up a rickety ladder to the upper story and then on to the flat roof. Lying on their stomachs, they surveyed the west end of Serat.

The Desert Gate was wide open, and everywhere there were screams of terror. There were hundreds of Chekaliga tribesmen on the walls and in the streets and alleys. There was little evidence of any organized resistance. Yandharan shook his head.

"I cannot understand it," he said. "As far back as anyone can remember, the Chekaliga tribes fought each other ferociously. Disunited, they have never had the numbers to threaten a city the size of Serat. What can have united the tribes against us like this?"

He scanned the western district, looking for some line along which he could set up a defensive perimeter. But the Chekaliga tribesmen were moving too quickly.

"This is hopeless. We only had a hundred or so men-at-arms to begin with and we are heavily outnumbered. We must delay them as long as we can to give our people time to escape. And we must get a warning to Tirut and to the king in Dreslin Center."

They descended back down into the dark house again.

"There is no time to waste," he said to his men-at-arms. "We will split up and head back toward the east end of town. Gather any of our people you see on the way. We will meet at the Tirut Gate. Set more fires; it will delay these scum."

When they emerged from the house, Caitlin stayed close to Yandharan, for she could not have found her way to the Tirut Gate through the maze of narrow alleys. He picked up a smoldering stake and led the way unerringly. He touched the stake to every thatched roof that they passed, starting a line of fires.

As the fires began to spread rapidly, the sounds of the war cries grew fainter behind them. Finally, they emerged from an alley into a small square that opened onto the main oasis. It was fairly large body of water, perhaps a hundred meters across, surrounded by a belt of sand and a few sickly date palms. It appeared to be quite deep, but it also smelled bad and had gray scum floating on the surface. Caitlin could not imagine how it did not sicken everyone who drank from it.

With a glance at Caitlin to make sure she was following him, he continued on through more twisting back alleys. Finally, they emerged into the small, dusty plaza that opened on to the Tirut Gate. Deputy Nambian was already there with thirty men-at-arms and about a hundred civilians. They had created a barricade out of debris and were crouched behind it, pointing crossbows toward the town.

A steady trickle of Serat inhabitants filtered through the barricade, heeding Yandharan's heralds and making their escape out of town. All carried bundles; some drove heavily laden horses and donkeys.

"Digaran has already led Mistress Zaibene's party away," said Nambian as Yandharan and Caitlin joined them. "As you can see, the people are heeding our heralds and fleeing. What are your orders now?"

"Our duty is to protect our people," said Yandharan. "We must defend Tirut Gate and maintain the safety of this escape route. We will hold this position for as long as possible."

Nambian, his men-at-arms, and the civilian volunteers looked dubious, but they did not contradict him. They settled into a depressing wait. The stream of refugees continued unabated. Some had just arrived in Serat from farther west. Many were injured and some were burned. Sometimes the fleeing crowds grew so thick that the men-at-arms had to step in to minimize the pushing and shoving. In between, there were periods of calm. At each lull, Nambian approached Yandharan and suggested retreat. Each time he was told to be patient.

When the attack came it was sudden, with no precursor war cries or drums. The only thing that saved them from being immediately overwhelmed was that the narrow alleys limited the number of warriors that could enter the plaza at one time. Nonetheless, the civilians pressed into service were no match for the hardened Chekaliga warriors and quickly began to be slaughtered. Yandharan fired and reloaded his crossbow with unthinking regularity. With the mass of Chekaliga warriors, he had no difficulty in finding targets. He exhorted his men as he fought. Nambian fought with grim determination, hacking with his sword.

Caitlin stayed low behind the makeshift barricade and out of sight of the onrushing tide, slashing or thrusting at each body that came over. She was soon covered with the blood of her victims. She found that the dead and dying bodies themselves began to form a protective barrier around her. Leaning against them, she looked as though she was mortally wounded herself, so fresh attackers ignored her till it was too late. The smells of close combat filled her nostrils— blood, sweat, and the more noxious bodily fluids. She had to numb herself against the sheer horror of what she was doing and lost track of time. She fell into an almost mechanical rhythm, wielding Nasht like she was in the training ring, feeling neither fear nor pain. She felt a hand touch her shoulder and whirled, drawing her long dagger with her left hand, before she saw the bronze badge and recognized Nambian.

"You must tell Yandharan to withdraw!" he cried. "He will listen to you! This is a hopeless and useless fight. There are no more—"

He stopped and coughed, his eyes bugging out. Out of the corner of her eye, Caitlin saw the Chekaliga warrior whose sword now ran with Nambian's blood. With pure reactive instinct, she sank her long dagger into the warrior's side. As she brought her sword to bear, the warrior gasped, "Don't kill me—please..."

She saw that he was barely more than a boy and hesitated. But the sight of Nambian's blood on his blade hardened her and she ran him through. As she did so, she noticed that he had a finely wrought gold chain braided into his hair. He had another warrior by his side, but he was unmoving, staring at what Caitlin had done with a horror-filled expression. As she pulled Nasht out and turned to face him, he disappeared.

Now there was a break in the action and she was able to survey the carnage around her. She could not believe how many bodies there were. Pitifully few of the Serat men were left alive. She was exhausted and could barely lift her sword arm. *The next charge must finish us*, she thought. *But I am the daughter of Deirdre d'Orr, named for my ancestor Caitlin the Unforgiving, the descendant of Simran the Merciless. I will fight till the end.*

She girded herself to face death, but she did not want to die alone. So she crawled through the bodies, hoping to find Yandharan or Dhanraj, even though the prospect of finding either of them gave her little comfort. For the only person in her thoughts was Greghar—and the realization that she would never see him again filled her with a deep sadness.

Yandharan was at the apex of the barricade, with half a dozen men-at-arms and a dozen dazed civilians. He looked gaunt and tired. He saw her, and a mixture of dismay and worry flooded into his eyes.

"Thermad's breath!" he cried. "How badly are you wounded? I did not want you to risk yourself—"

She looked down at herself and realized what a gory sight she was. She also knew that apart from a few nicks and scrapes, the blood was not hers.

"I am tired," she said. "But not injured. I have been luckier than most."

His relief was profound and he smiled, displaying his even teeth.

"The One God be praised," he said, spontaneously putting a hand on her shoulder pad. Then recalling his promise not to touch her without her permission, he withdrew it awkwardly. Just as he did so, a gravely wounded Chekaliga warrior raised himself from the ground behind her back and staggered to his feet. He raised his sword and aimed a thrust between her shoulder blades. Yandharan cursed and began to reload his crossbow, and Caitlin began to turn, trying to bring Nasht to bear as she did so. But they were both far too late and the Chekaliga drove his sword forward, striving to end one more life before his own was ended. She braced herself for the bite of the sword, but instead she heard a heavy thud as it struck a shield. One of Yandharan's men-at-arms had interposed himself between the Chekaliga and Caitlin. Once he had deflected the warrior's thrust with his shield, he ran him through and twisted his sword to make sure he was dead.

Caitlin breathed a sigh of relief, but Yandharan was much more demonstrative in his response. He came around her and clapped the man on the shoulder.

"Well done, man!" he cried. "Well done indeed! What is your name?"

"Rator," said the man-at-arms, bowing. "Rator of Karsk."

"Ah, I remember you now, Rator," said Yandharan. "You served with the Hilsons in the Zon Wars. I see that they trained you well. I will see that you are well rewarded when we get to Tirut."

"I ask no special reward for doing my duty, Collector," said Rator. He turned to Caitlin. "However, I hope that this small service will allow me the privilege of asking Your Highness a question. Your face is very familiar. Perhaps you have been a visitor to my hometown of Karsk?"

"I owe you my life, sir, and I hope I am able to repay the debt some day," said Caitlin, trying to evade the question. "But please do not address me with titles, for I am your comrade in arms, nothing more."

"The only repayment I ask is a response to my question," persisted Rator.

Caitlin had been to Karsk once, as a fresh graduate just out of the Academy. It had been a short but memorable mission led by Diana to collect the annual tribute. The visit was filled with formal ceremonies and balls as well as the politicking and subterfuge that the Hilsons always used as they tried to avoid paying the tribute in full. Caitlin recalled vividly that one of the cousins of the Duke of Hilson was sent to bargain over the payment and that instead of parlaying, Diana drew her sword Light and cut him down with one swift stroke. The tribute was paid in full within the hour.

She peered into the grimy face of this man-at-arms from Karsk, his features shadowed by the peak of his helmet. His accent was not that of a simple soldier—could he be a Karsk courtier? She had been introduced to dozens of nobles in that short visit, whereas there were only two squads of Zon huntresses on the mission. Though she concentrated hard, his shadowy features did not trigger a memory.

"I have had a nomadic life," she said vaguely. The fact that he had just saved her made her uncomfortable about lying to him. She was sure he would see right through her. "I think I may have been in Karsk a long time ago. But it was only for a few days."

"I had the pleasure of beholding Your Highness during that visit," said Rator, his steady gaze searching her face. "Forgive my boldness, but no man who saw your beauty could easily forget it."

The color drained from Caitlin's face.

"I am sure you are mistaking me for someone else," she said. "Where I come from, my looks are quite common."

"And where might that be, Your Highness?"

Yandharan listened to the exchange with pursed lips, but now he cut Rator off, turning to the surviving defenders.

"Every minute we hold them allows our people to get farther away," he said. "But there is nothing more we can do now. The next rush will be the end of us."

He raised his sword.

"We leave now, before the next attack!" he called. "We march for Tirut."

They did not need encouragement. Within fifteen minutes they were through the gate, putting distance between Serat and themselves as quickly as possible. Yandharan led them off the main Tirut road, over open country. They cut across the dunes and marched double-time. Within a few hours, their shortcut enabled them to catch up with the long, straggling caravan of refugees on the Tirut road. They rapidly reached the head of the column, where they found Zaibene mounted sidesaddle and guarded by Digaran and Yandharan's men. Binne rode beside her, mounted on Tagan. She cried out when she saw all the dried blood on Caitlin and would not be reassured till she held her in her arms. To Caitlin's intense relief, she had Rufus and Dhanraj's young bay trailing behind Tagan.

"I tried to be brave in the battle," said Dhanraj to Caitlin, once they were all mounted and moving at a brisk pace. "I was frightened, but I hid my fear."

Caitlin leaned over and patted his shoulder.

"They are bravest who conquer their fears," she said. "You need never apologize. You have courage to spare."

Dhanraj sat straighter in his saddle and tried to look modest, but his pride showed on his face.

"It is your courage that I admire, Cat." Yandharan's voice suddenly cut in, startling her.

"I do not need your praise," said Caitlin, realizing too late how rude she sounded.

She hoped her shortness would cause him to return to Zaibene's side, but he continued riding beside them. He did not say anything further, and the silence that settled on them grew oppressive. Binne saw the awkwardness and beckoned Dhanraj to her side. Yandharan waited till he was quite sure there was no one within earshot before speaking.

"Cat, you were safe on the remote Avedus ranch, where the only place you ventured was the tiny village of Hareskot. The Serat Oasis is only a country town, but even here you have been recognized. Tirut is a big city, the seat of a barony, with a permanent Zon Trading Guild fort on its outskirts. We often socialize with wealthy merchants and members of Zaibene's noble family. These are people who have significant interactions with the Zon."

Caitlin said nothing but rode on staring straight ahead.

"I cannot protect you if I don't know who you are. If you are Zon, if you have enemies, you must tell me."

She still did not reply and they rode on in silence, but she was thinking furiously. How much, if anything, should she tell him? By now he must be certain of her Zon identity. There was no point in attempting to conceal that any longer. But while she trusted him, she saw no reason to give him any information about the Sisterhood.

"I am Zon," she said at length. "But you already know that."

"A huntress?"

"I was one, yes."

"That man Rator has seen you in your past life. Who else may have seen you? Did you travel much to native courts? Did you visit Tirut?"

"No, I never visited Tirut. But I was stationed in Dreslin Center. And Alumus the Red Khalif and his followers count me as an enemy."

Yandharan whistled.

"You pick powerful enemies. He is the leader of the Themadan Mission and one of the most influential men in the One Land."

When she did not respond, he continued. "I thank you for telling me this. I will do all I can to protect you in Tirut."

With that, he spurred his mount and cantered over to rejoin his wife.

They rode steadily, traveling for much of night and erecting shady tents to rest during the hottest parts of the day. Yandharan and his men maintained order, ensuring that their stocks of food and water were distributed according to need and making sure that no one was left behind. They constantly scouted the rear, looking out for signs of Chekaliga pursuit.

The dunes of the Great Daksin Desert gradually gave way to dry scrubland and then to the foothills of the Mussadec Range. Now they came upon spring-fed streams and hillside meadows of sweet grass, raising everyone's spirits. The road climbed and then wound into Shard Pass, a deep cleft in the range. Passing through it, they beheld the waters of the Peril Sea. Down around Half Moon Bay stood the city of Tirut.

KITARA HAD JUST finished dining with some of her friends in the suite she shared with her husband, Cheval Jagus va Alsor, in Tirut Castle. She had been feeling very nauseous lately and even the thought of her favorite dishes was not appetizing. She had stomach cramps, and when she passed her hand over her belly, it felt warm. She mentioned this to her friends, and they giggled and brought up the issue of pregnancy. She giggled with them, but inwardly she panicked.

As soon as her friends left, Kitara summoned her personal maid, Rubya. She asked her about various womanly issues before bringing up the matter that weighed heavily on her mind.

"I suspect I may have conceived the Cheval's heir," she said looking down and affecting a shy look. "But I do not wish to raise the hopes of my husband or his noble father unless I am certain. Do you know of someone I can approach in confidence? Someone who is not connected to the castle?"

Rubya was a middle-aged woman with a kindly disposition, and she was touched by Kitara's bashfulness.

"The midwife who birthed my own three children is a discreet woman, my lady," she said. "I can take you to her. What time would be convenient for you?"

"Right now, if possible," said Kitara, keeping her eyes down, maintaining the appearance of innocence.

Fifteen minutes later, she was ready. She had a footman call for her coach and left the castle with Rubya. She was heavily veiled and covered from wrist to ankle in a black, shapeless shift.

The coach rattled through the winding streets and alleys till it came to a stop in a small square. Rubya led her into a shabby building and up a flight of creaking stairs. In a backroom cluttered with metal pans and a range of nasty-looking copper, bronze, and iron implements, sat a blowsy woman with white hair that was badly dyed black. Rubya went in first and spoke to her in a low tone. The woman then beckoned Kitara and motioned for Rubya to leave the room and wait outside.

"Well, my dear," said the midwife. "You may keep your veil on. But you must open your shift, unbutton your blouse, and unfasten your skirt if you wish for me to examine you."

She indicated that Kitara should sit in a chair in front of her. Wishing to retain her anonymity, Kitara did not speak but sat down and did as she was bid. As soon as she sat down, the midwife took hold of each of her ankles and set them on stools that were widely separated. Moving her own stool forward between Kitara's legs, she pulled down the unfastened waist of Kitara's skirt and pushed up her blouse.

Fifteen minutes later, she pushed her stool back, stood up, and looked down at her client with a smile.

"Do you have any children?" she asked.

Kitara shook her head.

"I hope your husband has the means to support a family," the midwife continued. "For your suspicions were well founded. You are indeed pregnant, though it is still quite early. There is a bit of warmth emanating from your belly. Perhaps your veins are close to the surface? In any event, I am sure it is nothing to worry about. It will be some time before you begin to show, if that is of any concern."

Kitara remained silent, but motioned for her maid, Rubya, to be recalled before standing and refastening her clothing. She departed abruptly, leaving Rubya to pay the midwife and follow her back to the coach. Based on the midwife's prognosis, she counted and recounted the days. As she sat in the bumping coach, she thought hard about how to take advantage of her situation. For there could be no doubt— the child she was carrying was Greghar's.

ANDROMACHE WAS IN the queen's private study in Chateau Regina. They sat on comfortable, high-backed chairs with a silver urn of *katsch* on the low table between them. The High Priestess's worry about Asgara's disappearance was plainly writ on her face. She was debating whether to tell Hildegard about it when the queen spoke.

"So Harald Shelsor is dead. Lady Selene's report indicates the circumstances were extremely suspicious."

"Yes, ma'am," said Andromache. "Every cell and system in his body was functioning normally, yet he developed a high fever and encephalitis. In the opinion of the attending medica, even these should not have killed him, yet he died. We have all the data in our processors in Repro. I have a team going over it, but they are baffled. It is a mystery."

"A pity," said Hildegard. "I liked the lad. He was well meaning and so amenable to our suggestions. Briga did well under his rule. But we can't change the past."

She took a sip of her *katsch* and her brows knit thoughtfully.

"As recommended by Lady Selene, I have installed Queen Esme as Regent, to rule in the name of her son, Crown Prince Axel."

"I thought the boy was dead as well—" began Andromache.

"He is in a bad way, and like his father, we don't know why. We have him on life-support systems in a secure location. Hopefully we can eventually find out what ails him. If he dies, we must take steps to install Esme as queen in her own right."

"You think she is the right choice?" Andromache looked doubtful.

"Five years ago, I would not have thought so," said Hildegard. "But that girl has matured since the Great Insurrection. Even as we speak, she is implementing Lady Selene's suggestion and marching to Tirut at the head of the Royal Blacks."

THE *DARLING THOMA* hove to in the Tirut roads. Greghar and Martius stood on the quarterdeck and watched the approaching pilot boat. Supported by Tar, Nitya made her way up from the great cabin below and joined them just as the pilot hailed them.

"Ahoy, the *Darling Thoma*! The harbormaster of Tirut sends his greetings. Do you have Lord Greghar and Lady Nitya aboard?"

"I am Captain Martius, master of the *Darling Thoma*," replied Martius, speaking through a voice trumpet. "Who asks for these gentlefolk?"

"The Chevalina of Tirut," responded the pilot. "She has ordered a special suite of rooms to be prepared for them at the Three Feathers Inn. I am to escort them there as soon as you drop anchor."

NINE

UNCOMFORTABLE MEETINGS

BODIL AXESSINA, THE Zon Resident in Daksin, slowly magnified the image of her face in the three-dimensional mirror. She smiled and frowned, carefully examining the faint lines on her forehead, looking for crow's feet around her eyes and for gray strands in her auburn hair. She tapped her wrist bracer, and an image of her face from the year before superimposed itself on the mirror, the differences between the two images highlighted with a reddish hue. She would turn 115 this year and though she still looked magnificent to barbarian eyes, the reddish hue on the mirror did not lie. Her most recent Excellence Board had given her just a marginal pass. She knew that she did not have long before retirement to Ostracis. *Goddess Ma!* she thought. *My mind is as sharp and agile as when I was a youthful seventy-year-old, and now I have the depth of experience that gives*

me perspective. If only I could slow the aging of my body! The thought of spending the last five or six decades of her life in retirement now haunted her every day.

She tapped her wrist bracer to summon her handmaiden to dress her. King Vokran of Daksin had called for an unscheduled meeting. While Vokran's message indicated that the meeting was to be "informal," she knew the Daksinis too well to go looking anything less than her best. She opened the analysis by Jordis Invarina, her Under Resident and read it while she was being dressed. Then she walked out of her apartments and took the antigravity shaft down to the courtyard. A squad of Palace Guardians, newly arrived from Atlantic City, was mustered alongside a brand-new Mark VIII airboat. Jordis stepped forward, looking composed and professional. Like most Zon, she was tall with an excellent figure and attractive facial features, but her skin was dark enough to pass for a native of Daksin. The sight of her second-in-command's dusky skin always irritated Bodil, but she forced a sweet smile.

"This is Seignora Megara Paurina," Jordis said, indicating the Guardian seignora. "You asked for her to attend you at this meeting."

Megara saluted, hand on heart, and her Guardians followed her lead.

"Indeed I did," said Bodil. "Both the queen and Cornelle Diana speak very highly of you, Seignora Megara. We have all heard of your exemplary service at the Brigon Residency during the Great Insurrection. I am pleased to welcome you to the Daksin Residency."

"Thank you, Resident Bodil," said Megara. "It is a privilege to serve under you."

She led Bodil and Jordis into the airboat and took a window jump seat beside them. The Guardian squad boarded after them. Megara had selected a pilot and copilot from among the squad, and they boarded through the fore doors, went through their checks, and powered up the engines. Megara looked out of the window as they rose above the Residency.

Sampore, the capital city of Daksin, was already old when the Zon first arrived on New Eartha. It was built on both sides of one of the major mouths of the Chamb River. The silted mud flats of the Chamb delta had been built up and reclaimed over the centuries to such an extent that the nearest swamps were now several kilometers from the city. Navdurg, a significant delta island, guarded the seaward entrance to the city, at the point where the brownish waters of the Chamb met the gray-green waters of the Warm Sea. Successive generations of Daksin kings had built it up with silt dredged from the river and crowned it with a guard castle. At its highest point, Navdurg now rose almost a hundred meters above the swirling waters.

The Zon appropriated the island after they conquered Daksin. They razed the superstructure of the barbarian castle, reinforced the old foundations, and built the modern, white Residency on them. Its shining battlements were festooned with wide solar panels and wind turbines rather than weaponry, testament to the long peace between Daksin and the Sisterhood. It was a short flight across the bustling Sampore harbor to Tapkotten Palace, the seat of the Bhoj kings of Daksin.

"The honor guard is mustered," said the pilot to Megara on the airboat comm. "I can see the commandant of the Daksin Lancers. They are ready to receive us."

Megara looked out of her window. All the requirements of protocol were met.

"Proceed with the landing," she said. "Deploy the baffles around the engine exhausts, let's not muss their fine uniforms."

"I hear and obey," said the pilot.

They landed and were received with due ceremony. Both the lancers and the Guardians presented arms. Then the commandant of the lancers led Bodil, Jordis, and Megara into the Reception Hall. Vokran II, King of Daksin and Chitgar and occupant of the Lion Throne, sat on an ornate, high-backed chair whose arms were carved lion's heads. He had a dusky-brown complexion and black, animated eyes. He was quite chubby and so bald that the skin of his round head shone. He wore fine silk breeches, but only a thin silk shawl around his shoulders, revealing rolls of fat around his middle and a substantial paunch. He had on an abundance of very heavy gold jewelry—necklaces, armbands, wristbands, and a crown circlet. Vokran's royal council and about a dozen of the most powerful Daksin barons were present and similarly dressed in their finery. Most of them had chocolate-brown skin and were much darker even than Vokran.

They all rose as the Zon party entered. Bodil gave Vokran the half bow he was due and made her prepared speech in Daksish. He gave his prepared response and signaled the stewards to bring out the refreshments. They approached the king and the Zon party first with trays of *phang*, a fermented rice wine. Only after each of them had taken a glass did they pass around the Hall serving everyone else.

Bodil was an old professional and she circulated, exchanging greetings and small talk in strict order of seniority. After the king, she moved on to speak with the chief minister, then the Baron of Kaylan, and so on. Jordis and Megara followed her, one at each elbow. From time to time, Jordis joined the conversation, but Megara just listened, getting a feel for the politics of Daksin.

After the appropriate amount of time, Vokran motioned to his herald, who clapped his hands and announced, "King Vokran welcomes the Zon Resident and her staff to the conference suite. Please follow me."

He turned and led the king out of the Reception Hall. The king was followed by two lancers in their colorful, beribboned uniforms, their spurs jingling as they walked. Bodil, Jordis, and Megara followed. They went down a corridor and entered a room furnished with a long conference table. The king seated himself at one end of it, and Bodil took the seat at the other end, with Jordis at her right hand and Megara at her left. Then the king's council entered and took the remaining seats. The herald closed the doors and took his place outside along with the two lancers.

"I thank you for accepting my invitation, Resident Bodil," said Vokran as soon as the door closed. "I imagine you have an idea as to why I have called this meeting."

"I understand that Your Highness is concerned about this season's Chekaliga raids."

"These are more than raids," he said, speaking slowly and controlling his temper with an obvious effort. "All the Chekaliga tribes are involved. There has never been anything like it! We have consulted all manner of scholars, monks, and deacons. They have pored over records going back hundreds of years. There is no precedent for such massed attacks."

"We have heard of the fall of the Serat Oasis, Sire," said Bodil. "But surely that is not our problem. The Southern Marches are the concern of King Harald of Briga and Resident Lady Selene."

"Resident Bodil, I have had dozens of messengers over the last week from all over our Borderlands, and every one brings the same story—villages burned to the ground, men butchered, women and livestock carried off. We have never faced depredations on this scale. Even the city of Siggar may be threatened. Surely you know of what is happening on our side of the border? Our treaty requires your Legions to keep these wild men in their lairs in the ravines of Chitgar."

"We have aerial intelligence," said Bodil, playing for time. "And we have received reinforcements from Atlantic City, under the command of Seignora Megara Paurina." She inclined her head toward Megara, who nodded at the king and his council. "The intelligence reports are being compiled as we speak. If they show incursions on the scale you describe, we will commit forces to battle."

"We are seriously disappointed, Resident Bodil," said Vokran. "Our tribute payments have been munificent and punctual. Is it too much to expect that you are at least as well informed about what is happening on the ground as we are?"

The meeting did not last much longer. The chief minister provided some further details of the attacks, and the Baron of Kaylan spoke forcefully, reinforcing the points made by the king. After the proper leave-taking ceremonies, Bodil and her entourage reembarked on her airboat and took off to return to the Residency. It was obvious that she was angry, and Jordis kept her eyes on the tips of her shoes. She knew that Bodil had very conservative Zon tastes, and that her dark skin was at least part of the reason that she was so often the butt of Bodil's wrath.

"Why do we know nothing of these raids in Daksin?" she asked. "Lady Selene seems to have detailed reports of the massed attacks in Briga."

"Resident Bodil, you will recall that we decided to suspend aerial reconnaissance last year to conserve power," said Jordis. "Three years ago we destroyed a large force of Chekaliga warriors and the last two years have been very quiet on this side of the border."

"Jordis, I wish you would collect better intelligence," said Bodil peevishly. "When *I* was an Under Resident, I always knew what was going on. If you would just do your job, we wouldn't find ourselves in such situations."

⌘

BODIL ORDERED A resumption of the aerial reconnaissance over northern Daksin and the Borderlands. They rapidly accumulated intelligence on the tribes' positions and strength, relaying everything they learned to Vokran and his council. But the more information they gathered, the less sense it seemed to make. The tribes seemed to be everywhere, indiscriminately sacking villages and ranches on both sides of the border. Then perhaps emboldened by their success at the Serat Oasis, they launched an attack on Siggar, a major Daksin city on the Kos, a tributary of the great river Chamb.

"The attack on Siggar has turned into a siege, Resident Bodil," said Jordis. "We have an airboat on station, and she is transmitting very good video. The attackers number about twenty thousand. Most of them are Ravan Chekaligas, but they are joined by a significant number of Kasar Chekaligas. They make up almost a quarter of their numbers."

They were in Bodil's study in the Daksin Residency. It was the beginning of winter, and the breeze blowing in through the open viewport was cool. But it was still mild enough that their temperature shields were switched off. Sampore's location on the shores of the Warm Sea meant that its temperatures rarely ever reached freezing.

"The Kasar Chekaligas have not raided since their forebears surrendered to the forces of Good Queen Sonia at the Bloodless Victory," said Bodil, surprised. "Since then they have tended their goats and stayed out of trouble."

"Well, no longer. They seem to have made common cause with their more aggressive cousins. According to reports from Lady

241

Selene, there were Kasar Chekaligas present at the sacking of the Serat Oasis."

"The Kasars have themselves been victims of Ravan Chekaliga raiders—they hate the Ravans! We selected Pallian, the Kasar chief ourselves, in part because the Ravan Chekaligas killed his father. Why, you and I took tea with him last year. I cannot believe he has turned into a raider, much less an ally of the Ravan Chekaligas."

"Be that as it may, ma'am, we cannot allow Siggar to fall," said Jordis. "We must take action."

Bodil heard Jordis's words, but her head was filled with the treatments and therapies she was undergoing to prepare for her Excellence Board. *Why must things become so unsettled just when I need to concentrate on myself?* she thought.

"I will not act unilaterally, Jordis. Vokran has mobilized two regiments and they will march tomorrow. The Baron of Kaylan has sent an express messenger to Kaylan City. The Kaylan troops will march as soon as they muster."

"But it will take them weeks to get to Siggar, ma'am," said Jordis. She strove to be patient, but it was hard. "I have been talking to Seignora Megara. She feels that—"

"We tell the military what to do, Jordis. We do not take orders from them."

"Ma'am, if Siggar falls without any action on our part, we will have failed to meet our responsibilities under the Treaty of Wolf's Head. If the Daksin barons believe that we will not protect them, they will begin to question the value of the Zon alliance."

Bodil's brow knitted. Jordis's words finally got through to her. Retirement was inevitable, but it would be so much worse to end her successful, if rather staid career with a disaster.

"Summon Seignora Megara," she said.

Jordis hid her relief and opened a comm channel to Megara. A few minutes later, she entered and saluted, hand on heart.

"Under Resident Jordis tells me that she has been discussing the situation in Siggar with you," Bodil said without preamble.

"Yes, Resident Bodil," said Megara. "The video indicates that they are using tactics unlike anything we have seen from the hill tribes before. In the past they almost always fought in the open field or attacked small villages and forts. They used the mobility and speed of their light cavalry to outflank and destroy forces that were sent against them. They never attacked powerful fixed defenses, and they never settled into sieges. However, at Siggar we have seen them using siege engines—catapults, rams, ladders, and wheeled towers."

"What has brought on this change?"

"We do not know, ma'am. But there are many things we must find out before we commit major forces to battle. Among other things, we need to discover what has happened to Pallian, the Kasar Chekaliga chief that you installed."

Bodil nodded.

Just then, Jordis's wrist bracer pinged, indicating an incoming comm channel. Megara stood to take her leave and give Bodil and Jordis privacy. Jordis opened the comm channel, listened for a moment and then made an urgent motion with her hands, indicating that Megara should stay.

"Wait a minute, seignora, while I will project a hologram," Jordis said. "I am with Resident Bodil and Seignora Megara of the Palace Guardians." She tapped her wrist bracer again and projected the hologram onto the center of the study.

A seignora in the uniform of the Pentheselia Legion appeared in the shimmering hologram. She was in the cockpit of an airboat.

"I am over Siggar, Resident Bodil," she said after saluting hand on heart. "Last night was calm, our monitoring equipment picked up only small movements and the situation appeared stable. However, the Chekaligas have just launched a major attack, and resistance has completed crumbled! There was almost no one to repel the attackers coming up the siege ladders and out of the siege towers. They are sacking the town now as I speak to you."

Bodil looked at Jordis accusingly.

"Jordis, I cannot depend on you for anything! I thought you said that we could depend on the Baron of Siggar."

"I don't understand it, Resident Bodil," said Jordis. "Baron Tuvaran of Siggar is a solid, dependable soldier."

"Is there any evidence of the tribesmen using advanced weaponry, seignora?" asked Megara.

"I am not sure what you mean. I said that they are using siege equipment—"

"I mean advanced technology. Have your monitors picked up any evidence of 'grators or laser pistols? And signs of gunpowder?"

"Why, that is impossible, Seignora Megara. The barbarians do not have—"

"Have you already forgotten the Great Insurrection, seignora? That is how the Ostracis Citadel fell and how the Aurora Citadel came very close to falling."

"We have no evidence of anything like that Seignora Megara."

"Very well."

Bodil addressed the Pentheselia seignora in the hologram.

"Take the airboat up to at least five thousand meters. Maintain your monitoring. Stay on station until you are relieved as planned."

Bodil nodded to Jordis and she cut the comm channel.

"Jordis, call Vokran and set up a meeting with him and his council," Bodil said as soon as the hologram faded. "They need to know this."

"I suggest we have a squadron armed with ready crews, Resident Bodil," said Megara. "Then if the Chekaligas march into the open on their way to Kaylan City or here, we can inflict heavy losses on them from the air."

"Make it so, Seignora Megara," said Bodil.

THE AIRBOAT FLEW at its normal cruising altitude of twenty thousand meters and the weather was good, so the flight was silky smooth. However, the hold was pitch dark, and Asgara was afraid that she would be found if she used her light stick. It was only minimally heated and she hugged herself in an effort to keep warm. A bigger problem was that the pressurization in the hold was significantly less than in the cabin and she had to work hard to keep alert and conscious in the thin air.

The landing approach was very steep and she clung to the restraining cables on the crates to avoid being flung forward. Once the airboat leveled off, the engines powered down and it was silent for some time. Then the cargo hatch was opened and light flooded into the hold. She shrank back against the bulkhead as she heard boots on the ladder. Crates were unlashed and raised to the deck on power hoists. As more crates were removed, she slid back toward the corner of the hold, hiding behind those that remained. But as the unloading proceeded, it laid open more and more of the hold. Then to her relief it stopped.

"We'll take a short break," she heard a voice say. "Let's get some *katsch* and then finish the unloading."

Asgara waited till it was completely silent before pulling herself up the ladder and peeking over the edge of the cargo hatch. The airboat was empty, so she pulled herself on to the deck. She was worried that if they kept unloading the hold they would find her, so she thought she had to find a new hiding place. However, the deck and cockpit offered no places of concealment.

The rear hatch was wide open, and outside she could see a very bright blue sky. She walked out on to the hatch and found that the airboat was about thirty meters above the Tirut Guild fort rocking gently on sky anchors. She looked down and saw that there were hundreds of people in strange garb milling about in the fort, dealing with a few dozen Zon traders watched by a handful of heavily armed huntresses.

There was a winch on the rear hatch with cables running down to a platform resting on the ground in the fort. Asgara hit the retract button and the winch whined, smoothly pulling the platform up. It automatically stopped when it was level with the airboat rear hatch. She stepped on to the platform and hit the deploy button and held on to one of the cables as it began to descend. The platform had been raised and lowered many times already, so it attracted no notice. Once on the ground, she found herself anonymous in the sea of mainly barbarian adults. Some were no taller than her.

She hoped they would take on some cargo in which she could stowaway to get to her final destination of the Daksin Residency. But her immediate concern was to eat: she was growing quite faint with hunger and a bit dizzy to boot. The flight in the thin air of the hold had not helped matters. She was about to reach into her pack and pull out an energy bar when she felt a hand on her shoulder. She looked around to see the thigh boots of a huntress's uniform.

"Who are you and what are you doing here? Show me your Guild fort pass."

Asgara did not look up and show her face, but bolted immediately. The huntress grabbed her pack, but Asgara shrugged out of the shoulder straps and left her holding it. She ran for the open gates of the Guild fort, dodging around barbarian traders. The huntress pursued her, calling to her colleagues at the gates. However, Asgara was small and lithe and managed to evade them. The huntresses stayed at the gates and did not pursue her outside into the barbarian crowd.

She found herself on a dusty, open space a few hundred meters across, between the walls of the Guild fort and the city walls of Tirut. There were even more barbarians here, crowding around stalls selling lower-quality merchandise than what was on offer in the Guild fort. They were more poorly dressed and fed than those in the fort. She spent a few minutes wandering around the stalls, but none of them were selling food.

Both the walls of the Guild fort and the Tirut city walls ran right to the sea. In between them was a small pebbly beach. There was a large gate in the city walls facing the Guild fort gate, guarded by liveried men-at-arms in shining chainmail and gleaming helmets. She thought she might be able to get some food in the Tirut, free from the risk of being apprehended by the huntresses. So she walked through the gates into the barbarian city. Hungry and tired, she walked almost a kilometer in a bit of a daze. She was soon walking past docks and saw dozens of strange barbarian ships with tall masts being loaded and unloaded. Brassily painted women, displaying plenty of cleavage and leg called out to every passing man. Raucous laughter spilled out of dockside taverns.

Everything was so new and different to her that Asgara would normally have been observing everything, soaking it all in. But now she was so famished and exhausted that she was not thinking very clearly, and little of what she saw registered. Then she saw what she was looking for—a small square with a cluster of stalls selling fruits, vegetables, bread, cheese, and other edibles. Across from the stalls was an imposing inn with a roped-off patio.

Asgara stumbled up to the first stall. It was piled high with all manner of fruit and was fronted by a big-bellied man hawking his wares loudly in Brigish. She was studying Brigish in one of her gifted classes, and while she was still not fluent, she could speak it well enough.

"Please, sir," she said, picking up an apple. "I am very hungry and hope that you will not mind my taking this. I am on my way to see my mother and will get her to pay you in a few days."

She turned away and was about to take a bite of the fruit when she felt him grab her collar and spin her around. He retrieved the apple with practiced ease but did not release her.

"Now here's a new one," the fruit vendor called out to his fellow stallholders. "She's coming back with her mother in a few days to pay!"

A small crowd quickly gathered. Asgara's dress and shift were stained with grass and blood from her dive from the speeder, as well as oil from the hangar trash bin. Grease and oil streaked her face and dimmed the brightness of her ash-blonde hair. Both her knees and elbows were caked with mud and blood. To the gathering Tirutans, she looked very like every other beggar girl in the streets, though her pale skin suggested she was from the north.

"Give her something to take to her mother, Joban!" called one of the other stallholders.

In response, the fruit vendor drew back his meaty fist and hit Asgara hard. She staggered away under the vicious blow and fell in the dirt of the street.

"I've had it with you young thieves!" he snarled, walking up to her prone form. "Here's something to think about the next time you want to steal!" With that he drew back his boot and kicked her heavily.

Asgara had never been physically chastised in her life, and in her current state, the shock of the beating almost caused her to pass out. However, she held on to her consciousness and dimly saw one of the other stallholders start toward her.

"Just to make sure you remember," he said loudly, and kicked her as well, driving her face into the mud.

She painfully crawled away, causing her knees and elbows to bleed anew. She got to the wall of the inn and rested her back against it. The crowd sensed the end of the excitement and began to drift away. The stallholders lost interest in her and went back to hawking their wares. No one paid her any further attention.

She sobbed quietly to herself for a while, but then wiped her eyes, creating more streaks of oil and mud across her face. Just when she was gathering the courage to stand up, a hand appeared before her with an apple in it. She shrank back, expecting to be hit again, but nothing happened. She looked up and saw a thin, balding man in brocaded robes, leaning down and offering her the apple.

"Take it," he said in a kindly tone. "I saw how that wicked fruit vendor treated you. I know that you must be hungry, and it is only right that those of us who can afford it should feed you."

Asgara looked into his dark brown eyes. He did not meet her steady gaze but blinked and looked away quickly. Her emotional acuity caused warning bells to go off in her head, but she was faint with hunger and ignored them. She took the apple and began to eat it hurriedly before he changed his mind. As she was eating, he sat down on the ground beside her. She felt him pet her hair and then her cheek as she ate the fruit.

"You are a beautiful child," he whispered. "Such pretty hair, such smooth skin."

Asgara kept eating as fast as she could. She was almost done with the apple when he put his hand under the blouse of her shift and began caressing her flat chest and stomach. She dropped the apple core and twisted away from him, saying, "I thank you for your kindness, sir, but I must return to my friends."

"Oh no," he said. "We have only just begun. One apple will not sate your appetite. I have something here for you to drink."

He produced a bottle of clear fluid and attempted to give it to her. When she did not take it, he held one of her thighs tightly and attempted to put it to her lips. As she struggled to free herself, his grip moved up her thigh.

"If you scream, the fruit vendor and his friends will come and beat you again," he whispered in her ear. "You had best come with me. We will make each other very, very happy."

"No!" she whispered desperately, as she continued to struggle. "Let me go! Please sir, I am good girl! I am sure that I cannot make you happy."

However, she did not scream, as she was afraid of attracting the vendors and being beaten again. Then she felt his fingers touch her underclothes.

GREGHAR HAD JUST completed his inspection of his room in the suite at the Three Feathers Inn, when there was a knock on his door.

Thinking it was Nitya, who was lodged in the next room, he called, "Come in! The door's open." But when he turned to the door, it was Kitara. She shut the door behind her and walked over to him, swinging her hips. She wore a colorful gown of Tirutan cami-silk with a hip-high slit and a matching scarf that she draped over her hair and around her throat so that it covered her bosom.

She unwound her scarf as she crossed the room and tossed it on the bed, revealing a neckline that plunged so low that it drew his unwilling eyes to it like iron filings to a magnet. She put her arms around him and pressed herself against him. Her gown was so thin and she held him so tight that she felt naked in his arms.

"Oh, Greghar!" she cried. "I have missed you so! It was so difficult to keep my distance on the ship, with you in the very next cabin. And then you went off to fight those horrible pirates and left me with my heart in my mouth! The men said you are a great warrior, a true leader of men. I have literally been pacing the battlements of Tirut Castle for days, waiting for my warrior love. You cannot believe how many excuses I have had to make to my husband to explain my behavior."

"It is very kind of you, chevalina," said Greghar, as she led him to the wide bed. "But I must tell you that—"

She put a finger on his lips.

"I must return to Tirut Castle within the hour or my husband will grow suspicious," she said. "So let us make the most of our short time together. And after we make love, I have the most precious secret to share with you!"

With that, she led him to the bed. As she snuggled in his arms, her intense femininity began to melt his reluctance.

"Chevalina," he began again. "My ward, Nitya—"

"Oh, don't speak to me of that pious faux virgin!" Kitara exclaimed, silencing him with a kiss so aggressive that he would have had to use violence to avoid returning it. "There! Tell me if she can kiss like that."

Before he could answer they heard a commotion from outside, beneath the window. Greghar used it as an excuse to get up from the bed. He went over to the window and looked out. With a muttered curse, Kitara got up and came to his elbow.

"It is nothing, love," she said putting an arm around him. "Just another thieving beggar girl. They are as thick as flies in Tirut, especially on market days. Come back to bed."

She tried to pull Greghar back inside, but he resisted.

"Just a minute," he said. "I want to see how this turns out."

As minutes passed, his eyes grew narrower. Finally, he said, "I'm going downstairs for a short while. I will be right back."

"But Greghar—" Kitara began. She stopped as the door shut behind him.

Greghar took the stairs three at a time and was out in the small square in a moment. He strode up to the outer wall of the Three Feathers and caught the man beside Asgara by the scruff of the neck. He pulled him off her and hit him hard in the face, knocking him to the ground. He picked up the bottle the man had been trying to put to Asgara's lips and sniffed it before smashing it against the wall. Then he drew Karya and put the point of the sword at the man's crotch.

"I should castrate you," he said through his teeth.

"You misunderstand me sir," the man gibbered, blood running from his broken nose. "I run a charity for young beggar girls—"

"So that is how you prey on children, is it?"

He crawled away from Greghar, and as soon as he got out of range of the sword, he rose and scuttled away as fast as his legs could carry him. Only when he had disappeared from view did Greghar look down at Asgara. He picked her up in his arms and seated her in the outdoor patio of the inn. He called for a server and when the man came, he ordered a meal for Asgara. She kept her eyes down but stole looks at him. He sat in silence, a decorous distance away from her.

"Will you not eat?" she asked him when a single plate of food arrived.

"I have eaten already," he said. "So I must excuse myself. But please do not tarry on my account."

In spite of her hunger, she ate slowly and carefully, engaging him in conversation in her stilted Brigish. Her precocity was quickly apparent, as she drew him to speak and politely pursued the topics that he raised. However, when she asked him about himself, he responded briefly, providing little specific information. He was surprised by how close and protective he felt toward this child, recalling his first meeting with Caitlin and Nitya.

When she was done eating, she felt much better. Even her injuries seemed to throb less intensely. She looked at him gratefully.

"I do not have a father, sir," she said. "But if I had one, I would wish for him to be like you."

"So she's a bastard as well as a thief, sir," the fruit vendor called over from his stall. "Have a care for your wallet!"

Greghar slowly got up and walked over to the fruit vendor. He saw the expression in Greghar's eyes and quailed. He wanted to run, but he could not abandon his stall.

"Now, now, sir, it was all in jest—"

"Men like you make me ashamed," said Greghar, speaking in a low tone. The fruit vendor cowered before Greghar's massive form, expecting a blow or worse. But Greghar's look indicated his contempt more clearly than any cuff. He returned to Asgara, took her hand and entered the inn.

As they stepped into the parlor, Kitara came down the stairs, her scarf again modestly covering her bosom and her head. She saw Greghar holding Asgara's hand and clicked her tongue in annoyance.

"Please, Greghar," she said. "This is the best inn in Tirut. As my guest, the landlord will accept anything you do, but it is not fair to bring beggars and thieves into his establishment."

"If it is a problem, I am happy to find other accommodation," returned Greghar. "This girl has been abused and needs care. I will not have her thrown into the street again."

Kitara came across the parlor and slipped her arm around Greghar again. She stood on tiptoe, but even so Greghar had to bend his head so she could kiss his cheek.

"Oh, Greghar, your kindness does you credit. It makes my heart grow even fonder. But—"

Just then, there was the sound of boots in the vestibule. Kitara disengaged herself from Greghar and ascended two steps on the staircase, rearranging her scarf. The landlord entered, wiping his hands on his apron, followed by Yandharan and Rator. All three of them stopped short when they saw Kitara, swept off their hats, and bowed deeply.

"Greetings, Chevalina Kitara," said the landlord. "I hope that you are happy with the way we are looking after your guests?"

Kitara smiled at him in response. He looked pleased but nervous, twisting his apron in his hands.

"What brings you here, Collector Yandharan?" she asked, glancing in the staircase mirror to make sure that her scarf was perfectly adjusted and her gown fell just right.

"I have been talking to landlord Biarus here, my lady," he replied. "For I have some guests of my own that I hoped to put up at the

Three Feathers. He tells me that there are some rooms on the lower level that are still available."

"Of course," said Kitara, taking the two steps down the staircase to allow the slit in her gown to widen and give them a glimpse of one eye-catching leg. She batted her eyelashes and spoke breathily. "You are my husband's most senior liegeman and your wife is connected to him by blood. Your guests are our guests."

She paused for effect.

"Indeed, I hear whispers that *you* are the majority owner of the Three Feathers. So I have you to thank for my guests' comfort."

"I would take it as a big favor if your ladyship would not circulate this information," said Yandharan.

Kitara nodded her head in assent.

"And I will ask a favor in return," she said, and then inclined her head toward Greghar. "But first allow me to introduce one of my noble guests, Lord Greghar, nephew of King Lothar of Utrea."

Again all three men bowed deeply. Asgara looked up at Greghar and tightened her grip on his hand.

"I bid you welcome to the Southern Marches, Lord Greghar," said Yandharan gravely.

"Lord Greghar has a soft heart," Kitara said, her expressive eyes moving from Greghar to Yandharan. "He has taken pity on this beggar girl from the market. I would be most grateful if you could find a suitable place for her. As you know, in the streets such girls get to thieving and worse. I will be happy to cover any expenses involved."

Yandharan polished his bronze badge with his sleeve and scrutinized Asgara carefully. Holding Greghar's hand, she felt safe. With revived self-assurance, she met his gaze with her habitual confidence and poise. She smoothed her shift, attempting to minimize the appearance of the rips. She fluttered her hands as she did so, a mannerism that was so like Caitlin's that Yandharan started. *She is dirty and bloody*, he thought, *but this is no beggar girl. Zaibene will not take kindly to her.*

Rator now spoke up.

"I stay with a widow when I am in Tirut," he said. "She keeps a respectable house and has children of her own. She will be glad to take the girl in if her expenses are covered."

"Who is this widow?" asked Yandharan.

"Lidill Ikren is her name, Collector. Her husband was an honorable soldier, but he was slain in the Zon Wars. So she is forced to take lodgers."

"Ikren," said Yandharan thoughtfully. "I had a deputy by that name, a very honest and brave fellow. He left to take service as a Hilson slayer in the Northern Marches."

He turned to Greghar.

"Lord Greghar," he said, with a slight bow. "I can personally vouch for this family. The Ikrens are not rich, but they are respectable. The girl will be safe there and well cared for."

I can stay with these people for a few days and recover my strength, thought Asgara. *Then I can stowaway in another airboat bound for the Daksin Residency.*

"Very well," said Greghar, reluctantly releasing Asgara's hand. Rator came up and took her. The two men looked at each other steadily for a moment, each expecting the other to speak.

"Lord Greghar, it is a pleasure to meet a fellow northerner," said Rator eventually. "As you doubtless gathered from my accent, I am from the colder climes. We are both far from home."

"Indeed we are," replied Greghar, but his attention was centered on Asgara.

Rator and Asgara walked out of the parlor. At the door, she turned around and waved to Greghar with a mature and sophisticated poise that was at odds with her childlike looks and unkempt state. Greghar waved back and felt a stab of sadness as she disappeared through the doorway.

"Why, Greghar, you charm all the ladies, no matter what their ages!" exclaimed Kitara.

Now Biarus the landlord bowed and said, "Chevalina, I pray you will excuse me. I must go and make sure that the rooms on the lower level are prepared for Collector Yandharan's guests." She nodded without looking at him and he left, bowing obsequiously.

"My lady, I should go with Biarus," said Yandharan. "I know the tastes and dispositions of my guests. I thank you for allowing them to share the inn with your distinguished visitors."

"I laud your concern for your guests, Collector," Kitara said. "I hope that we will soon see you and the lovely Zaibene at Tirut Castle."

He bowed and withdrew.

As soon as they were alone in the parlor, Kitara put her arms around Greghar and kissed him. His mind was elsewhere, but he took the path of least resistance, held her and kissed her back.

"My love, in just a little while, I must fly back to the castle," she breathed. "Come, let us spend these few precious moments in the privacy of your room."

THE BATWING DOORS to the parlor swung open, and Caitlin walked in, led by one of Yandharan's maids. Seeing Greghar and Kitara entwined, she stopped short. The maid bobbed a curtsey and scuttled out.

Greghar quickly disengaged himself from Kitara. He stood apart from her, shifting his weight from one foot to the other, unable to directly meet the shocked look in Caitlin's eyes. Kitara glanced from Greghar to Caitlin and immediately discerned a rival. Caitlin was unschooled in the complex intricacies of male-female relationships, but she nonetheless had feminine instincts and sensed the poison in the sweet look that Kitara gave her.

After a few moments of awkward silence, Caitlin gained control of herself and said, "Greghar, will you not introduce me to your beautiful friend?"

Greghar had eyes only for Caitlin, but he replied, "This is Chevalina Kitara va Alsor of Tirut."

Looking at the reality of Caitlin standing there, their years apart seemed to melt away. In that instant he realized consciously what he had thus far refused to admit even to himself—that refusing her when she had offered herself to him was the biggest mistake of his life. He now knew that he would do anything, give up anything, be anything, if only she would have him. He felt the old tightness in his chest, for he was afraid that what she had seen would cause him to lose her again, this time forever.

"Why, Greghar, now I am truly speechless," said Kitara. "It seems you know this warriorlike creature! Who is she?"

"I am Cat Avedus," said Caitlin before Greghar could respond. "My parents' ranch is in the far west of the Southern Marches."

"You are no rancher," said Kitara, wagging a finger. "I have seen you before. It was some years ago, when I was a lady-in-waiting to Her Highness, Queen Esme of Briga. You are the Zon officer who made a scene in one of the Royal Audiences. They say that you fought a gladiator in the fighting pits as the champion of a Yengar witch."

"You are mistaken, chevalina," came a voice from the top of the stairs. All of their heads snapped up to see Nitya. She began walking slowly down the stairs, leaning heavily on the bannister. Greghar ran up and met her halfway. She leaned on him gratefully as she made her way down.

"Why, it is the virtuous little lady-in-waiting from Utrea," said Kitara. "Who looks nothing like any Utrean I have ever seen—"

Nitya made a movement with her right hand, so small and unobtrusive that neither Greghar nor Caitlin noticed it. Kitara stopped speaking in midsentence and smiled blandly, first at Greghar and then at Caitlin.

"It has been a very agreeable afternoon, Greghar," she said. "I am pleased to see you and your ward so well settled in the inn." She turned to Caitlin. "Cat Avedus, I am happy to make your acquaintance. I hope that you enjoy your stay in Tirut. Now I must return to my husband in Tirut Castle. Good day."

She made her way out of the parlor, rearranging her scarf as she went.

"Caitlin—" began Greghar.

"That was quite a transformation," said Caitlin, cutting him off. "One moment she was draped around you like a python, the next she wished you good-day like she was your maiden aunt."

Before he could respond, Yandharan returned.

"Ah, it is good that you are here, Cat," he said, rubbing his hands. "I see you have met the Chevalina's high-born guests. I have set up your rooms on the lower level and they are quite fair, if I say so myself. I think you will be very comfortable here."

"Mantan, I actually know Greghar," said Caitlin. "We spent some time together in my *past* life." She emphasized the word *past*. "Collector Mantan Yandharan is a good friend," she continued, addressing Greghar. She put a hand on Yandharan's forearm and held it in a familiar grip. "A *very* good friend."

Greghar's fists involuntarily clenched.

"We live in dangerous times," he said. "Good friends are precious."

Yandharan was surprised by Caitlin's sudden show of flirtatiousness and looked from her to Greghar suspiciously.

"Cat and I are indeed good friends," he said, allowing her to retain her hold on his forearm. "I consider myself fortunate that she feels close to me. I have known her these past several years and have recently introduced her to my wife and family."

"You are married, then?" A note of relief crept into Greghar's voice.

"Yes, but he has proposed marriage to me, asking me to be his second wife," said Caitlin impulsively. "I am very flattered by this offer, since Mantan is well known as one of the most honorable men in the Southern Marches."

"Well, Collector, you could not have chosen better," said Greghar. His distress made his northern accent stronger. "They broke the mold when they made Cat. If she will have you, you are the most fortunate man in the world."

"Thank you for the endorsement, Lord Greghar, but you are telling me nothing that I do not already know."

He paused and turned to Caitlin.

"Now that I have settled your accommodation, I must return and see to my wife and children. I will send Binne and Dhanraj over with one of our maids."

Yandharan doffed his hat and bowed before turning to leave.

"Wait!" said Caitlin. "I will come with you. I can bring Binne and Dhanraj back in due course; there is no hurry. You need not tax one of your maids."

Yandharan smiled at her as she linked her arm in his and walked out with him.

NESTAR STOOD ON the quarterdeck of the *Black Sprite* as his helmsman guided the black-sailed carrack toward Hadoy's Inlet, just north of the port of Battara in Daksin. It had taken them almost two weeks of hard sailing from Tirut to get to this peaceful inlet.

Just south of Tirut were the Giants' Teeth, a line of rocks, reefs, and stony islands that extended hundreds of kilometers out into the Peril Sea. The narrow Strait of Gold was the only safe passage through the Giants' Teeth. This was dominated by the Baron of Tirut's forbidding fortress at Gold Port. Both the strait and the port were named for the tolls extracted from all passing merchant vessels, levies that made the Barony of Tirut the richest fief in the One Land.

Nestar had submitted to inspection at sea by one of the baron's toll ships. Without any trade goods aboard to value the inspection was quick, but even so the assessed toll was substantial. Nestar had paid it without complaint and they lost very little time in the process.

They glided into Hadoy's Inlet and hove to. As soon as the ship was at anchor, they launched a jollyboat. Nestar sat in the stern sheets as a squad of Skull Watchmen rowed them to the beach.

"I am sure we are in the right place," grumbled Nestar. "But I wish King Shobar's guidance was a bit more detailed. He asked me to look for a tower, yet directed me to this remote inlet."

The men ran the jollyboat on to the sand of the cove and handed their leader over the prow so he did not get his boots wet. The beach sloped upward and the top of the rise was covered with swaying palm trees. Leaving one man by the jollyboat, Nestar led the rest of them to the palms. Beyond the palms, the vegetation consisted of low brush, bushes and scattered clumps of trees. The coastal plain was quite narrow here, and the foothills of the Mussadec Range rose just over a kilometer from the shore. All of their eyes were drawn to the same thing. On the peak of the nearest hill was a soaring stone formation that looked so like a tower that it was hard to believe it was natural.

"By the One God," whispered Nestar.

He called up the rest of the men, leaving only a small watch crew on the carrack. They set off toward the stone tower with a mixture of anticipation and trepidation, completely unaware of what they were going to find. As they approached the hill, the sun began to go down, and the tower threw a growing shadow that pointed directly toward them. When they were about halfway between the shore and the hill, they entered a ring of stones, rough enough to be a natural formation, yet arranged to suggest that it was the work of human hands. Just as they entered the circle, the shadow of the tower reached them.

Nestar put up his hand, signaling them all to stop. He stood very still and looked around. The men looked at him so intently and expectantly that they did not notice the Chekaligas. More and more of the warriors appeared and moved silently, even their ponies making no sound as they completely surrounded the Utreans. Each Chekaliga warrior carried a light bow, and they all had nocked arrows.

"Greetings!" Nestar called in a booming voice. "I am pleased to see so many of you. I would speak with Grand Sab Kimr Ib Makhtoom."

The words were spoken in Brigish with very creditable fluency. Brigish was the most widely spoken of the barbarian tongues, but few Utreans spoke it so well. There a moment of silence before a rider with dusky skin paced his pony forward. He wore a brocaded tunic over his leathers, and his scimitar had a jeweled hilt. He had a fine-linked gold chain braided into his coarse hair.

"Who dares to ask for me?" he asked. His Brigish had a heavy Chekaliga accent.

"I come from the far north," said Nestar, in a deep, booming voice that was unnaturally loud. "To fulfill the prophesy of Chekaliga rule over all of Daksin."

"This is the well-known lore of my people," said Kimr. His flat, black eyes did not blink, and he showed no emotion. "Anyone could spout this."

"Lately you have seen Northmen in your dreams," said Nestar. "Have you not?"

"You are from the north land they call Utrea?"

"Indeed we are," replied Nestar. "We have come from there to lead you to claim the Lion Throne."

Kimr signaled the rider beside him, and he wheeled his pony and galloped off. He returned very slowly, still on his pony, but leading four men. It took some time for Nestar and his party to recognize Guttanar and his three surviving men. They all bore the marks of horrible torture. Obviously in great pain, they staggered forward under the prodding of Chekaliga spears.

"I have indeed seen you in my dreams," said Kimr, now stating it as a matter of fact. "These are your men. They have been kept alive so that they could be returned to you."

He grinned.

"My men have had some sport with them. I hope you will not mind."

Nestar stepped up to Guttanar.

"The Yengar wench was in your hands," he hissed in Utrish. "And our well-laid trap caught Greghar as well. Yet you let them escape us."

Guttanar looked down at the ground. Nestar put his hand under his chin and raised his head to look him in the eye.

"I did my best, my lord," Guttanar said, his voice fading to a harsh whisper. "But Greghar saw through our ploy. They were ready for us."

Nestar's expression grew darker.

"It was an easy task I gave you," he said. "Yet you failed me." He turned to Kimr. "If your men crave more sport, pray give them these men."

Guttanar clenched his jaw and looked to Nestar resignedly. However, the other men began to wail and beg Nestar to take them back, to save them from the Chekaligas. He was deaf to their cries, taking Kimr by the arm and leading him away, out of earshot.

"What is our destination?" asked Kimr as soon as they were alone.

"Bar-Dari," said Nestar. "You know the way?"

"Yes," said Kimr. "But it is a long and difficult march over the Mussadec Mountains."

"It will be well worth it."

IT WAS LATE evening in Atlantic City. Darbeni and Jena stood on the highest viewdeck of the Confederation Tower. While they savored the breeze, they tapped their temperature shields to raise them against the chill in the air. The light panels were just beginning to power up in the Lower Wards. Jena wandered over to one of the long visions set on an edge of the viewdeck and swept it around, zooming in on various points of interest in the city.

"Thanks for the wonderful dinner and the hospitality," said Jena without taking her eyes out of the long vision. "But I am sure you did not ask me to take leave and return to Atlantic City for the pleasure of my company."

"You have not found Princess Caitlin for me," said Darbeni, staying close to the center of the viewdeck and raising her voice slightly rather than approaching Jena at the edge. "But perhaps you were not the right person for that job. My mother has a much easier job for you to perform. One that is much better suited to your capabilities."

"What is it?" asked Jena without taking her eyes out of the long vision.

"We have a rather inconvenient ex-employee. We would like her to have an accident."

Jena turned around and looked Darbeni in the eye to make sure she was serious.

"You want me to kill someone here in Atlantic City? That's murder! If they find out, I'll be shot!"

"Relax. No one will find out. My mother is bringing her here in half an hour. We just need her to 'accidentally' fall over the edge of the viewdeck. The railings are low and the winds are strong. A tragic mishap like that could happen to anyone."

Jena looked dubious.

"Who is it?" she asked.

"Yukia Rabbina. She lured Princess Deirdre into the ambush where she was killed. Of course, we fired her immediately, but she cut a deal with the administration and got off scot-free. She deserves to die."

"Princess Deirdre was always kind to me when I visited Caitlin at Palace d'Orr," said Jena, running her fingers through her hair. She wandered around the edges of the viewdeck leaning over the low railing, oblivious to the strong breeze. "What is this worth to you?"

"Remember I promised you five hundred gold talents if you found Princess Caitlin. Well, that money is still sitting in my accounts. If you do this successfully, the money is yours."

"Very well. But remember I am recording all of this. If I am caught, I will drag you and your mother down with me."

"Oh, don't be so pessimistic. No one will ever know."

The minutes ticked by slowly. Jena was tempted to take a snort of *katsang*, but the drug made her a bit light-headed, so she resisted. Finally they heard the antigravity, and Vivia stepped out, followed by Yukia. Vivia was beautifully turned out as usual, but Yukia looked very different. Her confident demeanor was gone, replaced by an anxious look. Her clothes were well worn as well as several seasons out of date, and her makeup looked cheap.

"I am open to bringing you back, Yukia," Vivia was saying. "But you really need to convince my dear Darbeni. She controls the purse strings, you know. I am just a figurehead."

Yukia came up to Darbeni and bent her head respectfully.

"Chief Counsel Darbeni, I will do whatever it takes to be employed by Pragarina Enterprises again. I will do any show, even if I have to work under someone else. I know I can produce great content if you only give me the chance."

"We were thinking of doing a show on the Palace Guardians," said Darbeni slowly. "Seignora Jena here is our adviser. As you can see from her uniform, she is on active service with the Guardians. In fact, she is just visiting us from her posting at the Daksin Residency."

"I am pleased to meet you," said Yukia, approaching Jena and putting her arms out greet her as an equal. Jena took both her hands in hers and pulled her forward suddenly and sharply, causing her to stumble. She put her boot in the way, so Yukia tripped, arms flailing.

"I'm so sorry," said Jena, putting her hand on Yukia's back.

Yukia thought Jena was going to steady her, but instead the huntress propelled her forward with a strong push. As Yukia's stomach hit the railing, Jena leaned down, caught her by the ankle and tipped her over. Yukia screamed as she fell headfirst over the edge of the viewdeck. Her scream continued, declining into a long thin streamer of sound as she fell farther away from them. The Confederation Tower was much too tall for them to hear the impact of Yukia's body striking the street far below.

Yukia's obituary appeared on the comm the next day. It was written by Vivia's staff and was full of praise, highlighting her achievements as hostess of *Lives of Our Sisters*. It made no mention of her presence at the ambush that led to Deirdre's death. Nor did it make any reference to Yukia's unemployed status at the time of her own death. The obituary included a statement from Vivia in which she said, "We all remember the high points of Yukia Rabbina's life—a gifted hostess on the comm and a fine and generous colleague at Pragarina Enterprises. We will miss her terribly."

DIANA WAS FLYING on autopilot, listening to music from her personal store, when there was a ping in her earphones. She opened the comm channel and was mildly surprised to see the queen.

"Cornelle Diana, I understand you are bound for Sampore," she said.

"Yes, Your Highness. I am going to inspect our new forces in the Daksin Residency. Resident Bodil has also asked me to join her to discuss our response to the demands of King Vokran."

"Just so," Hildegard said, sounding uncharacteristically unsure of herself. There was a pause before she plunged ahead. "Cornelle Diana, are you aware that before her departure into exile, Princess Caitlin had a daughter that she left behind in Temple Heights Nursery? This daughter is now the d'Orr heiress."

"Yes, I did know that, ma'am. I also know that Seignora Megara Paurina is the child's legal mother."

"What else do you know about the case?" asked Hildegard cautiously.

"I was reviewing Seignora Megara's files for promotion, ma'am," said Diana. "I read everything in her record, including her performance as a mother. By all accounts, Seignora Megara has been an exemplary mother to the d'Orr girl."

"Yes, she has," said Hildegard, relieved that she did not have to explain everything. "And in return, Lady Asgara d'Orr loves Seignora Megara as though she were her real mother. But with her posting to the Daksin Residency, the child has been given over to the guardianship of Princess Andromache."

Hildegard paused to marshal her thoughts, and Diana waited patiently.

"Princess Andromache has just been to see me. Apparently, Lady Asgara ran away from Palace Saxe last night."

"Surely you have her on the security cams," said Diana. "A child should be fairly easy to find in Atlantic City."

"Unfortunately not, Cornelle. She is one of our most gifted children. She managed to avoid being caught on any of the security cams. We have no idea where she is. However, I think she is trying to get to her mother, Seignora Megara, in the Daksin Residency and that she has managed to get out of Atlantic City. She is clever enough to have stowed away on an airboat. There were only two airboats that were bound for Sampore today—one of them is yours."

"Let me call you back, ma'am," said Diana.

She turned to her copilot and said, "Search the 'boat. All compartments, the hold, the undercarriage bay, everything."

It was almost half an hour before Hildegard heard the ping of her private comm channel.

"Ma'am, we searched every centimeter of the airboat. She is not aboard now. However, we stopped at the Tirut Guild fort on our way. We unloaded cargo there, so if she was aboard, she could have gotten off to avoid being found."

"You have practical experience in these matters, Cornelle," said Hildegard. "What do you recommend?"

"We will return to Tirut, ma'am. I will speak with Baron va Alsor and get his people to begin looking for her."

"Be discreet, Cornelle," said Hildegard. "Any barbarian adventurer would know that a Zon child is worth a hefty ransom, and that a Zon heiress is worth even more."

"I hear and obey, ma'am," said Diana.

She cut the comm channel and put the airboat into a tight banking turn, heading back to Tirut.

TEN

CHE VA ALSOR BALL

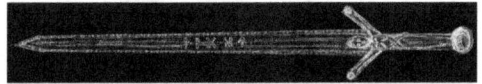

NEHEMUS VA ALSOR, the Baron of Tirut, paced the luxurious Limpore carpet in his private reception room, frowning. In his midfifties, he was recently widowed. However, he was still powerfully built and looked twenty years younger. He kept himself in prime physical condition through a combination of fanatical devotion to physical exercise and personal habits that verged on the ascetic. He had a full head of salt-and-pepper hair and a neatly trimmed beard.

The reception room was richly furnished as befitted the apartments of the richest baron in the One Land. His younger son, Cheval Jagus va Alsor, sat forward on a gold inlaid chair, watching his father's movements. Kitara walked beside her father-in-law, giving him her rapt attention.

"You are ever attentive to the interests of our house, my dear," Nehemus said. "Perhaps more so than some who were born into it."

271

"Father, you never see merit in anything that I suggest or do," Jagus said, his expression turning sullen.

Nehemus disregarded his son and continued speaking to Kitara, patting her on the cheek as he did so.

"Like you, I am suspicious of Queen Esme's motives. There are too many unanswered questions for my liking. Why has she brought the Royal Blacks to Tirut, instead of sending them to retake the Serat Oasis? With King Harald's death, she has declared herself Regent for Crown Prince Axel, but where is the boy? I fear she is thinking of usurping the throne for herself and is casting covetous eyes on our river of gold here in Tirut."

"You are so wise, my lord, and you put everything so well," said Kitara. "I see everything much more clearly after listening to you. It has made me think of a different spin entirely. Perhaps it will give Queen Esme pause to see the nephew of King Lothar of Utrea in your court."

Nehemus stroked his beard and put an arm around her waist affectionately.

"Ah, my dear, what a sharp mind you have," he said. "But you are too young to know minutiae of the Utrean House of Nibellus. The usurper Shobar murdered all the trueborn children of King Jondolar the Just years ago. King Lothar, the current occupant of the Masthead Throne is Jondolar's only sibling. I understand that Jondolar had a bastard son, who escaped—this Greghar must be that son. So while your idea of forging stronger ties with the Utrean monarch is laudable, I wonder how much love Lothar can have for his baseborn nephew?"

"Indeed father, what would your liegemen think if you brought the son of some brothel whore into our halls?"

Kitara let her scarf slip down to reveal her low-cut bodice, artfully making it seem accidental. She wore a necklace with a diamond pendant that nestled in her cleavage. She knew it would draw Nehemus's eyes to her bosom but pretended not to notice. She put her hand on his forearm and looked into his eyes earnestly.

"Greghar comes with a fine ship and a loyal crew. He has a lady-in-waiting to the queen of Utrea by his side—she has the unmistakable accent, carriage, and manner of a courtier. Surely this suggests that he has the favor of his uncle? And if your lordship points to the royal blood in his veins, how can your liegemen fault you?"

Nehemus looked at Kitara fondly.

"You reason like a diplomat, my dear," he said, smiling. "I agree—we have little to lose and potentially much to gain by hosting him."

He paused before going on.

"I have received an arrogant message from Lady Death, asking for an audience. Perhaps we can invite Greghar and her at the same time. Who knows, perhaps his presence will make her more civil."

"If it is civility you want," said Kitara. "Then don't hold an audience at all! Why not throw a ball and invite them both to it? In just a few days we will celebrate the twenty-fifth anniversary of your succeeding to the Barony of Tirut. It is fitting that your sons mark the occasion by hosting a ball in your honor. We can put up black bunting and some subtle marks of mourning so that you can host Queen Esme without any disrespect for her recent bereavement. The merriment may soften even Lady Death."

"A ball?" said Jagus. "That is the most foolish thing I have ever heard."

"On the contrary, my son, it is great idea. At a ball, it will be awkward for Lady Death to visit violence upon us as she often does. And since it will be in my honor, inviting Greghar gives him no special consequence. Yet we can still have the herald announce his royal connection, so that Queen Esme can see the respect being paid us by

King Lothar. Your wife is a clever woman, you should take lessons from her."

Jagus scowled. He stood up and gave his father a curt bow.

"I have an appointment with some friends, my lord. I must leave you now."

"I am tired of your so-called friends. All they seem to do is use you as an endless source of funds. Don't expect me to bail you out if you lose any more money at the gaming table."

Jagus stomped out of the reception room and shut the door behind him sharply. At the last minute, he caught it and closed it softly.

"I don't know what to do with Jagus," Nehemus sighed. "I give the boy everything, and yet he feels mistreated."

"Don't be hard on him, my lord," said Kitara. "He tries so hard to emulate his father. But you set such a high standard that when he cannot match it, he grows frustrated."

"Kitara, you are too good for him," said Nehemus, his voice growing thick. He put an arm around her waist again and drew her to him. "When your brother proposed you to us, I should have married you myself."

Kitara dexterously slipped away from him and rearranged her scarf to cover her bosom again.

"My lord, you are the dream of every lady in the One Land," she said. "How I wish I could put aside my devotion to Thermad and the One God! Then I could forget my marriage vows and follow my heart."

Nehemus sighed again.

"Your piety only adds to your allure, my dear. I wish that Jagus would recognize what a prize he has in you."

Kitara looked down at her feet modestly, drawing another sigh from Nehemus.

"I trust I can leave the arrangements for the ball in your hands," he said.

ZAIBENE HELD THE embossed parchment reverentially in both hands.

"*'Cheval Trianus va Alsor and Cheval Jagus va Alsor together with their wives cordially invite Collector Mantan Yandharan, Mistress Zaibene va Alsor Yandharan and their guests to the Anniversary Ball to celebrate Nehemus va Alsor's twenty five glorious years as Baron of Tirut,'*" she read slowly, savoring every word. "The list of invitees is very select. I have asked several of the wealthier merchant wives—very indirectly, of course. None of them has been invited. Clearly this ball is limited to best families. I hear that nobility are coming from all over Briga. "

"Those that can make it here at this short notice," agreed Yandharan. "Once again, I find myself elevated by your noble connections. I doubt whether Cheval Trianus and Cheval Jagus would have invited me if I were not married to their cousin."

"This is so incredible!" she exclaimed, too happy to boast anew about the superiority of her connections. "None of us heard even the slightest rumor before it was formally announced."

"Perhaps they wished to surprise the baron."

"Yes, yes, that must be it. I must go shopping! I must have a new ensemble—a gown, shoes, and scarf. Nothing in my wardrobe is good enough for such a grand ball. And I must see the jeweler for some new earrings. You must guarantee my credit."

"Of course, my dear," he said, sighing inwardly. He knew that Zaibene's shopping spree would be costly. She had inherited exalted connections and expensive tastes, but her own family had only modest means. She had brought no property to the marriage and only a small dowry. He made a mental note to sell some of his personal property and make a deposit with his goldsmith to cover her spending.

⁕⁕⁕

ESME LOOKED AROUND the richly appointed chamber in Tirut Castle, trying to conceal her irritation. She looked out of the wide window, trying to calm herself with the wonderful view of the harbor. It had already been a very long day and she was tired and tempted to lean back in her chair. But she fought the urge and maintained her ramrod straight posture, as befitted her status as queen. She wore a steel cuirass with gold trim over a tunic of soft chamois leather and leather breeches. A short sword hung on her belt. A black scarf of watered silk and a black armband made of soft velvet were prominent symbols of her mourning.

"Your Majesty, I can only advise, but I do so most vehemently," said Nehemus, smiling affably. "Campaigning, battles, and fighting are best left to the professional soldiers. As the recently widowed Queen of Briga, I understand that you wish to take the king's place at the head of the army. But consider that you are a young woman with no experience of war. Let my son Jagus lead our forces to retake Serat. It is his ancestral fief and his responsibility to fight for it."

"I am sorry, Baron, but my mind is made up," said Esme. "We march a few days after your Anniversary Ball, so I am disappointed that you do not see fit to personally lead your Kriggen Regiment and ride by my side. I see it as our responsibility to retake what is mine." She paused here to look at him with a challenge in her eyes, but he did not contradict her. "Where is your son?"

Almost on cue, Jagus entered with Kitara on his arm. Jagus bowed low and Kitara dropped a deep curtsey with a great show of deference.

"Majesty!" she said as she rose. "What an inspiration you are to us, dressed in such warlike attire!"

Esme looked from Nehemus to Kitara. She instinctively recognized the look that jumped into his eyes on his daughter-in-law's entrance. She glanced at Jagus, dressed like her in light armor and saw that he was quite oblivious.

"Pray sit down and join us, Cheval Jagus, Chevalina Kitara," said Esme. "We are pleased to see you."

Kitara took a seat and rang the bell. A steward hastened in and she asked for some refreshment. He left and returned with servers who rapidly laid out decanters of a very fine Mussadec wine and a selection of tempting hors d'oeuvres. They chatted about neutral topics till the staff left the chamber.

Nehemus cleared his throat and began in a serious tone, "Your Majesty, as you go off to war, I ask you to consider the future of the realm. It is far too heavy a burden for a beautiful young woman to bear alone. I ask that you consider taking a consort—one who can discharge the more onerous and inconsequential tasks that you perforce must do at the moment. Of course, any nuptial formalities must wait till you are out of mourning."

Esme looked at him and a ghost of her old vivacity played on her face.

"My dear baron! I am touched by your loyalty. To offer yourself and your riches to a poor widow!"

Nehemus looked horrified, as he realized too late how his words must sound to her.

"Oh no, Your Majesty!" He rose from his seat and kneeled. "I am not so bold as to press my own suit. I was thinking of other more suitable—"

"Why not, sir?" She gestured about her at the sumptuous furnishings of the chamber. "You are the richest man in the One Land and can aspire to the hand of anyone you choose. But perhaps you find me wanting?"

"No, no, Your Highness—" Nehemus stammered. "The truth is... the truth is..." His mind went blank and when she did not intercede to help him, he plunged on without thinking. "My heart is given to another."

Esme laughed. She knew he would like nothing better than to change the subject and bring up the name of the relative or ally that he hoped to betroth her to. But she was having far too much fun to oblige him.

"Come, come, sir. We high aristocrats know that love has nothing to do with marriage."

Nehemus took a deep breath and began to recover his wits. Still on his knees he said, "Ma'am, I am a simple baron, too far below you in rank to merit your consideration."

Esme laughed again, feeling genuine mirth for the first time in a long while. *I wish Harald were here to see me,* she thought.

"That is easily remedied. I can raise you to archbaron. I could even create you the Duke of the Southern Marches."

Jagus watched their exchange tongue-tied, but Kitara was not overawed. She had served Esme as a lady-in-waiting and knew her mistress's playful ways.

"As usual, ma'am, you delight in toying with us," she said. "But it does not behoove you to give my father-in-law false hopes."

Esme looked over at Kitara and beckoned her with a slight movement of her hand. Kitara came over and followed Nehemus's example, kneeling in front of Esme's chair. The queen put a hand on her cheek.

"As fair as ever, Chevalina Kitara," she said. "And just as sharp as you always were. You know me too well. We had such fun together, didn't we?"

"It was Your Majesty's indulgence," said Kitara.

"Well, let us put your father-in-law out of his misery. Baron Nehemus, I will not steal you away from your secret love. I hope she realizes how lucky she is. For in addition to being the richest, you are doubtless the fittest of my barons and the scourge of our enemies."

She rose. Both Nehemus and Kitara felt the sting of her last words.

LIKE MOST BARBARIAN coastal strongholds, Tirut Castle was built on a rocky headland that jutted into the sea. It dominated the city that was crowded around Half Moon Bay and centered on the harbor. The Baron of Tirut's colorful banners, emblazoned with his coat of arms of entwined sea serpents, streamed from all the towers. There were dozens of men-at-arms pacing the battlements in the bright uniforms of his Color Guard. Every eye in the castle was now on the Zon airboat that was just shutting down her engines and putting out sky anchors.

Diana lay back in the comfortable cushions of a club chair in the air-boat, looking out at the castle below. The airboat was crewed by a squad of armed Guardians in dress uniforms, but Diana herself was dressed in a long gown of local Tirutan cami-silk. The only elements of her uniform that she wore were the metal choker and wrist bracers engraved with the crossed swords of her rank. Her pale, flaxen hair was piled atop her head in the most elegant coiffure that the part-time beautician in the Tirut Guilt fort could manage. A white-gold armband fashioned like a coiled lasso and silver high-heeled slippers completed her outfit.

"I must voice my concern once again, Cornelle," said the squad seignora. "You have innumerable enemies down there in the castle. To go among them alone and unarmed is madness. Please allow us to escort you."

Diana stood up and stretched lazily.

"Tirut has always been more interested in money than war," she said. "The Straits of Gold pour such wealth into the city that they would never jeopardize it by doing me harm and bringing on Zon retribution. But I will take two Guardians with me in the pod for ceremonial purposes. And you may deploy the heavy 'grator to remind them that this airboat can destroy the castle."

Climbing into the pod, Diana settled herself into the plush passenger seat. Looking down out of the clear floor panels, she saw the honor guard drawn up to receive her. Her critical eye took in their shining helmets, burnished breastplates, and polished pikes.

Two Guardians climbed aboard the pod after her. One strapped herself into the pilot's seat, and the hatch hissed shut. The pod's small engine whined to life, the restraining clamps were released and they spiraled down to the castle courtyard, landing in a cloud of dust. As the ramp extended, the two Guardians emerged and took up positions on either side of it. They handed Diana down.

Tall and erect, she walked up to meet Jagus and Kitara, who came up through the lined honor guard to receive her. Jagus was dressed in a ceremonial military uniform, and Kitara wore a fine gown and expensive jewelry as befitted her status. They bowed to her, and Diana nodded rather than reciprocating. *Who does she think she is?* thought Kitara. *She is not the Queen Empress.* The three of them inspected the honor guard.

"Very well turned out," commented Diana. "My congratulations."

"Our Kriggen Regiment always does us proud," said Jagus. "Please allow us to escort you into the ballroom."

With Kitara on his arm, Jagus led Diana through the enormous entranceway into the ballroom. It was a cavernous chamber, brightly lit with countless candles. The walls were adorned with carvings and bright frescoes, and the ceiling was so high that it seemed like a sky. A large orchestra was at the far end on a raised dais. As soon as they saw Diana enter behind Jagus and Kitara, they stopped and began playing "The March of the Giants", the official anthem of the barons of Tirut.

Nehemus excused himself from the group he was chatting with and came forward to receive Diana. He smiled, and she gave him the half bow he was due.

"Welcome, welcome, Lady Death," he said, his tone jovial. "I am so pleased you are able to join us this evening."

"I wish to see you on business, Baron," she replied. "But this ball will have to do. I hope you will be kind enough to give me a private audience in the course of the evening's festivities."

"Nothing would please me more, Lady Death." He paused and appraised her for a moment from head to toe. "This is the first time I have seen you dressed for a ball. You must allow me to tell you how magnificent you look."

Diana gave him one of her characteristic smiles—one that did not reach her pale eyes.

"You are too kind, sir."

Nehemus crooked his finger, and a steward appeared with a tray laden with silver tumblers of finest Brigon apple wine from East Brosia.

"To the alliance between Tirut and the Zon Sisterhood," he said. "A partnership of equals."

"To our alliance based on mutual respect and trust," responded Diana.

They touched tumblers and drank. After a few more moments of formal conversation, Nehemus excused himself to circulate among his numerous guests. As soon as he departed, Kitara contrived to bring Greghar and Nitya forward. She poked Jagus, and he stepped up to Diana, uncomfortable under her daunting stare.

"Lady Death, we would like to present some of our noble guests, Lord Greghar, nephew of King Lothar of Utrea and Nitya, lady-in-waiting to Her Highness, Queen Lovelyn."

Greghar and Nitya stepped forward as they were introduced. Nitya curtsied daintily, demonstrating that she was on the mend from Guttanar's beating. She had ingeniously managed to cover her cuts with makeup. She wore a new gown cobbled together by the hands of the *Darling Thoma* from the odds and ends of a dozen different fabrics. The seamen had done themselves proud and it was a creditable effort that hung and fell well. To the noblewomen at the ball, it was still just a collection of rags, but Nitya wore it with such serenity and grace that the whispers that arose as she entered the grand ballroom soon died away.

Greghar bowed formally. Diana smiled at them both, and this time a hint of amusement lit up her eyes.

"To use the old cliché, we meet again."

"I hardly recognize you, Lady Death," said Greghar. "This is a side of you that I have never seen."

"You know each other?" asked Kitara, astonished.

"I have known both Nitya and Greghar Nibellus since they were children," Diana replied. "Greghar and I are such good friends that I once scarred his handsome face with my dagger."

Greghar smiled as she went on.

"Wasn't that fun, Greghar? Perhaps tonight we may do a different sort of dance."

"We certainly cannot fight, Lady Death," he responded. "For you seem to have forgotten your sword."

Kitara did not relish this rather familiar exchange. Conscious of Jagus by her side, she fought her temptation to compete with Diana for Greghar's notice.

"I am pleased to bring old friends together," she said. She looked at Diana thinking, *Surely her air of self-sufficiency and arrogance must negate her beauty; strong and desirable men want women they can be protective of.*

Kitara was about to draw Greghar and Nitya away under the pretext of introducing them to some other important guests, when the orchestra stopped. Before she could open her mouth, Trianus va Alsor, her brother-in-law and heir to the barony of Tirut, stepped onto the dais and clapped his hands to get everyone's attention.

"My lords, ladies, and gentlemen! The time has come to begin the night's festivities. I call on my dear father to come forward to cut the cake and say a few words."

No sooner had Trianus stopped speaking than Nehemus was at Kitara's side, putting a hand on her elbow.

"I pray that you will spare Kitara to cut the cake and then open the ball with me," he said to Jagus. He turned to the others. "This is the first ball I have attended since the passing of my dear wife. As a lonely widower, I must depend on the kindness of my sons to meet my social obligations."

"Of course, my lord," said Jagus. He did not sound particularly enthusiastic, but yielded his place by Kitara's side.

"You do me great honor, my lord," Kitara said, curtseying deeply. As she accepted Nehemus's arm, her expression was an arch mixture of deference and playfulness. She walked the fine line perfectly, stoking Nehemus's desires while remaining within the bounds of propriety. But unseen by anyone else, she shot Greghar a suggestive look over her shoulder as they left.

Jagus did not linger long and soon left to continue his duties as a host. Recognized as Lothar's nephew, Greghar had become one of the most highly ranked guests at the ball. It would be insulting to his hosts to stand through the opening dance. He knew that his duty was to Nitya and was on the point of asking her for the honor of her hand, when a familiar voice interrupted them.

"Lady Death, I am delighted to find you here," said Horus Matalus, appearing through the crowds. Diana turned to him in surprise and he saw her full form, unobstructed by other guests. He stared open-mouthed for a moment before continuing. "Why, you are a vision, a goddess come to life."

Diana grinned at him with genuine pleasure and pounded him on the shoulder pad of his ceremonial tunic. He staggered under the force of her friendly wallop.

"Horus, my old friend!" she said. "I hear your father has finally raised you from cheval to baron."

"True, true, when we last met in Firsk, I had the fiefdom, but not the title," said Horus. He glanced over at Greghar before going on. "I often think of the time we spent together in the Morning Room of the Gray Fort, for it is such a pleasant memory."

"I recall a much earlier time in Firsk," returned Diana. "Our first meeting when I gave you this."

She reached forward and ran a long finger down Horus's cheekbone, tracing a thin white scar. She allowed her finger to linger on his face possessively. Horus reached up, and covered her hand with his. She smiled, and allowed him to squeeze it.

"Lady Death, I will do anything—"

"I wonder at you, Horus!" His wife, Baroness Talia, appeared out of the crowd with two retainers, young men from noble Karsk families. "Seeking out and socializing with this whore of the Evil One! Have you forgotten how much pain she has inflicted on our families?"

Talia looked at Diana with hatred in her eyes. Her open display of venom surprised Horus, and he looked from his wife to Diana, unsure of how to proceed.

"So what brings you down to Tirut?" Diana asked to fill the awkward silence.

"Talia and I were visiting her cousins in East Brosia," responded Horus eagerly. "An express messenger arrived from her sister, Queen Esme, announcing the death of King Harald. As you know, the queen is here in Tirut with the Royal Black regiment, so we came down to condole with her. She is still in mourning, so she asked me to attend the ball to represent her. I am a baron, but I represent the crown!"

"You never cease to amaze me, Horus."

He could not tell whether she was pulling his leg, so he went on.

"Baron va Alsor has invited me to stand with Talia and take second position after him in the opening dance. I beg that you will join my party."

"I think that you should confer with your wife before issuing such invitations, Horus," said Diana.

Talia responded by turning on her heel and leaving them, followed by her retainers. Horus looked after her but then turned back to Diana with an expression that suggested he might drop all attempts at decorum. He opened his mouth to speak, but Diana forestalled him.

"Go to your wife, Horus," she said gently. "Or she will make your life miserable."

He looked at her for a long moment before saying, "She already does." But then he did as she suggested and left to rejoin Talia.

"How dare you insult me in public like this," Talia hissed when he returned to her side. Horus knew he would get no further enjoyment at the ball.

⊙∙⊙∙⧼∙⊙∙⊙

NEHEMUS AND KITARA jointly held the long silk-covered handle of the ceremonial knife and made the official first cut in the cake that had been created for the occasion. It was a massive tiered creation topped by "25" in runic numerals made of chocolate. As soon as they made the cut, Trianus led the eminent crowd in a round of hearty applause.

"My lord, Lady Death is reputed to be a great singer," Kitara whispered to Nehemus as the crowd applauded. "I suggest you ask her to give us an air before we open the ball. It will demean her status to that of a lowly performer, but it will be awkward for her to refuse."

"My dear, you are brilliant!" Nehemus whispered back. He squeezed her hand and mounted the dais, as the applause died down.

"My distinguished guests!" Nehemus spoke in a carrying voice. "I would like to thank my sons and daughters-in-law for putting on such a magnificent ball for me. I am a lucky, lucky man to have a family that loves me so dearly. And I thank you all for coming here from near and far at such short notice to celebrate with me." He paused and there was another round of applause. "We are fortunate tonight to have with us one of the best known singers in the One Land. Lady Death, we have all heard of your singing prowess. May I request you to favor us with an air before we open the ball?"

"It is an insult, Cornelle Diana!" said Nitya in a low voice. "They're trying to humiliate you!"

"I know," replied Diana without turning her head. But she moved forward with long, smooth strides. She gathered her gown above her ankles as she gracefully mounted the dais to join Nehemus. She regarded him for a moment before turning to the audience, that looked on with bated breath. There was complete silence in the huge chamber.

"My lord baron," said Diana. "I know that you barbarians consider a woman performing in public to be low class with loose morals. However, among my people, performers have high status. Hence, I accept your invitation as a Zon singer."

With that she turned to the orchestra leader and he gave her a pitch pipe. She used it quickly saying, "I'll sing a very simple melody in the middle C."

"That is a quite a range you've give us on the pipe," he said hesitantly.

"Don't worry, I can sing a cappella if I have to."

"We're professionals," replied the orchestra leader, stung. "Just sing—we'll accompany you."

Diana turned and looked out on to the multitude. Every eye was on her expectantly. Unthinking, Horus left Talia's side and pushed his way to the foot of the dais. As their eyes met, Diana took a deep breath and began with the chorus:

> *Duty calls, I must obey*
> *Duty calls, I cannot stay.*
> *Each time that we must part,*
> *It gets harder and harder—*
> *It breaks my heart!*

> *Each day is the first day*
> *Of the rest of my life.*
> *If I could only choose my way*
> *I would steer away from strife.*
> *I see the flowers, I see your smile,*
> *But then, duty calls, duty calls.*

> *On too many days and in so many ways*
> *I've fought and rolled the dice.*
> *A voice in my head says*
> *You've won, but at what price?*
> *I sheath my sword, I say, no more!*
> *But then, duty calls, duty calls.*

> *All that I see in front of me*
> *Is a long and lonely road.*
> *As I go on, I clearly see*
> *There's nothing ahead but woe.*
> *Being with you would set me free*
> *But then, duty calls, duty calls.*

Her powerful voice was rich and sweet at the same time, like warm honey. It filled the cavernous hall. Her pale eyes ranged over the audience, actively engaging them. But it was the pathos in her tone, her expression of longing that touched each and every person who heard her. The song was in Brigish, so everyone felt a personal connection to her words and the feelings she expressed. Nehemus looked upon Kitara with wistful eyes. Greghar thought of Caitlin. By the time she repeated the chorus, hundreds were swaying and humming along.

Horus was sure that she was singing to him. She had acquiesced a deadly insult to do so, and the enormity of her gift overwhelmed him. It made him unhappier than before and he felt his eyes mist over. He rubbed them before tears could form.

When Diana was done there was thunderous applause, dwarfing the earlier polite rounds of clapping. She bowed to the audience and asked the orchestra leader to come up and join her as the ovation rolled on and on. Then as quickly as she had come, she descended from the dais. As she rejoined them, Nitya thought, *She is learning how to love.*

AFTER A SHORT hiatus, the orchestra struck up the first bars of the opening dance of the ball. Kitara curtsied to Nehemus and gave him her hand to open the ball. The first dance was a stately minuet, and the baron led her down the line of privileged couples to open the ball. She gave Nehemus her rapt attention, and his pleasure at partnering her was obvious on his face. After they paraded the length of the aisle of couples, the ball was open. The music took on a bit more tempo, and all the assembled couples broke ranks in order of protocol and began the dance.

As representatives of Queen Esme, Talia and Horus were the first couple to follow Nehemus and Kitara. They were a stark contrast. She was graceful, but Horus's lack of coordination meant that they were often at odds with each other. He constantly threatened to crush her toes beneath his boots, and she was only saved from hurt by a combination of luck and quickness of foot.

Greghar and Nitya followed as the third couple in order of precedence. He raised Nitya's arm to begin and she gave him a radiant smile. Having spent his boyhood at court and being light and athletic on his feet, Greghar was an excellent dancer. And at the behest of Queen Lovelyn, Nitya had been an adept student of the Utrean royal dance master. The two of them had never danced together, but they were so in tune with one another that they fell into step almost immediately.

As soon as the piece ended and urged on by Nitya, Greghar bowed to Diana and led her out on to the ballroom floor for the second dance. While Nitya had become a good dancer, Diana was superb. She was used to leading, but Greghar had height and strength enough to hold her firm and get her to follow him. Within a few moments, her natural sense of timing had her in step. Thereafter they got better with every turn and were soon moving with such perfect balance and grace that even some of the other dancers slowed their steps to watch them. At the end of the dance, Greghar bowed to her again, and Diana executed a creditable curtsey.

"Thank you, sir," she said. "That was almost as much fun as a sword fight."

Nitya, Diana, and Greghar drifted into the adjoining dining parlor where an extravagant variety of food and drink was laid out. The older guests sat at tables here, gossiping and eating. Greghar flagged down a steward and took two glasses, water for Diana and wine for himself. Diana dropped in a cleansing tablet from her clutch before sipping it.

"They say that Nehemus is the richest man in the One Land," said Greghar. "This ball and this castle certainly give credence to that belief. Why, the furniture and decorations in Nordberg Castle look tawdry in comparison with what we see here!"

Diana did not respond, for she saw Nehemus himself approach them.

"You wished to speak with me, Lady Death." Nehemus's tone was courteous. "Shall we take a few minutes now? I hope your friends will excuse us?"

Greghar and Nitya nodded, and Diana inclined her head without reply. Nehemus took Diana's arm and escorted her into a narrow corridor. It was very long, with torches on brackets every ten meters or so. It climbed several sets of stairs, and the sounds of the ball faded away behind them. Soon they could only hear the echoes of their footsteps on the flagstones.

He led the way to a cozy round tower room with arrow slit windows that looked out to sea. He stepped over a high threshold and Diana followed him, hiking up her long gown. As he slid the door shut behind her, she drew a slim laser pistol from a thigh holster before she dropped the skirts of her gown again. She held the weapon behind her back.

"A convenient place for us to talk without being overheard," he said, taking a seat in one of the comfortable armchairs.

"If you say so," said Diana without warmth. She sat in the facing chair, casually dropping the laser pistol in her lap.

"What a distrustful woman you are, Lady Death."

"One of the secrets of a long life. I am sure you have not lived as long as you have by being credulous."

"So what do you wish to discuss? Our tributes have been paid on time and in full. Your Trading Guild runs very profitable operations here in Tirut. My lord's share of your commerce has considerably lightened the burden of the tribute payments."

Diana paused and studied his face, trying to predict how he would react to her request. *Asgara is worth a large ransom,* she thought. *But surely it is not enough for him to endanger his lucrative alliance with the Sisterhood.*

"Your alliance with us has been a model for the rest of Briga and the One Land," she said finally. "It is on that basis that I bring this request to you. As you know, we Zon value our children very highly. One of them has run away from home. We have reason to believe she is in Tirut."

"A Zon child loose in Tirut?" he threw back his head and laughed. "How droll! A Zon child will be conspicuous."

He leaned forward and put his arm by Diana's, contrasting her lightly tanned white skin with his swarthy coloring.

"I am aware of that," she said, not joining in his mirth. "I also know that Tirut is a trading port, full of foreigners from all parts of the One Land, with many paler-skinned folk from Utrea."

"Zon or Utrean, children do not survive long in the streets, you know."

"That is why I am asking for your help in recovering her." She paused. "We will richly reward anyone who helps in getting her back."

"I am sure that you wish to keep this information secret," said Nehemus, shrewdly. "It appears I did well to meet you here in this secluded tower room."

He reached over and pulled a long bell rope that hung by the arm of his chair. Diana heard it ringing at a great distance. She got up from her chair and stood loose limbed by one of the arrow slit windows, her pistol in one hand. A few moments later, there was a respectful knock on the door.

"Enter!" called Nehemus.

The door opened and Nehemus's personal valet entered and bowed deeply.

"Go to the ball and fetch Collector Yandharan," he said. "Tell him it is urgent."

The valet bowed again and disappeared. Nehemus looked at Diana, thinking to make some small talk, but she was staring out of the narrow window.

"Why are so many of your ships preparing for sea?" she asked suddenly.

"I am summoning a regiment from my vassal, Baron Lutus Terendor of East Brosia," said Nehemus. "Surely you are aware of the recent events here in the Southern Marches. The Chekaligas have taken the Serat Oasis. I must retake it."

"Queen Esme is here with the Royal Blacks. I hear you are mustering your Kriggen Regiment. How many troops will you mobilize?"

"This year's actions are unprecedented. We have never seen so many of the wild tribesmen acting in concert. Even tribes that have been peaceful for decades, like the Kasar Chekaligas have risen. I am thankful that Queen Esme is decisive like her father."

Diana digested his opinion, but did not respond. A moment later, Nehemus's valet was at the threshold again.

"Collector Yandharan is here, my lord," he announced, then turned and left. Yandharan stepped into the tower room and gave

Nehemus the full measure of respect. He glanced over at Diana and bowed to her as well, eliciting an acknowledging nod.

"I await your orders to return and retake Serat, my lord," Yandharan said.

"Yes, yes, indeed that is your responsibility as my son's liegeman. I am mustering regiments to enable you to do just that. But that is not why I have summoned you away from the side of the lovely Zaibene."

Yandharan bowed his head and waited for Nehemus to go on.

"Lady Death has given us a problem, Collector. Apparently there is a runaway Zon girl at large in Tirut. We need to find her and return her to the Sisterhood."

Noting the pistol that Diana held loosely in her hand, Yandharan put a hand on his ceremonial sword hilt.

"My lord, I will be happy to help in any way that I can. However, while I maintain a house in Tirut, it is not my native city. Technically I have no authority here."

"I have collectors aplenty here in Tirut, Yandharan," said Nehemus. "But they will all be constrained to work through official channels. The Zon don't want it widely known that there is a Zon girl wandering around the streets of Tirut. You can work discreetly and report directly to me. Your bronze badge will carry weight with the common run of people in the street." He paused and looked over at Diana. "And if you find her, the Zon will express their gratitude in gold."

"What does she look like?" asked Yandharan.

Diana tapped her wrist bracer and projected a life-size hologram of Asgara. The hologram buzzed and crackled softly before setting, brightening, and coalescing into a sharp image. Yandharan took a step back in alarm and almost tripped over the high threshold. Nehemus shrank back into the cushions of his armchair, whispering, "Sorcery!"

The hologram was Asgara's official school image, dressed in a pink uniform leotard, wearing the gold d'Orr band in her hair, identifying her as the heiress to the d'Orr tiara. However, barbarians knew little about the intricacies of Zon society, so this ornament meant nothing to Yandharan and Nehemus. Scrubbed, anointed, and made up, with her ash-blonde curls in a coiffure atop her head, she looked twice her actual age.

The initial shock wore off quickly, and both men stared at the hologram in fascination. Yandharan looked from the hologram to Diana and back again.

"I think I know where she is," he said finally.

"Take me to her," said Diana. "Let us leave right now."

Yandharan looked uncomfortable and addressed Nehemus.

"My lord baron, as you know I am here with my wife Zaibene, your kinswoman. She has been really looking forward to this ball and will be sorely disappointed to leave it so early."

"Is this Zon girl in any immediate danger?" asked Nehemus.

"No, my lord. She is safe in the home of one of my men-at-arms. A dependable man, who lodges with a respectable war widow."

"There!" said Nehemus, turning to Diana and smiling genially. "Yandharan will conduct you there early tomorrow morning. Let the child get a good night's sleep."

"Very well," said Diana, reluctantly.

THE HOUSE WAS at the end of a long, twisting alley in a poorer section of Tirut, where all the bins were overflowing with garbage. The smells of the refuse were almost as strong in the house. Asgara sat at the kitchen table, looking at the gray gruel, but she felt so sick that she had little appetite. She knew about germs and infection and had been careful to avoid drinking water and tried to eat foods where the risks were lowest. But she still felt queasy and weak.

Lidill Ikren came in carrying a cup of weak tea.

"Eat your supper, dear," she said. "You must keep your strength up."

Asgara looked at her with an annoyed expression. Lidill was plump with smooth, dusky skin and a pleasant face. She had been considered fairly attractive until a former lover had badly broken her nose. It had not healed well and now canted to one side. Asgara could not look at her without wrinkling her nose in distaste, an expression that Lidill found infuriating.

"It is your food that is making me ill," she said.

Lidill set down her cup and put her hands on her hips.

"Oh, forgive me, gracious lady. How may I serve you? Shall I order some shoots of orange grass from the Shoba Isles? Some Kaylan tea?"

"Just take me to the gates of the city," said Asgara. "If you let me go, I can take care of myself."

"Just eat your gruel, there's a good girl," said Lidill, cajoling.

"I told you to leave it on the fire till it boiled, but you didn't listen to me. So I won't eat it. It will make me ill."

"If you keep up with your high and mighty ways you can just starve, young lady," snapped Lidill, losing patience.

"Don't be angry at Asgara, Mama," Noki said as he wandered into the kitchen. "She's always so nice to me, not like the other kids in the lane."

Noki was Lidill's older son, and at ten, he was some years older than Asgara. But it was clear from even cursory observation that he was not normal. He had an unnaturally large head and eyes that slanted upward. His mouth and nose were small and his nasal bridge was flat. He walked with a loose-limbed, shambling gait. When he spoke, his mouth worked, and his speech was furry. But he was uniformly cheerful, and now he smiled brightly at both of them.

Asgara looked at him kindly, as she would at a particularly good-natured dog. She ruffled his hair and he beamed at her.

"You're a sweet boy, Noki," she said. "It's not your fault that you are retarded. It's your mother's fault, for she should have taken care of things when you were conceived and never had you."

Lidill's temper snapped and she slapped Asgara so hard that she fell off of her chair.

"I don't care that the chevalina is paying for your room and board!" she screamed. "I will not have you talking about my son like that!" She hugged Noki to her breast. "What do you know about him? He is the sweetest, best-natured child in the world. I wouldn't trade him for a hundred nasty bitches like you."

"Don't listen to her, Noki," she continued to her son in a soft voice. She shook her head angrily and hugged him tighter. "She is a spoiled, rotten girl. You will always stay with Mama."

Asgara put a hand to her face where an imprint of Lidill's hand was beginning to form. The blow was hard enough to disorient her, and the sharp pain drew spontaneous tears. It took a few moments for her to raise herself off the floor.

"You were cruel to bring poor Noki into this world!" she cried heatedly. "Don't you see how all the other children pick on him? Just this afternoon, they held his head in the horse trough—they would have drowned him if I hadn't stopped them. And for all your airs of respectability, you are just a whore from the gutter!"

"How dare you! Everyone knows that I am a respectable war widow. My husband was an honorable soldier, a fearless warrior. He was the only one brave enough to go after Princess Ice herself during the Battle of Aurora. His comrades were afraid of Zon magic and hung back, so he had to face her in single combat. They said she used sorcery to kill him."

Anger and her throbbing face made Asgara reckless.

"Then he was a failure!" she spat out. "It was my grandmother who killed your husband! All she had was her sword, and he was fully armed; I have read the whole story, many times."

Lidill grew still and the room became very quiet. Noki tried to hold on to his mother, but she silently disengaged herself and stood up. Asgara backed away toward the kitchen door as Lidill picked up a wicked looking knife from the chopping board and turned to her.

"You Zon bitch!" she hissed, advancing with the knife blade in front of her. "I should have known!"

Just then there was the sound of the front door, and Rator stumped into the house. He stood at the kitchen door, looking at the scene and hooked his thumbs in his sword belt.

"What is going on?" he asked quietly. "What are you doing with the knife?"

"Asgara said Mama should never have had me," Noki piped up. "What did she mean, Rator Karsk?"

"Nothing that need concern you," said Rator without looking at him. He looked at Lidill. "Did you strike her?"

"Yes," she replied sulkily. She put up her hand, level with her nose. "I am fed up to here with her lip."

"I see. Well, don't worry, you won't have her on your hands for much longer."

He adjusted his sword and sat at the table. Lidill brought him a fresh bowl of gruel, hunks of black bread, and a mug of beer. He waited for her to seat herself opposite him before he began to eat. He ate and drank with delicacy, a marked contrast to Lidill, who shoveled the gruel into her mouth and made guzzling sounds as she drank her tea.

As they were eating, Asgara went over to Noki. She put her arms around him and whispered in his ear, "I was angry with your Mama, Noki, not with you. You are my friend."

Noki hugged her back.

"I love you, Asgara," he said. "You are my only friend!"

"Where is our son?" Rator asked Lidill as they were eating.

"Vitor is asleep," Lidill responded with her mouth full. "It is late for him, you know."

"Has the girl eaten?"

"I am sick and tired of trying to get her to do anything," said Lidill with spirit. "She complains constantly about the food, her bed, the smells, everything!"

Rator turned to Asgara.

"You know where your bed is, child," he said, his tone level. "If you are not feeling well enough to eat, go to bed. I know it is a hard bed, but it is the best we can do for the moment."

Asgara stood and began to leave the kitchen without a word, with one hand on her cheek where Lidill had struck her. Noki followed her like a little puppy.

"One more thing," he called after her. She stopped and turned around. "Can you ride a horse?"

Her face finally broke into a smile.

"I love to ride," she said. "I ride very well. All the grooms say that I have one of the best seats in school."

"All the grooms..." mimicked Lidill.

"Go to bed," said Rator. "And can you be a dear and help Noki to bed as well? He may have wet himself. He should be changed before he goes to bed."

"I am sure I can," said Asgara. "I often changed my sister, though that was when she was very little."

"No, no, I will put him to bed," remonstrated Lidill, getting to her feet. "I can't trust my Noki to this little witch."

Rator stood and put his arm around Lidill's waist.

"I am sure she will take good care of him. Won't you, child?" Asgara nodded and led Noki away.

A look of sorrow crossed Lidill's face. "Every day I miss my dear daughter, Daril. She took such good care of Noki; I thought his future was secure. I often rage at the One God for taking her. For who will provide for poor Noki when I am gone?"

Rator was not listening. His lips were on Lidill's throat, and his hands slipped under her blouse to caress her full breasts.

"I have to leave later tonight," he breathed. "But we have a few hours to say good-bye."

Lidill's mind was elsewhere, and Rator's excitement was rapidly spent. Neither of them got much pleasure out of it. She waited impatiently for his breathing to slow and grow even. Then she cautiously reached over and pulled aside a corner of the thin curtain. In the shaft of white moonlight that shone in, she satisfied herself that Rator was asleep. She slid out of bed as softly as she could and padded to the kitchen. Armed with the sharp kitchen knife, she crept into the small storeroom where Asgara's narrow bed lay on the floor.

Lidill was by the bed when a premonition brought Asgara awake. She saw the blade of Lidill's knife glinting the moonlight and opened her mouth to scream. Lidill fell on her, choking off her cries with her left hand while she raised her right to strike. Asgara struggled and tried to twist away, all the while dreading the bite of the knife. Lidill cursed under her breath as she tried to keep the girl still as well as quiet so she could stab her.

AS FOOD AND wine flowed freely, the guests demanded more lively music, and the dancing grew more vigorous. Eventually most of them began to tire. Beginning with the elderly, they started to come up to Nehemus and take their leave. With timing born of experience, Greghar and Nitya waited for a decorous moment to pay their respects and take their leave of their hosts.

Nehemus stood by a window in the dining parlor with Jagus and Kitara by his side. Jagus felt as though he, rather than his father, was the third wheel, and he wore a sulky expression. Greghar and Nitya approached and made their bows.

"Allow me to express my heartfelt gratitude for your kind invitation, my lord," said Greghar. "It has been a dazzling ball and we have had a wonderful time. I have much to report to my uncle."

Nitya stood mute and demure, as was expected of a well-bred girl.

"Lord Greghar, it has been our honor to have you. I hope that we see you again and often. You will always find a welcome at Tirut Castle."

They were about to turn to leave, when Kitara broke with protocol and spoke up.

"Lord Greghar, I see that you have good offices with high-ranking Zon like Lady Death. I wonder if I may meet with you privately to discuss issues of mutual benefit."

Nehemus put his arm around her shoulders and looked down on her approvingly.

"I am at your ladyship's service," said Greghar.

With that they made their way out through the great hall of the castle into the bailey. A harried steward was calling for the carriages of impatient departing guests, each one thinking that their own departure was more important than that of anyone else. Greghar towered above the mass of guests and the steward noticed him immediately. Recognizing him as the personal guest of Kitara and knowing that he

would be conveyed in one of the great va Alsor coaches, he sent footmen to bring it around ahead of all the other queuing vehicles. Greghar
and Nitya drew irritated glances as they were ushered forward and
handed into the coach, superseding a long line of waiting worthies.

"Did you enjoy yourself?" asked Greghar as soon as they began
rolling.

Nitya reclined in the plush silk cushions and let out a sigh.

"I know you will think me shallow, but I cannot help enjoying
luxury," she said. "Ever since I was a little girl, I dreamed of dancing
at a great ball."

"Did it live up to your expectations?"

"It did and more. To tell you the truth, I was afraid you would be
ashamed of escorting a girl dressed in a gown made of oddments."

"You were the belle of the ball, Nitya. Surely you saw the looks
you got."

"Only because I was with you," she said, teasing. "For I know my
looks are unusual. But every woman wished she were in my shoes.
Especially your lady love, Chevalina Kitara."

Greghar flushed and looked out the window. They sat in silence
for a few moments.

"You were right," he said, turning toward her and taking both her
hands in his. "Kitara is a desirable woman, but it was my vanity that
made me yield to that temptation. I know now that I would rather
be the slave of Princess Caitlin than the consort of any other lady in
the One Land."

Nitya did not crow but gently extricated her hands and put them
on his cheeks.

"You must tell her that you love her."

"What would be the use of that? She was furious when she saw
me with Kitara at the inn. She will never forgive me now."

"You men are so stupid!" exclaimed Nitya. "If she did not love you, she would not care that you carried on with another woman."

"But she is Zon. They never associate with native men."

Nitya looked at him astutely.

"Greghar, you of all people know that is not true."

CAITLIN SAT IN a nook of the bar parlor of the Three Feathers, nursing a beer. It was quite late and both Binne and Dhanraj had retired, but the inn was still very lively. The va Alsor Ball had affected the whole city. It seemed like every innkeeper had engaged musicians and put on a party to take part in the celebrations in the castle.

There was a group of fiddlers playing a spritely tune backing a pair of singers, a man and a woman. The small dance floor of rough and pitted planks was crowded. Almost everyone was quite tipsy now. The mood was cheerful and the talk raucous. Caitlin had already turned down over a dozen invitations to dance. Now once again, a young buck caught her wrist and strove to drag her out, saying, "It is a crime to have such a pretty wench sitting through this party!"

She twisted her wrist free without difficulty, causing him to stagger back into the arms of his fellows. She smiled at him sweetly and said, "I am not much of dancer, sir. It would be shameful to waste your talents on me."

He was in too good a mood to take offense, and her smile mollified him further.

"You are the finest-looking woman I have ever seen," he said, raising his glass to her. "Just standing up with you would make me happy. Well, if you change your mind, I am available."

She was still smiling at the lad when over his shoulder she saw Greghar and Nitya enter. They stood at the edge of the parlor for a while, scanning the mass of people. Finally Greghar saw her, nudged Nitya, and they both came over, threading their way through the crowd.

"I am so happy to see you," said Nitya as they came up to the nook. She had to lean close to Caitlin to be heard above the hub-bub in the bar. She bent forward and pecked Caitlin on the cheek. However, as she did so, Caitlin spontaneously put her arms around her and enveloped her in a hug.

"You have grown into a beautiful woman," she said. "I barely rec-ognized you when I saw you here the other day. I hope that I may see some more of you."

"I apologize," replied Nitya. "It was not from lack of desire. We have been kept very occupied by our hosts at Tirut Castle."

"How was the va Alsor Ball?"

"I will let Greghar tell you all about it, for I am very tired. I hope that I may wait on you tomorrow."

She turned and left them together, glancing over her shoulder a few times. The musicians finished their set, the dancing stopped, and the general buzz of conversation grew louder. Watching Nitya's retreating back gave them both a cover for the awkward silence. Once she disappeared out the door, they looked at each other with con-trasting expressions. Caitlin's was cool and distant, while Greghar's was a mixture of discomfort and wistfulness.

"Princess Caitlin—" he began, but she silenced him with a gesture.

"I am Cat Avedus. For all practical purposes, Princess Caitlin has ceased to exist. In a few years, she will be declared legally dead, and that will be the end of her."

Nitya's words were fresh in Greghar's mind, and Caitlin's coldness made him reckless.

"She exists for me," he said. "Princess Caitlin is very real to me, for I love her more than life itself. Caitlin, on my honor—"

"Indeed, I thought you were a man of honor," she interrupted, bitterness seeping into her voice. "But I found that you are only a man, after all."

"My honor is my word," he retorted. "My word once given is never broken."

She opened her mouth to respond, but he put up his hand.

"But I cannot keep a vow that has never been made."

"I see," she said. "I thought that love implied a vow of exclusive regard. How foolish of me!"

She took a pull of her beer and averted her eyes from him. In so doing, she saw Yandharan enter the bar. She waved to him over Greghar's shoulder. He waved back and came to join them. He bowed formally to Greghar, eliciting one in return.

"Mantan, I am so happy to see you," she said. "I pray that you will have a drink with me."

Yandharan looked from Greghar to Caitlin and back again, sensing the tension. He looked doubtful.

"I do not want to interrupt anything," he said.

"No, no, Greghar was just leaving. Weren't you, Greghar?"

"Yes, Cat Avedus. I was just leaving."

Yandharan saw the look of defeat on Greghar's face. He looked back at Caitlin. He was perceptive enough to see that she was using him to hurt Greghar. But his desire for her overcame his wounded pride.

"In that case, I will join you," said Yandharan, taking a seat by Caitlin.

Before Greghar could leave, the musicians returned and the male singer rapped a tabletop to get everyone's attention. After a few moments, the volume of conversations eased, and he spoke up in a loud voice.

"We will begin our next set with a lovely ballad from the Northern Marches. I first heard it when I was up there, touring the Thal River Valley. It tells of the age-old story of a man's love for a woman that grows in spite of the rift between their tribes. I hope you enjoy it."

The fiddlers raised their bows, struck up the opening notes and he began to sing.

> *When I look into your eyes*
> *I see forever*
> *When you look into my eyes*
> *You will see*
> *That I am your man.*
>
> *When I saw you in my dreams*
> *I knew we were meant to be*
> *I know that to you this all seems*
> *So wrong, and I agree.*
> *But I am your man.*
>
> *Let us make a vow*
> *No matter that the world is against us*
> *To believe in each other and somehow*
> *Create from two, a oneness*
> *For I am your man.*

As the ballad began, Greghar was frozen into place. He turned back to Caitlin, and saw that she was looking at him too. The singer's voice had a magical quality and the ballad transported both of them back to their first meeting in Upper Thal when he had been willing to lay down his life for a woman he had just met. Images flashed through her mind of their time together, of riding, joking and sparring with him. She recalled the way he looked at her, the same look that was on his face right now. It was the look that she had treasured over their long years of separation. The coldness slowly drained out of her eyes.

"I loved you from the first moment I saw you," said Greghar, unmindful of Yandharan's presence.

"Why did you refuse me, then?" she whispered. "And if you love me, why did you betray me with another?"

"I was a fool," he said, his anger self-directed. "A proud fool, a vain fool. But I hope that you can find it in your heart to forgive me."

Yandharan quietly turned to leave.

"Mantan," she called after him. "Please do not think ill of me. You are dear to me, but—"

He stopped and turned back to her.

"How could I ever think ill of you, dearest Cat?" he asked. "When I pursued you, you told me the truth, that you loved another. I am glad that you did, for my dearest wish is for you to be happy and—" here he paused and smiled as he paraphrased the ballad, "—it is clear that I am not your man."

Now he did leave. He turned at the door of the bar and gave both of them a snappy wave before stepping out.

Greghar stood with his thumbs in his sword belt.

"Collector Yandharan is a good man, an honest man," he said. "And he is a man of means. All I have are my heart, my arm and my sword, but I offer them all to you. My heart is true, my arm is strong, and my sword is—"

"Karya, and I gave it to you," she said, with a sudden laugh. It broke the serious mood and he smiled. "Come into my nook and put your arm around me, Greghar. I know it is a sin to desire you...and I am stupid to trust you. But I love you."

ELEVEN

ESCAPE FROM TIRUT

STRONG HANDS DRAGGED Lidill off Asgara and flung her out of the storeroom. Rator did not speak but merely pointed at Lidill and made a violent gesture with his hand. She scuttled away, muttering under her breath.

"Get dressed and collect your things," he said to Asgara. "We leave immediately."

They left the city just a few hours after midnight. It was cold in the predawn darkness as they rode through the Shard Pass. From the pass, it was about a day's ride to the Daksin border. The actual boundary was mostly unmarked except for an irregular line of Brigon and Daksin border forts. Troops from both sides had patrolled the border, but they rarely bothered with civilians. With the Chekaliga depradations, they ventured out of their forts even less than usual. Everyone knew that as far as individual travelers were concerned, the border had always been porous.

Her mount was thin and bony, but Asgara did not complain. Rator saw from the first moment she took control of the horse that she had a fine seat. It was now over an hour after sunrise. The rising sun burned off the cold of the night within minutes and it rapidly raised the temperature. The heat and blinding glare reflecting off the landscape of sand and rocky outcroppings sapped the energy of even the most robust travellers. Rator could see that the long hours in the saddle had exhausted Asgara and now she was wilting in the heat. But he knew they were in the no man's land between the Southern Marches of Briga and the Daksin Borderlands, so he decided to push on for another hour to make sure they were over the border.

Asgara had asked him only one question when they started from Lidill's house in Tirut, and that was where they were going. When he said they were going to Daksin, she grew very cooperative and assisted him in his preparations for leaving. Lidill was very teary and hung on Rator's neck as he took his leave. She glared at Asgara when she asked Rator to hurry.

Rator had not ranged this area himself, but he had kept his ears open over his years of service in Serat and Tirut. He had heard that there were old ruins all over the Borderlands, most of them along the banks of an ancient dry riverbed. He had also heard that the desert sands gave way to rocky badlands soon after crossing into Daksin. So when they came upon substantial rocky outcroppings, he grew more confident that they had crossed the border.

Many of the outcroppings provided measures of shade from the punishing sun. He selected a particularly large one, almost a small hillock of stone, and found an overhang that created a shady retreat.

"We will stop here," he said to Asgara. "We will wait out the worst of the day's heat. You should sleep. Henceforth, we will try to travel as much as possible in the dark."

He quickly put up a small canvas tent and made out a bedroll for her to lie on. She crawled in and lay down.

"Thank you," she said to him, when he poked his head into the tent to check on her. "This is very comfortable."

He smiled at her in spite of himself.

He woke her around sunset. She sat up, rubbing her eyes at the unfamiliar schedule. They were soon mounted and on their way again before the white moon rose. They had been riding about an hour when she gathered her courage to begin a conversation.

"We are in Daksin now, are we not?"

He grunted, but after a few minutes he responded with more substance.

"How do you know that? Just guessing?"

"Just guessing," she lied.

They rode on in silence for a while. Then it was Rator's turn to reinitiate the conversation.

"We will be together for some time, you and I," he said. "These are unsettled times, and there is a war raging in this region. We will stand a better chance if we work together."

"Yes, you are quite right," she said tartly. "So you should begin by telling me why you are taking me away from Tirut. And why a northerner like you is going south."

Her precocity and acuity took Rator by surprise, and he stared at her, almost open-mouthed. Then he recovered.

"You think you are a clever little thing, don't you?" he replied. "Well, I can be clever too. I ask myself what a Zon child is doing, roaming around the streets of Tirut by herself."

Asgara laughed.

"If you think I am Zon, then I am doomed. For a barbarian man-at-arms would have only two uses for a Zon child—to trade her back to the Sisterhood for ransom or to express his hatred by doing her harm. Since you have not attempted to contact the Sisterhood in Tirut Guild fort, I must assume that you mean me harm."

"Enough of this wordplay," said Rator. "If I had meant you harm, I could have done what I wanted to you as you slept this afternoon. What is your name? Which Zon citadel are you from?"

Asgara kept riding and looked at him with a sidelong glance.

"My name is Asgara Paurina," she said cautiously. She knew that the d'Orr name was well known, even among the barbarians, so she omitted it. "I am Zon—what does it matter what citadel I am from? But who are you? From the way you eat and drink and from your gentle manners, you are no simple man-at-arms. In our Brigish class we have studied and listened to all the accents. You have a northern accent, but it is upper class. So tell me about yourself and why I should trust you."

Rator looked at her again thinking, *Are the Zon ever children? She looks like a child, but she speaks and carries herself like an intelligent adult.* He decided to treat her as one.

"I am well born," he acknowledged. "But I have lost everything. I have nothing now but my sword." He paused and smiled at her. "You seemed very keen to go to Daksin, so I am doing what you want. I have to meet some important people in the Borderlands. I will be frank with you—having a Zon child with me will give me a great deal of prestige with these people. After I have completed my business, I will take you wherever you want in Daksin."

Asgara looked at him steadily and he held her gaze calmly. She looked for signs of deceit, but there was nothing obvious. She suspected that he was not telling her the whole truth, but there was no way to find out. She sighed.

"I am going to visit my mother in Sampore," she said. "That is a long way on horseback. It will take weeks."

"All the more reason to get to know each other better."

"Where do you have your meeting?" she asked. "What is it called?"

"It is called Bar-Dari. It is an ancient ruined city. Do you know it?"

"We learned about it," she said. "A thousand years ago it was the capital of the Dhalian Empire, the seat of Larax and his Yengar allies. After Queen Simran the Merciless broke their power, she blasted the walls of the Dari Gorge and diverted the Dari River away from the city. Without water, the people moved away, the city shrank and eventually fell into ruin. The Dhalian Empire disintegrated and eventually the kingdoms of Briga and Daksin arose in its place."

Rator listened carefully.

"How big is this city?"

"Why, at its height, Bar-Dari had a population of almost a million. Today the ruins cover an area of over twenty square kilometers."

"You have been taught all this?"

She nodded. He scrutinized her carefully now. He caught sight of something around her neck that glittered in the moonlight. He kneed his horse toward hers, reached over casually and got his fingers on it with a quick snatch. It was a very thin necklace, the metal so fine that it was barely thicker than a hair. The necklace would have been virtually invisible to the naked eye; but for the brightness of the white moon, he would never have seen it.

She shrieked and tried to disengage his hand, but he held it fast. He tried to find the catch, and when he couldn't, he pulled at it. The metal cut into her neck, and she was afraid that it would sever an artery.

"Let me go!" she cried. "I will give it to you!"

He stopped pulling but did not release her. Eyeing him fearfully, she reached up and undid the catch. The metal chain pooled in his palm, the working so fine that the links were too small to be seen with the naked eye.

"A very fine piece of jewelry," he said, smug now that he had gotten his way. "It will pay for the supplies we will need for our long ride."

She rubbed her neck where yet another welt was forming.

GREGHAR AND CAITLIN talked and danced and then talked some more, unmindful of the lateness of the hour. She snuggled up to him in her nook in the bar and he held her, both of them oblivious to the frenetic crowd around them. They shared long and lingering kisses, as though to make up for their long years of denial and separation. Holding her in his arms, he was as nervous as a teenage boy and kept shaking his head, afraid that it was all a dream from which he would wake to bitter disappointment. The night was so blissful that neither wanted it to end.

They finally went to the room Yandharan had prepared for her. Greghar had had many women before, but with Caitlin everything— even his own body—felt new and exciting. She was like nothing he had experienced before, a heady mixture of virginal apprehension and sexual aggression. Acutely aware that she had never been in the arms of a man, he was gentle and patient. At length when she gave voice to her pleasure and cried out his name, he felt such great joy that it made him giddy.

As they lay entwined in each other's arms in the warm afterglow of their lovemaking, it slowly dawned on them both that they would never be able to recapture the wonder and magic of this moment. It made the moment sweeter, but it also filled them with an intense desire to prolong it. They whispered sweet nothings to each other cognizant that their togetherness—postponed for so long—was uniquely precious.

He rose in the early hours of the morning to return to his own room before anyone in the inn was up and about. He arranged her soft, flowing red mane on the pillow and kissed her lips lightly.

"Goodnight, my love," she murmured sleepily as he tiptoed out.

YANDHARAN LED THE way unerringly through the maze of small alleyways, some of them barely wide enough to admit their horses. His leather vest was buttoned up against the morning chill. Diana rode behind him on her white stallion, Hikon, and two Guardians rode behind her, 'grators unslung with safeties off. The alley they were in was long and winding, and it ran into a dead end. Yandharan drew rein, beckoned to Diana, asking her to ride up beside him and pointed to one of the shabby houses at the end of the alley.

"There is the house of Lidill Ikren. One of my men, Rator of Karsk, lodges with her. He brought the child into Mistress Lidill's care."

Diana wrinkled her nose in distaste as much from the overpowering stench in the alley as from the dilapidation of the dwellings.

"How can your people live like this?" she asked.

Yandharan did not reply but swung down from his saddle and strode up to the house he had pointed out. Diana followed him, patting

Hikon on the muzzle as she did so. Her Guardians dismounted and were at her back as Yandharan rapped on the door.

They had a significant wait before the door creaked open. Lidill peered out from the dark interior, shading her eyes against the light outside. Noki crowded behind her, smiling and waving at the strangers at the door. A much smaller boy stood on Lidill's right, holding her hand with a sullen expression that matched hers. Yandharan swept off his hat before he spoke.

"Greetings, Mistress Lidill. I am pleased to see you."

"Collector Yandharan," she said without emotion. "What brings you to my humble abode?"

"I am sorry to trouble you. I am afraid there has been a mistake. It turns out that the little girl that Rator of Karsk brought here is not a beggar girl at all. She is wanted by the Zon. We are here to recover her."

Lidill eyed him evenly, but when her gaze traveled to Diana and the menacing Guardians, it grew hostile.

"I have no reason to love the Zon," she said, and spat on the ground. "I will do nothing to help them."

Before Yandharan could reply, Diana stepped around him and caught Lidill by the throat. Noki cowered back, put his hands on his ears, and began to scream. The small boy on Lidill's right began to kick Diana's boots ineffectively. Neither boy's actions affected Diana in the slightest.

Her long dagger appeared in her right hand, and she pricked Lidill's throat with it.

"You will tell me what I want to know," she said in a low tone. "Or I will gut your idiot boy first and then smash the skull of the little one."

When Diana released her, Lidill shrank back and gathered both her sons to her protectively.

"Rator took her with him last night," she cried shrilly. "I don't know where they went. I don't know if they will return. I don't know anything!"

Diana looked down at her grimly.

"Search the house," she said over her shoulder to her Guardians. "Then search the adjoining houses and question the inhabitants. Shoot anyone who resists."

"Collector Yandharan, please protect us!" Lidill implored.

Yandharan spoke up in response.

"Lady Death, you must not harm this woman or her children. I can vouch for her good character. I am sure she has done the girl no harm."

The two Guardians shouldered past Lidill into her house. While they were searching, Diana looked down at Lidill with ill-disguised contempt.

"Tell me about this Rator of Karsk," she said.

The threats to her sons made Lidill much more cooperative.

"He serves as a man-at-arms," she said, her words coming out in a rush. "He serves the Collector here." She nodded her head toward Yandharan. "He lodges with me when he is in Tirut. He is a real gentleman with fine manners and speaks very genteel—not rough like the men around here."

"I see," said Diana, interrupting. "I assume you sleep with him. Are these his sons?"

Lidill held the boys tighter.

"I am not a whore," she said with some asperity. Then she squared her shoulders and continued. "I am a respectable war widow. I had two children—my dear Noki and a daughter, Daril—by my husband. Daril died some years ago of the black pox. Rator is good to me, and he supports us. Little Vitor is his son."

"Did he ever speak of other places?"

"He only spoke of Serat, Lady Death. But he is not from the Southern Marches. His accent is from the north."

"Karsk, obviously."

"I don't know, Lady Death."

"He is from the Northern Marches," interjected Yandharan, seeing the panic on Lidill's face as she hugged her boys. "When I recruited him, he said he had served in one of the Hilson regiments in the Zon wars. That's why we called him 'Rator of Karsk'. He is a dependable man and has served me well."

The Guardians were thorough in their search. It was over two hours before they returned.

"We searched the house, Cornelle," said the more senior one. "And questioned the neighbors. This Rator kept a low profile. No one seems to know anything about him, except that he serves as a man-at-arms with the Collector of Serat. However, we did find this."

She handed Diana a crumpled piece of parchment.

"Clever girl," said Diana. "She left a note in Pranto for us to find." She unfolded the parchment and read it to herself carefully: *I am Lady Asgara Paurina d'Orr. I am trying to make my way to the Daksin Residency to be with my mother, Seignora Megara Paurina. I am in the power of a barbarian warrior by the name of Rator of Karsk. He says he is taking me across the border into Daksin on horseback. I will take the first opportunity to escape him and continue on my journey. I beg my sisters who find this to tell my mother that I love her very much and not to worry about me.*

Diana looked at both her Guardians. They kept their faces blank, but Diana knew what they were thinking. The heiress to the oldest title in the Sisterhood was riding into the middle of the chaos and carnage of the Chekaliga uprising. *Like mother, like daughter*, Diana thought.

"Rator stables his horse at the Three Feathers Inn," put in Yandharan. "You may yet catch him there."

"Good suggestion," Diana said. "I'll go there myself."

GREGHAR FELT AS though he had barely put his head down on the pillow in his own room, when he sat up with a start. Someone was knocking on his door, and it felt as though they were striking his temples with a hammer. He looked out of the window and realized that it was still very early.

"Coming," he growled, as he swung his feet out of his bed. He padded to the door, the hardwood floor cold under his bare feet.

It was a servant in the livery of Baron of Tirut. He bowed obsequiously and would have bowed again except that Greghar asked him abruptly what he wanted.

"Lord Greghar, my mistress, Chevalina Kitara va Alsor of Tirut, invites you to wait on her for breakfast."

Greghar remembered Kitara saying that they should meet to discuss "issues of mutual benefit" as Nitya and he had left the ball. Now he was eager to see Caitlin again and the timing of this invitation was most unwelcome, but he could think of no good reason to refuse it.

"Please inform Chevalina Kitara that I will be along as soon as I can," he said, his lack of enthusiasm plain in his tone.

The servant hesitated, and tarried.

"Chevalina Kitara has asked me to wait on you, my lord," he said. "Her coach is drawn up outside, and I will wait with it. We will leave whenever you are ready."

"Oh, very well," he said with bad grace. "Give me a few minutes."

He quickly performed his morning ablutions and dressed. As he buckled on his sword belt, he half drew Karya from its scabbard, his face breaking into a grin as this gift from Caitlin recalled her presence.

"I will return as soon as I can, dearest Caitlin," he said as though she were there to hear him.

The coach conveyed him to the castle without delay, splashing through the puddles created by the overnight rain that now persisted in a depressing drizzle. He was impressed anew with the magnificence of the castle, the number of the men-at-arms and quality of their arms and armor. A rather pompous steward awaited him in the Inner Ward and received him with much ceremony. He led him through the long halls of the castle to Kitara's suite, where he announced him and withdrew.

In spite of the early hour, Kitara was dressed for the day, playing cards with a couple of her ladies. They played dutifully, but did not look particularly happy to be up so early. She threw her cards down when Greghar was announced and jumped to her feet. Seeing the surprised looks of her ladies, she restrained herself from running to him and said merely, "Welcome, Lord Greghar. How good of you to come so promptly. Please join us in a hand of cards before breakfast."

He approached and took a vacant chair at the table.

"I am sorry, my lady, I am not much of a hand at cards. You must forgive me. However, I will be happy to observe your play."

They played a desultory hand before Kitara rose and stretched, saying, "Oh, la! The cards are not going my way. I think I have had enough for now."

Her well-bred ladies immediately took the hint, rose, and departed with deep curtsies. As soon as the door swung shut behind them, Kitara put her arms around Greghar's neck and sighed, rubbing herself against him like a cat.

"It is a bore that we have to resort to such subterfuge," she whispered. "But there is no help for it, we must steal as many moments of happiness as we can. I will try to make them plentiful! Sometimes, I wish I had met you when I was single, at court in Dreslin Center. But on the other hand, the risk gives our relationship so much spice, doesn't it?"

He did not respond but stood in silence. After a few moments, she took his hand and led him to a window seat that provided a magnificent view of Tirut harbor. She unwound her scarf and put his hand on her bosom.

"Feel the beating of my heart. You always make it go pitter-patter."

He did not extricate his hand, but he did not make moves to take advantage of her obvious invitation either. She paused to marshal her thoughts before proceeding.

"My darling, I have great news and I hope you will be as happy about it as I am. I have just learned that I am pregnant—it is our love child, there can be no doubt. I have been to my astrologer, and he assures me it is a boy. The One God has blessed us."

She leaned into his arms and looked up into his eyes. His expression was neutral, but he allowed her to take his arms and drape them around her.

"I understand your reticence, my love. It is true that the boy will be brought up in this House and bear the va Alsor name. But what does that matter? That just ensures that he will have a title and wealth. You and I will know that he is ours, the living proof of our love."

Greghar's face was pained, for the revelation cast a pall over his joy from the previous night with Caitlin. He squared his shoulders, took his arms off her, and sat back against the wall. He looked out into the harbor, recognizing the hull and rigging of the *Darling Thoma*, moored at one of the quays.

"Kitara, I cannot carry on like this any longer."

She clucked understandingly and took his hand in hers again.

"Oh, don't worry on my account, love. There is little risk, for I have everything in hand. My father-in-law trusts me implicitly and delegates all manner of activities to me. I am to go on an inspection tour of Gold Port next week. I know a beautiful little island paradise in the Giants' Teeth; we can travel there separately. Then we can spend some days together in utter bliss—"

"No, no, Kitara," he said, throwing politeness and tact to the winds in his distraction and jerking his hand free of hers. "I am in love with Cat Avedus. I have always been in love with her. It was wrong of me to dally with you. I should never have done it. This pregnancy is a shock to me. I am sorry to burden you with it, for I cannot rejoice in it."

Kitara was so surprised that her mouth dropped open for a moment. Then as she regained control of herself, her eyes grew hard and her lips compressed in a thin line.

"In love! With that...that..." She stopped and a confused look passed over her face. There was something that she knew about this Cat Avedus, but there seemed to be a fog in her memory that blotted it out. She frowned for a moment and then gave up. "With that hulking, uncouth rancher girl who dresses like a warrior? You would give up my bed for her! What can you possibly see in her?"

"Kitara, you have everything—youth, beauty, wealth, a husband who loves you, and a family that cherishes you. Your life here in Tirut is complete without me. I ask you to forget our dalliance and return to your marriage vows. It is best for both of us."

"I don't need you to lecture me," she said, picking up her scarf. She played with it for a few moments, her expression becoming set. "Well, if I can't have you, then I will certainly not give you up to that redheaded bitch."

She paused, and her look turned malicious.

"I am a passionate creature, Greghar. I can give boundless pleasure to those who please me. But I can be as cruel as the Utrean winter to those who earn my hatred. You say you love that rancher girl. And I know you have tender feelings for Lady Nitya. Well, you will never see them again!"

She stood up and pulled a long gold pin from her hair, allowing it to cascade loose. She hooked her fingers in the neckline of her gown and ripped it open, laying bare her flimsy underbodice. Then she began to scream at the top of her lungs. Her cries triggered an alarm, and almost immediately there was a thunder of boots in the corridor outside. Greghar jumped to his feet and looked around the chamber desperately for other means of egress, but there was only one door.

"Oh, help! Someone please help me!" screamed Kitara when she heard the approach of the soldiers. The door was flung open and men-at-arms in shining light armor poured into the room, led by Quirus va Alsor, commander of the Color Guard. Kitara staggered over to him and collapsed into his arms.

"Oh, Quirus, oh, sir, I appeal to you as my husband's cousin," she sobbed. "You must defend my honor. I invited this man into my suite, thinking him to be a gentleman, but he has outraged my modesty. Please protect me!"

Quirus did not hesitate. He held Kitara in a protective embrace, simultaneously rapping out orders to his men.

"Arrest him! Disarm him and take him to the dungeons!"

The men-at-arms carried ceremonial halberds, unsuitable for combat in the confines of the chamber, so they advanced warily. Greghar drew Karya and made some rapid judgments. There were far too many of them. His sword would make them cautious, but if he fought, the result was not in doubt.

He ripped one of the curtains from the window frame. He wound it over his right hand in which he held Karya's hilt. With a few quick blows, he used the hilt of the sword to smash a large enough opening in the window for him to pass through. As he stepped outside on to the parapet, he heard Kitara's hysterical voice crying, "Quirus, send a troop to the Three Feathers inn. Arrest a red-haired wench who goes by the name Cat Avedus and a young woman called Nitya. They are this scoundrel's accomplices. Bring them to me in chains."

The drop off from Kitara's windows fell directly into the sea. Greghar looked around to see the men-at-arms almost upon him. That immediate danger completely drove his fear of heights from his mind. Sheathing Karya, he leaped out into space.

A MAID IN the kitchen of the Three Feathers Inn had just finished cleaning and drying a large metal tureen. Giving it a final rub with her dishcloth, she lifted the heavy pot to hang it on its hook when it slipped from her hands and fell to the floor with a crash. The loud clang reverberated around the kitchen and through the lower level of the inn. Caitlin's room was just adjacent to the kitchen, and in her dream she was continuing her enchanting night with Greghar, luxuriating in the feel of his arms around her. The noise rudely dragged her from her idyll, and she sat up with a start.

It was a gray and drizzly morning, but Caitlin was so happy that everything seemed perfect to her. *He loves me, he has always loved me,* she thought, and found herself grinning foolishly as she brushed her hair. She walked into the parlor with a light step, humming the melody of one of the airs she had danced with Greghar.

Binne and Dhanraj sat opposite each other, eating their breakfast. Binne smiled when she saw Caitlin's expression and demeanor.

"Why, my dear, you look like the cat that has found the cream jug," she said. "What has brought this on?"

"Nothing but sin can be so satisfying," said Caitlin mischievously.

"Sin is no joking matter," said Dhanraj, putting his spoon down.

She tousled his hair and sat down beside him.

"Oh, don't get all pious on me now," she said.

"No one deserves happiness more than you, my darling," said Binne.

Caitlin reached over and squeezed her shoulder.

"I have had such good luck. I could not have asked for a better mother than you."

"It is not luck," said Nitya, entering the parlor. "The good are drawn to you, just as those with evil in their hearts are moved to hate you."

"You are all dear to my heart," said Caitlin coloring at the praise. "I knew Nitya as a child, and she has now grown into the lovely girl you see before you. Nitya, Binne is my adoptive mother, and Dhanraj is her ward."

Binne stood and curtsied to Nitya, but Dhanraj sat and eyed her without warmth. Nitya looked abashed at Binne's show of respect, but when she met Dhanraj's dark eyes a quick look of understanding passed between them.

"Lady Nitya, we heard from Collector Yandharan that you were the toast of the va Alsor ball last night," said Binne. "Lady-in-waiting to the queen of Utrea!"

"I am just plain Nitya," she responded. "I have no title, it is only that Queen Lovelyn has been very kind to me."

"You are very late for breakfast," said Dhanraj, addressing them both. "Cat, I pray you will spend some time with me in the stables afterward. The horses have been sadly neglected the last few days. The grooms at these inns do as little as possible."

Caitlin nodded at him, smiling her assent. Nitya took a seat by Binne as a serving wench entered bearing a laden tray. As they ate, they talked. Nitya steered the conversation to neutral topics. She skillfully evaded Dhanraj's questions about her past and ignored his rather clumsy attempts to inject Daksish phrases into the dialogue.

They had just finished eating when there was the sound of the front door of the inn being flung open and tread of heavy boots in the vestibule. In short order, half a dozen men-at-arms stormed into the parlor led by a captain. The officer pulled out a parchment from his belt and began to read laboriously.

"Cat Avedus and Nitya of Nordberg, you are both under arrest for conspiring in an assault on the person of Chevalina Kitara va Alsor." He paused and pointed first at Caitlin and then at Nitya. "Your descriptions are unmistakable. Come with us quietly, and there will be no trouble."

Caitlin stood slowly, mentally sorting through their options when they were interrupted by a deceptively melodious voice.

"I would suggest that you and your men leave quietly, Captain." It was Diana who had entered quietly.

The captain turned on her. He and his men drew their swords. In response, Diana drew Light and Caitlin drew Nasht. Their beautiful long Zon blades glinted in the light coming in the window.

"We Companions are as one, are we not?" said Diana, addressing Nitya. The gold flecks in Nitya's irises glittered. She glanced from Diana to Caitlin, a wordless question in her look.

"I believe," said Diana.

"I believe," Caitlin echoed.

Diana approached the men-at-arms with Caitlin at her shoulder, their drawn swords at the ready. Transferring Light to her left hand, Diana drew her laser pistol and thumbed off the safety.

The laser pistol gave the captain the excuse he was looking for.

"We are too few to fight magic weapons," he said to his men. "Fall back! We must report this and get reinforcements."

GREGHAR DOVE DEEP and heard the sound of crossbow bolts striking the surface, so he stayed down. He swam strongly underwater, striving to put distance between himself and the castle. His lungs began to burn with the effort, and finally when he felt they would burst, he kicked for the surface. He stayed up no longer than necessary to gulp down a lungful of air before diving down into the green water again. The sharp-eyed men-at-arms in the castle saw his brief appearance. Again he heard the bolts striking the waves, but there were fewer this time and more widely scattered.

By the time he broke surface the second time, he was out of effective crossbow range. He picked out the *Darling Thoma* from the multitude of ships in the harbor and swam toward her with a steady, untiring stroke. The activity at the castle had drawn the attention of everyone in the harbor, and the crews of the ships at anchor in the pool thronged their decks to see him as he swam by. Some cheered him on, but most watched without expression. The crew of the *Darling Thoma* crowded by her rail and watched his approach, urging him on with shouts and gestures. They threw down a line when he drew near. He came up the line rapidly, and Tar hauled him aboard when he got up to the rail.

"We are prepared for sea," said Martius, even as Greghar took a towel from Tar and began to dry himself. "We were about to sail."

"Let us wait a short while," panted Greghar. "Nitya should be here soon, I am sure."

Martius nodded but gave orders to begin unmooring the vessel. As they were doing this, Greghar watched the castle and the harborfront esplanade with a worried eye. There was a lot of activity in the castle, flags were being raised, and signals sent out. There were a few bronze-badged deputies on the esplanade, and they stared at the *Darling Thoma.*

Greghar paced nervously, continually glancing at the hourglass on the quarterdeck. As the officer of the deck tapped and turned it to mark the hour, a troop of armored cavalrymen in the livery of the Baron of Tirut cantered onto the esplanade along the shore road. They fanned out, blocking each of the side streets leading into the open area by the water.

As Greghar and the crew watched, four horses suddenly burst out of one of the side streets. Diana led the way on Hikon, with Nitya seated behind her on the huge white stallion. Caitlin followed her on Rufus with Binne and Dhanraj close behind.

The cavalrymen converged, but Diana fired blasts with her laser pistol, killing two and creating a break in their line. She galloped through the break down to the waterside, scattering the sailors, traders, and trollops that were milling about there. One of the deputies tried to grab Hikon's bridle as Diana rode by. She took a boot out of her stirrup and her steel toe hit his jaw, knocking him senseless to the ground. She turned on to the quay, but did not slow down. As she approached the quayside, she whispered in Hikon's ear, and they soared over the gangplank and landed on the *Darling Thoma*'s quarterdeck, shivering her timbers.

However, the cavalrymen were now over their surprise. They reformed their lines and massed, so that Caitlin, Binne, and Dhanraj found themselves facing ranks more than four deep. Caitlin drew her laser pistol and got off two shots, but there were too many of them. Even as their two comrades fell, the remaining cavalrymen advanced from all sides, their long sabers drawn. Caitlin whirled Rufus and galloped back the way they had come, but Binne and Dhanraj were less nimble in handling their mounts. They found the troopers closing the circle around them. Seeing she could not escape, Binne turned her horse Tagan sideways to block the alley. This delayed the troopers enough to allow Caitlin to get a good head start and for Dhanraj to break free. Caitlin twisted in her saddle, about to pull up and return to them when she saw Binne cut down. Shock and grief were numbed by action as she spurred Rufus to a gallop. Dhanraj urged his bay to follow Caitlin as she disappeared around a bend in the lane. However, one of the troopers rode to head him off, and he had to pull hard on his reins to turn down a side alley to evade him.

"Cast off!" cried Martius. "Let us get under way!" He looked to Nexius, seeing with approval that the first mate was already for'ard, supervising the men up on the ratlines as they set the sails. The *Darling Thoma* began to glide away from the quay.

"No!" cried Greghar. "We must wait...we cannot leave without Caitlin—"

Diana swung down from her saddle and approached him.

"We can do nothing for them now," she said.

"Several of the baron's ships in the harbor are making sail," chimed in Martius. "Even now, we will have our hands full getting out to sea."

"But we cannot leave without Caitlin," Greghar repeated. "I will go back for her myself!"

He ran toward the rail, clearly intending to dive into the water and swim back to the esplanade, where the cavalrymen had now divided themselves into two groups. One proceeded in pursuit of Caitlin, and the other cantered up the quay from which the *Darling Thoma* had departed. Diana put her boot out, and with a quick move, tripped Greghar. He fell heavily to the deck, and as he attempted to rise, she struck his head with the pommel of her sword, knocking him out. Satisfied, she turned to Martius.

"I thank you for taking us aboard," she said. "But I must ask a further favor. My horse must be moved below decks."

"You did not give me much choice," said Martius, trying to sound gruff. He guessed Diana's identity and her reputation had his eyes darting to the laser pistol at her hip with unease. "Passage on my ship is not free, you know."

"A gold talent," said Diana. She drew a coin from a pouch on her weapons belt, and he took it eagerly. "One more when we get to our destination."

Tar picked Nitya up, his face aglow with happiness. She looked like a child in his enormous arms. The ship was slowly beginning to gather way. They were over fifty meters from the quay and it was falling further away from them with every passing minute. A few of the cavalrymen on the quay drew longbows and nocked ballistic arrows.

"Give over my cabin to Greghar and Nitya as before," Martius said to Tar urgently. "Take them below immediately. And get Lady Death's horse into the hold."

The bowmen on the quay launched their arrows. They arced over lazily, but the barrage was too sparse to do much damage, except by a lucky shot. The arrows fell into the sea around them, barely raising a ripple.

Martius turned back to Diana. "We are away from the quay. But the baron's vessels will attempt to prevent our departure."

He pointed to several ships in the harbor that were responding to the signal flags from Tirut Castle. Two large carracks had already hauled up their anchors and spread some canvas. They were moving slowly to cut off the *Darling Thoma* from the narrow gap in the seawall that protected the harbor.

"They can spread more canvas than us," said Nexius, stepping onto the quarterdeck. "We will be hard pressed to make the harbor entrance before them."

"I am more worried about those men-at-arms," said Martius, pointing.

A dozen soldiers in the livery of the Tirutan Color Guard were drawing the huge chain across the harbor entrance.

Diana drew her long-barreled laser pistol and jacked the slide.

"This will even the odds a bit," she said. "But it may not be enough."

"Look!" said Nexius. "Who are those men?"

Another large troop of men-at-arms was running along the top of the seawall. The Color Guard troopers saw them, but did not seem to consider them a threat. They continued their work securing the harbor chain. But then the newcomers formed a line and raised their crossbows. The attack was clearly unexpected and the Color Guard troopers saw that they had no chance. They put their hands up and were quickly disarmed. Their work on the harbor chain was undone and the harbor entrance was cleared.

"Those men wear the livery of the Baron of Firsk," said Diana. "They are Horus's men." She pointed to the quays by the castle. "Look over there. I think they're going to give us some more help. Rig a tow rope."

A large longboat came into view, pulling strongly from the quays. Horus stood on the prow, waving to them. The oarsmen rowed with power and timing, cutting through the water with efficiency and great speed. In short order they came under the bows of the *Darling Thoma*. Diana had run for'ard with Nexius in anticipation and they were ready with the heavy tow rope.

Two of Nexius's seamen threw the rope down and Horus's men secured it to the stern of the longboat. Then, they resumed rowing toward the harbor entrance, increasing the speed of the *Darling Thoma* significantly. The baron's carracks had had the advantage of position, but this was negated by the *Darling Thoma*'s increased speed.

"We'll get you to the harbor entrance before them!" called Horus, looking up at the Diana, Nexius and the crowd of seamen on the *Darling Thoma*'s bow. "But they may be able to shoot at you. Deploy some crossbowmen on the tops."

"We've already done that," said Diana, cupping her hands around her mouth to project her voice. "How did you manage to get your men ready so fast?"

"The Color Guard sounded the general alarm in the castle," said Horus, cupping his hands in like manner. "I brought my men down to the quays to support them. But then I saw you ride into the esplanade—no one but you could have ridden like that." Horus paused and glanced at the others on the bow before going on. "I thought you might need a little help getting out of here."

Their eyes met and Diana saw that he had much more to say to her. It remained unspoken, but she read most of it on his face.

The breeze was changeable and the baron's carracks lost way. Aided by Horus's longboat the *Darling Thoma* maintained steady progress and sailed through the harbor entrance, still out of crossbow range of her pursuers. Once beyond the seawall, Horus's men cast off the tow rope and it was rapidly pulled in by the seamen on the caravel.

"Thank you, Horus," Diana called out as their sails filled and they began to tack away. "Take care of yourself."

Her words were businesslike, but he thought he heard some tenderness in her voice. He stood as tall as he could on the prow of the longboat and gave her a wave that was more like a salute. She put her long fingers on her lips but did not blow him a kiss. He remained standing as the *Darling Thoma* bore away to sea. He shaded his eyes that remained fixated on Diana. Her flaxen hair marked her out even as the ship grew increasingly distant.

AS GREGHAR AWOKE, the first thing he felt was the throbbing pain in his skull. He ran his fingers over the back of his head tenderly and felt the lump, now grown to the size of a pigeon's egg. He groaned but swung his legs out of the hammock and onto the deck. He recognized the long swells and realized that they were on the open sea. He rapidly made his way up to the quarterdeck, where he found Martius and Diana standing by the helmsman.

"You had no right to prevent me from going to Princess Caitlin," he growled at Diana.

"She is not a helpless maiden," she replied. "Vasitha chose her to be one of the Companions. You must trust her to find a way out of Tirut on her own. You will achieve nothing by throwing your life away. Come, Nitya has much to tell us."

She led the way from the quarterdeck to the stern rail. Nitya was leaning over it precariously, tossing breadcrumbs in the wake and watching the seagulls diving in after them. She looked up as they approached.

"Vasitha has spoken to me," she said without preamble.

They waited in silence for her proceed.

"Malitha co-opts more and more temporal powers to his cause, magnifying his strength. The Dark rises and we, the Companions, are all that stand in its way."

"Invoke Vasitha and open the portal," said Greghar, nursing the lump on his head. "Surely this is his problem, not ours."

"Malitha has grown so powerful that he has sundered Vasitha from our world. We have tried, he from his side, I from ours, but we cannot open the portal. He cannot join our battle."

"Be that as it may, I refuse to continue being Vasitha's puppet. I have my own objectives and—"

"I know what your heart aches for," interrupted Nitya. "But believe me when I tell you that the triumph of Malitha will spell doom for both of you."

"You wish to be with Princess Caitlin," put in Diana. "So do we."

"Yes," agreed Nitya, putting a hand on Greghar's forearm.

She paused and surveyed the two of them for a moment in silence.

"Your bond with Vasitha is special, Cornelle Diana. Where must we go?"

Diana smiled. "Is there anything you do not know, young Nitya?" She paused and looked toward the shoreline. "We will steer for the port of Battara, then overland to the ruins of Bar-Dari."

"Even if she escapes from Tirut, how will Princess Caitlin know to come there?" asked Greghar.

"Believe in Vasitha, Greghar," said Nitya softly. "Princess Caitlin does. He will guide her."

"I WILL DO anything in my power to help you, Cat," said Yandharan, sipping his beer. They were seated in the secluded backroom of a tavern not far from his Tirut residence, out of the sight of prying eyes. "I have made discreet inquiries and have tracked Dhanraj to the Bermondy district of the city. Thereafter the trail goes cold, for the Bermondy ghetto is peopled by Yengars and Gandharas and they will not talk to lawmen."

"Hopefully he is safe there," she said. "But I must leave Tirut as soon as possible."

"It will not be easy, but I think I can use my badge to get you out of the city gates."

"You would sacrifice everything by doing that," said Caitlin. "I cannot ask that of you."

The look in his eyes was unmistakable.

"Cat, for you I would risk my life and fortune without a second thought."

"You forget your responsibilities," said Caitlin, softly. She put a hand on his arm, paradoxically making him feel worse. "Your wife and family will surely face retribution for your actions."

"Perhaps I can conceal my identity—"

"Perhaps," said Caitlin. "But I have a better idea."

An hour later they were at the gatehouse of the Daksin Gate, on their horses. Yandharan was resplendent in his Collector's uniform, prodding Caitlin who was astride Rufus and had her wrists in manacles. Her sword, Nasht, was in its scabbard on his lap.

"I have a prisoner for Chevalina Kitara," he called into the gatehouse in a loud voice. "I must speak with the gate captain."

One of the guards in the gatehouse came out and inspected the two of them carefully.

"I recognize you, Collector Yandharan," he said. "And your prisoner fits the description of one of those we were asked to look out for."

He went back into the gatehouse and reemerged with his captain.

"Why are you here?" asked the captain suspiciously. "Take her to the castle. She should be placed in the dungeons to await the chevalina's pleasure."

"I captured her just a few streets from here," lied Yandharan smoothly. "I require some of your men to come with me to make sure she does not escape again."

The captain digested this thoughtfully. As he did so, Caitlin suddenly reached over and grabbed Nasht. Yandharan pulled on his reins to turn his mount around, as if to snatch the sword back. However in the process, he interposed his horse between Caitlin and the gatehouse guards. She touched her spurs to Rufus's sides and galloped through the open gate. Travelers and tradespeople scuttled to get out of the way of the big red horse.

"Stop!" cried Yandharan, galloping after her.

As soon as she was clear of the gate, she gave Rufus his head. Yandharan spurred his horse as though he was in pursuit. The collector rode a fine horse but it was no match for Rufus; even if he had been in earnest, he could not have caught Caitlin. By the time the guards got their horses and thundered through the gate, she was out of sight. She was sure she could get to the Shard Pass long before her pursuers and Yandharan had assured her that it was still unguarded. *They will not pursue me into the arid Borderlands of Daksin,* she thought.

KITARA KEPT TO her bed for days, allowing only her personal maid, Rubya, into her bedchamber to see her. Nehemus came by her suite many times a day, usually with an herbalist. But each time she sent Rubya out to say that she was not ill, that she only needed privacy to recover from the shock of her assault. Jagus came by once, but when he was refused admittance, he did not return. On the fourth day, Nehemus came by once in the morning and once in the afternoon, each time looking more worried. He came by a third time that day, just after dinner, and stood in the suite's luxurious lounge. After taking a few nervous circuits, he knocked on the door of her bedchamber.

There was no response for several minutes, and he was about to turn and leave when the door opened. Rubya came out and bowed low.

"My mistress, the chevalina, begs you to enter, my lord," she said and stood aside.

Nehemus entered eagerly, but with a concerned expression, not knowing what he would find. He found Kitara in her wide, canopied bed. There was a silver bucket with a bottle of chilled Mussadec wine on a bedside table along with two goblets. She sat up in the bed when he entered, pulling the bed sheets up to her chin as she did so. She smiled at him nervously.

"How are you, my dear?" he asked, managing to keep the eagerness out of his voice, but unable to take his eyes off her.

She looked abashed and dropped her eyes.

"I am a simpleton and dupe, my lord. I fear I have brought shame on our house. I am embarrassed to face you."

He advanced rapidly and sat on a bedside chair.

"No, no," he remonstrated. "You are a dear, trusting thing—that is not a fault; it is something to treasure." He clenched his fists. "That filthy dog, Greghar, dared to assault your modesty! You, who are such a paragon of virtue! It is he who has brought shame on his house, not you on yours. I would love to squeeze the life out of him, slowly and with great pain."

"My lord, I am a weak woman," she said, with a tremor in her voice. "This assault has left me a mental wreck. Every sudden sound now makes me tremble like a leaf, and I even fear sleep for the nightmares that it brings. I long to be held by someone I trust. I have sent messages to Jagus, but he does not come."

Nehemus took her hands in his and held them gently. She lay back down on her pillows with a contented sigh.

"I have said it before, and I will say it again," he said with a trace of testiness. "That boy is a fool who does not recognize what a wonderful wife he has in you. Why, there cannot be another like you in all of the One Land!"

She gave him a nervous smile, looking up to him with big, innocent eyes.

"My lord, my husband is always good to me. He denies me nothing. I am a lucky woman to have one such as him as my husband and master. But he is a busy man and does not always have time for me. I confess to feeling the deep ache that comes from missing his touch."

"Surely he cannot stay away from one as beautiful as you?" Nehemus looked incredulous.

"He has much on his mind, my lord."

"Cards and dice," muttered Nehemus under his breath. "If he has been in the brothels, I'll have his hide!" He held her hands tighter.

She sat up immediately saying, "No, no, my lord, you must not fault him—" and as she did so, the bed sheets slid down to her waist. She wore a red, sheer negligee that left just enough to the imagination. She saw his eyes light up with a burning desire and in response she looked confused and mortified. She crossed her arms over her bosom and dropped her eyes.

"My lord," she faltered. "I long to nestle in your strong arms, for I would feel safe there. But my feelings for you are too strong. I fear I would not be able to control myself if I did."

One of her negligee straps fell off her shoulder, revealing more of her cleavage through her crossed arms. He hesitated no longer but rose from the bedside seat and sat on her bed. He put his arms around her and held her tight. After a brief interval, she took her arms out from between them and put them around his neck, rubbing her breasts against him. He kissed her tentatively, and she kissed him back with an ardor that stoked his arousal. Her mixture of innocent waif and wanton vamp was incredibly seductive. He could not have resisted her animal magnetism even if he had wanted to do so.

He paused to unbuckle his sword belt and draw his tunic over his head. When he took her in his arms again, she said in a timid voice, "Be gentle with me, my lord."

But once they were under the sheets, her expertise far exceeded his, and she got what she wanted very quickly.

Later as they cuddled, she whispered, "Pour us some wine, darling."

They sipped their wine and she fussed over him, marveling at his manliness. As he sought to reassure her of his protection she continued, her voice growing throaty. "Secure in your love, I can please you in more ways than you can imagine."

After they finished their wine, her hands and mouth caressed his body. As she dexterously aroused him again, he briefly wondered where she had learned these skills. But her adept ministrations soon drove these thoughts from his head.

The next morning, she rose early and stretched languorously. Nehemus was still stretched out on his back, deep in an exhausted slumber. He snored gently. She had been as good as her word, and Nehemus had had an active night. She looked at his peaceful features and sighed. She would have to stoke his passions and his ego regularly, but she was confident that she could convince him that this baby was his.

CHE MISSION HOUSE
OF ABAID

"WE ARE BEGINNING our descent to Bar-Dari, Lady Vivia," said the pilot over the airboat comm. "If you go to the obvservation deck, you will get a superb view of the old Dari river valley and the ruins."

"Thank you," said Vivia. She was with Darbeni in the dining parlor of her large personal airboat. She sipped her vintage *fitza* and nodded to her daughter. "Let us go and take in the view, darling. I haven't been to Bar-Dari in years."

"I haven't been here since I was brought on a school trip," replied Darbeni.

The two of them walked up to the observation deck, clutching their stems of *fitza* against the slight turbulence.

"Just descending through five thousand meters, your ladyship," said the pilot. "You can see the dry bed of the old course of the Dari River quite clearly over to port."

"Mother Ma!" said Darbeni. "That must have been a big river!"

"Yes, indeed," said Vivia, pointing. "You can see the old river bluffs—they are over a kilometer apart. But I have been told that in spate the river could cover all the land between them."

Darbeni glanced at her mother sharply, but Vivia did not elaborate.

As they proceeded lower, their view of the city resolved from a rough outline into distinct streets and buildings. It was an impressive city, with grand boulevards, huge public squares and concourses. Massive buildings dominated the city center and as the airboat glided lower, they saw the details of a uniformly grandiose architectural style. The hot, dry climate ensured that the city's buildings and infrastructure were preserved in good condition.

"I had forgotten how grand it is," said Darbeni. "It is almost as impressive as Atlantic City."

"Yes, it makes Dreslin Center look like a village, doesn't it? It is hard to imagine that they built all this without construct-bots. Just levers, inclined planes, pulleys, and human muscle."

"Don't forget slavery," said Darbeni.

"Where would you like to land, your ladyship?" came the pilot's voice over the airboat comm.

"In Dhalian Square," responded Vivia. "Just in front of the Abaidan Mission House."

The landing went off without incident and the egress ramp was extended. Vivia's personal maid, Naorina, stood by the ramp with two other junior maids.

"Would you like us to escort you, your ladyship?" asked Naorina as Vivia and Darbeni approached.

"No, no," said Vivia. "My daughter and I will be fine."

As they walked down the airboat ramp, Vivia's fine *kanjiam* scarf fluttered in the breeze. Darbeni gathered the pleats of her gown to prevent it from billowing up. The airboat had landed in the middle of the large square and it was a hundred meters to the massive Mission House. Thorny tumbleweeds skittered about in the wind that also threw up a fine dust, prompting them to shade their eyes.

Up close, the ruined nature of the city was much more obvious. Almost all of the buildings around the square had collapsed roofs. Most were just shells with one or more walls reduced to rubble. Choice stone fittings had been cut out and carted away. The wide boulevards that ran from the square were filled with debris.

Of all the buildings in sight, the Mission House was in the best condition. Its walls were virtually undamaged and it still had much of its high roof. Its tall towers still soared heavenward ornamented with intricate carvings all the way up to their spires. However, the glass was long gone from the windows. A few smaller ones yawned open, but most were boarded up.

"This huge edifice was a Yengar temple, built centuries before Thermad," said Vivia. She pointed upward. "See, on the tops of the spires, you can still see the trident of the Yengar god, Moksha. Thermad himself supervised the slaughter of the Yengar priests here and oversaw its conversion into the first great center of his Mission."

"But, Mother," objected Darbeni. "We were taught that the Yengars were allies of the Dhalian King Larax at the Battle of Rocky Scarp. He was a Thermadan. In fact, the Thermadan Mission became the official religion the Dhalian Empire."

"That is true, my dear," agreed Vivia, nodding. "The Thermadan Dhalian kings *did* make alliances with the Yengars in the centuries after the prophet's death. But these were always uneasy. While Thermad preached that anyone who accepted the Mission would feel the love of the One God, he explicitly excluded the followers of Moksha. He states quite clearly in Thermad Qura V: '*Love of the One God can save all the peoples in this world, except those who worship Moksha, for they are steeped in evil*'."

They passed through the portico of the Mission House and entered its dim interior. There was little left of the long rows of pews except for their stone bases. However, the long nave and faraway altar showed signs of more recent use. Darbeni put her hand on her mother's arm and Vivia patted it.

"Wealthy barbarians still organize religious ceremonies here from time to time," said Vivia. "Devout Thermadans are keen to be married here."

As they approached the altar, they saw candles and dried petals on it.

"This place is eerie, Mother," said Darbeni, shivering.

"Thermadans think that marriage vows taken here are particularly blessed," continued Vivia, as calm as ever. "For it was here that Thermad married his fourth and dearest wife, Taniyah. She was eleven years old on her wedding day and bore him seven children."

On one side of the altar there was a pulpit and on the other there was a carved stone seat grand enough to be a throne. Three substantial iron spikes were embedded in the seatback. Vivia ascended the steps toward it and Darbeni followed her. The throne was clear of dust and polished to a high gloss.

"This throne was made for Thermad," said Vivia seating herself on it and crossing her legs elegantly. She tossed her *kanjiam* scarf over her shoulder in her habitual manner. "But he never sat on it. The three spikes stand for the Three Refusals—the three times he refused to accept the formal leadership of the Mission he established. On the third refusal, he appointed Abaid, his chief disciple, to be the first Red Khalif and dispense justice from this throne. He exhorted him to preach from that pulpit and spread the Mission with 'the sword of peace'."

"How do you know all this, Mother? I don't recall learning this at school."

"Just stories I picked up here and there," said Vivia vaguely. She pointed. "Come and look at this stone by the right arm of the throne."

It was a cube of black rock about a meter high, elaborately carved with abstract, but symmetric shapes. The top of the cube sloped inward to a broad but narrow slit.

"What is it, Mother?"

"Thermad bequeathed his sword to Abaid. When Abaid left his mortal body, the sword was embedded in this stone. Every Red Khalif since then has taken the office with his hand on Thermad's sword."

"Isn't that sword in the Cathedral of Thermad the Divine in Dreslin Center?" asked Darbeni.

"I am pleased to see that you remember your history," said Vivia. "When Queen Caitlin the Unforgiving completed the Brigon Conquest six hundred years ago, Bar-Dari had declined to a dusty shell. But it was still the headquarters of the Thermadan Mission. She flew down here and killed the sitting Red Khalif—she personally shot him down, right here in front of this altar. Then she appointed a more amenable one. She moved all the valuable fittings and Thermadan artifacts from here to the Cathedral of Thermad the Divine in Dreslin Center, making it the new Mission headquarters."

Darbeni looked around the interior of the shadowy Mission House. She now saw the vacant cloisters, empty display shelves, bare pedestals, and pitted pillars shorn of their gold filigree. She imagined what it must have looked like in its heyday: all the walls covered with heavy tapestries, an abundance of gold and gilt, everything glowing in the light of thousands of candles.

"Thermad's sword, his tooth and the hairs from his head...we were taught that Willum Shelsor moved them to Dreslin Center," she said. "It says so in Caitlin Saga."

"That is one of the many lies that the d'Orrs inserted into our history," said Vivia. There was the clink of metal on stone. "Ah, here they are. Finally."

A warrior appeared in the entrance, blinking as his eyes adjusted to the dimness inside. He saw Vivia at the far altar and disappeared. A moment later, he reappeared, accompanied by about a dozen men.

Kimr ib Makhtoom led a group of his Chekaliga warriors, who kept their eyes down and carefully gave him precedence. They were all dressed for battle with dried blood on their faces. Nestar walked just behind Kimr, but looked straight ahead. His shaven head, full beard and paler skin were a contrast to the dusky, smooth-faced Chekaligas with their thick, black hair in braids. His light armor glinted in the dim light.

"I can see you are frightened, darling," whispered Vivia to Darbeni. "Return to the airboat and wait for me."

"But mother, what about you—" Darbeni began with a trace of panic in her voice.

"Don't worry about me." Vivia's whisper was soothing. "I know these men."

Darbeni tarried no longer, but hurried back down the nave. She saw the lust in Kimr's eyes as she passed him and pulled her thin shawl more tightly around her shoulders. Vivia waited till her daughter disappeared from sight before speaking.

"Welcome, Kimr ib Makhtoom," she said in a conversational tone. She did not rise, but inclined her head imperiously. "I am pleased to see you. You have begun well."

Kimr looked around the cavernous chamber suspiciously.

"High Mistress Lady Vivia," said Kimr, speaking Chekaliga Daksish. "I have driven out the weak willed Pallian. As soon as I did so, his Kasar Chekaligas accepted my sovereignty. They see that I wear the amulet of the Grand Sab inherited from my father—and just as you predicted, they have bowed to me as their liege. And once they acknowledged me, all the other Chekaliga tribes followed. United, we men of the ravines are invincible!"

"What of the mercenaries I sent you?"

"They have done an excellent job. Taking Siggar with its extensive fortifications would have been impossible without them. They set up and operated the catapults, the rams and the siege towers. Once they got my men to the tops of the walls, those cowardly Daksin men turned tail and ran!" He paused. "No city, no matter how well fortified, is safe from us now."

"Good, good," said Vivia. "Now you must march south and take Limpore and Sampore. Soon, you will be the master of all of Daksin and the Lion Throne will be yours."

She paused to look over at Nestar before going on.

"It does my heart good to see you so successful, for I remember you as a little boy, playing with a wooden sword while I visited your father." Vivia smiled, but her eyes remained cold. "Now you think that you no longer need me. That you can rule as King of Daksin and pay the mercenaries out of your plunder."

Kimr could not suppress the guilty look jumped to his face. He glanced over his shoulder at his warriors and then turned back to Vivia.

"That would be unwise, Kimr ib Makhtoom," Vivia went on, adjusting her *kanjiam* scarf.

Kimr felt her eyes boring into his. Candles on the altar spontaneously lit up. High up on the roof beams, hundreds more candles came to life, filling the chamber with a flickering light. A blue aura began to form around Vivia. It was faint at first, but grew steadily stronger till it radiated brightly in the Mission House. The aura seemed to magnify her size and stature. She raised her hand and naked fear showed on the faces of Kimr and all his warriors. Nestar had been detached, but now terror showed on his face as well.

Trembling, Kimr went to his knees. The Chekaliga warriors all followed their leader and knelt. Nestar hesitated, frozen on his feet for a moment. However, when Vivia turned her gaze on him, he slowly sank down to his knees as well.

"I accept your fealty," said Vivia, her gray-green eyes glittering. "Now rise. All of you."

They got to their feet with a creaking of leather and chinking of metal. Vivia's blue aura slowly pulsed like a living thing. The look on her face remained harsh.

"Fear me," she said. "And obey me. For I am Malitha's consort. Our instruments are positioned throughout the One Land. In Briga, in Utrea, in Daksin and even within the Sisterhood. The Thermadan Mission does our bidding. Soon, very soon, no one will be able to stand in our way. We will reward our adherents and crush our enemies."

"I thought you were Zon," Nestar mumbled. "But I see now that you are so much more. You are the overlord of my liege, King Shobar. Vasitha is our common enemy—"

"Yes, Vasitha!" Vivia snapped. "The traitor of Rocky Scarp! Who turned on his ally, King Larax, seduced by the wiles of Simran d'Orr. It is he who opposes the order we seek to create. Now he has created a new instrument of his own. If it is allowed to grow to maturity, it will destroy everything we stand for."

"Command me, Lady Vivia," said Kimr, mesmerized by Vivia's pulsing blue aura. "How can I serve you?"

"Vasitha's instrument is still young and weak," she said, her voice becoming a low hiss. "She is being brought here, to Bar-Dari. You can destroy her in this city, where Abaid raised the Mission to greatness."

"It will be done," said Kimr.

"It will be done," repeated Nestar.

She looked from one to the other. She smiled and her aura grew even brighter.

"Kimr, Nestar, do this and you will each receive a boon. Your most fervent desire will be granted."

Kimr hesitated. "High Mistress, I beg to reveal my most fervent desire. For it burns in my breast and unspoken it stifles me."

"Then speak, Kimr."

"I sent my brothers, Ghor and Tamr, to take the Serat Oasis in the Southern Marches of Briga. But in the battle, my youngest brother, Tamr, was killed."

"An honorable death for a Chekaliga," said Vivia. "You should be proud."

"Would that it were so, your ladyship!" Kimr clenched and unclenched his fists. "Alas, he died shamefully, begging for his life before being struck down by a *woman*. He has become a laughing stock, bringing shame on my family. I seek vengeance."

"Who was this woman? A victim who turned on him?"

"No, Lady Vivia. She was a socercess and struck him down with a magic sword."

"A swordswoman? Do you have more details?"

"Yes, your ladyship. I have brought Tamr's body-aide with me, he saw his master struck down. He was right by him, but managed to escape the sorcery."

Kimr beckoned and one of the Chekaliga warriors stepped forward diffidently.

"What can you tell me?" Vivia asked the warrior in fluent Chekaliga Daksish, her Zon accent barely noticeable.

"She...was...tall," faltered the warrior. But he gained confidence as he spoke. "She was surely a sorceress for she had the green eyes of a snow tiger and hair like flame! What's more, her sword blazed in the sunlight and had a spell engraved into its flat."

"Describe this spell."

The warrior went to his knees at the dusty base of the altar. He worked quickly, tracing out a pattern. They all watched as complex runes began to take shape. When he was finally done, he rocked back on his haunches and looked up at Vivia.

"That is what it looked like, your ladyship," he said.

It was only a fair representation, but Vivia saw immediately that the two sets of runes were in the ancient Artha-Pranto script. The barbarians could not read them and even Vivia had difficulty with the archaic letters. But after mentally sounding them out twice, she was sure. The two words were *"d'Orr–Nasht."*

"Kimr," said Vivia. "Our causes converge. Serving me, you will have your vengeance. Vasitha's instrument is the spawn of this green-eyed sorceress."

www.ingramcontent.com/pod-product-compliance
Lightning Source LLC
Chambersburg PA
CBHW070631180626
46817CB00006B/2098